Di Morrissey is Australia's leading lady of fiction. She planned on writing books from age seven, growing up at Pittwater in Sydney. She quickly realised you don't leave school and become a novelist. Di trained as a journalist, worked as a women's editor in Fleet Street, London, married a US diplomat and in between travelling to diplomatic posts and raising daughter Gabrielle and son Nicolas, she worked as an advertising copywriter, TV presenter, radio broadcaster and appeared on TV and stage. She returned to Australia to work in television and published her first novel, *Heart of the Dreaming*, in 1991. *Monsoon* is her fifteenth novel.

Di divides her time between Byron Bay and the Manning Valley in New South Wales, Australia, when not travelling to research her novels, which are all inspired by a specific landscape.

visit www.dimorrissey.com

DI MORRISSEY

MONSOON

MACMILLAN
Pan Macmillan Australia

First published 2007 in Macmillan by Pan Macmillan Australia Pty Limited
1 Market Street, Sydney

National Library of Australia
cataloguing-in-publication data:

Morrissey, Di.
Monsoon.

ISBN 978-1-4050-3818-8 (pbk.).

I. Title.

A823.3

Typeset in 12.5/15pt Sabon by Post Pre-press Group
Printed in Australia by McPherson's Printing Group

Internal illustrations by Francois Jarlov from *Under the Sign of the Blue Dragon*
Long Tan cross illustration by Paul Murphy
Internal map by Richard Adams

'I Was Only 19 (A Walk in the Light Green)'
Words and music by John Schumann
© Universal Music Publishing Pty Ltd.
All rights reserved. International copyright secured. Reprinted with permission.

Papers used by Pan Macmillan Australia Pty Ltd are natural, recyclable products made
from wood grown in sustainable forests. The manufacturing processes conform to the
environmental regulations of the country of origin.

Dedicated to Jim Revitt;
my uncle, mentor and mate,
who covered the Vietnam war for the
Australian Broadcasting Commission 1966–67.
Thanks for everything Jimbo!

Acknowledgments

For . . . Boris with much, much love. Couldn't get through each day without you!

. . . My daughter Gabrielle and my son Nick. I'm so proud of you both and love you more than words can say.

. . . All my family, especially my mother, Kay, who has always been there for me.

. . . For my other family at Pan Macmillan – Ross Gibb, James Fraser, Jane Novak, Jeannine Fowler, Roxarne Burns, Millicent Shilland, Liz Foster, the marketing team – Paul Kenny, Katie Crawford, the sales team and all the great reps, not forgetting everyone at the warehouse.

And for Nikki Christer – thanks for 13 wonderful years.

. . . Ian Robertson, lawyer extraordinaire, great and good friend – thank you.

. . . Liz Adams, you've turned into a wonderful editor as well as being a pal – thanks!

. . . Peter Morrissey who was with United States Information Service in Vietnam 1967–68.

For assistance with this book – Col Joye, Lt. Col. Eric Richardson (ret.), Jimmy Pham, Thi Duong, Chiquita Ho, Cath Turner, Gracie Nicholls. At Cockscomb – Gene Owens.

In Vietnam – Iain Finlay and Trish Clark, Carol Sherman and all at CARE Hanoi, Consul-General Mal Skelly, Quoc Nguyen, Mark Rappaport, Paul Murphy, Breaker Cusack.

. . . And thanks to long-time friend Kirsten Garrett who has shared so much of my journey.

And to all the Australian forces who served in Vietnam – THANK YOU.

DM

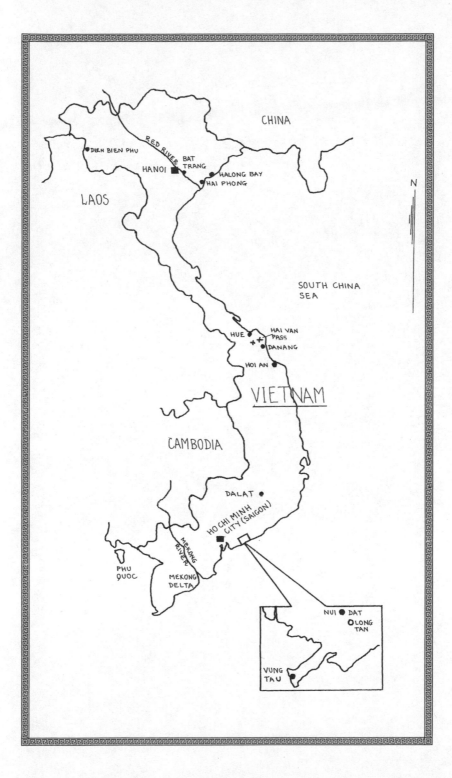

Prologue
South Vietnam, August 1966

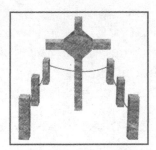

THE IROQUOIS HELICOPTER swept low over the broad curve of the Saigon River at the edge of Saigon city. The upstream harbour area was cluttered with large freighters and small coastal trading vessels, barges and the traditional wooden river boats that were homes as well as workplaces for thousands of river dwellers.

The scene had changed little over time, except that this year there were more warships than usual, a scattering of grey-hulled vessels ranging from river and coastal patrol boats to frigates. Their sombre presence and the overhead droning of helicopters were the symbols of a war that had already brought years of agony to the small South-East Asian nation.

And everywhere, upstream and downstream as far as the eye could see, there were hundreds of sampans and fishing boats moored together in floating villages or singly making their way to thousands of homes and enterprises by the water's edge. This river complex was part of the vibrant and rich region of South Vietnam.

Despite long-running post–World War Two conflicts, first with the French and now between communist and anti-communist powerbrokers in North and South Vietnam, the residents of Saigon carried on with their ceaseless bustle of commerce and politics at a pace that was increasing by the day. From the big entrepreneurs down to the humblest hawkers in the narrow lanes, there were new opportunities, and the locals were taking advantage of the boom times. By whatever means, legal or not, many saw the chance to profit from the war. Money was flowing as never before as the United States and its allies pumped resources into backing the anti-communist government of the South. No one knew what lay ahead, so they made the most of the moment.

Further down the coast, from his seat beside the helicopter pilot, Australian entertainer Col Joye gazed down at the sluggish brown Mekong River snaking its way towards the sea. Tom Ahearn, an Australian reporter travelling with them, tried to take a photograph.

'Where's the river start, mate?' Col asked the Australian army pilot.

'Comes from Cambodia. And, before that, the backblocks of Laos. The densest jungle and remotest villages you can imagine. Beats me why the French fought so hard to hang on to their old colony there. Dry season you can't get all the way through but most of the time you can. 'Specially now.'

'Bit of a back door that'd be hard to patrol, wouldn't it?' asked Tom Ahearn.

The pilot glanced back at the journalist and at the famous rock and roll singer beside him whose world was so far removed from the distant jungle. He gestured to the horizon. 'There's really a bloody big highway down there, under the trees, and even in stretches under the ground. A highway for the Viet Cong and their backers up north. That's what makes this stoush a bit different. It's hard to figure out friend from foe, until they start shooting at you.'

'Yeah, I heard the enemy over here wore pointy hats and black pyjamas. Seems to me the whole damn country is wearing pointy hats and black PJs!' said the singer.

The journalist made a quick note of the comment in his notebook.

They flew almost at tree-top level. 'Why so low?' asked Col, his apprehension making the pilot grin in response.

'Making it a bit safer, mate. We've gone past any Cong sniper before he's even heard us.'

The chopper flew beneath thunder clouds that hung heavy, leaden and sodden. Most days a solid wall of water was dumped over the jungle, rice paddies and river, but quickly, as now, the sun burned through the grey clouds making the damp air steam, insects surge and men sweat in their uniforms.

'It's really quite a beautiful scene,' said Col as the patchwork of rice paddies gleamed in the sunlight.

'Yeah, but every acre down there is part of a war zone,' Tom reminded him.

They landed at the Australian base camp helipad at Nui Dat, where the rest of Col's band – the Joy Boys – and singer Little Pattie were watching their gear being transferred from the other aircraft to a line of military Land Rovers.

As they waited to set off Tom gestured to his tape

recorder hanging in a bag from his shoulder. 'Col, could I have a bit of a yarn to you about this story I'm doing on troop entertainment?'

'Sure thing, mate, want to do it now or when we get to the camp? Might get a bit busy then.'

'How about I jump in the Land Rover with you to the camp? I'll grab some of the concert and a few comments from the troops after.'

'Hop in, Tom.' Col clambered into the front of the large Land Rover. Two of the Joy Boys were already in the back.

As they moved off from the edge of the airstrip and into the remains of the abandoned rubber plantation that made up part of the base camp, Tom gazed at the distant jungle-covered hills that now seemed so threatening. Beneath the low mountain spread, much closer to the camp, he could see a few thatched huts and some water buffalo in fields. It looked so peaceful.

'Man, it's steamy. My shirt's shrinking on me,' said one of the band.

'Don't take it off and throw it,' Col advised his lead guitarist. 'This audience is all blokes.' He grinned. 'Got your dancing shoes on?'

The two members of the band, who favoured long pointy-toed winkle-picker shoes, eyed the army boots and the jungle green pants they'd been issued. The civilian shirts they were to wear on stage had been the only concession by the army to showbiz glamour. Tom glanced at his own fatigues and army boots and smiled.

'The fellows are really looking forward to your show,' said the driver. 'It'll be a big audience. Some of the Sixth Royal Australian Regiment have just come straight in from the perimeter.'

'Been much action around here?' asked Tom as they set off down the dirt road.

'Been fairly quiet. Bit of action to the west. Few mortars were lobbed in at the base last night, probably a few stray Viet Cong having a go. D Company 6RAR are having a quiet snoop around. Nothing to worry about, I reckon.'

Tom had his large tape recorder balanced on his lap and he held the microphone close to Col. 'What are your feelings about doing a concert for the troops here at Nui Dat, especially as there's been a bit of action near the base camp?' he asked.

'We're happy to do our bit for the men who are up here in the middle of it all. Bring them a taste of home,' answered Col. 'We're here to bring some fun to our troops. Remind them what Australia is all about and that the folks back home haven't forgotten them. No big message, just a few laughs and a singalong.'

The driver swung the Land Rover onto the worn track through the base to a slight dip in the landscape where a stage had been built and some tents erected for performers and their equipment.

The raised dais was screened with green canvas and the sound equipment was set up to one side, the big amplifiers facing the crowded audience who were sitting on the ground, chatting, smoking and laughing. Tom began describing the scene into his tape recorder.

'Let's do it, eh?' Col picked up his guitar.

As Col was approaching the stage three soldiers – two Australians and a New Zealander – jumped from a Land Rover.

'G'day, Col . . . ah, listen, mate, when's the show going to finish?'

'When we sing "Clementine",' answered Col. 'You blokes in a rush?'

'We nicked the colonel's Land Rover so we want to get it back before he notices. Love your music, mate.'

'Enjoy the show.' As Col leapt onto the stage Tom stepped in to get more comments from the three soldiers who were happy to help, provided they remained anonymous.

'Col Joye and the Joy Boys, Little Pattie . . . What a ripper. Couldn't miss this.'

'Even if there's a very irate colonel awaiting your return?' said Tom into the microphone.

'She'll be apples, sport. One of our mates has arranged a little diversion if we don't get back on time,' laughed one of the Aussie soldiers.

Tom's next question was drowned out by a roar and cheers from the men as Col Joye launched into 'Bye Bye Baby'.

The performers ran through their hit songs as requests from the audience written on lolly wrappers, playing cards and scraps of paper were passed forward.

There was thunderous applause as diminutive singer Little Pattie came on stage, simply dressed in a skirt and blouse, her bouffant hair giving her extra height. A bundle of bouncing energy, she radiated fun and humour, every man's favourite little sister.

Half an hour into the show Tom leaned over to shout in the ear of a sergeant manning the sound boxes. 'Did I hear a few rockets, or was that feedback from the amps?'

'Bit of a blue going on near the base. They've sent a platoon out to check. She'll be right.' One of the soldiers tried to ask Col for an autograph but the lanky singer was belting out popular songs from the hit parade. It wasn't so long ago these men in the audience had been home, keenly following Saturday *Bandstand*. The music brought back good memories for them.

Although entertained by the performance, Tom was aware that some of the men to one side were moving away from the crowd and he noticed a message being handed to some of the brass down the front. There was a rumble and Tom glanced up at the sky where thunder clouds had covered the afternoon sun.

'It's not just thunder, mate,' said one of the men. 'That's some Viet Cong trying to have a go.'

'Where are they?'

'Out in a rubber plantation, few miles down the track. I heard about it from one of the blokes who went out last night.'

At that moment the heavens opened and the band and Little Pattie were hurried into an armed personnel carrier as rain began to fall. The boys stripped off their stage shirts and were handed army shirts as the torrential downpour became a constant curtain of water. Holding his camera and tape recorder inside his shirt, Tom joined them.

'Sounds like something's happening near here. The brass are having a pow wow; no one would speak to me.'

'Hop in with me, Tom, I'll yarn to you,' offered Col.

They jumped in the vehicle behind Little Pattie's and the band.

'Jeez, are we going to be able to fly out in this weather?' Col asked the driver.

'It'll stop soon. Like a bloody tap going on and off. It's monsoon time.'

'Hurry up and wait, eh?' said Col.

'Yeah. This doesn't look too good,' said Tom, wondering if he would get back to Saigon in time to file his story. He was trying to think of a solution when the Land Rover's weather flap was wrenched open and a grinning, dripping sergeant stuck his head in.

'G'day, Col. I'm Tassie Watts. Listen, could you nick

7

back and say hello to the blokes in my Land Rover? They missed the show. Just say hello, like.'

'It's flaming wet out there, mate.'

'We're parked right behind you. Just take a tick. Boost morale no end, do us a favour, eh?' The sergeant reached to help Col. 'Hang on to me shirt and run.'

'Coming, Tom?' called Col.

Pulled along by the sergeant, Col kept his head down, and Tom followed, clutching his gear inside his shirt as the red mud sloshed over his boots. A Land Rover weather flap opened and Col was manhandled into the back as Tom jumped in next to the driver. In the back two men held Col, one pinning him down.

'Got 'im! Take off, Rusty.'

'What the . . . ?' began Col as the Land Rover lurched and did a U-turn, sliding along the slippery track. 'What's going on?'

Tom could only watch helplessly from the front seat, wondering what was happening.

'We've kidnapped you, Col,' said Tassie cheerfully. 'We're from 5RAR. We had to man some outposts so missed the show. Thought you could at least say hello to the blokes.'

Tom burst out laughing and Col joined him. 'Well, I guess we're not going anywhere else in this rainstorm.'

For the next few hours Col went from tent to tent, yarning to the men who were just elated to talk to some-one from home and not because he was a big name. Tom tagged along, recording snatches of the conversations, asking the men questions, knowing he had a far more colourful story than if they'd left Nui Dat on time.

'You're bloody terrific, Col,' said Tassie, well pleased his plan had been so successful. 'The way you ask where a fellow is from and then you say you've been there or know the area. Makes them feel real close to home.'

'Me and the Joy Boys have toured all over Australia, so, yeah, we've been everywhere,' grinned Col.

'Hey, Col, come in here and see us!'

In a large tent a guitar was produced and men crowded around Col to sing their favourite songs until Tassie stuck his head in a tent flap. 'Hey, Col, HQ are screaming at me to get you back. Let's go, mate. Where's that journo bloke? Let's go!'

As the Land Rover bounced and swayed through the mud Tassie explained, 'Been a bit of enemy fire so HQ is sweating on getting you out. They said get you back no matter what. You too, Tom,' he added.

'Listen, Tassie, tell 'em it was my idea. To see the blokes,' said Col.

'Aw, she'll be right.' Tassie peered through the windscreen. 'It's coming down again. Thought it might clear up before dark. No such luck.'

They skidded to a stop and through the rain Tom could hear artillery fire close by.

As they jumped out of the Land Rover Col looked at the empty helipad. 'Where're the others?' he asked.

'One of the Chinooks got out with quite a mob. Your lot will probably be back in Saigon in their cosy hotel, mate.'

'I don't fancy hanging around here,' said Tom.

At that moment a barrage of Australian and New Zealand artillery fire went over their heads into the jungle from the unit behind them. Col and Tom got back in the Land Rover and as they sat and waited they hoped none of the shells fell short or the enemy on the other side of the hill got closer.

'With all this stuff coming down on them, the VC will pick up their mortars and run,' said Tassie. 'Little but lethal. Hard to pin 'em down.' He lit a smoke, his cheerful face now grim.

In the gathering dusk the tropical downpour eased as

another vehicle pulled up beside them and a burly officer stepped out.

'Hello there. I'm Max Smith, the chaplain.' He shook hands with Col and Tom. 'You can't get out so you'll have to spend the night. You can have my bed, Col, and we'll find a tent for you, mate,' he said to Tom, who nodded his thanks.

Col went to protest; the chaplain waved a hand. 'Don't worry about it, mate. They're calling in the dead and missing: I won't be sleeping tonight. Follow me.'

Tassie gave a rueful grin. 'Sorry about the detour, Col, but it meant a lot to the boys.'

Col looked at Tom. 'You're getting a bit of an exclusive, eh?'

The chaplain pulled up at a row of standard green canvas tents. 'There's your stretcher bed, there's your bunker hole. Nick in there if there's any action.'

Col and Tom looked at the small and very wet pit next to each tent. 'Fat lot of good that's going to do me,' commented the tall rangy singer.

'We might be doing a bit more digging,' remarked Tom, ducking into his tent.

'Well, thanks, sir,' said Col.

'Call me Maxie. Here, you might need this too.' He handed Col his pistol. 'See you both in the morning.'

'Listen, Maxie, this is clearly a big story. I can't just go to bed. Is there somewhere I can find out what's going on?' asked Tom.

'Well, I don't think the base command will tell you even if they know, but I guess you can ask.'

Col was sitting on the stretcher bed tying his shoelaces as Tom stuck his head inside the tent next morning. 'How'd you sleep?'

'Not bad. Should've slept on that pistol, might have been softer than the pillow. But thanks. How'd you get on at the base?'

'They were very tight lipped, but I stayed all night. It's all happening at a rubber plantation only a couple of miles away from here,' said Tom. 'Long Tan is a place our boys have been through many times without problems, but it seems the Viet Cong have been burrowing there for ages. A hundred or so blokes from Delta Company from 6RAR ran into what probably amounted to a full enemy battalion.'

The chaplain wandered over looking tired and grim.

'What's the latest?' asked Col.

'They've taken some casualties,' he replied. 'Radio contact with them was lost for a while. The Kiwi artillery moved in with support fire. We're flying the most serious casualties to Vung Tau. I suggest you two go up to the command post and clean up and have breakfast.'

At the mess they ate a bowl of cornflakes each, wondering about the men who'd been trapped in the Long Tan rubber plantation.

'Wouldn't be much protection behind a couple of rubber trees, would there?' Col said to Tom.

A chopper pilot came past and asked Col how he was doing.

'Better than a lot of the men, I'd say. I'm Col Joye, how are you, mate? This is me mate Tom, the journo.'

They shook hands and the pilot suddenly looked at Col and exclaimed, 'Christ, I thought you had too much hair for a captain.' He pointed at the pips on Col's borrowed shirt and grinned. 'My chopper's back. It's been out dropping Chieu Hoi leaflets. Bloody stupid idea. I wouldn't surrender if a bit of paper fell from the sky promising me amnesty and hot dogs, or whatever those

Yanks from the Information Service are saying. Anyway, I can get you out.'

'We're ready, mate.' Col put down his bowl of half-eaten cereal and followed the pilot and Tom to the waiting chopper.

In Vung Tau, Col and Tom found the rest of the entertainers waiting for transport to Saigon, who were pleased to see them.

'Where've you blokes been?' asked Little Pattie.

'Took a bit of a detour,' grinned Col.

Tom turned to Col. 'There's some wounded Aussies from Long Tan in the base hospital. I've arranged transport to go and see them.' He stuck out his hand to farewell Col.

'Hey, we'll come with you. You right, love?' said Col, looking at Little Pattie, who nodded in agreement.

At the base hospital they did the rounds, sitting at bedsides, lighting a cigarette for the injured, yarning about home and families.

A harassed young doctor finally bore down on the party demanding they get the hell out of the hospital and announcing that the transport back to Saigon had been organised.

'You could be bringing in an infection, for God's sake,' he declared angrily. 'Please go.'

'Ah, Doc, we're just having a yak, doing the men a bit of good, I reckon,' protested Col.

He found Little Pattie holding the hand of a soldier lying quietly, his face creased in pain.

'We're being turfed out, love. We've got a lift back to Saigon, it seems.'

The soldier in the bed down from Little Pattie gave them a weak wave. 'Been nice seeing someone from home, mate. Thanks for coming. Your show must've been beaut. We heard it, y'know. In that rubber plantation before we got hit. We could hear the music.' He held out his hand and Col gave it a firm shake.

'Thank you for what you're doing up here, mate. Hope you get home real soon. Where're you from?' asked Col.

'Sydney. Maroubra. You know, Little Pattie's song, "Stompin' at Maroubra".'

'Ah, know Maroubra well. Good beach you got there.'

'Catch a wave for me when you get back, eh, Col.'

'I'll do that, mate. What's your name?'

'Sergeant Phillip Donaldson, 6RAR.'

'Good on yer, Phil. See you back at home, keep your powder dry, eh?'

'I'll try, mate. See ya.'

Col stopped by a bed where Tom was talking to a soldier and making notes. 'Hey, Tom, go talk to Phil over there. Reckon he's got a story for you.'

'Great. I'll do that, Col.' Tom went and pulled up a chair beside Phil's hospital bed and shook his hand. 'You've come out of Long Tan?'

Little Pattie tugged gently at Col's sleeve. 'We have to leave. I don't want to miss another ride.'

'Too right.'

As they were about to leave, the harassed young doctor grabbed Col's hand. 'Listen, sorry I was so abrupt. I've been up all night. It's tough, seeing so many badly wounded. And losing men.'

'Understood, Doc. Look after me mate Phil over there. And the rest of 'em.'

The doctor wiped his hand across his eyes. 'We try our best, Col. That's all we can do.'

Col turned and gave Tom a wave. 'Nice travelling with you, mate. Keep the stories coming, eh?'

'I'll do that, Col. Good luck.' Tom turned back to

Phil Donaldson, who tried to recount what he'd seen and felt as his mates had been killed beside him.

Maroubra, Sydney, 2006

Phil Donaldson put the letter down on the kitchen table, opened the refrigerator door and stood staring into the brightly lit shelves of food.

'You hungry, love?' His wife, Patricia, went to fill the kettle.

'Nah.' He slammed the fridge door shut.

'Who's the letter from, pet?' asked Patricia.

'Nothing important.' But then he turned at the doorway. 'It's from Tassie Watts. Wants to get some sort of a reunion happening. But I'm not interested.'

His wife stared at his hard expression, recognising the symptoms of the painful memories washing over him. Now he was right back. Back in Vietnam. The place he could never leave behind. 'Might do you good, love. See your old mates and, you know, talk about things,' she said gently.

'There's nothing to talk about.' He left the room.

Sighing, Patricia Donaldson turned on the kettle, emptied the teapot and stood at the table staring down at the letter tucked back in the envelope. Slowly she reached for it and drew out the single sheet of paper.

I

Sydney, July 2006

TOM AHEARN SPRAYED WATER from the garden hose around his roses in the late morning winter sun. He was proud of his circular bed of roses backed by deep blue summer hydrangeas along the back fence. After his roses he was most proud of his tomatoes and spinach. Although he had owned his Sydney house for thirty years there had been little time to attend to home maintenance or the garden. Now he was enjoying doing these things in his retirement. Not that he was retired totally, he was quick to point out. He worked from his home office and kept almost as busy as he ever had been as a journalist and broadcaster.

Meryl watched her husband from the kitchen window as she poured their morning tea, set out the homemade Anzac biscuits and carried the tray to the old table on the verandah. Tom was a fit sixty-five, which he put down to his regular walks and occasional big bush hike. He'd had a few health problems which he would have ignored if Meryl hadn't pushed him into the doctor's. High blood pressure had been pinpointed along with an overdose of stress and a dicky knee from his intensive squash games years before. Now that he was on medication, watched his diet and had his knee replaced he felt better than he had in decades. But Meryl knew he was still a bit frustrated with life. While he wrote a column for the local paper and was active in the residents' association and local politics, he missed his career as a foreign correspondent.

'Tom, tea.'

He turned off the hose and joined her at the table. 'Going to be a magnificent display come spring and summer,' he said, waving a biscuit towards the roses. 'That early pruning has set them up beautifully.'

'I'm sure they'll be stunning,' said Meryl, who always wondered at the way the chopped-back, dead-looking wood sprouted fresh green leaves and miraculous blooms come the warm weather. 'How're the vegies coming along?'

'Abundantly. Thought I might make a stir fry tonight,' he said.

'Wonderful. I'll put my feet up while you cook your Asian delights,' said Meryl with a smile. Stir fry wouldn't decimate the kitchen. When Tom took it into his head to recreate some of his favourite dishes from his years in the East, it could become a major – and messy – production. The desserts were the worst. Sticky rice and gula Malacca, when the sago and palm sugar had boiled over on the stove, still haunted her.

The phone rang and Tom sauntered inside to answer it as Meryl poured a second cup of tea, noting the knitted tea-cosy could do with some running repairs. Tom's tea

16

was cold when he returned some time later, thoughtfully holding the portable phone which he put on the table.

'You were on the phone for ages. Who was it?'

'The old war horse himself – Alistair Knight.'

'Your old chief of staff? I thought he'd gone to God yonks ago.'

'Good lord, no, he's as spry as can be. He's eighty-two going on fifty-two.'

'So why was he calling you out of the blue after all these years?' asked Meryl.

Tom gave a quizzical smile. 'Aha. I could have another assignment. Well, not really, but an intriguing invitation.' He paused for dramatic effect before satisfying his wife's curiosity. 'Remember I told you about my time at Nui Dat in Vietnam?'

'The time you and Col Joye got kidnapped?'

'Yeah. Well, sort of . . . I was an extra bod that the Aussie command wasn't expecting at the time,' he chuckled. 'That was forty years ago. Incredible how the years get away from us so easily. Anyway, there are plans afoot for a couple of big reunions. One in Brisbane, one at Long Tan, near Nui Dat.'

'Long Tan,' said Meryl.

'That battle has never been given its due recognition,' said Tom, suddenly serious. 'Alistair reckons this anniversary could change that. As I was there he wants me to write about it. It's hard to believe that one hundred and eight men held off several thousand VC in that rubber plantation at Long Tan . . . ' His voice trailed off and he wandered into the house.

Meryl took the cups into the kitchen and as she was rinsing them music suddenly roared from their ageing stereo. She stood there listening, her wet hands tightening on the edge of the sink, eyes closed as Redgum's big hit 'I Was Only Nineteen' came to the final verse.

And can you tell me, doctor, why I still can't get to sleep?
And why the Channel Seven chopper chills me to my feet?
And what's this rash that comes and goes, can you tell me
   what it means?
God help me, I was only nineteen.

Tom walked into the kitchen as Meryl dabbed at her eyes with a tea towel. 'It's still such a moving, painful song . . .'

He nodded. 'Hardly any of them were over twenty at Long Tan. Eighteen young blokes died.'

'So you're going to Brisbane then, to this Long Tan reunion?'

Tom put his arm around her. 'I thought I'd go back. To Vietnam. And Long Tan.'

*

From: Sandy Donaldson (SandyD@VietHOPE.com)
Sent: Wednesday, 4:41 pm, 6 June 2006
To: Patricia Donaldson (PatriciaD@Austmail.com.au)
Subject: End of an era!
Hi Mum, I can't believe my time here in Vietnam with HOPE is coming to an end. I really love these people and the country. I'm at a bit of a loss about what to do next. I'd like to stay with HOPE, I think they're such a worthwhile NGO program . . . and another country doesn't appeal so much after here. But if I sign up for another year or so I worry I'm kinda out of the mainstream. You keep saying I shouldn't leave marriage and babies too much longer, but I am only 28! I'm due for a meeting with Cherie (the director) tomorrow so that might throw a bit of clarity on the situation. luv me

Sandy pushed the send button and then, in the twilight, changed into cotton shorts, a T-shirt and running shoes and walked down to Hoan Kiem Lake in the centre of Hanoi to think about her future. She loved the tranquil scenery there – weeping willows, kapok trees, the clipped grass, the neat path that wound around the lake. Seats faced towards the islet on the southern end with its lonely-looking Tortoise Tower, topped by a red star. The Ngoc Son Temple on a pretty island at the northern end was connected to the path by the Rising Sun red bridge.

When she'd first arrived in Hanoi she'd joined the tourists who came to watch the sunrise and the crowds of locals exercising around the lake before work, intending to do the same. But the sight of hordes of energetic Vietnamese – even quite elderly men and women – meditating or exercising singly, in groups or with family members, was too diverting and she found herself stopping to watch and enjoy their activity rather than exercising herself. They were jogging, power walking, doing all forms of aerobics, gymnastics, dance, martial arts, tai chi or even playing a spirited game of badminton. Ladies swinging their hips in a suggestive aerobics class and another group learning traditional fan dancing waved to Sandy, inviting her to join them.

Sandy would laugh and wave back, concentrating on a fast walk around the perimeter of the lake, planning her day or letting her mind drift. Afterwards she would stop for a coffee at one of the trendy cafes that had sprung up in the park and in the Old Quarter. The French had left a legacy of wonderful baking and sometimes she had a delicious croissant or bought a warm baguette from one of the bread sellers who sold them from the back of his bicycle or from a basket carried on her head.

But as the lake area and the nearby Old Quarter became more familiar to her, and she felt quite safe in the city, Sandy changed her walk around the lake to the early evening before dinner.

She loved the local food and ate out with friends and colleagues several nights a week. At lunchtime she bought a bowl of the famous Vietnamese pho soup from the sidewalk kitchen run by Mrs Han down from the HOPE offices. The tiny woman cooked over a small charcoal brazier, tossing in ingredients from the baskets that hung on either end of a long bamboo pole which she carried to the early morning markets to get vegetables and freshly made noodles. From sunrise to dark she crouched by her makeshift stove turning out pho, the delicious traditional soup based on her grandmother's secret recipe. Pho was once considered peasant food but had become iconic in Hanoi. Customers perched on short blue plastic stools around Mrs Han. Sandy had come to understand the Vietnamese obsession with this seemingly simple meal that was a tradition like chicken soup – a dish redolent with nostalgia, comfort and identity.

A large pot of green tea was always ready to be splashed into small beakers. It was a social exchange between those eating, those waiting and friends who came to gossip, squatting on their haunches around Mrs Han. After school her young daughter sat beside her chopping vegetables on a small plastic board and washing plates and tea mugs in a large bowl.

Depending on her mood and the company, Sandy also ate in small cafes, hotels, or in tucked-away eateries known only to locals who made a habit of eating out on a regular basis. The food was fresh, cheap and tasty so Sandy avoided the more expensive restaurants catering to tourists and offering upmarket Vietnamese food, international cuisine and French wines.

She had her favourite hangouts but her 'regular' spot was Barney's Bar. It was run by a jovial American draft dodger who'd lived in Denmark and Canada before wandering around Asia. He'd hiked into Vietnam in the early 1980s before tourism had been embraced by the communist government.

Barney Stuart had a loyal clientele of expats, Vietnamese business people and American and Australian ex-servicemen. Barney was the jovial host and bartender, and always had a suggestion about what to try. Mrs Lai Stuart, his wife, a pretty Vietnamese woman twenty years younger than her husband, supervised the cooking and menus. When she appeared from the kitchen she was always dressed in her long ao-dai, the traditional figure-hugging ankle-length dress with deep splits to the waist worn over loose flowing pants. It was quickly apparent that Lai was the business brains behind Barney's. The two had been together for years and it was Lai who had suggested that Barney open the bar in Hanoi with her as the official owner, as she could see that the influx of visitors and the loosening of the communist restrictions presented a good business opportunity.

Sandy jogged home from the lake, her route so familiar that she recognised the street hawkers on their patch, the shop owners and the itinerant businesses that set up to catch the night-time passers by. Families were out and about, children playing on the crowded footpaths as mothers shopped, prepared food or spread out trinkets, cigarettes, Tiger Balm, and other small souvenirs to sell to tourists. Coloured lights, strung haphazardly outside shops and along streets, twinkled, and candles flickered at outdoor altars. Incense sweetened the air.

Sandy had overcome her initial shock at the chaotic traffic as wave after wave of bicycles, cyclos, motorcycles, scooters, cars and trucks in tooting congestion filled the streets. But as she ploughed into the mayhem of the endless writhing traffic dragon to cross the road she still had made no future plans.

At work the following morning Sandy made herself a cup of coffee in the kitchen that served as a staff room in the HOPE headquarters in Hanoi. She always liked coming back here after being out in the field. The double-storeyed house with its open courtyard was narrow, reminding her of an upturned matchbox. Like most houses in old Hanoi, it was built in the days when the width of the site dictated the land rates. Homeowners added extra floors with balconies or extra rooms behind the frontage, sometimes separated by alleyways and sometimes sharing central courtyards. Sandy thought the colours of the HOPE building were like a hand-tinted photograph – fading greens and yellows, burned sienna and red picking out the fretwork and curling Chinese corners on the roof, while shutters and an iron lace balcony was an architectural remnant of the colonial French.

The walled courtyard that divided the HOPE front offices from the rear was open with a small fountain, shrubs in tubs, and a weathered table and chairs. It was a place for informal meetings, for the staff to smoke during coffee breaks, as Cherie Mitchell, the HOPE country director and health fanatic, had banned smoking indoors. Off the rear of the courtyard were two bedrooms, a bathroom and toilet used for emergency staff accommodation.

Sandy had spent her first few nights in Vietnam here before finding the tiny flat she now rented. Those first few days had been warm and welcoming thanks to the local staff and the overseas volunteers who worked for HOPE. She immediately felt part of a family. It had been interesting learning from her compatriots their reasons for wanting to join a non-profit, non-government aid organisation. HOPE, dedicated to helping people in developing countries, was partly funded by the Australian government and by public donation so their budget was limited.

While not having consciously planned her career to

arrive at this specific place and opportunity, her first meeting with Cherie had made Sandy realise how she had been instinctively working towards this goal for years.

'You went overseas as a youth ambassador straight after getting your degree in fine arts. Where did you see your future heading?' Cherie had asked her new recruit four years previously.

Sandy looked at Cherie smiling across the desk and formed the answer to the question. 'I wanted to travel, see the world, but not just as a tourist or doing odd jobs to pay my way. I wanted to contribute in some way, so I joined Australian Volunteers International and later Youth Challenge Australia. I was sent to the Solomon Islands. Then I travelled on my own to India and worked for the Indian Archaeological Society. I also helped out in several charitable organisations there. So when I came home and heard about HOPE, I applied. I was thrilled to be appointed here as this part of South-East Asia is new to me.'

Cherie ran an eye over a page of Sandy's file. 'You have of course completed the required reading and groundwork about Vietnam before arriving,' commented Cherie giving Sandy her prepared pep talk. 'While the emphasis of HOPE is alleviating poverty at the community level through rural, economic, health and agricultural projects, I hope you'll make the most of the chance to learn about the culture of Vietnam. This is a unique opportunity to get to know a country and its people by working among and with them.'

Those words came back to Sandy now as she carried her coffee to the old table in the sunny courtyard. She had indeed become immersed in the culture, customs, cuisine and lives of Vietnamese friends and colleagues. Her initial two-year contract had been renewed and she had signed on for two more years to work on different projects as well as stints in the HOPE offices in Hanoi and Ho Chi Minh City.

Sandy had worked on rural projects involved with providing clean water and sanitation to villages, and flood mitigation in the flood-prone Mekong delta, as well as education programs at several orphanage centres. She was now well qualified to move into international development programs or, as Cherie had suggested, perhaps international relations or the Australian Foreign Affairs Department. But none of these suggestions appealed to her at present.

Cherie joined Sandy, planting a large bottle of water on the table. She studied the tall blonde girl with her wide green eyes and pretty face. To the Vietnamese, Sandy epitomised the healthy, outdoorsy Australian poster girl. But Sandy's usually friendly smiling face was clouded.

'You look pensive, Sandy. Still mulling over your next move? You don't have to leave us, you know. But I sense you want a change.'

Sandy looked at the director, who'd been her boss for the past four years. In her forties, Cherie Mitchell was a typical expat Australian who had lived and worked abroad for twenty years. She'd travelled widely, only making flying visits home to see family. She had no children of her own but had been briefly married to an American engineer she'd met on a project in South America. When he expected her to return to the US with him and settle down as a housewife and raise a family, Cherie realised their life goals were radically different and they parted. There were stories of her various liaisons over the years, but she was discreet and it seemed to everyone she put her job first.

Sandy didn't want to be like Cherie; she wanted a husband and children at some stage. But also a job that stimulated her.

'A change, but not radical. I like seeing results from my efforts and I really like this country. I just can't imagine fitting in to an office routine in Australia. My girlfriend Anna back at home suggested I go and work for indigenous communities in the outback, but it'd feel too remote after being here.'

'Frankly, Sandy, what I think you need first is time out, a break, a holiday.'

'I haven't saved money to go anywhere expensive,' sighed Sandy, thinking time out with no obligations would be pleasant – for a short time. You didn't work for an NGO to make your fortune. 'I'm not very good at doing nothing. Never been one for hanging in a hammock or lying by a pool.'

'You know, you should take a holiday here. Travel round Vietnam; there are lots of places you haven't seen, or haven't had time to enjoy. And it's still inexpensive to be a tourist here. Do it now before this place starts to resemble Singapore or Thailand,' said Cherie with a mock sigh.

Sandy sipped her coffee. When she'd gone to regional areas on HOPE business she'd always made a mental note she'd go back to explore some day. 'I would like to see more of Vietnam. Even to just spend time here in Hanoi. I'm always so busy with stuff to do when I'm here . . . '

'There you go. Why not ask a friend to come over and travel with you? You'd be a great guide,' said Cherie, taking a swallow of water and getting up. 'You might also want to think about sharing your insights with the new intake of volunteers who arrive in the next few weeks.'

Sandy nodded, remembering her first weeks here as a new volunteer and how green she'd been. No matter how much you read about a country, the reality was so different, more powerful. She had worked hard at learning about the history of Vietnam, a country that had seen seven hundred years of warfare. While she'd been well briefed by HOPE before she left Australia, when she arrived in Vietnam, Sandy had realised that one was never really prepared for the culture shock – good and bad. Her time in India had meant many adjustments, but somehow she had known what to expect, and there wasn't such a language barrier as in Vietnam, although she spoke Vietnamese quite well now. Yet so much of her training had not really prepared her for on-the-job reality. She could have done with some hands-on, nitty-gritty advice from an experienced worker when she'd first landed in Hanoi at HOPE headquarters. So she readily agreed to share her experiences and insights with the new arrivals.

This idea of cruising around the countryside sounded terrific. And sharing the journey with someone else would be even better. Cherie's plan was a good one and the obvious choice of travelling companion was her long-time friend Anna.

It was a logical choice, not only because of their close friendship but also because Anna was half Vietnamese. Anna had been born in Sydney to a Vietnamese mother and an Australian father, and the two girls had gone to school together and remained close friends.

Anna had laughed when Sandy told her she was moving to Vietnam. 'Tell me all about it. I don't know anything about the place. But I'll really miss you.'

While Sandy sent long and what she hoped were interesting emails about her adventures in Vietnam, Anna had responded in detail about life in Sydney. She worked as a public servant at the local council and was wrapped up in her boyfriend, Carlo Franchetti. Ever since Anna had met Carlo, he had dominated her life. While Anna hadn't been swept off her feet initially, she told Sandy she found him attractive in his dark heart-throb Italian way. But he was persistent. Within weeks he had become the centre of Anna's life to the point where he decided where they would go, who they would meet and what Anna should wear.

When Sandy had finally met Carlo on a trip home she'd thought him handsome too – but, boy, did he know it and flaunt it. Sandy thought that Carlo was trying to smother Anna and that she hadn't had a chance to assess her true feelings about him. Sandy had kept probing Anna.

'What can I do, Sands? He adores me, he spoils me, he's gorgeous . . . I mean, I'm lucky, aren't I?' said Anna.

'Just don't let him boss you around so much.' Sandy didn't want to say there was something about Carlo, but she couldn't put her finger on it. She felt Anna had given in too easily, almost as if she was afraid to pass up the opportunity in case no one else came along. So Sandy had taken it upon herself to flatter and praise her beautiful best friend, but Anna had laughed it off.

'You're the queen bee in our crowd, Sands.'

Sandy tried again. 'Anna, you're a real catch; don't take up with someone who wants to own you. You want some freedom, come with me for a girls' night out. I go back to Vietnam in a few days,' she'd pleaded.

But their night out had been spoiled by Carlo texting Anna every twenty minutes, complaining he missed her, asking her what she was doing and suggesting that she let him come and pick her up and take her home. Sandy and their friends had finally persuaded Anna to tell him good-night and turn off her phone.

The next day Anna told Sandy that Carlo had been waiting for her at her father's house when the taxi had dropped her off.

'That's outrageous. He's too possessive, Anna.'

'He was just worried, that was all.'

'Anna, you should see other people, put a bit of space between you,' advised Sandy. 'He's your first serious romance but it doesn't mean he's it forever.'

While Carlo was sugar sweet and charming to Anna's girlfriends, Sandy saw a side to his nature that she didn't like. He seemed threatened by Sandy, as if they were competitors for Anna's attention, and she knew he had been pleased when she returned to Vietnam to work.

Within a year Anna and Carlo were living together in an ad hoc arrangement. Anna still kept some clothes and her bedroom at home, telling Carlo she had to keep an eye on her widowed father, but she frequently overnighted at Carlo's flat. Carlo worked as a partner in his father's import business and regularly visited his large family, where he was the apple of his mamma's and sisters' eyes. He told Anna he had big plans for their future, and marriage would have to wait till they were financially set up.

Sandy didn't like the sound of this but Anna brushed aside her concerns, saying he was attentive and caring, a good lover and had big plans for them. Sandy bit her tongue, but to her it seemed that Carlo Franchetti was all talk and exaggeration. She was yet to hear of any of his great ideas coming to fruition, so she told Anna to hang on to her job and keep her savings away from Carlo.

Over the four years Sandy had been in Vietnam, her trips home had been short and crowded. In the brief times she had been alone with Anna, Sandy had seen that Carlo was exerting more and more influence over her friend, but thankfully Anna continued working and laughed at Sandy's concern that she might marry Carlo.

'Your lives are so enmeshed. Does he assume marriage is inevitable? Do you want to spend the rest of your life with him? With his family?' asked Sandy.

Anna had told Sandy about his large extended family and how Anna felt she was at the bottom of the pecking order. She was expected to cook his favourite Italian dishes and to learn to speak Italian in order to converse with his mother, who spoke little English, and his grandmother, who spoke none at all.

'I guess I'm considered part of the family. Carlo says

marriage should wait until he's hit the big-time. But his father hates the fact that we sort of live together – I'm not pure,' grinned Anna.

'God, it sounds like the 1950s,' said Sandy. 'What's your dad say?'

'He's okay with our living arrangements but I don't mention any future plans. Easier that way.'

Sandy liked Anna's father, Kevin Fine, a down-to-earth Australian and a hard-working garage mechanic who was also a relief taxi driver on weekends. Anna enjoyed her widowed father's company too and made it a habit to spend Friday nights, which was Carlo's boys' night out, with him. She would cook dinner and watch TV, play a game or drag him off to a movie.

As Sandy finished her coffee, Cherie's suggestion started to take hold. If she could persuade Anna to come over and have a decent holiday with her, it would not only be fun, but it might give Anna a breather from Carlo and let her reassess their relationship. Sandy decided to send her a long email.

Initially Anna dismissed Sandy's idea, but Sandy was persuasive, arguing that Anna's visit would help her through a time of transition, of indecision, and surely it would be an interesting experience for her to see and learn something of her mother's homeland.

Anna replied that although her dad approved, she couldn't possibly leave Carlo and he was against the idea.

Sandy was appalled that her friend wouldn't take a holiday because her boyfriend didn't agree. She decided to call Anna's father and talk it over with him.

'Jeez, it's good to hear your voice, Sandy, love. We

miss you round here, but I hear you're going great guns over there.' Kevin was fond of his daughter's best friend. And when Sandy expressed her concerns about Anna's relationship with Carlo, Kevin quickly agreed with her. 'You're spot on there, Sandy. That Carlo is very foolish. He's spoiled by all the women in his family and expects Anna to fall into line. I reckon it'd be a terrific thing for her to have a proper holiday with you. And frankly, I've always thought she should visit her mother's country.'

'Do you know anything about her mother's family? Where they came from?' asked Sandy suddenly.

'Not really. I've got some papers of Thu's. I've been waiting for Anna to show some interest, didn't want to force it on her. But I always thought one day, y'know, when she has kids of her own, she might want to know more.'

Sandy had a fleeting thought that if Anna married Carlo there'd be trips home to Italy, not Vietnam. 'Listen, Kevin, try to persuade her. Say I need my best friend with me. We'll have fun together.'

'I bet you two will. I'll try to talk her into it. I've got a bit put by, I'll throw some dollars in the kick as a bit of an early birthday pressie.'

And to Sandy's surprise, Anna finally agreed.

At Sydney Airport Carlo cursed as a parking attendant waved him away from the No Standing zone outside the departures terminal.

'It's all right, Carlo, just leave me here. You don't have to park and come in. It's chaos,' said Anna, who didn't want him to argue with the parking attendant.

'Baby, are you joking? You're going away from me for three weeks and you think I'm just going to leave you

30

on the footpath? Never. Get a trolley and I'll park and I'll be with you in a flash.'

'I can manage my bag. Sandy told me to travel light.' Anna sighed in resignation. 'I'll see you inside then.' She pulled her bag along behind her and joined the check-in queue. She was at the counter when Carlo joined her and began flirting with the check-in girl looking after Anna.

'Come on, you can do better than that, a beautiful girl like you. Don't tell me you don't have some pull around here . . . Bev.' He read her name tag and leaned over the counter in front of Anna who shrank back, embarrassed by his obvious cajoling to get her a better seat. 'This girl is going to Vietnam for the first time,' argued Carlo.

'Look, the best I can do is the bulkhead seat, give you more leg room.' Bev smiled at Anna.

'Thank you. That would be lovely.' Anna nudged Carlo as he was about to press for an upgrade.

In an airport cafe Carlo put a coffee in front of Anna and sat next to her. 'Look, I could have got you into Business. I was just getting warmed up.'

'It's fine, Carlo, just save the famous Italian charisma for when I really need it.'

'You gonna miss me, bella?' He picked up her hand and nuzzled her ear. 'I'll be horny as hell by the time you get back.'

'Do you good,' she chided. 'You could do that work at your dad's place he's been asking you to finish for ages. Work off some passion in the yard and shed.'

'What about you, dream of me at night, eh?' he whispered in her ear.

'I'll miss you, of course. But Sandy has a lot of trips worked out. I'm starting to get a bit excited,' said Anna, a fact that had just struck her now she was actually on her way. She wished Carlo had let her dad bring her out

31

to the airport as he'd offered. 'Carlo, you should get back to work. I might go through Immigration and browse in the duty free.'

He pulled away and downed his short black in one gulp. 'You trying to get rid of me? Don't you let Sandy lead you into any trouble. You're my woman, remember that.'

Anna stood and kissed him quickly. 'Of course. Don't be silly.'

'Call that a kiss? C'mon, babe. Kiss me like you mean it. This one's gotta last.' He pulled her to him, his hands on her bottom pushing her pelvis into his as he kissed her passionately.

Anna bought a bottle of perfume as a gift for Sandy and a book to read on the flight.

The Immigration officer glanced at her departure card and opened her brand-new passport.

'First trip away?'

'Yep, I'm visiting my girlfriend. She works for HOPE, the aid outfit.'

'Good one. You got rellies over there?'

'Not that I know of . . . it's just a holiday.' Anna was slightly uncomfortable at the awareness she looked Vietnamese.

'How long you plan to stay?'

'Three weeks.'

'It's a great place. Went there last year. Terrific food. Nice people.' He stamped her passport and handed it to her. 'Have a good trip, love.'

There was a less friendly reception when she landed in Hanoi. Tourists were herded by officials in unflattering khaki uniforms. There were also police or army officials, she wasn't sure which, holding guns. The women officers wore the same uniforms as the men and were brusque and unsmiling. There was a lot of standing around in a cavernous cement space with posters on the walls which she couldn't read. She followed an English sign to claim her baggage and waited with the other subdued passengers from her flight.

Finally, after every scrap of official paper was scrutinised, she headed for the exit with a wave of jostling travellers. An official checking luggage stickers spoke to her in Vietnamese and she shook her head.

'Sorry, I don't understand.'

Two more officials at the exit waved her through, one making a short comment to the other. She heard the words 'Viet Kieu'. She would hear them much more in the coming weeks.

Through the sea of pushing passengers, drivers touting for business, and hotel and tourist operators waving placards with names on them, she spotted the tall figure of Sandy, her blonde hair a beacon in the sea of drab colours. They hugged, each surprised at how happy they were to see the other.

'C'mon, Kim from our office is here to help. Is that all your luggage? Good girl.' Sandy linked an arm through Anna's and waved at a smiling young man standing by a car.

'Welcome to Vietnam. I hope your visit is everything you want it to be.' Kim spoke with an American accent.

'I haven't thought that far ahead yet,' smiled Anna. 'Is this your home?'

'I wish it were: I love it very much here. I'm American. I work for HOPE also,' he answered rather formally.

'Kim's from Hawaii. Anything you want to find in Hanoi, Kim's the man,' said Sandy as they approached the car. 'You take the front seat and experience the full impact of driving in Vietnam,' said Sandy, and Kim laughed.

Anna quickly understood what they meant as they left the airport and made the forty-five minute drive into the city. Soon she stopped stamping her foot on the non-existent brake, cringing and drawing to one side as vehicles and bikes, a hand span away from the car, surged around them as they wove through the haphazard traffic.

'At least we're all going in the same direction. Are there any road rules?' she asked Kim.

'Some. The problem is that only fifty per cent of drivers have a licence so you just have to take your chances. Stick your hand out and wave and jump into a space as soon as you see it,' he explained.

Anna gazed at the pretty women seated on their motor scooters, some dressed in the traditional ao-dai, some in casual pants and blouses. They wove through the traffic with poise and skill. Some wore hats, kerchiefs over their faces and long gloves to protect their skin from sun and pollution.

'The women don't like getting sunburned,' explained Sandy. 'White skin is preferred. The Bondi look doesn't work here. A tan means you work outside in the fields, a peasant worker.'

The motorcycles and scooters fascinated Anna. Couples with several children perched in front and behind, and people carrying impossible loads of brooms, food, bunches of flowers, crates of chickens, even several huge live pigs, careened past. Close to the centre of town cyclo drivers seated behind their passengers furiously pumped their pedi-cabs to keep up with the flow of the traffic.

They passed the untidy remains of a huge flower market now almost deserted after its five am start. Anna was experiencing strange feelings as she looked at the women on the sidewalks and in the traffic, and recognised traits and similarities to herself. The swish of their long hair, their delicate frames, their facial features, even mannerisms fleetingly glimpsed. She was seeing flashes of herself in a thousand mini mirrors.

Sandy leaned over the seat and touched her shoulder. 'It's always a bit over-the-top when you first arrive. You'll adjust.'

Anna simply nodded, hypnotised by the bustling street life, the throng of people and traffic, the tall narrow multicoloured buildings, the open-air markets.

'It can be a bit overwhelming. But there are oases in this city. I love Hanoi,' said Sandy reassuringly.

'It's still the real Vietnam,' agreed Kim. 'With a lot more western comforts. I worry tourism is going to change it too much. Like Saigon.'

'What does "Viet Kieu" mean?' asked Anna suddenly, and Kim glanced at Sandy in the rear-vision mirror.

'It has several meanings, literal and inferred. Basically it means foreign-born or half Vietnamese and also means Vietnamese who live overseas,' said Sandy. 'You'll be regarded as a foreigner no matter what you look like. It'll be up to you to ignore it, or to try to bring the two pieces of your family history together somehow.'

Sandy hadn't expected this to come so early in Anna's visit. Foreign Vietnamese, those born or living outside the country who had privileges and opportunities but no awareness or knowledge of their heritage, often earned the scorn and ire of those living in the country who had inherited the past as well as the future of a now-united Vietnam.

Anna recalled the friendly exchange with the Australian Immigration officer and the snide remarks of the North Vietnamese airport officials. 'It's not my land. I have no connection with this place. Australia is my home; it's all I know,' she answered.

There was silence in the car for a moment, then Kim said warmly to Anna, 'It can be an advantage to blend in when you can. You might discover Vietnam brings you all kinds of gifts.'

Anna thought it an odd remark.

Sandy leaned forward and touched her friend's shoulder. 'We're here for a good time, right? I've worked hard since I've been here . . . now it's time to play a bit. We both need time out.'

Anna thought Sandy was referring to their jobs, but Sandy was thinking more of Carlo. She desperately wanted Anna to have fun, feel free and adventurous. And loosen the ties to Carlo.

Anna was obviously thinking of him too. 'Do mobile phones work okay here? I must text Carlo and tell him I've arrived safely.'

'Some places, no probs,' said Sandy easily. 'Let's settle you in to my flat. It's no palace, but it's comfy and a great location.'

Kim joined the conversation. 'So, Anna, what kind of shopping do you want to do? Vietnam has many wonderful things to buy.' He broke into a recitation of hot spots for tailored clothes, lacquerware, antiques, pirated DVDs, places to eat, places to see.

Anna began to relax. She was with her best friend in a place that offered interesting sights, great food and shopping, and a chance to share their lives as they always had. She realised how much she'd missed that. Anna pushed aside the uncomfortable business of her genetic links to this place. Yep, she was here for fun. And she intended to make the most of it.

2

WITHIN A WEEK ANNA knew her way around the centre of Hanoi and had her favourite coffee bar, noodle shop and pho maker where she and Sandy stopped after their morning walk around the lake. Sandy had taken Anna to the lake at six on her second morning in Hanoi and she'd so enjoyed the scene that Sandy decided they should walk there every morning. Their evenings were taken up with eating out and meeting friends from HOPE, and, it seemed to Anna, there was always a friend of a friend from home passing through.

Sometimes they met for drinks in the plush modern surrounds of five-star American-style hotels where some friends stayed. Other times they met at the more modest hotels, many of which clung to their French heritage with small metal-grille lifts, tiny balconies and dining rooms presided over by maître ds who called everyone madame or monsieur. Or else they hung out at trendy bars frequented by foreigners and the business elite.

Anna, not a sophisticated foodie, as Kevin's mother had raised her on plain Australian fare, found the cuisine on offer a continuous gourmet safari. With Sandy now on her break the girls indulged in occasional long lunches trying French or Italian food as well as local dishes. Anna watched men and women cook at stalls, over a brazier on the street, in markets, in large noisy outdoor restaurants, in tiny food shops. Sometimes she and Sandy cooked for themselves at the table in small cha ca restaurants, dipping vegetables and fish pieces in the bubbling spicy broth.

'I think I'd like to learn to cook properly,' Anna confided in Sandy.

'Perfect place to do it! There are cooking schools and courses proliferating like mushrooms,' said Sandy.

Anna spread her arms. 'So many interesting people everywhere you look . . . doing things, starting businesses. No wonder the Vietnamese are so successful everywhere they go.'

Sandy smothered a smile. 'Yep, industrious and entrepreneurial right down to a woman sewing, cooking or selling produce off the pole on her back, or a cyclo driver dreaming of one day owning a taxi. And with the government loosening restrictions on free enterprise, big business is booming too.'

After browsing through a street full of silk shops and tailors Anna sighed. 'It's too confusing. All those fashion magazines and assistants trying to push me into this or that design. Or else they expect me to wear the ao-dai and when I don't understand what they're saying they give me pencil and paper to draw an outfit like I'm an illiterate kid.'

Sandy laughed. 'Tailoring shops are pretty competitive. Wait till we go to Hoi An, it's probably cheaper down there.'

Sandy was working on an itinerary to show Anna more of the country and decided the first trip out of Hanoi should be to one of the great natural wonders of the world – Halong Bay.

'So what's there?' asked Anna as they threw their small bags into Kim's old car.

'Did you ever see the film *Indochine* with Catherine Deneuve? That was before tourism hit the area,' said Sandy. And when Anna shook her head Sandy smiled. 'Try to imagine fifteen hundred square kilometres of jewelled waters with over two thousand limestone islands soaring out of the sea.' She was still surprised how little Anna knew about Vietnam or the fact that she hadn't bothered to do any homework on the country before jumping on a plane to visit.

Kim had offered to drive them on the three-hour trip to Halong Bay. He thought he would then go hiking in the Cat Ba National Park while the girls spent the weekend on Halong Bay. They'd all drive back together after he'd visited a fish farm project in the port of Hai Phong.

Just outside Hanoi the car slowed as it threaded through the crowded street leading into Bat Trung, where two adjacent villages formed the commune famous for its ceramic production.

'What's that smell? And look at the pollution,' commented Anna from the front seat.

'It's from the coal-burning kilns,' said Kim. 'They're replacing them with gas-burning ones now, but it's not a clean place yet.' He pointed to a pile of coal pats drying along a wall. 'That'll soon be a thing of the past.'

'Look at the dirty buildings from years of coal fires,' said Sandy.

Anna studied the blackened bricks, the sooty roofs and the darkened wood of shops displaying all manner of ceramics from incense burners to bowls and vases, while others looked like they held more antique treasures. 'Those places look interesting.'

'This Red River delta area has been famous for its ceramics since the fifteenth century. It's the kaolin clay that came from the local provinces,' said Kim. 'See, there's the river.'

'Wow, can I take a photo?' exclaimed Anna.

They left the car and picked their way through the traffic as workers busily loaded wide wooden sampans with piles of cream-and-blue ceramic pots. The boats, already low in the water, had their roofs strengthened with wood and timber to take the weight of the pottery.

'We're only thirteen kilometres from Hanoi so the pottery is sent downriver to the exporters. Or people carry it on bicycles to shops in Hanoi. Some of those ceramic pots could well end up in garden nurseries in Sydney,' commented Sandy.

After Anna had taken photos of the broad stretch of the Red River bustling with activity, Sandy led her down an alley to a small factory. Through a side door they entered a workshop where several potters were kneading the grey-white clay while two girls were delicately painting flower designs on large vases ready for glazing and firing in the large coal-fired brick kiln.

Sandy greeted the head potter who pointed to the rear of the workshop. Anna followed Sandy to a small studio where an elderly man with a shock of white hair and strands of hair on his chin that hung in a wispy beard waved a hand and rose to greet her.

'This is Master Potter Thinh. He's very famous in the village,' Sandy told Anna. 'He was one of the first people here to start reproducing the antique glazes.'

Mr Thinh gave a slight bow and greeted Anna in Vietnamese.

She smiled, saying, 'Thua Bac,' the greeting of respect that Sandy had taught her.

Mr Thinh led them both on a tour, proudly showing off shelves stacked with figurines, vases and bowls waiting to be fired. He pointed at details, from the traditional dragonfly and taro plant decoration to the graceful curve of the lip of a vase.

'These are made by Mr Thinh's students. He is a great teacher who uses the traditional methods. We've also helped him start classes for women in the rural parts of the province to make pottery at a co-operative. Handicrafts are proving to be a great income for women, and a popular export,' explained Sandy.

Anna was entranced with a vase decorated with water lilies. The glaze was cracked and tinged brown, giving it an old patina. 'This looks very old.'

'Mr Thinh worked out how to imitate the old glazes. Years ago this sort of work was sold as genuine,' said Sandy. 'And even now there probably still are unscrupulous dealers passing them off as real antiques in Hanoi and Saigon.'

As Anna carefully replaced the vase on the shelf, Sandy noticed a large plate that certainly looked old, even down to the chip on the edge. It was painted in blues and greens with two fighting cocks in its centre. She studied it for a moment then picked it up and turned it over.

'Is this one of yours, Mr Thinh?' asked Sandy.

The wizened old man gave an impish smile and shook his head.

'Your very best student?' asked Sandy.

'Ask him if it's for sale,' said Anna.

Again the old man shook his head and gave Sandy a rapid explanation. Sandy's eyes widened.

'He says it's genuine. Really old. A lot of plates like this were sent from Vietnam to China in the fifteenth and sixteenth centuries. He said he has learned a lot by studying it.'

'Where did he get it?' wondered Anna.

'I'll try to ask diplomatically.'

Sandy and Mr Thinh chatted some more and then Sandy thanked him and said goodbye, echoed by Anna.

'So what did he say?' asked Anna.

'He says old pieces turn up in this area occasionally. Farmers dig them up in a field, but that one came from the sea.'

'As in a shipwreck?' asked Anna. 'Or dropped overboard in the river perhaps?'

'Could be. He said a young boy sold it to him. He wouldn't give Mr Thinh any details. Mr Thinh has adapted the pattern for other pieces.'

In the street they spotted Kim outside a shop and he led them back to the car.

'It won't take too long to get to Halong Bay,' said Kim. 'We have to meet the people who run the boat trip. And I have a date with an old friend in Halong City before I go over to Cat Ba Island for the weekend, while you're on the boat.'

Anna marvelled at the procession of rice paddies, lushly wet green, red mud bank arteries dividing paddies and directing life-sustaining water to the rippling green rice shoots. Some were tended by the lone figure of a farmer with oxen and plough, or by women bent over, occasionally a baby tied to their back. Others were empty save for a tiered stone family mausoleum in the centre, a monument where ancestors stayed close to their family.

They passed townships, villages, thatched huts hidden among palms, and waterways on which men and women in conical hats poled narrow open boats, fish farms, houses on stilts in marshy reaches and small temples. Everywhere families were on the move – by motorbike and scooter, bicycle and on foot.

Anna was disappointed to find Halong City a resort town of ugly high-rise apartments, hotels, holiday accommodation and casinos.

Sandy decided against visiting the resort of Cat Ba town next to Halong City, preferring the natural beauty of the bay. 'Once we're on the boat we'll leave all this commercialisation behind,' she promised Anna.

'You two should come hiking with me,' said Kim. 'Cat Ba National Park is fantastic – there's amazing wildlife, interesting caves like the one used as a secret hospital during the war, and very challenging hikes or walks.'

'We're thinking something more cruisey, thanks,' said Sandy, knowing Kim's penchant for difficult hikes. He dropped them near a long jetty stretching into the bay. 'We'll meet you on Sunday afternoon. Thanks for the ride,' she said.

'Are we on that?' Anna pointed to the replica paddle steamer at the wharf. It was over fifty metres long, its three decks filled with international tourists and the French crew in crisp white uniforms. The paddle, just for show, was behind a swimming deck.

'No way. We're on the *Harvest Moon*. Captain Chinh's old junk that he's had renovated,' said Sandy. 'There are a lot of new junks being made just for tourist trips, but I like to go authentic where possible.'

'I hope that means a loo,' said Anna.

'There he is, the yellow and red sails.' Sandy pointed to a wooden junk with red sails and a yellow moon design on them that was manoeuvring its way to the jetty as the tourist-packed paddle steamer motored away.

They boarded on a wobbly plank laid from the jetty steps to the deck of the junk. A smiling young man swung their bags on board.

'Meet Hung, new crew man. Good sailor,' beamed Captain Chinh, giving Sandy a welcoming wave.

'Anyone else coming along?' asked Sandy, and Anna looked around, wondering where'd they'd fit anyone else given the space. But once she followed Hung below deck she was surprised at the space in the broad-beamed old vessel. Sandy and Anna shared a little cabin with two single berths and a good-sized porthole above. A shelf and a small dresser with deep drawers and a large carved storage box that smelled of sandalwood was big enough for their belongings. Off the room was a tiny compact ensuite with a toilet, basin and handheld shower.

'Cute and comfy,' observed Anna.

'We're lucky: there's only one other person on board, an older Aussie fellow,' said Sandy.

'Do local people come on these trips?' asked Anna. So far at the jetty she'd only seen foreign tourists. 'Is there a local wealthy upper class taking to the water?'

'You bet. We'll probably spot some of the luxury boats that look like they've just left Monaco or the Riviera. Let's go and sit on deck as we head out. You haven't really seen what it's all about.'

Hung settled them in sling-back deck chairs in the wide bow and handed them a glass of soft drink and woven conical stiffened cane hats with bright nylon ribbons attached to the inside.

'Very practical and won't blow off,' said Sandy.

Anna was surprised at how light the hat was as she tied the ribbons under her chin.

Hung put a tray of crisps, tasty dried nuts and seeds, and some fresh fruit beside them and showed them where the icebox was, filled with cold drinks.

Captain Chinh, wiry with sun-crinkled skin, wearing voluminous shorts, a T-shirt and the ever-present conical hat, was in the stern guiding the *Harvest Moon* out into the bay when the other passenger came out and went to talk to the skipper and take some photographs. He was in a short-sleeved batik shirt and a battered cotton hat that reminded Anna of her dad's old fishing hat.

Anna gazed at the striking scenery about her. She'd seen the ragged grey outlines of granite and limestone against the skyline, but as they left the horseshoe curve of the shoreline she realised they were sailing into a strange world of startlingly different geography. The sea was emerald and from its smooth surface exploded thousands of bare peaks eroded by sea and wind into craggy sculptures. Others rose out of the sea dripping dark green vegetation like a mantle over one shoulder. Another cluster looked like the gnarled fingers of a giant's hand, the palm cupped below the surface.

'It's said a monstrous dragon ran to the sea from the mountains and his tail gouged out the landscape, which filled with water. Supposedly there are periodic sightings of the mythical marine monster – the tarasque,' said Sandy.

'Vietnam's answer to the Loch Ness monster? I can believe there's something down there – it's so eerie,' said Anna. 'Beautiful, but mysterious.'

As the shore disappeared Captain Chinh cut the motor and, under sail, they glided between the strange monoliths. Leaving the steering to Hung he came up to the bow to introduce the other passenger.

The girls liked him immediately. He had speckled grey hair, an open friendly face and a well-modulated

Australian accent. 'I'm Tom Ahearn. Quite amazing, isn't it?' He nodded at the sheer grey sculptured walls rising out of the sea close to them.

'Listen to the birds,' exclaimed Anna.

'We were thinking you could get lost among all the peaks and islands,' said Sandy. 'They look alike to us, but each peak is quite different when you study them.'

Captain Chinh smiled. 'I know every place here. Lot of caves for tourists to see. Tonight we stop in special place. You see tomorrow, magic one. You take kayaks, okay?'

'We're up for a paddle,' said Sandy, and Anna nodded.

'Tomorrow you come with me, Tom. Hung watch boat.' Captain Chinh had everything arranged, it seemed.

'The water is like glass, more like a lake. But then it's a really huge bay, and out there – the Tonkin Gulf,' commented Tom. 'You two travelling around the country?'

Sandy answered. 'I've been living here for four years. It's Anna's first visit from Australia. I'm due to move back there so we're being tourists. Your first time here?' How many times had Sandy had this conversation with visitors who crossed her path at popular spots in Vietnam?

'I was here in the war,' said Tom. 'Never got to the north, of course. What've you been doing here?' he asked Sandy. So she told him about HOPE and he nodded. 'Bloody good outfit. NGOs do a terrific job. Young people like yourself getting in and mixing it with the locals. Achieves more than some of the aid bureaucrats, I reckon,' said Tom. 'And, Anna, you have family ties here?'

Anna didn't really want to talk about her family, but he asked so gently, so sensitively, that she said, 'My mother's family came from here. My mother was a refugee in Australia but she died when I was young.'

'Sad start to a new life,' he said gently. 'When you say "here", you mean this province or just Vietnam?' asked Tom.

'She was from the south, that's all I know. I don't know which village or anything. I'm just being a tourist with Sandy.'

'Where're you from, Tom?' asked Sandy to shift the attention from Anna.

'Sydney. Northern beaches. What about you?'

'Anna and I grew up in Maroubra – we've known each other since kindy.'

'Nice one,' said Tom, grinning and leaning back in his seat. He then turned to Captain Chinh. 'How long have you been in the tourist business? Did you refit the *Harvest Moon* or take over a going concern?'

'This boat been in my family long time. We fishing people, do many things, always live near sea. Hung, my nephew, he learning tourist business at university,' said Captain Chinh proudly. 'His idea make this tourist boat. People better than fish,' he laughed.

The girls exchanged an amused glance at Tom's hearty burst of laughter.

'You told me we're having fish for dinner. Fresh, I hope?' said Tom.

'Hung catch this morning. He lives in fishing village over there, you see tomorrow.'

'So he's on university holidays?' said Sandy. 'Where's he studying?'

'Number one university in Hanoi. He work with me, make money for next year study,' said Captain Chinh.

Tom excused himself to go to his cabin and unpack some of his gear. Captain Chinh went to the galley to prepare dinner. The girls moved to the stern to dip into the icebox near Hung.

'Can I get you something, Hung?' asked Sandy.

'No, thank you. Help yourself. I put your drinks in there to keep cold,' Hung added and Sandy opened the lid.

'The white wine is chilling nicely. Looks like Tom brought some beer.' Sandy handed Anna a lemonade. 'So what are you studying, Hung?'

'I'm in my second year of economics and business administration. I work with Uncle when I come back here in the breaks.'

'Where's your family?' asked Anna.

He motioned over his shoulder. 'In the village. It's a fishing community; you'll see tomorrow. Tourists like to go and look at it.' He smiled.

'It's a small village with floating houses,' said Sandy, thinking he'd come a long way from such a remote village to study at university and speak English as well as he did.

As if reading her mind Hung added, 'I live with Uncle's younger brother's family in Hanoi. They took me in when I was young. I have brothers and sisters but I am first son so I was chosen to be educated.'

'Congratulations. You must have been a smart kid,' said Anna and they all laughed.

'What is the word in English for too smart?' asked Hung.

'Precocious? No matter, you made your mark early. What do you plan to do?' asked Sandy.

'Tourism is big business in my country now. I would like to start my own travel company. For visitors coming here. But I would need much money. There are many places visitors never see. The national operators are good but I would like to make tours for small groups. Special trips to special places.'

'For the niche market, you mean?' said Anna and Hung smiled, filing the phrase away.

For the next hour he guided the *Harvest Moon* past the more spectacular monoliths, occasionally passing another tourist boat with an exchange of waves and smiles. He pointed to the paddle steamer in the distance.

'Those big boats cannot get so close, or go through some of the narrow passages,' said Hung. He pointed out one huge outcrop that had a small forest on top spilling down one side where soil had collected over the years. There was a scrap of rough beach with a sampan pulled up onto it.

'There's a roof in the trees. What's that near the top?' asked Anna as she glimpsed the late sun shining on a flash of gold.

'It's an old pagoda.'

'Whose boat is that?' said Sandy.

'Maybe there's someone visiting the old Buddhist nun who lives on the island.' Hung steered the junk around the outcrop, which came between them and the setting sun, and busied himself adjusting the big red sail.

Tom joined the girls, helping himself to a bottle of local 333 beer. 'Magic, isn't it? Chinh says there'll be a mist tonight. Make it interesting, eh?'

'Creepy maybe. You mean we're stopping round here?' said Anna.

Before Tom could answer, Hung and Captain Chinh began reefing down the sails and with a splash, an anchor was dropped from the bow.

Because it was a still evening they decided to eat on deck rather than in the small saloon below. Hung set up a table and put a heavy tablecloth over the flat hatch cover to use as a serving table. Lanterns hanging from the rigging were lit and, along with the red and green mooring lights, they splashed the glassy surface of the still dark sea with sparkling streaks of colour.

'Is this very deep here?' asked Anna.

'Very deep. Some places too deep to measure,' said Captain Chinh.

'It has a mysterious air about it, doesn't it,' said Tom.

Anna shivered. There were no other boats or lights in sight, just the looming peaks encircling them, dark against the evening sky.

Captain Chinh served them fried fish and grilled eggplant with spicy minced pork topped with fresh coriander, followed by bananas dipped in batter, fried, and sprinkled with sugar. Dinner was praised by all.

Candles in glass jars threw a soft light on the table as Captain Chinh accepted one of Tom's beers. Sandy topped up the wine glasses as Hung took away their dishes.

Tom leaned back in his chair. 'This is the way to appreciate a place. Chinh, you didn't finish the story you were telling me. Sandy and Anna might be interested.'

Captain Chinh pulled a cigarette from his top pocket and lit it, then took a swallow of beer, enjoying the anticipation on the faces around the table.

'Long time, long ago in Vietnam we have famous ladies . . . they fight for our country, we honour them in stories. Most famous is Kieu, very beautiful story, very sad. Also famous Trung sisters, one husband killed by Chinese and the sister start big rebellion and send Chinese out of Vietnam. But some years later Chinese come back and so sisters kill themselves drowning in a river.' He took another drag on his cigarette. 'And Lady Trieu, another very brave lady, she fight off Chinese invasion. She go to battle on elephant, all dressed in gold armour and white shoes made from elephant tusk – yes, ivory. Yes, she very brave lady, only nineteen.'

Only Nineteen. It brought back the echoes of Redgum's song to Tom. He didn't mention it; Sandy and Anna were probably too young to know it.

'I've heard of *The Tale of Kieu.* A very famous epic love story,' Sandy said to Anna.

'Do tell,' said Anna.

50

'The scene is medieval times and this young girl sacrifices her own true love to save her family. Her life becomes a procession of lovers, husbands and bad men but her spirit remains pure, so she is finally reunited with her first love and her family.'

'So a happy ending?' asked Anna.

Captain Chinh and Sandy shook their heads.

'No, some call her a prostitute, but, despite preserving her own spiritual honour, she can't go back to the way it was before. Only in her heart and memory,' said Sandy.

'Loss and nostalgia for what was. There'd be a lot of that after the war, wouldn't you say?' Tom asked Captain Chinh, who grasped the meaning of the question but struggled to find words to express his answer. Finally he summoned Hung, who translated the older man's explanation.

'*Que huong* means the village you come from, *ky niem thoi tho au* means young memories before bad times. These are things wished to go back to after the war. Vietnamese people are very family and community people, and being displaced and losing their home and relatives make them very sad,' said Hung, looking at his uncle.

'I'm thinking Kieu's story sounds very contemporary,' sighed Sandy. 'There are a lot of lost young people in western society who have made choices that haven't worked out but can't go back.'

Captain Chinh rose and excused himself to check the boat then bunk down. 'Hung stay here and watch the wind and the sea. But it will be safe. Very calm,' he assured them.

'Anyone for a cuppa? I brought some tea bags from home with me,' said Tom.

'I'm happy with the wine for now. But I'd love one in the morning, thanks, Tom,' said Anna. 'I can't come at green tea for brekkie.'

After Tom bade them good night, the two friends sat on the deck watching the light of the rising moon glimmering behind what they'd named Pagoda Peak.

'What's that?' Anna pointed to a faint drift of moonlit white swirling between the smaller peaks jutting from the sea around them. They watched it waft down and across the sea, blurring the crevices and intricately weathered cliff face closest to them, like a distant sprite.

'It must be mist like Tom said. I feel the temperature dropping. I think I might hit my bunk,' yawned Sandy.

'This is looking scary. I remember years ago some old black-and-white movie on TV,' said Anna. 'There was a ghost ship, covered in moss and wispy white stuff floating in this weird fog; no one was on board. I think aliens had got them. This does seem like we're on another planet.'

'Oh, for god's sake,' laughed Sandy. 'There's probably a dozen boats around the corner. Most of them moor out here for the night. It's a two-day excursion, remember.'

'You'd think we'd hear noises . . . sound carries across water,' said Anna.

'Come to bed.' Sandy put down her glass. 'Good night, Hung.' She waved at the dim outline of Hung sitting cross-legged on the deck. He lifted an arm, the red glow of a cigarette in his hand.

Anna woke wondering what time it was, aware of the gentle swing of the old wooden junk on its anchor chain. She lay there for a short time but felt wide awake. She listened to the unfamiliar noises, a slow symphony of creaks and slapping water. It was as if the old junk was wheezing in its slumber. A metal clink, a soft thud, and was that a footfall? Hung in the galley making tea? Anna waited a few more minutes but, knowing she wasn't going to get to sleep, decided to go up on deck. She went through the main saloon with its dining table and built-in long seats that doubled as storage. A small wall lamp glowed. She quietly climbed up the wide ladder, but before stepping out onto the deck she glanced around. There was a soft breeze; the moon was high but filtered through the light mist that drifted low above the surface of the water. She glanced to where the green light hung on the starboard cross arm and suddenly imagined that the nearby craggy peak spearing out of the sea was wavering. At first glance it seemed that the monolith might crumble and fall but it looked more like it was swaying, an illusion caused by the sea mist.

It was eerie and she was about to turn and go below when she heard the soft murmur of voices. Was Captain Chinh taking over his shift from Hung? Dawn seemed a long way off.

Anna poked her head above the raised cockpit, looking through the rigging, and saw the slim outline of Hung, but the other shape was not Captain Chinh or the Australian man, Tom. Snatches of conversation came on the wind but she didn't understand what they were saying and wished Sandy were there to translate. There was something about their body language, the lowered urgent tone of voice, that seemed conspiratorial. Had this other man been on board since they left Halong? Softly Anna moved down the port side of the boat towards the stern, leaving the men amidships.

It was then she noticed a wet rope fastened to the railing and saw a wooden boat tied to the side. A large cane basket secured with rope was in the bow of the small boat and she wondered if it contained supplies to be hauled aboard the junk. But why so late at night?

The short muscular man talking to Hung flicked his

cigarette over the side. Anna quickly hunched over so as not to be seen and tiptoed back the way she had come.

Lying on top of her bed sheet as it was so warm, Anna strained to hear noises up on deck, but the creaking of the wooden hull, occasional thuds from the rigging, soughing wind through the open porthole, Sandy's gentle breathing and other unidentifiable noises made her imagination race. Finally, when she heard Captain Chinh making his tea in the galley before relieving Hung at sunrise, she dozed off.

Sandy, dressed and fresh, called Anna for breakfast, and when she'd showered and joined everyone on deck, Anna couldn't help but glance over the side to where she'd seen the little boat tied up. There was no sign of it. Nor the large basket. A late-night visit from one of Hung's relations, perhaps? But she didn't mention it to anyone as she accepted one of Tom's tea bags and tossed up whether to try Captain Chinh's pho or the assorted breads, fruit and sweet rice, or just a mini packet of muesli. Sandy had become addicted to the strong chicory roasted coffee dripped into a cup with a liberal dollop of condensed milk.

'Were you in the army, Tom?' asked Sandy as Hung began stacking life jackets and water bottles on the deck ready for the day's outing.

'Felt I was on the occasions I travelled with them. No, I was a foreign correspondent for Australian radio. Wrote articles every now and then as well.'

'Really?' Sandy was surprised and immediately interested. 'So you're back as a tourist or a journalist?'

With chopsticks Tom deftly fished out a small piece of beef and bok choy from the hot broth in his bowl. 'I retired a couple of years back. But once a journo, always a journo. Thought I'd update myself. I've been asked to do a couple of stories. There's a lot happening here.'

'From a political, economic or tourist point of view?' asked Anna.

'They're pretty well all entwined,' said Tom. 'Initially I agreed to come to be part of a reunion and my curiosity got the better of me, so I've come early to see the changes since the war. The stunning scenery, its diversity, its people, make Vietnam pretty attractive. To businesses as well as tourists.'

'You like what you see, Mr Ahearn?' asked Hung.

'I like, Hung, I like,' said Tom, smiling. 'I'm looking forward to this kayak expedition.'

After breakfast two kayaks and an open canoe were towed to the *Harvest Moon* from the village. They were surrounded by a flotilla of wooden boats filled with women and children, some with babies tied to their backs or across their chests in a cotton cloth sling. All were exuberantly selling food, shells, hats, postcards, necklaces or silk scarves as souvenirs. Standing on the deck, Tom flipped coins into the water and young boys were over the sides of their boats before the money had hit the surface. Several enterprising kids had paddled out in old rubber inner tubes and the water fight for coins became noisy and competitive.

There was a lot of good-natured banter as the locals watched Anna and Sandy climb down a ladder to a small wire platform just wide enough for two people to stand on. Hung held the craft steady and helped Sandy and Anna settle in the middle of each small yellow kayak, handed them both a paddle and pushed them off. Tom settled in the stern of a slightly larger canoe, and Captain Chinh lightly stepped into the centre and set off. Tom had a paddle that he cheerfully dug into the water following the captain's lead.

Sandy and Anna handled their kayaks with ease and skimmed across the sunny calm morning water following Chinh and Tom. Then they paddled into deep shadow as they rounded Pagoda Peak and went behind a smaller out-crop that hid a narrow slit in the rock face. Captain Chinh stroked confidently through it. Sandy and Anna paddled through the opening to find themselves in another world. They were in a beautiful broad chamber where it was dim and cool, the water strangely luminous. With a deep plunge of his paddle Chinh took a turn around a wall of rock, disappearing from sight. Sandy paused, glancing to see Anna was behind, and did the same.

They had turned into a passage cut by centuries of wind and waves and suddenly they came out into an incredible light green lagoon, surrounded by dripping moss-covered limestone walls. The huge sheet of water was brilliant and calm. Far above, there was an opening to the sky. A fairytale grotto. They glided across the vast chamber only to find another smaller grotto. The tower-ing walls shone in the reflected light and across an overhang marched an army of stalactites.

Captain Chinh and Tom stowed their paddles and drifted, Tom reaching for the small digital camera in his pocket.

'Wow,' breathed Sandy as Anna drew alongside.

'This is unreal.' Anna trailed her fingers in the crystal water. 'Better than being in a cathedral at dawn. So cool, clear and calm.'

Captain Chinh and Tom drifted by. 'Stunning place,' said Tom. 'How deep, Chinh? Anyone know what's down there?'

'Very deep. No fish.'

'Can we swim?' asked Anna.

'Yeah, and how do you get back in the kayak?' said Sandy. 'Just enjoy the view, Anna.' She caught Chinh's eye. 'How far back does it go? Can we get out the other side?'

'No boat go through. You take picture and we go,' said the captain. 'Not many people see this place. Just special people. You special.'

Anna and Sandy exchanged an amused glance. Tom, looking through the zoom of his camera, pointed to one side of the grotto. 'There's a ledge there. Someone could stand on it. Is this tidal? Does the water come up higher?' he wondered.

'Little bit. When moon right,' answered Captain Chinh. 'You take picture and we go.' But he paddled close to the ledge, raising himself to see it more clearly, then sat down again and turned the canoe away.

Anna and Sandy manoeuvred their kayaks, handing Anna's camera to Tom to take a picture of them both. The flashes glittered on the craggy stone walls as if studded with jewels, illuminating the two friends holding hands in their orange life jackets.

Captain Chinh firmly dipped his paddle in the water and led them back into bright sunlight and the openness of the bay, where the brooding peaks dwarfed them all.

'That was amazing,' said Sandy.

'Sure was, though I kept thinking that a monster could rise up, or a whirlpool start or something,' said Anna.

'There are stories from many years ago of people disappearing in such places, never to be found,' said Sandy mysteriously.

They headed across the bay to where a finger of water led into a cove. Along one side was a small rough beach littered with boats, fishing nets, bamboo fish and crab traps, empty fuel drums and rubbish. Next to it, jutting into the shallow water, was a collection of thatched and wooden houses on stilts, mostly small with narrow verandahs only wide enough for two or three people to sit on woven straw mats. Below, pontoons sagged next to fenced water 'paddocks' and rickety ladders led up to the fronts of the houses. As they drew closer Tom burst out laughing.

'The floating farmyard!' He reached for his camera to take a shot of the small fenced pens on stilts above the water. One held chickens, another a fat pig.

'What are in the fenced cages in the water?' asked Anna.

'Big fish for eating. In the tanks are shrimp,' answered Captain Chinh.

Anna watched a girl sitting on the edge of a sampan moored next to her dwelling as she washed her hair, pouring a bucket of water over her head. 'Do you reckon the loo, bathing, washing and so on is dumped into the water?'

'Of course. No sewerage or plumbing here,' answered Sandy.

'Yuk. I've changed my mind about a swim.'

'Ah, don't worry, the catfish clean up everything,' said Tom.

The girls howled at him and even Captain Chinh laughed. 'This old-style village. Over there, that Hung's father house.'

There were several boats tied up and people sitting in the open doorway smoking and eating. They glanced at the tourists and Anna suddenly wondered if one of the men was the one she'd seen on the boat with Hung last night. As if to confirm it, the man acknowledged them with a slight nod.

'Are they Hung's relatives?' she asked.

Captain Chinh shrugged. 'Yes, and some people from the mainland. They do business.'

Anna was about to ask what kind of business would be conducted in such a small out-of-the-way village, but the others were stroking strongly back towards the

Harvest Moon as another batch of tourists in kayaks and tenders headed into the cove to see the floating village.

Back on the junk Hung had prepared food and, with Captain Chinh in command, he took a canoe, waved goodbye and skimmed across the water to visit his village.

When the three Australians were alone, Tom took another look at the photos he'd taken, then handed the camera to Sandy.

'What do you make of this?' he asked, showing a photo of the grotto in the large viewing screen.

'Pretty. The light in the water is great,' said Anna.

'Yeah, but look at the ledge I pointed out. Above that.'

'There are steps,' exclaimed Sandy, taking a closer look.

'Odd, don't you think? Where would they go? Who'd access them from the cave?' asked Tom.

The girls studied the picture. 'Weird. Ask Captain Chinh,' suggested Sandy.

'What about the old nun at the temple up the hill? How does she get up and down to get supplies?' asked Tom.

'How do we know there even *is* an old nun at the pagoda?' added Anna.

'Let's go and look!' joked Sandy.

'I'll go have a yarn to Chinh,' said Tom. 'You chat up Hung when he comes back.'

'Well, we don't have anything else to do this afternoon,' said Sandy. 'Might cost more, an "extra" excursion.'

'Be a great view from up there. Tom looks fit enough to make it up to the pagoda,' said Anna.

'Let's talk to Hung when he gets back.'

Returning from his village with fresh fish, Hung was

relaxed about their idea and shrugged. 'It is not a very impressive pagoda but the walk winds around so it's not a steep climb and it's a shady walk.'

'So let's do it. I'd like to talk to the old nun. She must get lonely. How long has she been there?' asked Sandy.

'She was a novice near Dien Bien Phu, but fled when the French were defeated in the early 1950s and the communists took over. She finds this place very peaceful. Occasional tourists visit her and my family take her food. She is nearly blind but manages to cook and look after herself and the temple.'

'Heavens, poor thing. What can we take her?' asked Anna.

'Just make an offering: that will please her. Fresh fruit. After the spirits have eaten she will enjoy the fruit,' said Hung.

'So how do we get up there? Surely we don't have to climb up from the grotto?'

Hung gave a slight smile. 'No one uses the grotto; it was once a place for . . . ' he struggled to find the right word and finally Sandy attempted to help.

'Smugglers? Pirates? Shipwrecks? Bandits?'

Hung nodded. 'Yes, very many bad men sailed all around South-East Asia in old times. Also when rich Chinese refugees left Vietnam after the American war they too were robbed.'

'And so were some very poor people,' added Sandy.

After lunch Hung took them across the bay in the *Harvest Moon*'s motorised rubber ducky. At the base of the outcrop Hung jumped into the water and dragged the boat onto the beach. Then Hung, a small bag slung across his back, led the way over the rocky foreshore to where the track began.

They threaded their way between boulders, the cliff face bare and windswept, until the track curved upward and there were suddenly straggly, struggling trees. It seemed they were walking in corkscrew fashion, slowly ascending, watching carefully where they stepped.

Eventually Hung paused and pointed at the view through a break in the high rocks beside the track. They took a breather and leaned on the rocks for a view of the bay spread out below. Tom took more photographs, murmuring repeatedly, 'Great shot.'

Within minutes they were in a thicket of old trees that had weathered years of wind and sun, sinking roots between cracks in the rock in search of soil and water. Then, through the trees, they glimpsed the small pagoda, its red and gold paint cracked and faded. Hung hurried ahead to alert the elderly nun of their arrival.

As they stood admiring the incongruity of what Sandy had instantly christened the Temple of Nowhere, Tom announced that he would take a look at the pagoda from the other angles on a path that seemed to circle it. 'Bound to find something worth shooting.' He took off, and Sandy and Anna answered Hung's wave and walked up the steps to the pagoda.

There was a small cobbled courtyard of beach stones in front of a stone arch etched with Vietnamese letters and religious symbols. They left their shoes at the open doors and stepped inside the dim cool room with its large decorated altar. Incense was burning; candles flickered next to a small offering of rice and nuts. To one side of the main shrine were smaller carvings and a doorway through which they heard Hung's voice.

He came into the main room, leading a tiny woman in a simple brown robe. Her head was shaven and she walked carefully as if she knew rather than saw the way.

Hung made the introductions as Tom joined them. Sandy touched the woman's hands, speaking quietly, and the nun smiled and led them to wooden seats in the courtyard.

'She says it is good to feel the soft hands of a woman,' said Sandy.

Hung wandered off as Sandy translated questions from Tom and Anna, piecing together the story of the nun, who had been raped and bashed, yet spared when others with her died. Since she had left Dien Bien Phu, where the French had made their last stand against the communist forces, she had prayed each day and observed the rituals of her faith.

Sandy told them how the little nun came to this bay and was told of the deserted temple and how she'd asked to be brought here to thank the ancestral spirits who had watched over her. Local people came on feast days and ceremonial occasions to pray and make offerings at the temple on the hill, and gradually word spread and it became something of a pilgrimage to visit the nun living simply in a small hut beside the old pagoda. Visitors came away enriched by the woman's piety and faith for she had suffered so much adversity and seen so much horror but remained serene.

When Sandy asked her about her blindness. She told them in a mixture of French, English and Vietnamese. 'I do not miss seeing very well. I see shapes, a little light, a little dark. Enough for my needs. I believe the taking of my sight is a blessing. I see in my mind those things I wish to see: good people, lush rice paddies, blue sky and sea, my cooking pot, yellow star fruit and pink water-melon. When I taste food I remember good times with my family, my sisters and my brothers. When I hear your voices, I remember friends and teachers. In this place I see and hear and remember what is good. The spirits come and speak with me. I am not alone.' She smiled. 'And how may I help you?' she asked simply.

'We came thinking to help you, Mother,' said Sandy softly, summing up what they all felt. 'But you have given us far more.'

Hung had chopped the fruit and gave them each a bowl of sweet sticky rice and the fruit on top as an offering. They followed the nun to the altar, where in turn they set a bowl at the foot of the statue of Buddha, lit sticks of incense from the burning candles and, with hands clasped, bowed three times and offered a silent prayer.

'We should go back now,' said Hung quietly. 'I will wait outside.'

'Can I take your picture?' asked Tom, and he led the old nun to the doorway.

Anna was deeply touched by the atmosphere and lingered before the shrine, trying to settle the many emotions she felt.

Suddenly the nun was beside her, touching Anna's arm and smiling. She handed Anna another stick of incense, and guided her hand to the candle flame. 'Pour votre famille,' she said softly.

Anna's hand shook, making the candle flicker. She placed the sweet burning stick in the brass bowl filled with sand and stood as the nun prayed, bowing deeply.

The nun straightened and from the folds of her robe she withdrew her hand and, taking Anna's, placed a small object into her palm, folded her fingers over it, patted it and turned away.

Anna was strangely moved and she stood there, studying the altar, before opening her hand. Lying in her palm was a tiny green jade Buddha.

Sandy came back inside and spoke softly, not wanting to intrude too abruptly on her friend's meditation. 'Anna, we've got to leave now. Hung says something to do with the tide.'

Anna nodded, then pointed to the altar set with

63

offerings. 'Look. Isn't that like the plate we saw in Mr Thinh's studio?' She pointed to a plate that held nuts and dried herbs and a roll of folded palm leaves.

Sandy lifted up the plate and examined it. 'It is too. And it's old, not an imitation. Now where do you suppose this came from? It's museum quality.'

Hung appeared behind them. 'That plate came from our village. It is for offerings.'

'Hung, it's very valuable – it's old, very famous Vietnamese porcelain,' said Sandy.

He showed no reaction. 'We must go or the tide will cover the last of the beach; it can be dangerous getting back to the boat.'

'Are there any more ceramics like this in your village?' Sandy asked Hung.

'There might be. There are stories of treasures hidden in the crevices of some of the cliffs,' he said. 'Come, let's go.'

'Hung, if any more ceramics or porcelain come into your village, please, take them to a museum or a reputable art gallery,' said Sandy. 'They are worth a lot of money.'

'If things are found they will be sold quietly.' He went outside and motioned to Tom to follow and set out towards the track back down the hill. In the late afternoon sunlight they watched the elderly nun make her way unaided around the back of the pagoda.

'Hung knows more than he's letting on,' whispered Sandy.

'What's that?' asked Tom.

'There's a very old porcelain dish on the altar. Hung says it was found in the floating village.'

'Doesn't sound likely. Unless it was in a shipwreck like the haul of Chinese porcelain that was found in the South China Sea somewhere a few years back. Fetched a good price at Christie's,' said Tom.

'Hung had a visitor late last night. Someone paddled over from the village with a huge bamboo crate,' said Anna.

'Probably dried fish, or local hootch,' said Tom.

'You're the journalist. This could be a story, Tom,' said Anna.

'That nun is a story. What an incredible old bird,' he said. 'She's even got a vegetable garden going round the back.'

Kim was waiting at the wharf when the *Harvest Moon* returned the next morning, and Sandy introduced him to Tom before Sandy, Anna and Tom effusively thanked Captain Chinh and Hung for the trip.

'Can we give Tom a lift back to Hanoi, Kim? Better than the bus he came down on,' said Sandy.

'Of course, plenty of room,' agreed Kim, taking Tom's backpack and stowing it in the boot.

'We're going back via Hai Phong,' Kim told them. 'It's where the fish project is that HOPE is involved with. I have to check on how things are running.'

'Is there anything else there?' asked Anna.

'It's a big sea port, very industrial, but the city has some lovely colonial architecture – it's like Hanoi used to be. Still a little sleepy and great seafood.'

By the time they had taken in the sights of Hai Phong, they decided to stay for lunch and found a shady court-yard restaurant specialising in local seafood. Sandy began asking Kim about his hiking trip and what wildlife he'd seen in the national park.

Tom turned to Anna. 'So, Anna, what's your story? What do you think of Vietnam?'

3

THEY WERE THE ONLY people left in the shady courtyard of the little restaurant. The owner settled himself at a table inside to eat his lunch. The clatter of dishes and chatter drifted from the kitchen. The jangle of bicycle bells and car horns in the street seemed far away in the somnolence of the early afternoon.

Tom stretched. 'If anything the food in Vietnam is even better than I remember. Simple rural cuisine but served with sophistication.'

'Yeah, well, it's not that "simple". Some of it takes hours, even days to prepare,' said Sandy.

'This is a nice little place, more for westerners, but I wouldn't call it sophisticated compared to some places in Hanoi,' said Kim. 'Not that I can afford to eat at the Metropole or some of the other tourist restaurants.'

'I haven't had any desire to eat upmarket. I've only been in Hanoi a week, and I'm bowled over by what a lovely city it is,' said Tom. 'When I was in the south all those years ago Hanoi was far away and a closed city inhabited by communists and the North Vietnamese regular army. I imagined a grim, regimented place shattered by the war. But the city is charming.'

'It might have had a lot of masters from the Chinese to the French but they've left interesting and beautiful buildings. Unfortunately the ugly cement jobs that are around are souvenirs of the Soviet alliance,' said Sandy.

'I like the energy: everyone is active and there are so many young people,' said Anna.

'The majority of the population are under thirty-five,' said Kim. 'Baby boomers don't rule here!'

'Talking about young entrepreneurs, are you going to check out your fish farm people?' Sandy asked Kim.

'Yes, would you like to come along? The project is the first of several like this for HOPE. The co-op is planning to move up to freezing and exporting fish and shrimp.'

'We won't be long: it's near the harbour. Or you could stay here, have some dessert, coffee, a cold drink,' Sandy suggested to Anna and Tom.

'That sounds good to me,' said Tom.

'I'll keep you company, Tom,' said Anna. The fish farm might be a worthy project but it didn't appeal enough to trail around after Sandy and Kim on HOPE business. She found Tom easy to get along with and so she picked up the menu to choose a dessert.

While they waited for sweet sticky rice and coconut to finish the meal, Tom sipped his beer. 'So, Anna, is this a holiday, a girls' own adventure or a pilgrimage?' He unconsciously slipped into journalistic mode.

Anna smiled. 'It seemed a good idea at the time. Although I admit I did initially need a bit of persuading. Anyway, I took leave, kissed the boyfriend goodbye and was on a plane not long after Sandy emailed me.'

'Ha, boyfriend. Serious? He didn't want to come here with you?' asked Tom.

'No way. Well, Sandy didn't invite him. Sandy thought it would be nice to have time out together, like we did as kids. She's always been the ringleader. I don't think she likes Carlo much. He's Italian. This place doesn't hold much interest for him.'

Tom studied the beautiful girl sitting opposite, her long straight black hair, dark almond eyes, high cheek bones and full lips an indication of her Vietnamese heritage. But her tall elegance, the same open and healthy vitality as Sandy, her sense of humour and her friendly manner came from her Australian upbringing. He'd seen what close friends the girls were and he wondered how Anna felt about her best friend not appearing to like her boyfriend.

'You said you and Sandy met in kindergarten. Were your families friends?'

'Our fathers are both in the car business so became friends and, living in the same street, Sandy and I played together, started preschool together. Sandy's mother has always kept an eye on me since my mother died, though my dad's mum stepped in and lived with us and raised me.'

'So you and Sandy are a bit like sisters.'

Anna paused, thinking back to those days, which, while mostly carefree, were also dotted with a few unpleasant incidents. If it hadn't been for Sandy and her mother, Patricia, Anna might not have coped with them as well as she had.

Maroubra, Sydney, 1985

It was a holiday and they were at the beach. Two big umbrellas, a carpet of towels, an Esky filled with cold drinks, chilled prawns and fruit, paper plates, plastic containers of sandwiches and rolls.

Anna watched her mother, Thu, take out her favourite food – savoury cucumber, meat, spiced tomatoes and green herbs chopped and rolled in the fine soft steamed rice flour sheets. As Thu poured a dipping sauce into a small bowl the men pounced. Sandy and Anna squealed and reached for rolls with both hands, fearful of the grownups polishing them off.

Anna nibbled delicately; Sandy finished hers in quick gulps then began digging into the prawns, peeling them expertly, handing every second one to Ashley, her younger brother.

With the arrival of Thu's aunt and uncle, more Vietnamese food was unpacked and Anna's grandmother had to admit she was getting a taste for 'those fiddly things'. Making minced pork dumplings, stuffed savoury pancakes, rice rolls and the other varieties of appetisers that Thu produced was far too much trouble for Grandma Fine. 'A ham, lettuce and tomato sandwich is plenty for the beach,' she said. She had contributed fruit cake left over from Christmas, but ate a good share of the Vietnamese food – 'just to taste'.

Along the beachfront and in the park and under trees, barbecues sizzled with spitting meat despite the heat. These were manned by red-faced men clutching beers to their sagging bellies while women fussed with picnic food. It was tradition; it was the Australian way. After all, it was Australia Day. Some of the picnickers preferred wine, olives, cheeses and salami eaten with thick bread ripped by hand, others the thin white sliced variety wrapped around a sausage dripping with tomato sauce.

To the two little girls it was a joyous day of feasting, playing in the cool wet sand, supervised rides on small waves on Sandy's rubber boogie board, and exploring the rock pools at the far end of the beach.

Phil Donaldson was not present. His car yard stayed open on public holidays in case people with time on their hands came to browse and perhaps buy. Sandy's mother, Patricia, was sorry he was missing the fun: it was so hard for him to relax.

But what had been a sunny happy day turned sour as the girls trailed back from the water with Kevin and saw their families hastily packing up their belongings and the picnic. Grandma Fine was holding Ashley and was on her feet arguing with a circle of jeering young men. Thu was kneeling, hastily stowing items in a basket helped by her aunty, while her Uncle Quoc spoke quietly to the young men who merely laughed at him. Their voices were raised and people on the sand near them stared curiously, laughed behind their hands or pretended not to notice.

Kevin broke into a sprint, shouting, 'Hoy, what do you think you're doing?'

The leader of the group shouted back. 'Telling the chinks to bugger off. Go home where they belong. This is 'Stralia. 'Stralia day, for Aussies, not slopes.'

His voice was slurred and as Kevin, thickset and angry, formed a fist and drew closer, an elderly man put down his book and got to his feet, protesting at the young men's language.

The boys kicked sand over the food and, still calling out, raced drunkenly away, laughing, pleased with their efforts.

'You all right, love?' Kevin bent to help a teary-eyed and shaking Thu.

'Evil little devils. We should call the police. Disgraceful behaviour,' snapped Grandma Fine. 'They need a good walloping.'

'What happened? What happened?' chorused Anna and Sandy, racing up to their families.

The girls were shushed and led away by Grandma Fine.

Kevin drove home, grim faced. There'd been a rushed farewell to Uncle Quoc and the others. Patricia, Sandy and Ashley hurried up the street, Patricia making Sandy promise not to say anything to her father. 'We don't want to upset him.'

'But what were those boys saying? Why was Aunty Thu crying?' persisted Sandy.

'They were drunk, and stupid.'

'If Dad was there I bet he'd have bashed them up.'

'Fighting gets you nowhere. They were just being cruel and rude. Forget it.'

But Anna never forgot it. She had the feeling that her family was somehow at fault.

Anna and Sandy remained good friends. They shared toys, wore each other's clothes and were in and out of each other's homes as if they were their own. They shared secrets, made plans and played together at school.

Anna studied hard for it had been drilled into her by her mother, aunty and uncle that doing well at school would help her to become a success in the world and make her family proud. Australia was a land of opportunity they kept telling her and she understood that meant she had to work harder than the other students.

However, soon Anna was making excuses to stay at home and spend time with her mother, who wasn't feeling well. More and more Thu took to her bed and the house was strangely quiet. Kevin or Grandma Fine did the cooking, and there were no more delicious smells or tasty treats.

Often, when there were still gatherings of her mother's Vietnamese relatives and friends at their home, Anna would hear them speaking in their homeland tongue, a language she didn't understand. Nor did her father. It was an odd bond between father and daughter: their lack of knowledge of that little country far to the north across the sea that Thu, with her uncle and aunty, had crossed at such great risk.

South Vietnam, 1978

She could not look back. Her mother's sobs, the howls of her baby brother, the pale face of her middle sister, the grim face of her father with tears running down his cheeks as they stood in a tight pathetic group, were too hard to see.

They had shared their last meal together in the small house where her family lived. Her father had explained once more the importance of the journey Thu now faced with her young brother. He took her to one side. 'Thu, you are our first born and a clever girl. We are not safe in the south any more since the Americans have gone and now the communists are here. Your Uncle Quoc worked with the Americans, so he could be killed. He must leave Vietnam with Aunty. You go with them and start a new life. Then one day we will follow.'

'Why is little brother Van coming too? Uncle said it will be dangerous escaping in a small boat.'

'I want my son also to start a new life. He is nine and will be a big help to you one day. You will have each other. Listen to your Uncle Quoc, say your prayers and do not forget us.'

'But Father, when will you come? When will we be together?' cried Thu, trying to stop the little-girl tears and be a strong nineteen-year-old.

'Uncle will find a way to send word to us. Keep safe the gold and precious stones from your mother. Protect your brother and keep your honour.' He kissed Thu's forehead and put his arm around her weeping mother, who took a small gold crucifix from around her neck and placed it around Thu's own.

There was a hasty round of hugs and handshakes then the little cart, pulled by an ox, disappeared down the dirt track past paddies and plantations. Sacks of rice and bundles of dried bamboo sticks were cleverly stacked on raised boards and the fleeing family hid beneath this false floor as Uncle urged the ox forward, the perfect image of a simple farmer taking produce to market.

After several uncomfortable days, the cart stopped and Thu shook Van awake. 'We are near the sea; smell the ocean,' she whispered.

Thu had heard discussions about the plans and knew that money had changed hands. She suspected her father only had enough money to send his first-born child and his first son. He had given Uncle Quoc money and food for them, so Thu hid the little jewellery pouch inside her top. She knew her father had arranged for them to escape on a fishing trawler.

However, they had to wait many months before a boat was able to help them escape.

It was a moonless night when the old fishing boat left the harbour and headed out to sea. Holding hands, Thu and Van silently watched the dim lights of the coastal villages fade in the distance until Van asked where they would sleep. A sheet of plastic was all Uncle gave them, which Thu wrapped around them both, as now the sea was rough, the wind peeling back the waves, and rain threatened. Aunty had whispered that it was not wise to travel so far out to sea in the monsoon season, but Uncle reminded her they had no choice. It was time to leave.

Two other families were packed in with Thu and her relatives. They were all tense. Fear of the unknown travelled with them. Thu hugged Van tightly until he fell asleep with his head in her lap.

The rains came the next morning, and the sea and the sky were joined in a streaming mass of water. Van was seasick; he couldn't keep food down and became feverish. Thu and her aunty wiped his hot forehead with a wet rag. When the monsoon rain stopped, the sun was hot, making their damp clothes steam and saltwater crusted on their skin.

Van was pale and shaking and Thu began to pray for him. She reached around her neck and unclasped the gold cross necklace which she pressed into Van's clammy hand, telling him, 'This will protect you, Van. We are going to a happy land, where we can all be together and have a house with many rooms, plenty of food. You will go to school and have friends. Just a little while longer, dear brother. Be strong.'

After several rough days at sea they were settling down for another night when there was an urgent command from the captain. He had sighted another craft moving in on them at high speed and ordered the adults to hide under the fishing nets, the children to get below into a concealed and cramped hideaway near the bow. Thu went to go with Van but was pulled back roughly by the captain and told to get under the plastic sheets among the nets and fishing pots.

There was arguing and shouting between the passengers and Uncle told Aunty and Thu to keep down and hide their faces. 'There is a boat coming; it could be pirates. Keep one thing to give them and hide the rest.'

Shakily Thu slipped a gold ring on her finger, then tightly rolled the pouch and put it on top of her head, twisting her long hair in a topknot over it.

A large and fast white boat came alongside. Commands were shouted and the trawler slowed. Armed men jumped aboard the trawler, pulling out those hiding on board, demanding money and valuables in broken Vietnamese.

Below in the bow, Van heard his sister scream and he rushed up onto the deck and saw his aunty cowering as a man stood over her demanding her jewellery or gold. But what frightened Van more was the sight of two men dragging Thu up the side of the white boat now tied alongside. She was flung down roughly by two men. Her screams stabbed into his heart and he ran towards the other boat, but one of the pirates laughed and lashed at him with a heavy machete. He felt a sharp sting, blood gushed from his shoulder and he fell down screaming.

On the big boat, Thu was thrown on a pile of canvas, her clothes slashed and ripped from her and men took turns to throw themselves on her, panting and thrusting, ripping into her body as she was held down by her arms, and her ankles spread-eagled.

She squeezed her eyes shut, biting her lip till it bled to stop from crying out in agony. She had heard Van scream and knew he had tried to rescue her. So she suffered in silence, hoping these men would leave her and that Van would not see or understand the horror that was happening to her. She kept her face averted, eyes shut and head still, suddenly afraid of her hair tumbling down and revealing the pouch tied in it.

It seemed to Thu these men pummelled and pumped and thrust and tore her in two for an eternity. But then it was over and with a kick they shouted at her to get back on the trawler. She staggered to her feet, clutching the remnants of her top and the slashed cotton trousers, now stained with blood.

'Jump, Thu, jump to us!' shouted her uncle, standing on the deck ready to catch her.

Stumbling, she swung her legs over the side and crashed through his arms on the rocking trawler as the powerful engine of the pirate boat was gunned and with a surge of white water it roared away.

Uncle took his cotton blanket and wrapped it around Thu, who was frantically looking for Van. Everyone was shaken; all had lost some possessions, but they were grateful they were alive as, silently, the trawler captain restarted the engine and set a fresh course through the rolling sea.

Thu knelt beside Van as Aunty held him, trying to stem the bleeding, murmuring prayers and sounds of comfort.

Uncle begged the captain for help but was dismissed with a wave of the hand. He turned to the others on the deck. 'Does no one have medicine, bandages?'

They shook their heads, frightened at what had occurred, each now more fearful than ever about what the future held, glad that their family had not had to bear the brunt of the pirate's brutality.

Darkness fell and Aunty and Thu took turns sponging Van's face, holding his wound together, mopping at the seeping blood with a cotton blanket and washing it in a bucket of seawater.

Van kept asking Thu what had happened and calmly she kept reassuring him she was all right, whispering in his ear, 'They never found the pouch with our gold and precious stones.'

Van showed her the cross around his neck and gave a little smile. 'He protected us.'

Thu winced, trying to blot out the memory of what had happened and ignore the pain in her body and her heart. 'Yes, it is over now. Soon we will arrive at the happy land. Sleep, Van.'

Thu rocked her young brother in her arms through the night. She hummed him songs her mother sang, and for a little while she felt at peace again, before the nightmare of the men raping her returned.

She dozed off and in the morning light she gazed at the peaceful sleeping face of her brother. But he was dead. Slipped away from her during the long night hours when she'd tried to push away the bad dreams and cling to the memories of everything beautiful she'd known and loved.

She cried and cried, rocking him, holding him tightly to her bruised body. Aunty and Uncle tried to console her, but throughout the day she refused to let Van go. At sunset, when the seas became calm, she agreed. His little body was wrapped in Aunty's sarong, and Uncle offered up prayers as Thu lifted her mother's crucifix from Van and hung it around her neck. The boy was slipped silently over the stern of the boat as the family huddled together, facing the land from which they'd fled.

Thu hoped the wise one would guide Van to his next life where there would be happiness and contentment.

She stopped counting the days until one day an island appeared on the horizon. Slowly it came closer: waving palm trees, silver sand and a pristine lagoon. There were figures on the beach to meet them, people speaking Vietnamese, huts and buildings among the trees.

'This is a new country; this is an island paradise,' said Aunty.

'It is only the first stop on our new journey,' replied Uncle.

'Where are we?' asked Thu.

The trawler captain, now friendly and pleased to be

delivering his cargo safely, said, 'This is Pulau Bidong, off Malaysia. I've told them that you are refugees; you must stay here until you are processed.'

Looking at the temporary buildings that had sprung up, even a church and a temple made from scraps of tin and wood, Thu wondered how long they would wait here.

Weeks passed. Thu watched the scenic tropical island change from being a rough camp, home to people with nothing but the clothes on their backs who ate any wild creature they could catch, to a much smarter settlement known as mini Saigon. Under the supervision of the International Red Cross and the United Nations High Commission for Refugees, houses, offices, shops, schools, a post office, a church and a temple were quickly constructed. Food became the local currency and entrepreneurs flourished. Malaysian fishermen, although banned from having contact with the island, smuggled goods to quiet coastal spots where refugees would paddle a raft or canoe out to meet them.

Each day Thu would visit the crude cement monument, shaped like a ship's bow, that commemorated those boat people who didn't cross the sea safely to this shore. Stone tablets were engraved with the names of family members and Van's was added.

Uncle Quoc got work as a labourer and was paid in food parcels, and Aunty set up a small hairdressing stall to help feed the family. Thu studied hard with a teacher who had taught in a university in Saigon and began to learn rudimentary English, as they all hoped the day would come when their applications for asylum would be approved.

Thu kept to herself, rarely mixing with people her

own age, and only Aunty and Uncle, her family now, knew the shame she felt over what had happened to her. And still she blamed herself for Van's death.

Then suddenly their struggle on the island was over. They were among the lucky ones to be processed quickly and were taken to the mainland with their few possessions and flown to Australia.

It was a dramatic change. They were cold, overwhelmed by the city of Sydney, did not understand the customs or the language, which sounded to Thu utterly different from the English she had learned from a professor on Pulau Bidong. But soon they connected with friends who had already settled in.

They struggled, worked hard, studied at night, sharing a small house in the inner city. Here it felt like a transplanted Vietnam – the signs were in Vietnamese; the shops were owned by Vietnamese and sold food, silks and clothes that were familiar. Uncle opened a little shop, Aunty worked in a large hairdressing salon and soon they began to save for the day they could bring over Thu's family.

Thu worked in a shop, though initially she had been mistaken for a boy, being slight and shy with short cropped hair. But by the time she celebrated her twenty-first birthday she had blossomed into a beautiful young woman, although she was still shy.

By this time Kevin Fine had already noticed Thu at Mass each Sunday. He asked the priest the name of the Vietnamese family. He was told they were boat people. Hard workers, nice family.

Kevin had never been a believer in fate, but when Thu began walking past his garage repair shop he would wave and greet her.

At first she merely nodded and passed by, embarrassed by the cheerful greetings from the big Australian man who seemed older and a rather rough character. But then he introduced himself to her uncle and aunty at church and gradually he was able to coax a smile from Thu. When he offered to look at Uncle's troublesome old car, the friendship was sealed.

On her way to and from work Thu would pause outside the repair shop and try to appear comfortable with Kevin's good-natured banter. She soon came to realise he had a good heart. He took to dropping around to their house to chat with Uncle and was finally invited to share a meal.

Kevin became a regular in the household. He loved Aunty's food and slowly Thu came out of her shell and agreed to go to the movies with him. Saturday afternoons became a regular date. Sometimes she took him to different Vietnamese restaurants in Cabramatta, or he took her across the harbour on the ferry to Manly – though being on the water brought back bad memories for her. On one trip Thu shared her experiences of the dreadful sea voyage and how much she missed her family.

Kevin was gently comforting as little by little Thu told him her story. He dropped an arm around her shoulders. 'You're in the best country in the world now, Thu. And if you'll let me, I'll look after you. We could start a new life together.'

It was an awkward proposal that didn't register with Thu for a moment as she reflected on what Kevin was saying. 'You mean, me . . . and you? You mean . . . ?'

'Get married. What do you say, Thu? I reckon we could make a go of it.'

'We are very different. Very different history. Different people,' she began.

'I'm not hearing a no,' beamed Kevin. He hugged her. 'Listen, love, we have a lot more going for us than a lot of couples I know. I'm thirty-one. My mother's nagging me to settle down. I've just been waiting for the right girl to come along. You're the one.' He gave her a passionate kiss, unlike the restrained kisses they'd so far exchanged.

Thu, flushed and smiling, began to be practical. 'What will your mother say about me? And you must speak to Uncle.'

'Don't you worry about Uncle. He'll be sweet, I reckon. And my mum is going to love you, guaranteed.'

Thu spoke to Uncle but when Kevin came to ask for Thu's hand, Uncle was not as instantly receptive as Kevin had expected. He spoke formally and seemed a little restrained.

Kevin finally took the bull by the horns. 'What's the problem? Don't you think I'll look after her? We're both Catholics. She's had a tough life and she deserves some happiness. We can be happy together. Have a good life,' said Kevin. The idea Thu might not marry him had made him anxious and brought home to him how much he loved and wanted to protect the girl he thought of as his 'little bird'.

Uncle lowered his head and clasped his hands. 'Kevin, I speak for Thu's father as he is not with us and she wants you to know . . . everything.'

'What's to know? I'll take her just as she is, Uncle,' said Kevin vehemently.

Slowly, not looking at Kevin directly, Uncle told him about the attack – he could not use the word rape – that Thu had suffered on the boat when they escaped. He finished by saying softly, 'For some men in our country, she would not be a good wife.'

'Bullshit! 'Scuse me, Uncle.' Kevin's anger and pain over the incident flared again. 'Poor Thu. She's already told me. But I love her and that's all that matters.'

Uncle felt a smile breaking out and he reached for Kevin's beefy hand. 'You are a good man, Kevin. Thu is a lucky woman.'

Kevin's face broke into a huge grin. 'Bugger me. I'm the lucky one! So it's all right, we can start planning the big day? Nuptial mass, the full works!'

Uncle nodded and called for Aunty to bring the best rice wine. The men toasted each other and by the time Thu arrived home from work, her future husband and Uncle were flushed and very jovial.

It was a formal wedding. Thu wore a crinoline of lace and a small tiara. Kevin was in a tux with a red bow tie and cummerbund. The reception was at a Vietnamese restaurant with Vietnamese food, Australian beer, and an Italian crooner and his band.

Nine months later Anna was born.

They settled in a house in Budge Street, Maroubra, and within a month Kevin had met Phil Donaldson after the owner of the car yard where Phil worked began to employ Kevin as a mechanic. Discovering they lived in the same street, the men began to socialise. Initially Thu was shy and simply put food in front of the men as they talked cars on the back patio. But when Phil's wife, Patricia, discovered they had little girls the same age, she insisted they have family get-togethers. And so an enduring friendship was born.

Sandy followed Kim into a large airy building near the port of Hai Phong and was surprised to find they were in a kind of floating, open-air model farm with tanks in the centre. Water was sluicing through the tanks and monitoring equipment was mounted on one platform where a man was dipping a net into the water and dropping small shrimp into plastic tubs.

'This is an odd place for a shrimp farm, isn't it?' commented Sandy. 'Who owns this one?'

'It's a trial model. You know I've been involved in research into shrimp farm practices, well, now some solutions are happening.'

'It's been an environmental disaster for Vietnam, hasn't it?' said Sandy. 'Even though it's a booming industry.'

Kim shrugged. 'Yeah, a big export for the big guys, but at a huge environmental cost to the country. Hopefully projects like this will lead to more sustainable aquaculture management. The head of the research institution involved has come over from France.'

He went to a glass partitioned office where two men were talking, rapped on the door and both were waved inside.

'Hello, Professor Truyen,' said Kim.

The professor smiled and extended his hand.

'This is my associate from HOPE, Sandy Donaldson,' said Kim introducing her to the visiting Vietnamese professor.

The professor turned to the man at the desk. 'Kim, this is our French director, Doctor Petiere.'

'Please, Jean-Claude. Delighted to meet you, and Miss Donaldson.' His French accent, debonair looks and warm smile oozed Gallic charm.

'Call me Sandy.' She smiled, shaking his hand.

Professor Truyen excused himself saying, 'Jean-Claude will show you where our operation is up to.'

'So, Kim, have you had a chance to look around? While the problems are still with us, we hope this model will provide a few solutions. Convincing the government, the international donor community and indeed the poor farmers this is the way to go is the next challenge.'

HOPE, like other agencies in the country, had a myriad of projects at various stages of development. While Sandy knew about the work Kim and the HOPE volunteers had been doing with farmers who were struggling to make their shrimp farms profitable and sustainable, she'd been busy with her own projects and hadn't taken in the details of how it was all going.

Jean-Claude came around the desk. He was in his mid to late thirties, very lean and brown, with dark hair and light-green eyes. Sandy immediately thought that if he hadn't spoken she would have picked him for a Frenchman anyway. There was just that air of insouciance, of clothes that sat like an Abercrombie and Fitch advertisement – classy, elegant, yet very casual. She noted the blue shirt with rolled sleeves was fine linen with a quality finish, and had a small emblem embroidered in white on the pocket. It didn't look like a locally made garment. She wished she wasn't wearing a T-shirt and faded cotton drawstring trousers.

He was smiling into her eyes, noting her quick assessment. 'And what is your involvement with HOPE? It is an excellent non-governmental organisation. I presume you do not work with Kim or you would have met the professor before, yes?'

'No, well, I mean yes.' Sandy was furious that he made her feel flustered. 'I have been working with HOPE for several years but not with Kim. My contract has just finished. Sadly I'll have to leave Vietnam soon.'

'Hard to tear oneself away from this country. It has a way of getting under one's skin, eh? Perhaps you will find another opportunity here.'

'I hope you don't mind me bringing Sandy along; I always value her input,' said Kim. 'I think what you're doing is important, and more people should know about it,' he added, trying to ease the slightly uncomfortable connection between Jean-Claude and Sandy.

'Know about the problem, or the solution?' asked Jean-Claude, still smiling at Sandy.

'One follows the other, doesn't it?' said Sandy. 'I'd love to understand more.'

'Then come with me.' He led the way to the outside tank. 'How long will you be in Hai Phong? Where are you based?'

He chatted amiably as Kim stopped to greet the man bending over the tubs of shrimp. Sandy was curious.

'What is the main problem with the shrimp farms? People hoped that helping farmers set up small ponds as value-add use of their land,' she said.

Jean-Claude dropped his smiling demeanour. 'Shrimp aquaculture has developed rapidly here with little foresight, planning or regulation. They haven't looked at the problems encountered by other countries, such as Thailand, which leapt into this in a big way years ago. Consequently we are now dealing with enormous environmental and social problems.'

'So what are you doing?'

'We're testing better means of raising shrimp using more traditional methods, researching sustainable ways of keeping them healthy without polluting the water or resorting to indiscriminate use of chemicals and antibiotics.'

'You're putting me off those nice big tiger prawns I see in our market,' said Sandy.

'Indeed. I eat only the shrimp I know are raised in properly run farms.'

'Well, how do you know that?'

'There has to be certification and proper labelling. Not an easy order here,' said Jean-Claude. As Kim joined them Jean-Claude asked, 'Kim, would you like to see the latest results? Sadly there are some depressing reports from the Mekong. Erosion, deforestation, destruction of mangrove habitats: the overall picture is quite grim. I believe many farmers wish they'd stuck to growing rice. They were swayed by greed, a quick return, and now they are suffering. They've lost everything.'

While Kim and Jean-Claude flipped through a sheaf of papers and talked statistics, Sandy looked at the tiny creatures milling in their thousands in the big tank. In several large containers shrimp fry still at the larval stage were being readied to go into the main tank where their growth would be closely monitored.

The man tending the tank smiled at her. She greeted him and in Vietnamese asked what he thought of shrimp farming.

'I was a shrimp farmer. I turned over my paddies to raise them.' He gave a shrug. 'The money I borrowed is all gone. Shrimp have very big mouths: they have eaten my house and all my land. I wish I could go back to growing rice.'

'What happened to your shrimp?'

'The same as many others. They got a disease and after a few years the ponds are no good. I did not have the money to make fresh ponds. And now the land is spoiled.'

Kim joined Sandy. 'I have to spend a few moments going through these papers and chat to Jean-Claude. Do you want to wait? Or I could meet you back at the cafe.'

'You are welcome to sit in with us, Sandy,' said Jean-Claude as he put the papers back in the folder.

'I'd love that. Sure you won't mind?' Sandy couldn't immediately explain it, but the shrimp industry interested her. The story of the old farmer, now working on the model farm, had touched her. She recalled the initiative to subsidise programs such as aquaculture but had heard the government only released 'good news' stories. Even though Kim was involved in the project she thought she would like to find out more. She wished Tom, the journo, was here. He'd be reaching for his notebook.

Jean-Claude took her arm. 'Sandy, you are most welcome. And feel free to contribute. Half an hour, and we'll be done.'

Sandy was thoughtful as she and Kim walked back to join Anna and Tom at the cafe. Although her official work with HOPE had ended, she realised she couldn't easily walk away from this country. Not only would she have to leave the projects she'd been involved with – especially the orphanage school down on the coast – but there were still so many areas where she could see help was needed. More strongly than ever she now questioned whether her time here was over.

4

ANNA STROLLED SLOWLY THROUGH the Old Quarter while she waited to meet Sandy. It was day's end and she found herself falling into the rhythm and flow of local people around her: those finishing work, those setting up for evening trade, those who were refreshed, holding toddlers in pyjamas, chatting with neighbours, or going out for a meal, even if just simple street food. The relentless traffic seemed to have a communal purpose – everyone was anxious to get home, or to their destination, before darkness. Tourists were not obvious, it being siesta time after shopping and sightseeing before heading into the nightlife of Hanoi's restaurants, hotels, shops and bars.

The maze of thirty-six streets dating back to the thirteenth century where craftsmen formed guilds and businesses side by side in a single area charmed Anna and, as Sandy had pointed out, it was a convenient way to shop. Many of the old crafts and trades had died away to be replaced by European boutiques, or silk shops, or shoes, or lacquerware aimed at tourists as well as locals.

But what Anna loved about the Old Quarter was its bohemian atmosphere generated by the French colonial architecture and the concentration of artistic endeavour. Hang Ma – Paper Street – intrigued her with its shops selling colourful paper replicas of everything one could desire to take into the next life. It seemed a shame to Anna that the miniature paper motor cars, jewellery, furniture and clothes were all to be burned in offerings to ancestors. But there were modern paper goods on sale too, so she bought some greetings cards and a pink and an orange paper lantern for Sandy to hang in her courtyard.

The sidewalk was narrow and Anna was frequently forced to step into the street as the pavement was jammed with small business operations of incredible variety. A man could set up a bicycle or motorcycle repair shop, lining up spare parts, tools and bicycles in various stages of repair on the footpath. Often a barber or a letter writer merely set up a chair, a table or a mirror and was in business. Shopfront dentists and pharmacists had their waiting rooms on the street, chairs lined up for customers to wait their turn. Stacks of postcards, T-shirts, plastic goods, food, clothes and souvenirs were displayed and sold on the street. Women squatted with baskets of sweet bean cakes or fresh produce to sell.

In the next block, shops which catered more for tourists displayed merchandise behind glass windows with large signs announcing *Air Con*.

Anna skirted a cluster of huge and elaborate flower arrangements on easels and in large containers framed by ribbons and placards. They stood outside a small art gallery, its freshly painted walls hung with an exhibition of modern art. A few people were standing inside admiring the bold canvases. Although Sandy was the art aficionado of the two, Anna stepped inside on impulse. She was welcomed by a beautiful shop assistant in an ao-dai.

She greeted Anna in Vietnamese, then French, then, with a little giggle, in English. 'Welcome to our exhibition. Would you like to meet the artist, Mr Bien Dinh?' She gestured towards an earnest young man talking to a small group of people.

'Not just now, thank you. I'm only looking. This is very dramatic work. Very abstract and unusual,' commented Anna.

'He is up and coming. Many foreign people buy his work. You like modern art?' the assistant asked.

'I don't understand modern art very well. I prefer traditional art,' said Anna, making conversation.

'Ah, old masters, you want good copies old art?'

Anna shook her head. She'd seen the tiny art shops where teams of young painters sat by their canvases copying famous classics – Rembrandt, Botticelli, Monet, Picasso. Reproductions of their works were lined up for sale for a few dollars. Anna recalled something Sandy had said about a friend who had a gallery that specialised in antiques, ethnic and anthropological work. 'I suppose I mean more realism, crafts and art from Vietnam.' Anna was repeating what Sandy had told her.

The girl nodded. 'Traditional. Yes, Vietnamese people very artistic. Our old artists trained under the French, but since 1950s our artists start to combine western and Asian art. Now modern art very popular.'

'I've never seen a city with so many art galleries,' said Anna. She'd also noticed that there were a number of bookshops and how everyone read a local newspaper.

A voice beside Anna added, 'The art and intellectual life here is very healthy. Hanoi is very cultural.'

She turned towards the low-key American accent and found an attractive man in his thirties smiling at her. He held out his hand. 'Rick Dale. Are you a visitor or do you live here?'

'Anna Fine. I'm staying in Hanoi with a friend. I was just passing . . . ' She suddenly wondered if this was an invitation-only function, as trays of rice rolls and cold drinks were offered around.

'Come and meet the artist; everyone is welcome at these things. Hanoi is exploding with galleries, artisans, craft places. It's good, but let the buyer beware,' Rick said, steering her towards the painter before she could object.

'I'm afraid I'm a neophyte in this scene. My friend, whom I'm staying with, is more the expert.'

'It's always interesting to hear the expert's viewpoint. Where is your friend?'

'At her office.' Anna didn't have time for details, as Rick introduced her to the artist who gave her a soft handshake while avoiding her eye. Sandy had told her this was a sign of respect and humility: a strong hand-shake and bold eye contact was considered arrogant in Vietnamese society.

'Congratulations on your show. Er, what is the theme of this exhibition?' Anna was fishing, as some of the geometric cubist-style paintings, while colourful, didn't convey much to her. Rick gave her a smile as he translated her question.

Bien led her to the largest canvas and explained to Rick, 'This is my dragon series. This one represents the nine dragons of the Mekong River which is the most important river in Vietnam.'

'At the delta the river splits into nine tributaries,' explained Rick.

Anna angled her head. 'I see it.'

'It's a dragon with the beak of a phoenix. It is said that the largest one, the ninth dragon, held incredible powers,' said Rick.

The artist moved to the next painting. 'And here is the descending dragon at Halong Bay.'

As Bien pointed, Anna could see the interpretations of the limestone peaks rising from the blue paint representing the bay. 'Of course, I see it now. We just went there. It was a wonderful experience,' she said.

'It's pretty stunning scenery, that's for sure,' said Rick.

'Yes,' said Anna quietly. But she was thinking of the little nun in her lofty remote pagoda.

More people had arrived and were pressing around the artist, so Anna thanked him and followed Rick to a table where there were cold drinks.

'How long are you here for?' Rick asked Anna. 'By your accent you're an Aussie?'

'Yes. My girlfriend Sandy has been working here so I've joined her for sightseeing before we go home.'

'Is that Sandy Donaldson who works for HOPE?'

Anna was surprised. 'How do you know her?'

'The expat community in Hanoi is very small. I'm sure Sandy will show you some great places.'

'Absolutely. We have an itinerary worked out. I think Hoi An is next.'

'That's a popular place. Make sure you get off the beaten track though. I've travelled through most of this country: there are still a lot of unspoiled areas, but for how long?' He sighed. 'One of the islands off the central coast has a five-star resort – very elegant, very upmarket. However, now there're plans for five more international big-name resorts along the beach. The fishermen are being moved inland, away from their boats and nets, and soon there'll be more visitors a year than to Bali.'

'Goodness, tourism is certainly taking off. So what do you do here?'

'I've just finished my PhD and I'm working for a New York gallery sourcing artworks. It's an interesting job that allows me to travel and indulge my passion for antiquities. I buy for private clients.'

'So is there a big market for Vietnamese antiques?'

'Yes,' said Rick warmly. 'Almost everything has a market. Some through the front door, some through the back door.'

Anna raised an eyebrow. 'What do you mean by the "back door"?'

Rick laughed. 'Ah, Asia. Someone always manages to turn up at the back door with what they whisper is a rare find. Such things are hyped as antiques, but genuine ones are thin on the ground.'

Anna thought back to the old ceramic plate at master potter Thinh's as Rick chatted about places to see and things to do.

'Well, excuse me, I'd better go and help our star, do some translating now a couple of tourists have arrived,' he said. 'Enjoy Hoi An. I go down there often; it's got a very good little museum. I'll give you some tips on Hoi An if you'd like.'

Anna smiled at him. 'That'd be great. I can be the expert for a change!'

Anna walked to the lake where she was to meet Sandy, bought an ice-cream and sat on a park bench to watch the after-work joggers on their circuit of the calm and beautiful water. She was beginning to love the moods of the lakes in Hanoi, particularly Hoan Kiem. Sometimes misty and melancholy in the early morning, sometimes golden and mellow like now, or sparkling blue green in the middle of the day. But there was something special about sunset as the pace of life slowed and the twisted tree trunks cast shadows across the water. No matter how many people clustered around the rim of the lake, each appeared to be in their private cocoon, their own little world.

Anna had enjoyed her afternoon, especially the art exhibition and meeting Rick Dale. She finished her ice-cream and wandered across the lakeside park to the Italian cafe where she was meeting Sandy. In two days they were going to Hoi An, the pretty and historic town south of Danang. Rick had told her that it had become something of an arts and craft centre and had given her some good ideas about places to see and she was keen to ask Sandy what she thought.

It occurred to Anna that even though she was on holidays and playing at being a tourist, it was more than that that made her life here so different, so relaxed and interesting. There wasn't the pressure she felt at home and, with a guilty start, she realised she hadn't thought of Carlo as often as she usually did. She resolved to borrow Sandy's laptop and send him a long email about all she'd seen. She had a sneaking feeling that Carlo wouldn't be at all interested in what she was doing in Vietnam, but she still wanted to let him know that she missed him.

Sandy was in the HOPE offices checking her emails and messages and touching base with everyone. Although she was officially off the payroll, it was hard to sever all ties. She still had a desk with her coffee mug and HOPE computer as the new staff hadn't yet arrived.

Sandy had tried to explain to Anna how the attitude of the local staff reflected that of Vietnamese people – family came first. And HOPE was surrogate family. The

Vietnamese staff adopted and included the westerners in the minutiae of their lives. There was a protocol involved in meeting people for the first time which continued into the relationship where personal inquiries about families, their wellbeing, activities and health had to be dealt with before the business at hand. Sandy had initially been shocked at being asked her age, until she realised it was necessary to give them the key to the proper form of respectful address.

She had passed these details on to Anna, who had listened but made no comment. Sandy was surprised that while Anna was becoming quite fascinated with all the facets of life in Vietnam, she still didn't seem to relate to the people personally.

Sandy walked to the lake, where she met Anna. They hopped into one of the pedicabs to go to Barney's Bar, where a farewell drinks gathering had been arranged for Sandy.

The popular bar and cafe was brimming with expatriates, local business people and a group of trendy young Vietnamese. It was something of an institution in Hanoi. It started as a small cafe in the ground floor of an old French building that combined Parisian wrought-iron balconies with Vietnamese decorative trimmings. Unlike most houses, it was set back from the pavement which allowed space for several tiny tables and chairs. A recent addition of sliding doors melded the interior with the outdoor tables and conversations and patrons flowed from the pavement to the tiny bar in the rear of the long main room. The kitchen was hidden behind the bar where a narrow staircase went to the private quarters upstairs.

The building was painted ochre yellow with red trim and the sign *Barney's* was in turquoise. But the colourful exterior was no match for the inside walls and stairwell which were covered with paintings. Even some of the old wooden tabletops had been used as canvases for landscapes, portraits, modern art and calligraphy. The cafe, in a previous incarnation, had been a hangout for artists back in the mid 1920s and for students from the Ecole des Beaux Arts de L'Indochine, which later became the Hanoi College of Fine Arts. Students would trade a painting for a meal. When Barney took over he had inherited hundreds of paintings stacked in the small rooms upstairs. Lai was tempted to throw the pictures away but, being the businesswoman she was, thought perhaps she might be able to sell them to one of the little galleries springing up in the district. Fortuitously the first place she walked into was a tiny art shop owned by an American, Charlie Ralston and his Vietnamese business partner, Miss Huong.

When Miss Huong went through the collection she recognised that many were by great Vietnamese artists who had begun experimenting with western and Vietnamese styles. She negotiated the sale of most of the paintings and encouraged Barney and Lai to protect the ones painted on the cafe walls and tables, for the artists were all famous names now. Barney had kept a lot of paintings against Lai's wishes, which were hung in the upstairs quarters. Miss Huong made it a habit to drop into Barney's to check on his collection. Following the quaint custom of the past, art students short of cash continued to drop in to Barney's offering to trade one of their works for a meal.

Tom Ahearn waved from a table to one side where he'd managed to hold several empty seats. An older western man with a younger Vietnamese woman were seated with him. The table next to them was filled with Sandy's friends from HOPE.

Barney, big shouldered, flushed face, his clipped moustache speckled with drops of perspiration, hurried to the girls. 'Howdy, Sandy. You're popular: you've got two tables – Kim and the HOPE lot and your pal Tom.'

'You'll have to table hop,' grinned Anna. 'Quite a gang here.'

'Miss Huong and Charlie Ralston are here,' said Barney.

'Great, that Charlie is quite a character,' said Sandy.

She was swept into the HOPE group as they pushed the two tables together. Anna sat opposite Tom who introduced her to Charlie and Miss Huong

'Charlie runs a pretty famous gallery here and Miss Huong is his business partner and curator. Sounds like they have a very impressive collection,' said Tom.

'Where do you find things for your gallery?' Anna asked Miss Huong.

'I source them from all over the country: ethnic minority villages, the hill tribes. At present I'm searching out some pieces for a New York gallery and their representative Mr Rick Dale.'

'I met Rick at an art show earlier,' said Anna. 'It's quite a coincidence.'

'Not really – Hanoi can be a small place even with four million people,' said Charlie.

Barney took orders and relayed them to Lai behind the bar, who looked as cool and calm as he was flustered.

'Barney's short handed,' commented Tom. 'Reckons he should be socialising with the customers.'

'Arguing, more like it,' said Charlie. 'There's always some debate going on now Australian vets are trekking in here more and more. Barney was a draft dodger: didn't believe the war was justified. Doesn't always endear him to some of the veterans.'

'What about you? Did you get out here during the war years?' Tom asked Charlie.

'I was a medico. In the last years of that mess. But it

97

gave me a taste of the Orient. I found private practice a bit tame so I made a career of working abroad wherever I could. Was in some pretty primitive areas . . . that's where my interest in tribal art started.'

'How long have you been here in Hanoi?'

'Once the kids were at college my wife and I decided to leave New York and live abroad and get serious about my collecting. Came here in 1991 and came back to stay in 1995. Then I met Miss Huong and she persuaded me to start a business.'

'He was retired, had a house overflowing with thousands of objects – thought he was a collector, but I said he was a dealer,' said Miss Huong with a smile.

'I didn't know what I was doing. Miss Huong is the business brains and she has the best eye in the country, too. Trouble is, I never want to part with the things she finds.'

Anna was intrigued. 'When you were here during the war, were you interested in Vietnamese history or art or anything?'

Charlie gave her a smile. 'Funnily enough, I was. I got to fly into villages to treat civilians and that was where I first saw a lot of ethnic minorities and their tribal pieces – grave carvings, shamanic objects. Hard to come by stuff like that now.'

Kim stopped by the table and caught Anna's eye. 'Want to swap places? The office group wanted to say farewell to Sandy in a more informal way.'

'No, I'm fine; you all carry on. I'm being entertained here. I'll squeeze by the table in a little while.'

'What about you, Tom? Were you here in the war?' asked Charlie.

'I was a journalist and radio correspondent down Saigon way from sixty-five,' answered Tom. 'Hung out with the Australian forces at Nui Dat a fair bit, but managed to see quite a lot of the country in the south.'

'So, you on a nostalgia trip? Like so many are doing now?'

Tom paused. 'You might say that. Not so much a personal odyssey though. I'm doing a bit of a look-see for an old newspaper editor friend. He thought I might like to cover a reunion of the boys who were at the battle of Long Tan, a big Aussie rout of the Viet Cong that's never really been properly acknowledged. It's the fortieth anniversary coming up.'

'I know about Long Tan,' said Barney, who'd joined them. 'Often have some of the diggers who were there come through these days. I know a couple of Aussie guys who now live at Vung Tau.'

Tom's interest was instantly aroused but Anna jumped in, saying, 'Sandy's dad was at Long Tan, I think.'

Tom swung his attention to Anna. 'Really? Now that's very interesting. Wonder if he's coming over for the anniversary.'

'I don't think so. It's the John Cleese rule at her folks' place – "Don't mention the war".'

Tom was thoughtful and glanced over to where Sandy was laughing with her ex-workmates. 'I'll have a yarn to her about that later.'

'So, you covering this anniversary from a personal or professional viewpoint?' asked Charlie.

Tom gave a grin and finished his beer. 'Seems it might be a bit of both. I was in the area at the time. Anyway, I thought I'd come and see what'd become of the country since the war. I never got up here to the north, of course. I reckon the Long Tan reunion will be a good story.'

Anna leaned forward. 'You know, Tom, my dad has always said that Sandy's dad, Phil, should come back. However, I don't know if he's coming. Talk to Sandy.'

'I'll do that.' Tom paused as if to raise something with Anna but thought better of it. 'It's past my bedtime. You party on. Nice to meet you, Charlie. Miss Huong, after what you've told me, I'd like to see your gallery.' Tom shook hands with Charlie and Miss Huong, then dropped his hand on Anna's shoulder. 'How about I treat you and Sandy to coffee tomorrow?'

'Great. See you here – not too early, Tom,' laughed Anna.

Tom hailed a cyclo and gave directions to his hotel. He sat back in the balmy night air as the driver weaved through the less frenetic traffic on streets lit by ribbons of coloured lights strung outside late-night shops and eateries. It was so peaceful, calm, non-threatening. Not for the first time in recent days he reflected how at home he felt in Asia. Even though his home was in Sydney, he'd always enjoyed assignments in Singapore, Japan, Indonesia and Far Eastern countries.

He imagined Saigon, now called Ho Chi Minh City, was even more bustling than Hanoi. He'd read so much about it as a tourist Mecca bursting with capitalist energy rather than the communist ideology that had once dominated the north. Hanoi was full of surprises and he was enjoying the city immensely, but he looked forward to going back to Saigon, the city he had known early in the war after the Americans and their allies put in hundreds of thousands of troops to combat the Viet Cong guerrilla army and regular army units that infiltrated down the Ho Chi Minh trail from the north.

Tom paid the driver and nodded to the concierge.

'Good evening, Mr Ahearn. Have a pleasant evening?'

'Indeed. Thank you.'

It was a modest but smart hotel and Tom saw that the main bar was packed with international guests. For a moment he was tempted to join them for a nightcap, but dismissed the idea. He felt really tired.

In bed he tried to sleep, but memories were stirring. Yes, he would ask Barney for the names of the Aussie vets living at Vung Tau. Names and faces swirled in his head. He'd definitely talk to Sandy about her father, too.

As he slowly dozed off to the gentle hum of the air conditioner, his mind suddenly focused on a name . . . Phil Donaldson, Sandy's old man. Something stirred deep in his memory . . . that name. But he rolled over and was sleeping before his mind completed the memory search. Other images took over in dreams that made for a restless night.

Saigon, 1965

'Attention, all passengers. We are approaching Tan Son Nhut Airport in Saigon. Please fasten your seatbelts. Our descent to the airport will be a little steeper than you are probably used to on commercial flights elsewhere, but please do not worry about it. The procedure is actually designed to enhance your safety. Cabin staff, please check and prepare for landing.'

Tom Ahearn closed his book on the history of Vietnam that had absorbed him since taking off from Singapore, checked his seatbelt and looked out of the window at the landscape far below.

'What the bloody hell am I doing here?' he asked himself, knowing that the odd landing procedure was designed to make it harder for Viet Cong snipers in the jungle to score a hit.

Only a couple of weeks ago he had been leading a

great life in Singapore building up a good reputation for delivering to editors back in Sydney and Melbourne a steady flow of stories about the island state and its multiracial neighbour, Malaysia. There was the occasional serious piece looking at the minor but long-running hunt for a handful of communist guerrillas hanging out in the hills of Malaya, but covering a real war had not been on Tom's agenda. Then suddenly Australia had boosted its military presence in South Vietnam from advisors to a full-on infantry battalion, with more on the way.

The First Battalion Royal Australian Regiment had just arrived and were settling in alongside the also newly arrived American Rangers of 173rd Airborne Regiment at Bien Hoa, near Saigon. And up the coast at Danang some four thousand US Marines were setting up camp. Tom's editors back home wanted coverage of the escalation.

So, no more tennis sessions with mates at the Tanglin Club in Singapore for a while.

As they bounced down the runway, there was a light-hearted cheer from the passengers. Tom looked at the strange scene that rolled past as they headed for the terminal – a seemingly endless sprawl of military aircraft of all kinds, scores of military vehicles going in all directions and great long lines of new buildings for storing the tools of war that were pouring into the country. He knew that from this airfield planes were delivering a massive aerial bombing assault on North Vietnam: Operation Rolling Thunder.

In the terminal there was utter chaos as hundreds of men in uniform mixed with hundreds of civilian passengers in a scramble for luggage and taxis. He was glad to reach the Caravelle Hotel in the centre of Saigon. One of his tennis mates from Singapore, Neil Davis, an Australian cameraman for an international TV news agency, had booked him a room. Neil had an office in Saigon and a flat in Singapore to which he retreated for 'R and R', rest and recuperation. Neil loved the war as any reporter loves a good story. It gave him a big buzz, but he never dropped his guard and he knew all the tricks of survival in the jungles and the paddy fields of the war-torn country. He had become something of a legend in the process.

The desk staff at the Caravelle apologised when Tom checked in. His room wasn't ready; the staff had yet to clean it. The previous occupant, another correspondent, had moved out only that morning, heading for Singapore.

'She'll be right, mate,' said Tom.

'Pardon, monsieur?' responded the booking clerk.

'Forget it. Look, I'll just dump my gear in the room and go for coffee, okay.'

He went up to the second floor and found the room busy with cleaners who were all smiles and bows as he waved the key and told them in halting French that he would leave his gear and let them get on with their work. He opened the wardrobe and found a green canvas haversack on the floor. To his surprise it was half-full of ammunition. He looked at the leader of the cleaning team with a raised eyebrow.

'Maybe you can use it, sir. The last man here had many guns.'

'Did he now,' said Tom, a little puzzled that a non-serviceman should be in the arms business in some way. A pencil was all he wanted to carry into the field. 'Okay. Thanks for the offer. I'll go for a walk and come back in an hour or so.'

'Thank you, sir. So sorry,' replied the head cleaner.

Tom went back down to the front of the hotel and took in the scene across Lam Son Square. Nearby was the imposing white National Assembly building, empty of real democracy. And then a little way down Tu Do Street was the more inviting outdoor terrace of the Continental Hotel. Neil Davis had recommended the colonial-style Continental as a drinking hole so Tom headed there, hoping that a few drinks and lunch would lift his spirits.

He took his beer to a table with a good view of the street which was busy with a steady flow of motor scooters, usually with at least two people on board, often with two adults and two little kids. There didn't appear to be any road rules. The women overwhelmingly favoured the traditional ao-dai and wore large conical straw hats to protect their fair complexions.

Their beauty immediately captivated Tom. It wasn't as if he had limited experience of the feminine charms of Asian women. It was a year since he had sailed from Sydney to Japan to report on the Olympic Games in Tokyo. Before the Games he'd spent two months wandering the main islands of Japan taking in the culture and lifestyle of people in remote mountain villages as well as big cities. He'd had some tantalising affairs with a few Japanese women in Tokyo who were fluent in English and well established as 'career ladies', an emerging force of university graduates who were breaking down the old and formidable barriers of discrimination.

After the Games he had drifted around Taiwan for a couple of weeks, which he'd found rather boring. Everyone was so intent on making money and regarded foreigners with suspicion.

Hong Kong was a better scene, even though the border with China was still like the Great Wall of China. You could look over the fence, but forget about trying to get in. He'd met some wild young Australians working for British companies in the colony, all intent on eating, drinking and screwing themselves into oblivion as often as possible. There was an endless supply of compliant women.

And then there was a swing through Thailand, the highlight of which was a memorable romance in Bangkok with a 'liberated lady' who owned a shop selling fine Thai silks to locals and tourists at different prices. The tourists usually thought they got a good deal and no one disillusioned them. Tom got his silks for free. Got a free bed as well.

A celibate trip down the Malay Peninsula led him to Orange Grove Road in Singapore and the chance to build his base for future operations. Financially it was imperative to knuckle down to hard work and continually produce stories to revive the ailing bank account. And it was all going nicely until the war in Vietnam went wrong and became a major international struggle by western democracies to stop the march of the communist bogey.

'Such is life,' reflected Tom as he finished his beer. He looked around and waved a finger at a waiter standing beside a potted palm on the terrace. The waiter, in immaculate black and white with bow tie and a neatly folded serviette over a forearm, glided towards him. Tom was surprised to see how old he was. Probably been with the hotel all his life.

'Yes, monsieur, would you like another drink?'

'With all these Yanks in town I assume you have some bottled American beer?'

'Indeed we do. Which one, sir?'

'Surprise me.'

He smiled and gave the table a wipe. 'I haven't seen you here before, sir. You with the diplomatic corps?'

Tom chuckled at the assumption. 'No, I'm a journalist. Flew in this morning and still in a state of shock.'

'Ah, phong vien,' responded the waiter.

'Meaning?'

'Sorry, sir, our word for people of your profession. Welcome to the war and our city. Where are you from?'

Tom was enjoying the exchange. He liked the old fellow and decided that he could be a good contact further down the track. Life had taught him that blokes like the old waiter usually heard a lot of enormous interest and knew more than they ever let on.

'I'm Australian. You know, that land with the kangaroos.'

Another smile. 'Ah, uc dai loi . . . sorry . . . '

Tom interrupted. 'I can guess: that means Australian. Now how about that drink?'

When the waiter returned Tom paid him with American dollars. 'Keep the change, friend.' It was a hefty tip. The waiter wouldn't forget him.

After lunch Tom decided on impulse not to go back to the Caravelle until he saw Mr Minh. Neil had told him about Mr Minh, the tailor who provided foreign correspondents with the smart safari suits that were something of an unofficial uniform. The military gear for operations in the field had to be purchased on the black market.

Tailor Minh had rooms in Tu Do Street. He had Tom measured up in minutes and announced that the three suits, in excellent cottons and three different colours – olive, fawn and navy – would be ready for a first fitting in two days. Some more dollars changed hands.

'Might as well score a few more runs – get my accreditation cards,' said Tom to himself as he went back into Tu Do Street. He consulted a map Neil had given him in Singapore marked with the locations of the press offices of the American and Vietnamese armed forces. At the Vietnamese office he filled in a form and handed over a couple of passport-style photographs.

'Be ready in four days, sir.' Remembering Neil's advice Tom slipped the Vietnamese clerk a few dollars. 'Ah, thank you, sir. Maybe it could be okay tomorrow afternoon. Please check with me.'

At the American forces press office it was easier. 'Call back tomorrow afternoon, Mr Ahearn, before the five o'clock follies. I'll have it ready,' said the Marine lieutenant.

'Five o'clock follies?' Tom raised a quizzical eyebrow.

'That's what the press call the daily briefing on the war by our staff here.' He gave a half smile.

Back at the Caravelle Tom went upstairs to his room and began unpacking. Opening the wardrobe he found the haversack of ammunition still there. 'Welcome to the war, Tom,' he said out loud and, after scratching his head, decided to take the bag to the five o'clock follies the next day.

Much later in the evening Sandy and Anna returned home. Giggling softly they fumbled with the lock on the gate leading to the courtyard in front of Sandy's apartment. The families on either side were sleeping; all was dark save for the dim light bulb outside Sandy's door.

'Feel like a cup of tea? A nightcap? Food?' offered Sandy, and Anna shook her head.

'Couldn't eat a thing. Fun evening. They're a nice bunch.'

Sandy kicked off her shoes and curled her legs up on the sofa. 'Yeah, I'll miss them. Still hasn't sunk in that I won't be working with them again. Really feel a bit adrift, y'know.'

'Something will come along. Wish I could swap jobs with you,' said Anna.

'Do you really? I thought you liked what you were doing.'

Anna settled into the cane lounge chair. 'I do. I like my job; I think I'm good at it. But this holiday is making me realise how boring it can be.'

'Perhaps you need a change. And what about Carlo? Is marriage on the horizon?' Sandy asked.

'I don't know, Sands . . . When I'm with him, it's lovely and it all seems sort of, well, inevitable. But here . . . things seem different,' said Anna hesitantly.

'No absence making the heart grow fonder?'

'Not really . . . I suppose it's all the excitement of a new place, being with you . . . Once I go back I'm sure things will be fine. What's happening tomorrow?' Anna changed the subject but Sandy wasn't to be deflected.

'Anna, are you sure? It just seems to me . . .' she paused but then, emboldened by the few drinks she'd had, went on, 'Look, you're my best friend and I don't want to see you throw yourself away on someone who doesn't fully appreciate you.'

'That's not true. You don't really know him, like I do –' began Anna with some heat.

'I know what I see,' said Sandy flatly. 'Look, sleep with him, do stuff with him, live with him if you have to, but don't marry him. I think you'll regret it. That's all I have to say. As a friend.'

Anna was silent for a moment. 'Why do you say that?'

'Because I see a change in you. Don't be such a door-mat! I think he dominates you too much.'

Anna sighed. 'Listen, I don't want to get into all this stuff. I hear you. Let's leave it at that.'

'Why? Why don't you want to get into this stuff, Anna?' Sandy got up and headed for the fridge in the kitchenette. Then she tried a bit more gently. 'If you're the least bit unsure, now's the time to get out. It's because I care about you, Anna. I think you're too good for him.'

'Thanks for those words of advice,' replied Anna somewhat tartly. 'You don't know Carlo. He's ambitious, got a great personality and has big plans. I'm lucky; he could have any girl he wants. We have fun together, most of the time.' Anna took the glass of wine Sandy handed her. 'And what about you, Sands? Where's all your love-life advice come from? I thought you told me everything. Is there something I don't know?'

'Not really. I wish.' She tried to laugh but it sounded hollow. 'I told you about Andy, Canadian guy that was working here. He did a number on me. Engaged to a girl back home. How was I to know?' She raised her glass. 'To blokes. They can be shits sometimes. We just have to find the genuine ones. And, most important, not settle for second best.'

'Ah, it's too hard, Sands. Forget it. Let's make the most of our time together here. Neither of us will probably ever come back. So here's to . . . good times.' Anna raised her glass and took a large gulp.

Sandy did the same. But she could tell she'd rattled Anna. And she was glad. She wanted Carlo out of Anna's life more than ever before. Anna could do better. Sandy might not have seen or talked to Carlo except for a brief visit, but she could see what was happening to her child-hood friend.

Anna felt uncomfortable. Sandy had irritated her and she didn't like it. She changed tack. 'I had an interesting talk with Tom before. Did you know he was planning to come back and cover the anniversary of the battle of Long Tan?'

'Long Tan? That's where Dad was.' Sandy closed her eyes for a moment. 'Mum says that's been the third party in their marriage – bloody Long Tan.'

'Well, I mentioned it to Tom. He wants to talk to your dad.'

'Oh yeah? Good luck. He never talks about the war.'

'Tom says a lot of vets are coming over. Don't you think it would be a good thing for him to come here?'

asked Anna, glad the conversation had moved away from Carlo.

Sandy was serious. 'Anna, you know how my dad has been since we were little . . . moody and stuff. Mum says it's because of what happened in the war. Dragging that all up . . . I don't think that's a good idea.'

Anna saw the sadness in her friend's face. 'Okay. But at least talk to Tom.' She suddenly realised that the cause of the sadness in both their families had to do with this country and its history.

5

In the cool courtyard at the rear of Barney's Bar, a few tourists lingered over a late lunch. It was siesta time and Barney took the opportunity to join Tom, Anna and Sandy. He ambled towards them with a cold bottle of lager in his hand.

'Barney looks tired,' commented Sandy in a quiet voice.

'Hiya. Mind if I join you guys?' Barney lowered his large frame onto a chair. 'I'm beat.'

'A busy day?' asked Tom.

'Most days are busy. Lai is taking a nap. Few problems on the home front,' he said with a sigh, and took a large drag on his lager.

'Sorry to hear that, Barney,' said Sandy, who didn't want to pry.

But Barney wanted to talk. 'Hey, not with us. She's great, we're great. It's our daughter in Canada. Having a few relationship problems at university. Lai's pretty worried.'

'We've all been there,' said Sandy.

'It's more that she's with the wrong crowd,' said Barney. 'I think we'll have to go over and try to sort things. Anyway, enough about us, what're you guys up to? Heading to the central provinces, eh?'

'Yep. I'm taking Anna with me to Hoi An, then to Danang. There's an orphanage that HOPE has an interest in near there. I guess we'll go to Hue too.'

'Got to see Hue: magnificent buildings. Though so many were bombed,' said Tom . . . he paused. 'Don't want to rabbit on about the war.'

'Why not? Most of the Australians and the Americans who come in here do nothing else. It's therapeutic,' said Barney.

'Were you there before the big 1968 Tet offensive then?' Sandy asked Tom.

'Yeah, I set out from Saigon to see what was happening in the war right up to the demilitarised zone near Hue which marked the border between the two Vietnams. North Vietnam was in the hands of the communists under Ho Chi Minh. The south was run by an army general, one of several who had held power after President Diem was toppled in an army coup in 1963,' said Tom. 'It was clear to me that the Australian effort at Bien Hoa was a sideshow to the fast deteriorating scene up north.'

'How'd you get around?' asked Barney.

'I hitched rides in choppers, bombers and C-47 transports fitted out with banks of machine guns. Our view that the war was changing was spectacularly confirmed when I saw first hand the massive build up of American forces through the port of Danang.'

'For sure,' said Barney. 'What sticks in my mind is that Buddhist monk setting fire to himself to protest against the policies of the South Vietnamese government.'

Tom looked down into his glass of beer. 'That photo of him went round the world and had a huge impact.'

Sandy nodded. 'The little blue Austin car he drove to Saigon is now in the Thien Mu Pagoda in Hue with the picture of him alight. It's very moving.'

Anna was quietly listening. Tom lightly touched her arm. 'Be sure and go to the pagoda for me. Light a stick of incense and say a prayer.'

'I'll do that, Tom.' But she was thinking how little she knew of Vietnamese history. Tom's reminiscence was another reminder of the many cultural and emotional moments that had assailed her in this country.

'So when are you heading to Saigon, Tom?' asked Barney.

'Same time as Sandy and Anna leave for Danang. Then I'm home to Sydney. I want to stay longer but I can't miss my wife's sixtieth birthday.'

'What are you giving her?' asked Sandy.

'I've bought some nice silk, a few trinkets. Have to give it a bit more thought,' confessed Tom. Then he asked the young women, 'Would you like me to call your folks when I'm home? Say I saw you, what a great time you're having and so on?'

'Sure, that'd be nice,' said Anna.

'I've been in touch with my folks pretty regularly via email,' said Sandy. 'But I'm sure they'd appreciate a call.'

Tom picked some peanuts from the bowl on the table. 'Sandy, your dad was at Long Tan. What're the chances of him coming over here for the fortieth anniversary?' he asked.

'None, I'd say. The war left a lot of scars. He tries to

forget it and I don't think Mum would want old wounds opened up either,' said Sandy firmly.

Tom was thoughtful. In spite of Sandy's warning he'd still like to meet her father. 'How about I phone your dad, Anna?'

'Go ahead and give him a call. I feel I've been neglecting him a bit, so he'd like to hear.' It occurred to Anna she'd also neglected Carlo because she was so busy and having such a good time.

'So will you be coming back to Vietnam, Tom?' asked Barney.

'I reckon. I'll hit Saigon, Vung Tau and head home and be back in the country for the Long Tan anniversary in August.'

'Why don't you bring your wife with you?' suggested Sandy.

'Be a great birthday present,' added Anna.

'Now there's an idea. Thanks, girls. I might try to do that. I'll stay in touch with you, of course.' He stood up. 'Have a bit of souvenir shopping to do. Catch you later.'

Barney watched Tom settle his bill and chat to the young waitress. 'Temporary staff are proving a big problem. Guess I'll have to close this joint while we're away in Canada.'

'That's a shame. You'll lose a lot of business. How long do you plan to be away?' asked Sandy.

'I don't quite know . . . probably two weeks.' Barney paused. 'When're you two heading home?'

Sandy laughed. 'Hey, don't look at us, Barney. No way could we take this over for you.'

Anna looked at Sandy. 'Why not? The chef is here and you have waiters and some bar staff.'

'But the whole business side of things . . . ' Sandy couldn't believe Anna actually sounded serious. 'And you have to go back home.'

'I have some leave owing. I can extend my stay. My ticket is good. I just have to tell the office.'

'And what about Carlo?' Sandy raised her eyebrows.

Anna's effervescence evaporated. 'He won't be thrilled.'

'Whoa,' exclaimed Barney. 'It's really great of you to offer and it would help us a lot. But I understand you have family, a life . . . '

'Do you think we could handle it?' asked Sandy, suddenly seeing a way to stay longer in Vietnam.

'Hell, yes. The chef is a bit temperamental, the staff unreliable, but between the two of you – should you agree to do this – I know you could cope. Have a bit of fun. Lai and I would show you the ropes, of course.'

Sandy and Anna looked at each other.

Sandy shrugged. 'Why not?'

'It'd really help us out,' said Barney.

'It's a deal,' said Anna. 'Can we start when we get back from our trip?'

The winding river was narrow this far from the sea. The wooden sampan moved sluggishly, the painted eyes on the prow seeing their way past rice paddies and the leaning stakes of the small shrimp ponds. The man on the stern dipping the long pole into the muddy bottom was dressed like most men on the river – dark pants and loose top, a conical straw hat shadowing his face.

The narrow old boat was low in the water, laden by a cargo of heavy baskets and boxes under the woven bamboo canopy. The man stroked lazily, in no hurry. He kept to the centre of the river away from the river banks where men and women worked in the fields or around thatched houses or at the water's edge. No head lifted; no attention was paid to the familiar river scene.

As darkness fell and the lights of the township

glittered in the distance, the boatman bent to his task, pushing more strongly and the little craft surged forward. He passed the edge of a town where cafes, bars and shops shone with light, activity and laughter. He steered out of the colourful reflections on the water and guided the sampan alongside a string of narrow planks that formed a rather unstable walkway to the bank. He tied the craft to a couple of leaning posts and hurried along the planks into the shadows of a dimly lit building.

Soon two other figures emerged and the sampan was hauled close to the shoreline footpath. The three men unloaded the cargo and carried it on their backs through the gate of an old house. It was a house that had stood by the river for centuries. Floods had been through it and the house had seen many generations of one family live and die.

The house, which surrounded an inner courtyard, was filled with heavy antique inlaid furniture, paintings, vases, photographs and memorabilia and a large ornate family altar. The interior wooden beams of the house were dark with age, smoke and weather. Stairs, ladders and steps led to other levels where rooms and floors formed the jigsaw that created an imposing and gracious home.

The men panted with the exertion of handling the weighty baskets so carefully. The moon was rising as the sampan, job completed, slipped silently down the river, a dark shadow on the shining water.

It was a short flight to Danang, and Anna and Sandy peered down at the beaches as the plane skimmed over the deep-water port.

'The beaches look nice,' commented Anna.

'There are resorts and hotels springing up. It's good weather most of the time except for the occasional typhoon during the monsoon season. This used to be a big military base in the war,' said Sandy. 'It's an interesting drive over the high pass into Hue.'

'We're trying out Hoi An first,' said Anna. 'That's a heritage town too, isn't it?'

'The ancient town is lovely, untouched. It was a big trading port about five hundred years ago. So many wonderful old buildings were bombed in other parts of the country but Hoi An was lucky to be spared. It's world heritage listed.'

'So when are we going to visit your orphanage? Is that on the way to Hoi An?' asked Anna.

Sandy chuckled. 'It's not exactly *my* orphanage. HOPE helped get it established. It's outside Danang, down the coast a bit. You can't help but get attached to the kids. They're so sweet. Many of them suffer birth defects and were just abandoned. Agent Orange has a lot to answer for.'

'Even a generation or two on it's still affecting people? What's happening with compensation or some kind of help for them?' asked Anna. Since she'd been in the country she'd become aware of the claims being made by victims' groups and Vietnamese government lobbyists for compensation. The Vietnamese wanted the US government to acknowledge that the use of the defoliant Agent Orange had not only affected soldiers but poisoned the countryside and its people.

'Yeah. A hell of a legacy. America is going to admit total liability because of the cost.' Sandy looked out the window and added quietly, 'The legacy of that war continues in all manner of ways. Everywhere.'

Anna nodded but didn't answer. She knew Sandy was thinking of her father.

The landing was bumpy. 'Bit of a cowboy at the helm,' said Anna with a grimace.

Sandy quickly spotted the driver holding a placard with their names on it. 'We'll get him to twirl us through Danang, but I think we should go straight down to Hoi An.'

'Lunch and a swim sound good to me,' said Anna.

Sandy had booked them into a hotel overlooking the river and Anna was glad that it was fifteen minutes out of Hoi An. The streets of Hoi An were packed with tourists on foot and on bikes, crowding the shops and cafes. There was a casual air as though everyone was there to enjoy themselves.

'It's just like a holiday town. I thought I was relaxed in Hanoi, but this seems to be a real party place,' Anna said, noticing the abundance of young tourists, back-packers and crowded cafes. 'Looks fun.'

'We're booked into a bit of a sleepy joint, but it's quiet and comfortable. If we want to splurge we could go to the Royal Hotel at Cua Dai Beach,' said Sandy.

The spacious units of the River Resort all faced the river and were clustered among palms and lawns landscaped with flowering frangipani and hibiscus trees. Anna and Sandy had a second-floor room, and when Anna flung open the doors to the balcony she exclaimed at the view over the rice paddies and the river where a lone fisherman was pulling a net into his sampan. They were pleased to be at the far end of the resort, away from the noisy pool, dining verandah, hotel spa and bar.

'There's a small village right next door. What a contrast,' said Anna, looking down at thatched huts, chickens, a penned pig and several dogs. Sheets of blue plastic sheltered communal outdoor areas where cooking pots simmered and several men lay in hammocks as children played along the sandy paths.

'I think some of the staff come from that village,' said Sandy. 'Let's hit the pool.'

After a refreshing swim they jumped on the hotel shuttle bus into town and wandered through the maze of shops before heading to the waterfront where colourful cafes lined the path along the river. From balconies and at outdoor tables you could watch the water traffic gliding by.

'Everyone's got something to sell,' said Anna as women with laden boats called out, offering all sorts of handicrafts, clothes, fabrics, toys, souvenirs or food for sale. Other sellers pedalled past on bicycles, cheerfully ringing their bells to catch the attention of prospective buyers. The locals smiled and chatted and seemed relaxed about selling their wares, persuading tourists to join tours or to visit a particular shop or business.

The girls settled at a small cafe at the end of the strip. The front entrance was covered with a thick drooping vine and upstairs a bright red balcony railing added a dash of colour. Sitting at a table just inside, which caught a slight breeze off the river, Sandy ordered cold drinks and studied the menu while Anna read the noticeboard fluttering with For Sale signs, share trips and accommodation and travel tips from backpackers. At the rear of the restaurant was a courtyard with an internet cafe and travel agency. On a blackboard was chalked the daily special: *Swedish Meatballs and Beer. At 7pm Karaoke.*

'Dishes from around the world. I think I'll stick to the local food,' said Sandy, turning over the International Menu to the Regional Specials on the back.

'Me too. I'd love to learn to cook some of these dishes. They're different from what Aunty used to make,' said Anna. 'I never paid much attention.'

'Too busy learning to make pasta?' queried Sandy with a raised eyebrow, quickly adding, 'Just joking. This is the place to do it. Cooking schools everywhere.'

'Why don't we do one while we're here then?'

'Sure, let's book in for a course tomorrow. And we have to get some clothes made. Did you bring your favourite shirt and pants?'

'Yes. I'd love some silk outfits in those pretty colours you see everywhere. But there're so many places, streets of them,' said Anna.

'I've got it covered. Know just the place. We'll go after lunch.'

It was Sandy's turn to pay so while she was talking to the cafe owner about cooking schools, Anna wandered across the cobbled road to the edge of the river. There weren't so many boats about now or people plying the river to trade and sell. It was siesta time. A sensible idea in the tropics, she thought. But a figure walking along some planks to get into a sampan caught her eye – a slim young man in cut-off cotton trousers, bare chest and the classic cone hat. While she couldn't discern his features, there was something familiar about his figure and movements. She watched him cast off and push the boat away with the long wooden pole then, midstream, he shipped the pole, crouched in the stern and pulled the starter cord on a small outboard motor. As the boat sped past her, she recognised the young man with the long tiller tucked under his arm. It was Hung from the *Harvest Moon* junk.

'Hung!' She waved and ran a few steps. But if he saw her he gave no indication and she realised he couldn't hear her over the noisy motor.

'Hey, let's walk off lunch and hit the tailor,' said Sandy, adjusting her dark glasses.

Anna turned and walked back. 'I just saw Hung. You know, from the junk on Halong Bay. What do you suppose he's doing down here?'

Sandy shrugged. 'This is a tourist town. Chasing

business. Who knows? Come on; let's do the clothes bit.'

In the Miss Rose Silk Shop the girls were draped in lengths of fabric, and rivers of satin and silk were unrolled along the big table in the centre of the tiny shop.

'No, no, I don't want to look at the picture books, thanks,' laughed Anna. 'Just copy these clothes in these materials.'

'You so pretty, so pretty,' began one of the girls, stroking Sandy's blonde hair. But when she smilingly answered in Vietnamese the shop girls became more businesslike.

Finally they agreed on the outfits and fabrics and measurements were taken.

The girl who was measuring Anna gave her an appraising glance. 'You wear ao-dai?' She pronounced it *ao-zai*.

Anna shook her head. 'No, not for me. Nowhere to wear it,' she added as she eyed the green satin trousers and long patterned green silk tunic top of the ao-dai the seamstress was wearing.

'You can wear. You Viet Kieu, more better. Not like . . . ' she angled her head towards two weighty German ladies who were trying on the classical ao-dais they'd had made.

Anna nodded in agreement. While it was a flattering garment for slim Vietnamese women, it didn't look as graceful on the lumpy European women.

'This one special for Vietnamese lady. You very beautiful; you try.'

Sandy overheard the conversation. 'Great idea, Anna. Go on, get one. Surprise your father.'

'Oh, and where will I wear it? To a fancy dress ball and go as a Vietnamese?' said Anna, but there was no humour in her tone.

121

'Lighten up, Anna . . . it's the world's most sensual outfit, if you ask me. God, Ralph Lauren and any number of designers have used the ao-dai style in collections. I have one I wear on occasions here. I just wish I looked as good in it as the local girls. Curves and blonde hair don't do it justice.'

An older woman glided towards them. She wore the darker colours of a married woman – deep violet tunic and black silk trousers, her long hair twisted on top of her head. Her tunic top had the popular raglan-cut sleeves that buttoned on the diagonal on one shoulder, different from the other neckline styles which Anna had noticed. This ao-dai had a slightly scooped neckline that showed a heavy gold necklace. Like all ao-dai, the tunic's split extended above her waist – showing a flash of flesh above the trouser waistband. The full pants almost touched the floor and the tunic sections floated about her as she moved. The bodice hugged her breasts and rib cage, showing off her narrow body.

She smiled and took Anna's hands and in perfect English said quietly. 'I am Madame Nguyen; this is my silk shop. To wear the ao-dai, it must be fitted correctly. You are married?' When Anna shook her head, she went on, 'Pastel colours for a young unmarried woman. The school-girls wear white and older ladies like me, dark colours.'

'No dark colours for me?' asked Anna, who'd never thought of herself as a pastel person.

'On rainy days,' smiled Madame Nguyen. 'Now choose best quality material. Modern girls are so busy, they like synthetic, no iron. For you, nice silk. Heavy one, yes?'

Madame Nguyen was gentle but persuasive and, before she knew it, Anna was holding a pale cream and a rich chocolate silk fabric up to her body. Madame Nguyen turned her around to face the mirror.

'Dark trousers, and the milk-coloured tunic shows off your skin and eyes. This is the one for you.'

And so Anna paid the deposit on her clothes and on two shirts for Carlo as a surprise. She'd packed one of his favourite shirts to have copied even though he had dismissed the idea of having clothes made in Asia, as he considered nothing matched Italian tailoring.

Sandy had ordered pants, shirts and a skirt.

Well satisfied with their afternoon they set out for their hotel and another swim.

'Did you notice the jewellery, the rings, that Madame Nguyen was wearing?' said Anna, as they walked from the shop.

'How could you miss them? They were serious rocks. She mentioned she had more than one silk shop. Must be money in it,' answered Sandy. 'What did you make of her?'

'I liked her at first, but then I started to feel she was a bit like a snake. Her kind of lazy, slithering movement, hissy voice, those sharp eyes, the shiny clothes, glittery jewellery. If I was a man in bed with her I wouldn't shut my eyes in case she wound around me and strangled me.'

Sandy burst out laughing. 'Anna! My god. She's a shrewd businesswoman, that's all. I bet she has smart private clients. Now I'll check out the cooking schools. You book us into the spa for a massage or a facial,' said Sandy. 'It's a quarter the price of home.'

Sandy chose the Blue Gate Cooking School. 'It's all morning. Then we get to eat what we make. We go to the markets, buy the ingredients, then get a shuttle bus to the school – it's an old place on the river that's been kitted out with kitchen, big tables, a deck – sounds nice. There'll be about fifteen of us. We have to meet at the Blue Gate Cafe in the Ancient Quarter at nine.'

*

Those in the cooking group were tourists from all over. Anna and Sandy were glad they weren't the only young people. The older couples had been to Vietnam before and were keen to show off their knowledge to the first timers. With notebooks, water bottles, cameras, shady hats and shopping bags the group trailed out of the cafe to walk to the markets, led by Mr Bach and Miss Tan.

'Feels like a school outing, doesn't it?' smiled a young American woman walking beside Sandy and Anna.

By the time they reached the small streets leading into the food market, Anna and Sandy had learned that Josie, the American woman, and her husband, Trent, came from New Jersey and were on their honeymoon. An older English couple had always wanted to visit the Orient, while two German ladies were on their third trip.

The side streets around the main market were jammed with people looking at the overflowing stalls, people selling from mats and baskets on the streets, or wandering vendors, mostly women, with a shoulder pole bent with the weight of a basket at either end filled with fresh produce or homemade delicacies.

It was mid morning and the market had been in full swing since sunrise. As Mr Bach explained, 'Vietnam is a nation of markets, daily ones, some speciality ones and others that happen once a year for a big festival like Tet.'

'Many recipes are kept secret, passed down for generations,' Miss Tan said. 'Some are given only to sons as daughters might give them to their in-laws.' She went on to explain that the rituals around food bind families together. 'Traditions, whether it be food used in ceremonies, for worship, or eaten at certain events and times of the year, unite us. Flavours, recipes and ingredients might vary from the north to the south, but the memories of certain dishes prepared by family, or an old woman at a stall in a market, or at a certain favourite eatery, last through life.'

124

'I love the markets,' said Sandy. 'When I first arrived I used to go with one of the local girls from the office. I'm still learning what all the different things are. So much of it is seasonal and local to various areas.'

'Do you cook much?' asked Anna, rather surprised. Sandy wasn't known for her culinary skills.

'Just the basics! You know me. So many dishes here take hours or days to prepare.'

They were led in a straggling group into the big covered market area. Cameras and notebooks came out to record details of vegetables, dried spices, pickled food, brightly coloured mounds of rice and a variety of noodles.

'It's an art show,' declared Anna.

Women crouched on stools or sat on plank beds before their displays of foods, which were artistically arranged on trays, in bowls or in cones of colour. Dressed in cotton pyjamas, they gossiped loudly as they bundled beans and leaf plants, or sifted seeds, lentils or dried foods by tossing and shaking them on a fine bamboo tray or sieve. Some giggled and flashed welcoming smiles when the group stopped before them, while others turned shyly away from the cameras.

Rainbow fruits – small bananas, longans, persimmons, tangerines, pomelos, starfruit, mangoes, kumquats, dragonfruit and huge watermelons – all looked mouthwatering in the heat. There were gasps and groans as they passed through the meat section where pigs' heads and trotters, and chunks of raw and bleeding flesh were laid out on slabs or hung from hooks, exposed to flies and dust.

They stepped carefully on the wet floors as they sloshed into the seafood area close to a canal where small fishing boats, sampans and canoes were tied up. Fishing baskets were piled high and spread in front of every seller were tubs and plastic buckets full of wriggling, squirming, flapping fish and eels. Live crabs and large shrimp were tied in mournful bundles. Bowls of tiny school fish and freshly cleaned fish were laid out ready to cook.

Miss Tan picked through the fish while Mr Bach chose small crabs and mussels, which were ladled into plastic bags. As the two instructors consulted their list of ingredients, Anna took a photo but turned when a voice hailed Sandy.

'Bonjour! Such a surprise. Nice to see you again, Sandy.'

'Jean-Claude! What are you doing here?' Sandy laughed. 'I was just thinking of you as I looked at those shrimp – are they safe to eat?'

Anna glanced at Sandy as the good-looking Frenchman came towards them.

'They're still alive, so fresh. Unfortunately for them.' He grinned at Anna. 'I am Jean-Claude. I met Sandy a few days ago.'

'When Kim and I went to the shrimp farm,' explained Sandy to Anna and then made the introductions. 'Anna Fine, Jean-Claude Petiere.'

Anna shook hands. 'Ah, the shrimp doctor. Sandy told me about the problems with the shrimp farms. Are you working here in Hoi An?'

'Danang. But I have been visiting a few farms around this area. How long are you here for?'

'A couple of days. I'm showing Anna around and visiting an orphanage. We thought we'd go over to Hue as well.'

'Would you both like to join me for dinner this evening?' he asked with a warm gesture of open hands.

Sandy glanced at Anna, who smiled agreement. 'Well, that would be lovely. We're staying out at the River Resort.'

'I'm at The Royal. They have a very nice ocean-side

terrace and it's close to your end of town. Say seven o'clock?'

'Wonderful. We'll see you there, then,' said Sandy. 'Here's my mobile number in case there's a problem.'

'There won't be.' Jean-Claude tucked Sandy's card in his pocket and for a moment Anna thought of Carlo and his regular text messages and suddenly missed hearing from him. Jean-Claude grinned at Anna. 'Enjoy your cooking course.'

'Thank you. I look forward to seeing you tonight,' said Anna.

'Au revoir. Until this evening.' He swung through the market and Sandy and Anna hastily followed their group to the shuttle bus waiting to drive them to their cooking school.

They teamed up with Josie and Trent, the American couple, for the cooking demonstration and participation. While Sandy drew the line at turning tomatoes into a perfect rose or a carrot into a swan, Anna enjoyed everything, from preparing dishes in fine detail to learning customs associated with serving food.

Mr Bach gave some additional social commentary. 'Since *Doi Moi* – the renovation of the country that began in 1986 – there has been a return to our traditional customs and values, like religion and many food rituals.' He gave a small smile. 'The new rich people want to have big weddings and funeral banquets like in the old days.'

Following Miss Tan's deft hands and swift instructions the group learned to prepare rice noodles with grilled pork rolled in sweet spices, fried spring rolls, steamed shrimp pancakes, noodle and crab soup topped with tangy mint, green papaya salad and sweet rice cakes. A lot of the food preparation had been done in advance but the three hours flew by quickly.

'Now is the best part – we eat,' said Mr Bach.

On the large verandah of the old house that over-looked the river, the western tables and chairs had been pushed to one side and woven mats were set on the floor with four tiny stools at each corner. Large trays, bowls and chopsticks were set out and everyone chose a seat.

'I'll never get off this darn thing without help,' laughed a heavy American woman as she lowered herself onto the tiny plastic seat.

'Sit on the floor if you prefer. Or perhaps a cushion,' suggested Miss Tan. 'We sit at the four corners of the mat and the food is placed in the centre on the tray – usually an even number of dishes for luck. Rice is served by the mother or the first daughter-in-law.'

Serving chopsticks were placed on each dish and everyone helped themselves, putting small portions into their bowls and adding chilli paste or nuoc mam, the fish sauce that Vietnamese use liberally on nearly every dish.

'Families like to eat together; it is a tradition. We help ourselves to each dish but it is polite to serve food to others,' said Mr Bach.

Sandy leaned over and dropped a portion of spring roll onto Anna's rice. 'Nice custom, eh? Did you write down the recipes?'

'I did. I'll try some of them out on Carlo when I get home. Such healthy food. But I'm not going to eat much tonight!'

They dressed up for dinner with Jean-Claude. Both had treated themselves to a massage and facial, and so they drifted up the white stone steps of The Royal into the marble foyer feeling very relaxed.

'Wow, this is certainly five-star,' said Anna as she looked around at the antique furniture, the exquisite flower arrangements, the beautiful women staff in ao-dais, the expensive boutiques. Through the colonnades that led to the upper terrace they could see palm trees and a stretch of blue ocean gleaming in the sunset.

'Look at that view!' exclaimed Anna.

'I could learn to love this lifestyle,' declared Sandy.

'Hello there. How lovely you both look.' Jean-Claude strode towards them.

Both girls stared at him, breaking into smiles at the sight of the tall and handsome Frenchman in white linen pants and a pale blue shirt slightly revealing a tanned chest. His hair was damp and as he kissed each of them on the cheek they caught the scent of a fresh tangy citrus aftershave.

He was good company and after champagne aperitifs they moved to the sheltered lower garden terrace where trees were floodlit, frangipani flowers carpeted the grass and candles fluttered on the elegant tables set discreetly apart.

Over dinner they talked about the challenges of working in a foreign country.

'Something I'll also be able to experience,' said Anna. Then they told him about running Barney's Bar for two weeks.

'Is there no end to your talents? I shall be sure to stop by, of course.'

'What about you, Jean-Claude? Who do you work for?' asked Anna.

Jean-Claude expertly eased an escargot from its shell. 'I work for a private company. At the moment I answer to the head office back in France, but within the country we have local staff and I attend monthly staff meetings in each office, and we also have a series of meetings on program management and program quality so staff can share what they are doing in various sectors. How does HOPE work, Sandy?' he asked.

'HOPE is quite hierarchical. Our accountability is

not just to our donors, but most importantly to our partners and beneficiaries. Cherie Mitchell, our director,
reports directly back to Canberra.'

'Sandy, you don't work with HOPE any more,' Anna
reminded her.

Jean-Claude laughed and held up his wine glass for a
toast. 'To your next life, Sandy! What will it be? Your
own restaurant?'

'Good Lord, no! I have no idea. Except it won't be a
desk job. Or in hospitality. Barney's is strictly a favour
and a bit of fun.'

'And you, Anna?' asked Jean-Claude.

'Oh, my life seems very boring compared to you two.
A desk job, a steady boyfriend, future all mapped out.'

'Says who?' retorted Sandy.

'Have you not found being here, making connections
with your heritage . . . interesting?' asked Jean-Claude.

Anna looked away from his intense green eyes. 'Yes,
interesting. As all tourists find it, I'm sure.'

'What about you, Jean-Claude? How do you find
Vietnam?' asked Sandy suddenly to change the subject.
Everyone was always keen to hear a Viet Kieu story.

Jean-Claude gave Sandy a swift glance and lifted the
bottle of wine to refill their glasses while he decided how
to answer her direct question. He put down the bottle
and twirled the stem of his glass. 'I have a connection
with this country too. My maternal grandfather lived
here and worked for the French administration. My
mother lived here when she was very little but left before
World War Two broke out. I was born in France but
grew up in a house filled with Vietnamese furniture, art
and photos. We had a Vietnamese maid who cooked
Vietnamese food.' He paused. 'Because my family were
part of the colonial regime, I feel a great bond with this
place.'

'Is that why you feel you have to help the country? What business is your family in now?' asked Sandy.

He gave a wry smile. 'Seafood. My father has a processing factory in Boulogne. So we have a long history connected to seafood. I originally came here looking for export opportunities but have temporarily switched to improving the Vietnamese aquaculture industry because it's been overexploited.'

'So you're working for your family's company?' asked Sandy.

'Yes, but I'm taking it in new directions.'

Anna stood up and excused herself to go to the ladies' room. The reality was she felt uncomfortable and couldn't quite explain why. Maybe it was a sense of guilt because she had no deep knowledge of a country with which she had very close links. Unlike Jean-Claude's family, she had grown up with no meaningful acknowledgment of her Vietnamese heritage. For Jean-Claude the link was cultural, for her biological and yet he knew more and felt more connected to Vietnam than she did.

The soft lights, perfumed candles and fresh flowers were calming as Anna stared at her reflection in the mirror in the elegant ladies' room. She looked at her image, taking in the features that made her different from most Australians. The slanting almond-brown eyes, the high cheek bones, the sleek dark hair all combined to give her an exotic Eurasian appearance. The outline of her mouth, the curve of her eyebrows, the shape of her head she saw all the time in Vietnamese women here.

She recalled how often Kevin Fine, her father, told her that Thu, her mother, had been very beautiful, and her genes had produced another beauty. Anna wiped her eyes with a tissue to dry her tears. She suddenly felt there was a stranger lurking there within the image, a woman she'd never known but who lived with her day and night.

Where and who was the real Anna? It was an issue that had scarcely raised its head while she was growing up in Australia. Only a few instances stuck in her memory, an argument at a beach, a taunt or two at school.

Now she was becoming curious about her mother, long dead. The few memories Anna held of Thu were warm and loving – a small child embraced by her mother's arms, comforted by a soft voice, songs and smiles. For the first time Anna thought deeply of her mother as someone who had grown up in this country, who had relatives and friends and a whole life here before she had fled as a teenager with Uncle Quoc. Anna wasn't even sure where Thu had lived. What markets, what temple, what places had she visited? Anna was finding this all very unsettling. Something inside was telling her that she had to know more.

When she returned to the table Sandy and Jean-Claude were still talking about Jean-Claude's family.

'My grandfather was an administrator in Hue. But when he returned to France after the French left he missed this country very much. Perhaps when you get to Hue you might like to see the house where he lived?'

As he was writing on the back of his business card, Sandy looked up. 'What's wrong?' she asked Anna, who had an odd expression.

'I just went past that antiques boutique in the lobby. They've got a plate like the one we saw at the potter's in Bat Trung. Mr Thinh's old platter.'

'What, the genuine one? The one with the fighting cocks?' asked Sandy.

'This one has a fish on it but looks old and has the same glaze.'

'Surely someone isn't copying them and hoodwinking the tourists,' said Sandy, looking puzzled.

Jean-Claude looked at them. 'Are you interested in ceramics?'

'I am. Along with other old objects. We visited a famous potter the other day and he had one lovely genuine piece. It seems odd there could be another one similar,' said Sandy.

'There are some expert forgers around. And one hears rumours,' said Jean-Claude.

'What kind of rumours?' asked Anna.

'Ah, fakes, stolen stuff, secret caches, shipwrecks. I've heard of fishermen pulling up things in their nets. But there's money to be made with fakes as well as genuine pieces.'

'Really? Sounds like a movie,' said Anna.

'Let's have a look at it when we've finished our coffee.' Sandy smiled at Jean-Claude. 'It's been a wonderful evening.'

'Superb food,' agreed Anna.

'I suggest a walk along the beachfront another time as it's very pretty. Early in the evening they light flame torches and sell trinkets. Or you can sit out the front of the hotel and have them bring cocktails to your lounge chairs, if you're feeling decadent.' Jean-Claude smiled. 'I rough it round the country a bit, so I enjoy a little luxury now and then.'

'We're definitely coming back,' said Sandy, standing up.

There was one American man browsing in the antiques shop in the hotel lobby as Anna pointed out the plate to Sandy while Jean-Claude went to arrange a car to drive them the short distance to their resort. The shop assistant was careful about handling the plate when the girls asked her to lift it down onto the counter. She shook her head when Sandy peppered her with questions and finally retreated to the rear of the shop to get the owner.

They were surprised as Madame Nguyen appeared and, recognising the girls, gave them a charming smile.

'So you have been dining here? A beautiful hotel, isn't it?'

'Indeed,' agreed Sandy. 'Madame Nguyen, is this your shop?'

The elegant Vietnamese businesswoman lifted her shoulders and spread her hands in a very French gesture. 'I have several businesses. My family come from here and we have an old house by the river. We have lived in it for many generations. My family are collectors so it is full of antique furniture, paintings and photographs. It gives me an interest. You are enjoying Hoi An?'

'Yes. Very much.' Sandy indicated the old plate. 'Is this a real antique? It must be very valuable, and very expensive if it is.'

'It certainly is genuine.' She lowered her voice, flicking her eyes towards the American. 'A lot of very rich people come here. We also have a shop in Hue.'

'With more plates like this?' asked Anna.

She gave a tight smile. 'There are still rare objects to be acquired in a place like Vietnam.' She lifted her voice a little as the American came closer. 'This you would only find in a museum in America.'

Curiosity got the better of the American man listening to their conversation. 'That plate is museum quality? How much?' he asked without any preamble.

Madame Nguyen turned away from the girls and gave him her full attention. 'This is over four hundred years old . . . very special. See here: the mythical winged fish . . . very special story in our country. This is best Vietnamese pottery, not Chinese . . . ' She launched into her spiel as the girls excused themselves and left.

Jean-Claude was waiting at the entrance. 'I have a hotel car to drive you back.'

'Thank you,' said Anna.

'The pleasure is mine. So did you buy the plate?'

Sandy laughed. 'Not likely. It's worth a lot more than I can afford. I'd like to know its provenance and where she got it.'

'Yes, it could be interesting,' smiled Jean-Claude. 'Enjoy Hue. When are you leaving?'

'Two days' time,' said Sandy, making an executive decision. 'As soon as we pick up some new clothes from Madame Nguyen's silk shop.'

'Get a good driver. Storms, high winds and rain are predicted. Be a good thing to leave the coast.'

'Unfortunately we have to come back to the coast near Danang to see the orphanage HOPE supports. When do you leave, Jean-Claude?' asked Sandy.

'Depends on the farmers, an aquaculture specialist and the weather. You have my card if you need to contact me.' He kissed both of them on each cheek and watched them go down the flight of steps to the waiting car.

As the car turned out of the circular driveway, Sandy looked back and saw Madame Nguyen walk from the hotel lobby past Jean-Claude at the entrance, acknowledging him with a smile and a slight nod of her head. Then their car swept around the corner and the elegant white hotel was out of sight.

Anna leaned her head back against the seat. 'Man, this country is one of contrasts. He's nice, eh? Will you contact him again, do you think?'

Sandy didn't answer for a moment. 'I'm sure we'll run into him somewhere. It's how it is here.'

'Seems so. Creepy seeing Madame Nguyen again tonight.' Anna said it lightly but she was thinking that perhaps, when they returned to Hanoi, she'd call her father and ask him some questions. Or maybe she'd wait until they went to Saigon. They planned to catch up with Tom Ahearn in the south and she felt sure he'd be willing to help her should she decide to do a little investigating.

Saigon, 1965

It wasn't a restful first night in the South Vietnamese capital for Tom Ahearn, despite a solid round of pre-dinner drinks and a long meal enriched by some good French wines with a group of foreign journalists and photographers he'd met at the bar of the Caravelle Hotel. They worked for Reuters and Associated Press of America which, like news agencies from all over the non-communist world, were expanding their bureaus in Saigon. A 'real war' made good copy, and the folks back home wanted to know how 'our boys' were going.

The conflict was no longer a low-key backblock shootout involving those holding rival political ideologies. Following the departure of the French, the former colony was divided into the communist-dominated North and the Democratic Republic of South Vietnam. It was getting serious now that the Americans and their allies were committing significant front-line units in a desperate effort to put some real steel into the defence of South Vietnam. The years of military advisors trying to lift the combat quality of the South Vietnamese government's regular forces just hadn't been good enough. To make that really clear, communist guerrilla units in the south were already active on the outskirts of Saigon and Tom could see that without even leaving the hotel. It was a sort of after-dinner treat, a standard offering to newcomers, to glimpse some action from the hotel roof while enjoying a nightcap or two.

Led by a small group of journalists and hangers-on employed or freelancing to make their names and dollars from the war, they filed up to the rooftop, and, as usual, the Viet Cong guerrillas obliged with their nightly show. A few mortar shells fired into distant defences lit up the sky with bright flashes and drew an equally bright artillery retaliation that lasted for only a few rounds. Then everyone on the roof applauded and the city went quiet again . . . apart from the late hum of scooters and motorbikes from the nearby streets.

After another round of drinks Tom fell into bed in his underpants and slept uneasily, waking frequently to fresh echoes, real and dreamed, of the war on the horizon.

He rose early, showered, made a cup of instant coffee, then, wrapped in a towel, stood at the window looking out at the sprawling roads already busy with thousands of scootering locals going about their normal lives.

'Normal lives!' mused Tom to himself. 'Jesus, I don't think anything is normal here any more.' He recalled that when the counterinsurgency campaign had begun several years back, 'Win the war by '64' had been a wonderful slogan in true Yankee advertising style. Now it was a joke line among journalists who attended the daily military briefings, the five o'clock follies. Ah yes, the follies. Must get cracking, he resolved. He dressed quickly and headed to the dining room for breakfast.

His first call was to the Continental Hotel, where he sought out the old head waiter he had met the day before whom he hoped would become a useful ally in this strange city.

'I need to change some American dollars for local cash. You know, unofficially. Perhaps you can help? For a fee, naturally,' said Tom with a smile.

'Of course, Mr Tom. I know an Indian gentleman with excellent connections.' He quickly wrote an address on a drink order pad and tore off the sheet. 'Mr Dema also helps your friend Mr Davis, who you mentioned to me yesterday. Any time during the day.'

Tom slipped him a five-dollar note, then went to the hotel lobby and consulted a street map. The address was only a ten-minute walk from the city square and Tom strode out, telling himself that the brisk walk was good exercise. But he was sweating from the humidity when he arrived.

A rather nervous small Indian man opened the door. There was a quick exchange of names and, in a bedroom that also served as an office of sorts, money changed hands. Dollars for dong. It was illegal, of course, but the blackmarket rate of exchange for US dollars was more profitable, so practical Tom had decided that the method was necessary.

He then took a taxi to Cholon, the predominantly Chinese area of Saigon, to a shop that his drinking mates of last night had recommended as a good place to pick up military gear for field operations. He bought an American field uniform, from boots to helmet, several shirts, shorts and webbing, all fitting nicely and costing little.

'You want some Australian uniform?' the bustling Chinese dealer asked as he listed the prices. 'And I have very good medical kit, very new, just in from Yankee stores.'

Tom was astonished. 'Give me the medical kit. And where did you get Australian military gear?'

'Relative in Singapore. Relative in Australia. Very easy to buy and ship.'

Tom bought a couple of Australian kits, wondering whether the Viet Cong used mail order too, or simply sent someone into Cholon to buy what they wanted.

Later he called at the Australian Embassy to register his presence in the country and to get the address of the Australian military task force HQ, which was being cobbled together in a hurry to cope with the build-up of forces.

In a nondescript part of town, behind solid brick walls topped with barbed wire he found a sweating, mustachioed Australian Army major settling in at a broad wooden desk adorned with a cluster of family pictures and a little display of Australian, American and South Vietnamese flags.

The officer beamed when Tom was escorted in to the office. 'Welcome to Saigon. You're my first customer. Major Harry Brown . . . Call me Harry. Now, how can I help?'

'Accreditation for the Australian base is at the top of my shopping list. Picking up the Viet and Yank tickets from the bureaucracy later today.'

Major Brown shrugged. 'No can do, mate. We're not issuing accreditation cards. The others you mentioned will get you through most of the barricades you'll run into.'

Tom was taken aback. 'You're not accrediting journos? Why not? It's a bureaucrat's dream scene for controlling who goes where, and when.'

'Well, mate, it's like this, but don't quote me. According to the brass, who listen to the pollies back home, we aren't at war so we don't have war correspondents.'

'We're not at war? Hell, I saw it last night.'

Major Brown was unperturbed. 'Care for a cuppa? The pot boiled just before you arrived. Bushells tea from back home. And some Scotch Fingers.' He went to the sideboard and busied himself. 'No, you see, we're involved in a pacification campaign, not a war. We're helping the local lads maintain the peace. Guerrillas don't represent an invading army, if you get my drift.'

Tom groaned. 'I'd love that cup of tea. Hope it's a strong brew.'

'Yes, just give me a bell or drop in whenever you want to get down to where our boys are in action or holding the fort. Working alongside the American airborne lads at the moment, as you know, but we'll soon have our own little pad of operations. Can't say more. Sugar?'

At the five o'clock follies a couple of hours later Tom waved his new American and Vietnamese accreditation passes at the guards standing by the door to the hotel auditorium. There were a couple of hundred correspondents gathered for the daily briefing by officers on what had been happening across the country. It was a controlled and sanitised briefing, as one of his dinner pals had described it the previous night, with emphasis on wins and limited information about setbacks. A young Australian from Reuters at the table had added that the fun started when Question Time gave the reporters a chance to get behind the glossy façade and barrage of 'utter bullshit'.

Before Tom could get inside, one of the American guards tapped him on the shoulder. 'That pack you're carrying, can I please have a look inside? Can't be too careful, sir.'

Tom nodded agreement and plonked it on a desk by the door. The Marine sergeant unlaced the flap and did a double-take. With raised eyebrows he tried to make sense of the weird collection of ammunition.

'I'd like to donate it to the war effort,' said Tom, straightfaced, when their eyes met.

The guard picked up a handful of bullets and there was a pregnant pause. 'Could you please explain, sir?' Another Marine guard moved towards them to see what was going on.

'Look, I'm sorry, I was just making a joke. I found them in the wardrobe at my room in the Caravelle. Seems the last occupant, another correspondent, liked to go into the field well armed. He's been given another assignment and moved on . . . left this behind and, well, it's just not me.'

'You're not going to carry a weapon, sir?'

'Oh yes . . . a pen and pencil or two.'

There was another blank look from the guard, who did not look amused.

'I thought it'd be best if I turned it all in here. You'd know what to do with it,' Tom said affably.

'Thank you, sir, we'll look after it. Do you want the bag?'

'No, thanks.'

The follies lived up to their reputation. Poker-faced American officers read out summaries of briefing papers distributed to the newsmen as they arrived, sometimes adding details of updated enemy casualty figures, or giving a verbal report of a recent engagement. It was an overwhelmingly 'good news' scene. It demonstrated to Tom that the only way to get a realistic picture of what was happening was to get out in the field, get around the country, and see first hand just what was being achieved in the conflict, which was unlike any war he'd read about. There just wasn't a defined front line. The 'front' could be anywhere in the city, or the country . . . and the insurgents called the tune.

The highlight of the follies show came at the end of Question Time, when a reporter from a New York paper rose to a little round of applause and chuckles. The correspondent beside Tom explained, 'Joe is a star act every day. Always fires a good shot to end the show.'

'Captain, is it true that there's a tense situation developing in relations between men of the one seventy-third Airborne and the Australians operating alongside them? Something to do with the Australians being able to drink beer when they're in camp, but the Americans being forced to drink Coke or water?'

There was a burst of laughter.

The briefing officer stayed straightfaced. 'I'm not across that issue, Joe. I will certainly make inquiries.'

More applause, a clatter of seats and a wave of

conversation signalled the show was over. Tom caught up with the senior briefing officer who was still gathering up his files.

'What're the chances of getting down round Bien Hoa where the Aussies are operating with your men?'

'I'm sure something can be arranged,' he drawled.

It was easier than Tom could have imagined. A lift in a supply helicopter was arranged for the next day.

He quickly observed that defending the huge air base being developed at Bien Hoa during the massive round-the-clock build-up of American strength involved a lot more than having a strong perimeter. The allied forces mounted frequent assault missions against suspected Viet Cong bases in the nearby jungle and swampland. Strikes were made even further out in a prime target area known as War Zone D. The zone was subject to heavy blanket bombing but the enemy wouldn't go away. They just bunkered down and kept digging tunnels and an underground network that housed barracks for thousands of fighters.

Tom spent a couple of days getting to know the officers of the Australian First Battalion and their neighbours, the American paratroopers. Despite Tom's lack of combat experience, the Americans offered to take him on an operation to find an enemy base they had identified by monitoring radio transmissions. The force included a company of Australian troops so Tom joined a chopper carrying some of the Aussies into the swampy jungle at dawn.

Dressed in a mix of American and Australian army uniforms and feeling a little foolish in the American-style helmet, Tom shut his eyes for the first few moments as he made his inaugural jump into the war from a helicopter that hovered low over an abandoned rice field. He promptly fell over and sank into a mire of stinking mud.

An Australian corporal assigned to keep an eye on him grabbed his arm and pulled him up. 'Come on, mate, run like hell for that line of rubber trees. And keep as low as you can.'

They made it without a shot being fired.

'Thank you, Victor Charlie,' panted Tom as he flopped down beside the corporal on the edge of the rubber plantation.

'Yeah, the bastards must have slept in.'

Then, slowly and very carefully, the troops fanned out and began to move forward, looking for any sign on the ground that might indicate the underground target. The plantation yielded nothing and they moved into the jungle nearby.

'Keep your mouth shut,' whispered the corporal, 'and try not to touch anything that looks a bit out of the ordinary. Could be a booby-trap.'

They crept forward. Tom started to sweat profusely, not just from the heat, and began shaking with fear. Suddenly firing broke out far to the left and everyone threw themselves to the ground.

'VC machine gun,' snapped the corporal. 'They've hit the Yanks out on the far flank, I reckon. Keep your head down.'

Almost immediately the Americans began retaliatory fire, but Tom couldn't see any enemy. The Australians held their fire until suddenly a few men in black pyjamas were seen scurrying through a thicket of jungle. A deafening roar of automatic rifle fire from all around him made Tom squirm. Bullets whined overhead. 'Oh shit,' he gasped. Then as suddenly as all hell had broken loose, it was quiet. The shooting stopped.

'I think we got 'em,' said the corporal. 'Stay low.'

There was a shouted call for medics from the American lines. Along the Australian line there was a silent hand signal from man to man that confirmed no one had been hit.

A sergeant crawled up to Tom. 'You stay put. A few of us are going out to see what we hit up there. Okay?'

Tom nodded vigorously.

The Australians moved forward with trigger fingers ready to fire, covering each other in carefully prepared tactics so well drilled into them that they didn't have to think about what they were doing. Simply keep eyes open and keep moving. They soon came across the bodies of three Viet Cong. Nearby they found the entrance to a short tunnel from which the VC had fled. It wasn't the complex they were hoping to find, only the beginning of another hideout. The force that had hit the American flank had disappeared into the jungle and were probably already back in well-concealed underground bunkers. They left behind fifteen dead comrades. Five Americans were dead, six wounded.

Tom stood and watched the body bags and wounded on stretchers lifted into a Chinook helicopter.

The corporal quickly shook Tom's hand. 'Hop aboard; they'll drop you back at base.'

Tom nodded. Words for once seemed inadequate. All he managed was, 'Good luck, mate. And thanks.'

The corporal gave him a thumbs up as the rotors roared to life.

Tom found it hard to reconcile the casual chaos of the military in Saigon with its blackmarket, gung-ho mentality, compared with the life and death reality being played out in the paddy fields.

Now Tom had his story.

6

AFTER JUST A COUPLE of days in Hoi An, Anna had become intrigued with the village next to the River Resort. There was a young waiter who walked from the village to work in the terrace restaurant overlooking the river each morning. In the evening he returned to his small garden.

'Do you think we could go through the village, pretend we're taking a shortcut?' Anna asked Sandy.

'What for? It's only ten little houses and a sort of communal area at most,' she said.

'I know it's not a tourist thing, but it gives a better idea of what this place is about rather than the buzzy market and the shopping area where all the hotels are, or even the Ancient Town – which is lovely but touristy now. Ask Trung, our breakfast waiter. He lives there. It's right next door.'

Sandy had seen Anna taking photos from their balcony and thought it a great idea to experience some local life. So when she next spotted the young man, she chatted to him in Vietnamese and discovered he was a student saving money to go to classes at night. He agreed to take them to see his family in the small commune next door.

At sunset the girls walked with Trung along the sandy path beneath the palm and frangipani trees at the rear of the resort. He stopped by the pig in its outdoor pen and threw in a bag of scraps from the hotel kitchen. Sandy and Anna followed him past several houses where men wearing sarongs relaxed in doorways or squatted together under a tree, smoking and talking, but fell silent and stared with frank curiosity as the two foreign women passed by.

At Trung's small house his mother, sister and an aunty were gossiping and preparing the evening meal. They shyly welcomed the unexpected visitors, but relaxed as Sandy chatted to them in Vietnamese and Anna handed over the small gift of French chocolates they'd brought. Children, smiling but shy, edged closer.

The women turned to Anna asking questions of the Viet Kieu, which Sandy answered. They were curious about Anna's story and nodded sympathetically as Sandy related what she knew of Anna's family.

Anna immediately won their interest by asking about the dish they were cooking and so the women made space for her in their circle around the low plastic table outside the house where a gas ring burned beneath a large wok.

Sandy explained they'd been to a cooking school and the women laughed, saying they'd show them how to make fried noodles and spring rolls for free.

Trung, now wearing old shorts and a T-shirt, asked the two friends if they would like to go down the river with him to check his father's crab pot and fishing net.

'I would,' said Sandy.

'I'll stay here and watch the way they make these dishes,' said Anna. 'I'll manage with sign language.'

'You're really into this cooking thing, aren't you? There could be fish for the main course if Trung has any in the trap.' Sandy had a sudden thought. 'Hey, you could do some of the cooking at Barney's!'

'I don't think so,' laughed Anna. 'But at least I'll have an idea of what people are ordering!'

Sandy followed Trung to the edge of the river, where his wooden long boat was drawn up to the bank. She sat in the middle and when comfortable gave a thumbs-up signal. Trung pushed off and from near the stern began poling them down the river. They glided past several rice paddies, a few thatched houses and then some more solid homes that faced the river with their small landings on the river bank. There was a bicycle path alongside the river and an occasional food stall. Around a bend in the river a small fish pond was staked out. Overlooking it were sizeable homes with tiled roofs, balconies and high fences. These houses had ornate trimmings and smart gardens complete with altars next to the river-bank landings. Obviously it was a new and expensive neighbourhood.

'Who lives in these houses?' asked Sandy.

'Rich people. Merchants, business people,' answered Trung. 'Some high-up government people.'

'Local people? Tourism has done a lot for Hoi An. Money there, eh, Trung?'

A partly finished block of apartments came into view from behind a screen of palms. 'Another resort, or for local people?' asked Sandy.

'Holiday place for rich Vietnamese people. Some come from city. Madame Nguyen is building.'

'Madame Nguyen the silk shop owner? She's building it?'

Trung nodded. 'She Hoi An rich lady. She do much business.'

'Obviously. What sort of business?' Sandy turned around to look at Trung, who gave a quick smile.

'Any business. She clever lady for make money.' He shipped the pole and reached for a rope floating in the water near bamboo poles jutting from the river.

Sandy helped him pull up the trap, which had several fish in it. Then Trung hauled in an old net secured to another pole and was delighted with the catch of small silvery fish. Sandy couldn't help thinking that at home they would have been used for bait or thrown back but she knew these would be cut into tiny fillets and the head and bones used for stock and soup.

As they headed back fluorescent lights shone from the new homes but when they reached the little settlement where Trung lived only a few dim light bulbs glowed. Hanging in the trees and from poles outside the huts were coloured silk lanterns swaying gently, casting slow dancing shadows in a rainbow of colours.

'How pretty,' exclaimed Sandy.

'My mother and aunty they work with two other families to make. Since tourists come handicrafts help them make money.'

Anna looked animated as one of the women chatted to her in very broken English. 'Are we eating fish for dinner then?' she called to Sandy.

'Trung has a few. What do you mean, "we", Tonto?'

'We're invited to stay and eat with them. They're so hospitable. I love learning how to cook all this stuff.'

'I prefer eating it,' said Sandy.

'It's not just the cooking. These women are very funny. I've had lots of advice.'

'Love advice?' quizzed Sandy.

'Kind of. I might be missing a few finer points without you to translate, but they say they could find a husband for me. A good fisherman.'

Sandy laughed.

Trung cleaned the fish at the river's edge as his father sat beside him smoking and watching him work, chatting quietly. Sandy watched them for a moment, thinking how fishing skills had been passed down by river men, father to son, for generations. She wished she and her brother, Ashley, were close to their father. She'd never had any father–daughter experiences like camping or sport, or trips away together, just the two of them. Her father had never sat proudly in the front row of the audience for a school play or concert, but had reluctantly been dragged along on a few occasions, when he had stood at the back. When she'd taken her bow and looked up he had always already gone.

Anna followed one of the women inside to help with the food. Immediately the other women peppered Sandy with questions about Anna's family. Where were they from? Was she going to see them? Would she take her relatives to Australia? Did she send money back to her family?

Sandy answered as best she could, knowing the Vietnamese strong sense of family. She wondered if these thoughts had occurred to Anna.

It was becoming quite dark when the men joined them, smiling shyly, curious but welcoming, recognising at once that Sandy's language skills and Anna's being a Viet Kieu made them more than the usual run of tourists. When they learned Sandy had been working with HOPE, the discussion turned to the changes in their villages and farms and the growth of Hoi An. While they welcomed the prosperity tourism brought, they lamented the loss of the small farms which had been bought for

149

accommodation, shops, businesses and the infrastructure that went along with meeting the needs of visitors. An older man puffed on his cigarette and expressed some annoyance with young people for wanting to be 'modern' by aping western fashions and fads.

'He says young people are losing their traditional customs, music and manners. They want money to buy things they see on TV or that tourists have instead of appreciating what they grow and make themselves,' explained Sandy. She added, 'When I first came here I went to a village and asked about helping the poorest families and the head man said they didn't have any. They grew their own food, worked together, made their own clothes, entertained themselves with stories and music. A couple of years later when I went back, he told me they were all so poor. They wanted big TV sets, western food and clothes, and jobs where tourists were. Without these things they now considered themselves poor.'

'Did you tell them the luxuries we have at home don't make up for the rich things they have here – like close-knit families, the sharing, the communal way of life, a strong work ethic, respect and devotion to ancestors?' said Anna quietly.

Sandy glanced at her friend in surprise but translated the comment and there was a lot of head nodding in agreement.

Trung brought the fillets of fish to his mother, who called everybody to the large woven straw mat to eat next to a pot bubbling over a charcoal brazier. The fish pieces were dropped into the stock pot along with fresh greens and then spread over rice in bowls, the first helpings handed to Sandy and Anna. Plates of crispy duck and chargrilled eggplant topped with a spicy sauce tasted as good to Anna as anything she'd had in the local restaurants.

'What was down the river?' Anna asked Sandy as they ate.

'It's pretty and quiet. Rice paddies, some small fish farms and an amazing housing development. The biggest is owned by our Madame Nguyen.'

'Really? The silk business must be profitable.'

At the mention of the shop owner's name, one of the women spoke up. 'Her family have lived in Hoi An many generations. She buys things to sell in Hoi An and Hue.'

'Like what?' asked Sandy.

Trung spoke sharply to his mother. 'She has many businesses,' he said, then lowered his voice and added, 'People bring her old pieces, special things that she sells to dealers.'

'And where do these people find them?' asked Sandy, suddenly curious.

Trung shrugged. 'I hear stories. Boats go to her house at night. Madame Nguyen has shop in Royal Hotel and she talk about gallery in Hue.'

'I think I'll pay another visit to that antiques shop in The Royal before we leave for Hue,' said Sandy, then turned to Trung. 'Could we visit Madame Nguyen's house? There are some very old homes open to the public in Hoi An. It would be interesting for Anna.'

'Yes, but not Madame Nguyen's,' said Trung.

'And what about the little museums here? I've been told they're very good,' said Anna.

Trung nodded. 'Museum of Trading Ceramics in famous old house. Easy to visit. Hoi An very famous as trading port years ago. When Thu Bon river silt up Danang become number one port.'

They talked and drank coffee until it was bedtime for the children, when they thanked the family for their hospitality and Trung escorted the young women back to the hotel.

'It big honour for my family you visit our house,' said Trung as they shook hands.

'And for us too, Trung,' answered Sandy.

Back in their room, Anna stood on the balcony and looked down into the quiet cluster of thatched houses that was the small, close-knit community. A dog barked; there was a squawk from a chicken; a child cried briefly; and the soft sound of a mother singing to children drifted up in the still night air.

'That was a different evening,' commented Sandy as she prepared for bed.

'Yes. Very special. They're nice people. You know, at one point I thought it was like being in a caravan park back home. Before Uncle Quoc died he and Dad and other friends sometimes took me to a lakeside park in the summer holidays and it was like living in a small community,' said Anna.

'There are a lot of villages, bigger of course, like that all over this country. Maybe we should go to the hill country and see the minority tribes. It seems people rather than museums are your cup of tea,' said Sandy.

Anna headed for the bathroom as Sandy got into bed. 'No, we'll go to the museum. I know you're interested in old plates and antiques. Shall we go back to the shop at The Royal?'

But the next morning when the girls dropped in to the antiques shop, the old ceramic platter had gone.

'Sold to a rich American,' Sandy told Anna. She raised an eyebrow. 'Madame Nguyen must have influence. It's not easy to get permission to take antiques out of the country.'

'You're not going to buy one; why so interested?' asked Anna.

'I don't know. Mr Thinh so treasures the one he has. It seems odd to find these old ceramics popping up for sale when they're museum-quality pieces.'

'And don't forget there was one in the pagoda with the little nun in Halong Bay,' Anna reminded her.

'Now that I can understand. It's probably been there for a hundred years, an heirloom given by a family perhaps. Well, let's hit the beach before the rain comes.' Sandy pointed at the gathering clouds. 'Might be a wet drive over the mountain to Hue.'

Sandy had rented a car to drive the few hours over the Hai Van Pass to Hue. They started in steamy humidity as they drove back towards Danang. Clouds gathered over the tips of the Marble Mountains, making them appear dark and sinister.

'Those peaks are said to represent the five elements of the universe – water, wood, fire, metal, earth,' said Sandy. 'The largest one has some of the finest Buddhist cave sanctuaries I've ever seen.'

Anna once again sighed in wonder at the contradictions of the vista that filled the windscreen. The dark and rugged mountains produced the material for magnificent gleaming marble artifacts and as they drove past they saw rows of marble shops stacked with statuary and headstones.

From Danang they drove up Highway One towards Hai Van Pass. Anna gazed down at the stunning scenery to where a beautiful beach glittered in the curve of the green peninsula. Lushly forested ravines rushed down the mountainside towards the South China Sea. Then suddenly the coast was out of sight and a faint mist began to swirl down from the peaks.

They continued in silence as Sandy concentrated on the narrow road. At the top of the pass they stopped to relax with a coffee from a tourist cafe but the car was instantly surrounded by women and children offering souvenirs.

'Postcards and pearls,' said Sandy. 'Let's get a coffee.'

'Pearls up here? Are they any good?'

'They're farmed off Danang. Not in the same league as pearls from Broome. But you might find some with a decent lustre. They're cheap enough.'

While Anna bargained for a pair of simple pearl earrings, Sandy ordered coffee and talked to a tour guide driver who had just driven up the range from Hue. He told her that the weather was worsening and bad storms were predicted.

The strong coffee dripped from a filter into the small cups half filled with sweetened condensed milk. They drank quickly, anxious to get on the road before the weather got too bad.

'What's that on the rise over there?' asked Anna.

'An American command post from the war. It was a radar station. They could monitor three Indochinese countries from there,' said Sandy. 'C'mon, let's hit the road.'

'I want to take a photo but the cloud has wiped out the view.'

'Buy postcards,' said Sandy, waving goodbye to the cafe owner and tour guide.

Anna held up a plastic envelope of scenic views from Hai Van. 'They threw it in with the earrings,' she laughed.

Normally there were tour buses, private cars and guides ferrying tourists to the pass, but it was deserted as the rain began to pour in a constant stream. Sandy drove carefully, unsure about the condition of the car's brakes. They didn't speak for a while until Anna asked, 'When are we going to visit the orphanage? It's not far from Danang, is it?'

'It's just inland from the coast. We'll visit it after Hue because I want to take some of the girls to the coast before an informal celebration for the older girls. You know, acknowledgment of reaching puberty.'

'A rite of passage thing? You're really emotionally

attached to the orphanage, aren't you, even though you're not working for HOPE anymore,' said Anna, glancing at Sandy who was concentrating on the mountain road.

Sandy's face softened and she smiled. 'It's been wonderful to see the place grow and get a school going and have better facilities for the kids. It's rewarding when you see something positive happening. A lot of the time you never get to see projects finished.'

'I can understand that. Sands, you're obviously very attached to Vietnam. Is that why you don't want to go home?'

Sandy didn't answer immediately. She'd gone past the living with the folks at home stage. 'Of course I'm going home. To visit. Then I'll apply for another position somewhere else, I guess. It's hard just to walk out of this country and sever the ties overnight.'

Anna knew what was running through Sandy's mind. Her mother was sweet, but she was a woman dominated, sometimes crushed, by her husband's moods. Sandy and her father certainly also had their moments. Anna suspected Phil Donaldson disliked his daughter working here helping the Vietnamese people. Anna felt uncomfortable with him as well. While he had always accepted Anna as Sandy's friend and the daughter of his best mate, she knew he had never warmed to her. Occasionally she had caught him staring at her with a cold hard look that she didn't understand.

'You should be proud of what you've done here,' said Anna.

'Thanks. I've tried to be a good humanitarian. By and large the ordinary people are wonderful, hard working and quite ingenious, but it's hard when you see so much money is being wasted by inefficient bureaucrats, and knowing corruption exists and seeing the degradation of the countryside.'

'But the orphanage is a success. So you'll keep in touch with the woman running it even when you leave Vietnam?'

'Yes. I might try setting up some sort of support group at home to raise funds to send back.' Sandy stopped talking as a strong gust of wind hit the car. 'Hai Van separates the climate between north and south, so it's a bit unpredictable around here,' she said.

'Oh great,' said Anna nervously. 'Look, we're almost down. Let's hope the weather is better in Hue.'

They decided to splurge and checked into a refurbished French colonial hotel.

'Get the floor,' giggled Sandy as they stepped into the elevator to go upstairs. The green carpet decorated with a border of bamboo leaves had 'Good Afternoon' woven into the centre. Sandy glanced at her watch. 'One-fifteen. Do you suppose they'll change it tonight?'

'We'll find out.' Anna stepped out of the lift and began walking down the passageway, pausing to look at the old photographs of the original French owners and famous guests taken in the late nineteenth and early twentieth centuries.

'Look at the Lounge Bar. I feel I should be wearing a tea gown,' said Anna as she pushed open the heavy doors with etched glass panels.

'How 1930s!' exclaimed Sandy. 'It's immaculate. It must all be original furniture. A bit gloomy though. Don't think we'll be eating in here.'

'It looks like it's only for cocktails. Though the view of the bridge over the river is pretty spectacular.'

'Great, the rain's stopped. Let's get a cyclo across to the other side and find some place to eat. I was only here once before for a meeting and didn't have time to see much.'

*

Settled in a small restaurant with some maps and brochures they planned their itinerary for the next two days.

'Why don't we go to the area Jean-Claude told you about?' said Anna. 'Where his grandfather lived.'

'It's amazing any of the old colonial residences escaped the wars. His family must have been wealthy French officials. Having Mandarins to tea and negotiating exports and so on,' mused Sandy.

'Is he rich then?'

'I have no idea.'

'But you like him,' persisted Anna.

'I hardly know him. But yes, I think he's nice.'

'Other than the Canadian, have you had many romantic flings while you've been over here?' asked Anna. 'All the red-blooded idealistic volunteers flung together in an exotic country, helping to save the world, finding themselves in coups and hot spots.'

'You read too many novels,' said Sandy. 'It's hard enough finding a casual root with a western bloke let alone a committed root.'

They both burst out laughing.

'Limited fraternising with the locals?' asked Anna archly. 'No wild parties?'

'It's frowned on. And certainly no sex, drugs and rock and roll. This country is serious about drugs. Do drugs and you'll wind up on death row.'

'Carlo would never make it working in a place like this,' said Anna. 'Or me. Feeling – or knowing – you're being watched all the time.'

Sandy looked surprised. 'Carlo doesn't do drugs – does he? Jeez, Anna, be careful.'

'No! Of course not, I didn't mean it like that. He's such an entrepreneur, he'd feel restricted by the atmosphere, the government rules, the cultural subtleties, the odd way they do things.'

Sandy didn't press the point of Carlo's entrepreneurial methods and activities. In her view Carlo was more talk than action.

Anna also wanted to shift the conversation away from Carlo, knowing how Sandy felt about him. 'If you feel attracted to someone, such as Jean-Claude who's intelligent, nice and definitely good looking, why not go after him? Even for a fling.'

'What's the point of a fling, as you put it? A waste of time and emotional energy,' answered Sandy.

'Maybe you wouldn't feel so lonely, and it's good to feel loved and wanted, even briefly.'

'Look who's talking. Anna, you've clung to the same man just because he's there. You know I think you could do better. You should shop around more, have a few flings yourself!' countered Sandy.

Anna looked cross. 'I'm not like that. Okay, let's change the subject. Where are we going this afternoon?'

Sandy noted, not for the first time, that when the subject of Carlo came up, Anna changed it. 'I'd like to see the tomb of Emperor Tu Duc: it's supposed to be beautiful. And maybe we can squeeze in the Thien Mu Pagoda while the weather is holding up. The hotel has a tour guide with a car that's very reasonable.'

The driver suggested they go by boat to the pagoda and dropped them at a landing where dozens of brightly painted wooden dragon boats offered sightseeing trips. He said the river trip was really worthwhile, would take only fifteen minutes or so and he'd meet them at the pagoda.

The trip down the Perfume River was as pretty as promised. The scenery and the river traffic enchanted Anna and she snapped photos of bulky sampans laden with building supplies and of smaller boats filled with rural produce being paddled by women. She particularly liked a shot she got of a sampan with a man paddling at the stern, a woman cooking over a small fire on the bow and children and a dog peeping out from under the woven rush canopy.

The Thien Mu Pagoda was crowded with tourists as Sandy and Anna followed the guide up flights of steps, pausing to admire the seven storeys of fine traditional architecture and the high octagonal tower. The guide reeled off in reasonable English the pagoda's history, explaining that it had been destroyed and rebuilt several times.

They walked around the grounds but the young boys training as monks, their hair cropped and shaved, took little notice of the visitors as they chanted their lessons. While it was an impressive and fascinating place, Anna suddenly remembered the near-blind nun back at the Temple of Nowhere hidden on the tiny island in Halong Bay. I wonder how she's going, mused Anna, contrasting the size and atmosphere of the two pagodas.

When they came to a chamber where a reverential group stood before a battered little blue car Anna caught her breath.

'It's the car of that monk – the one who burned himself to death, isn't it?' she said softly. Anna was surprised at how moved she felt and noticed the same reaction from those around her, especially the Vietnamese who lifted their hands in prayer and bowed their heads. On a wall behind the car was a framed photograph of the dreadful incident that Tom had told her about in Hanoi.

'Let's go inside and light some incense,' suggested Sandy. Anna nodded and the girls stepped out of their shoes and went into the main temple to pray at the altar under a Buddha's benign gaze.

During her moments of silent reflection, Anna was conscious of an emotional stirring that defied immediate explanation, but it was accompanied by images of the old nun and the island temple far to the north.

In the late afternoon, as the sun beamed from behind the remaining clouds, they drove through several villages to arrive at the beautifully landscaped grounds of the tomb of the Nguyen monarch who had reigned long and in imperial luxury.

'Emperor Tu Duc chose this as his resting place, which he designed and enjoyed for fifteen years before his death in 1843,' said the guide as they entered the grove of pine trees interspersed with large frangipani trees, which were smothered in fragrant flowers.

'There's a palace for his concubines and wives, his own palace . . . and look at that gorgeous setting,' said Sandy as they came to Luu Khiem Lake. 'Look! The path is made of ceramic tiles like the ones at Bat Trung – where we visited Mr Thinh.'

The pretty lake was covered in lotus flowers and an airy pavilion was built over the water facing a romantic island in the centre where wild game was hunted. They wandered among the other royal tombs and temples, marvelling at the elaborate complex.

'Nice to know where you'll spend eternity,' said Sandy.

The guide nodded emphatically, then gave a conspiratorial wink. 'The biggest surprise is his mausoleum. This way, please.'

They walked between the honour guard of stone elephants, horses and diminutive mandarins and guards, all shorter than the very short emperor, and came to an open-sided pavilion sheltering a massive stone tablet.

'The emperor wrote the story of his life,' said their guide.

'One way to make sure only the good stuff goes down in history,' commented Anna.

They entered the emperor's walled sepulchre where a giant stone tomb was mounted on a plinth.

'This is the surprise. His remains are not in here,' said the guide, looking pleased.

'Where are they?' asked Anna.

He shrugged. 'No one knows. He is buried with a large fortune so they were afraid of grave robbers and kept it secret. The two hundred servants who buried him were beheaded. He had no children and so his dynasty ended.'

'You wouldn't want to have been a servant,' said Anna.

'Yes. Must have been hard on their families,' agreed Sandy.

On the way back to the hotel Sandy pulled Jean-Claude's business card from her bag, and showed the driver the address he'd written on the back.

The driver nodded. 'I can go there before the hotel. It is where there are many old French homes. They were not destroyed in the last war. But too much of Hue is gone from American bombing in the 1968 Tet Offensive.' He shook his head. 'The communists took the city for nearly four weeks and many, many people – merchants, monks, Catholic priests, academics – all were murdered. A very cruel time. Some of my family died. Then US and South Vietnamese bombed Hue, so much of the old citadel, the Forbidden City – all destroyed.' He shrugged. 'Now people come here and wish to see what was here before the wars.'

They pulled up outside a three-storeyed white house that, while in some disrepair, still had an elegant air of grandeur.

'That's a mansion,' said Anna. 'Stand outside and I'll take a picture.'

Sandy reluctantly posed, wishing Anna wasn't such a

shutterbug. But she couldn't help wondering if Jean-Claude had ever had his picture taken outside what was once his family home.

The guide glanced at the house as they got back in the car. 'French people built some beautiful places in Vietnam. Some French people very good people, but it is not good to have foreigners run your country.'

As they returned to the hotel, Anna sighed, 'Been a full-on day. I'm on information overload. Thanks, Sandy, it's been great.'

'For me too. It's such an interesting country. So many contrasts.' She laughed as they stepped into the elevator and pointed to the floor where the carpet now read 'Good Evening'.

The next day they spent at Thuan An Beach, some fifteen kilometres from Hue, exploring the near-deserted island at the mouth of the Perfume River. It was too rough from the previous day's storm to swim so they found a small kiosk, bought some food and went beachcombing.

On the way back to Hue they stopped in a small village for Anna to take a picture of the massive brown ceramic jars stacked against walls of houses.

'Nuoc mam, the local fish sauce, is marinating in them,' explained Sandy. 'Vietnamese tomato sauce. They put it on everything. Some villages are famous for the soy bean sauce they ferment in similar jars.'

But what fascinated Anna most were the elaborate mausoleums, graves and family crypts strung along the ocean side of the road. 'It's like the city of the dead!'

'It's keeping up with the Joneses, Viet style. They all try to outdo each other. A lot of boat people left from here and send money back to maintain and build them,' said Sandy. 'I've heard some wild stories from villagers.'

'Like what?' Anna settled back in the car as Sandy relayed another of the titbits of information she'd gathered during her time in Vietnam.

'Most families bury their dead relations in coffins, at the edge of rice paddies. Then after three years the bones are taken out, cleaned and put in ceramic jars and placed, if they can afford it, in a shrine or mausoleum.' Sandy smiled. 'One villager told me how they went to dig up the coffin and heard banging inside as it swilled around in the water, so he got a gun and pumped bullets into it.'

'What was inside? Sounds gruesome.'

'For starters, ten fat dead catfish that had swum into the coffin.'

'The fish were banging around?'

'Yeah, along with several frogs that had dived into the eye sockets with their legs sticking out. They had got so fat on the fishes' remains that they couldn't get out, so they swam around dragging the skulls with them.'

'That sounds gross and not very reverential.'

'There are many different customs. The Buddhists prefer cremation. But this village man told me their custom was that the reburial had to be done in the early hours of the morning before sunrise, when the spirits aren't around. Can you imagine creeping round the rice paddy in the dark, digging up and burying bones?'

'No, thanks. Seems a lot of time is spent keeping spirits happy here.'

'It's true. You don't want them feeling slighted and coming around bothering you.'

They left Hue and drove back over the pass through the Truong Son mountains towards Danang, heading along the coast road in a blustery wind.

'This area must have the worst weather in Vietnam,' commented Anna.

'We're turning inland soon. The orphanage is close enough to the coast to take the girls to the beach today.'

'What goes on at the ceremony tomorrow?'

'It's a way of making the girls feel they are growing up. Dancing, music, games, fun stuff. Each girl gives up something from her childhood – a small toy if she has one, a ribbon, a lock of hair – and she is given a symbolic gift of womanhood: red fruit, rice dyed pink for fertility and paper shoes as a means of walking into the next stage of her life.'

'Nice. Do boys have a similar thing?'

'More or less. I've never been to one; it's men only. Kim went once. I could ask him. Even those of us not involved in the orphanage project take an interest,' said Sandy, and again Anna wondered when Sandy was going to put her work with HOPE behind her and move on with her life. The stint of running Barney's Bar when they got back to Hanoi would be good for her.

The orphanage was on the outskirts of a village surrounded by palm trees next to a narrow river. A water buffalo was dragging a plough through a rice paddy and behind the long low buildings were neat garden beds and animal pens.

As Sandy drove up, several young children raced outside excitedly waving. A young Vietnamese woman, about the same age as Sandy and Anna, followed them out, holding a smaller child on her hip.

Sandy greeted the woman and introduced Anna while a little girl tugged at her, chattering as fast as a monkey.

Anna patted her head and turned to Sandy. 'What's she saying?'

Sandy gently shooed her and the other girls back inside where curious faces were gathered at the open window of a school room. 'She's asking if you have come for them, are you her mother.'

'Oh. Do people adopt kids from here? Foreigners, I mean?'

'No. This is not one of the government-approved adoption orphanages. HOPE set this up for kids in the surrounding area who have been abandoned, or whose families can't feed or care for them but who come and visit. Some kids are just too damaged and are a liability to poor families who need them to work. If they have a disabled baby they try again for a healthy one. And so it goes on,' sighed Sandy.

Anna and Sandy were shown to a small room with two narrow beds, a mosquito net and windows with open shutters.

'This is the VIP quarters. We share the girls' communal bathhouse. It's basic but clean. Dump your stuff and I'll take you on a tour.'

Anna was subdued as Sandy took her around the various buildings – two school rooms, two dormitories furnished with simple frame beds and cots, a kitchen and dining area and three rooms for staff on night duty. The staff were from the local villages and knew most of the children's families.

'It's very much a local co-operative, isn't it?' said Anna. 'But there are no frills. No play equipment, no proper desks.'

'Compared to what they had before, which was nothing but a lean-to shelter with a local woman trying her best to feed the homeless ones, this is five star.'

'I see why you want to keep involved with them. It'd be good to fundraise to get them extra things. It's so hard seeing some of the children with the birth defects . . . '

Anna found it hard to speak. The sight of the handicapped children shocked and upset her. 'Why isn't more being done? Compensation, help, money . . .' she began.

'There are a lot of good people helping with various charities and aid programs for children and other victims.' Sandy tried to sound upbeat. 'These kids are amazing. It's lovely to see them mingle as one family, all accepting each other. Now, there are the four girls who are taking part in the ceremony tomorrow. Come and meet them before we go to the beach.'

Despite the ominous clouds and murky sky they set off for the coast in high spirits. Three girls were in the back, while Phuong, a slim girl, squeezed in the front next to Anna as Sandy drove. They sang, teaching Anna 'The Song of the Blackbird' in what Sandy called the tinh tang style of the Hue dialect. One of the girls in the back seat pulled out her bamboo flute to accompany them.

They pulled in to a village, just a few scattered houses that over-looked a sweep of beach. It was off the beaten track and few visited the area. Sandy explained they would eat at a small kiosk on the beach.

The beach was windswept and deserted. White choppy waves clawed at the shore. In two teams the girls raced the kites they had brought with them against each other, higher and higher, dipping and diving, the bamboo flute attached to one of the kites singing like a bird, the other like a musical deep-throated frog.

Anna had her camera out and took some dramatic photos of the tiny kites high above the churning sea against the thickening clouds.

'I don't like the look of that sky. I think we'll have an early lunch and head back,' said Sandy.

The girls giggled as they ate their lunch at the little

seaside kiosk. The owner soon closed his shop as rain began to spatter and the nearby village became ominously empty. Before Sandy and Anna had shepherded the girls to the car, it was streaming tropical rain and the day had disappeared behind black clouds.

Sandy started the car and turned away from the beach along the small road that ran beside the dykes rimming the rice paddies.

'Do they ever overflow?' asked Anna, looking at the solid curtain of rain that almost obscured the fields of rice where the water channels were rushing with brown water and palm trees fringing the paddies were being lashed by the wind.

'Sometimes. I think we're far enough now from the ocean not to worry about huge waves.'

'This wind is a bit much,' said Anna nervously as she felt the car blown sideways. 'I can't see a thing. Where's the road? If you can call it that.'

There was a crunch and the car swerved and came to a thudding halt. The girls squealed and Anna gripped the dashboard, trying to see out the windscreen through the streaming water.

'Have we hit a tree? I can only see leaves and stuff.'

'Not sure, I'll look.' Sandy pushed open the door and for a moment Anna thought it would be whipped off by the howling wind. Sandy fell back into the driver's seat, wrenching the door shut. 'Damn! There's a tree down across the road.'

'Track, you mean. I haven't seen another car since we left the orphanage.'

'It is pretty rural,' admitted Sandy, pondering what their next move should be.

'Rural!' snorted Anna, peering at the shapes of the palm trees that were flailing wildly. 'It looks like we're surrounded by swimming pools.'

The four girls looked scared and the one in the front touched Sandy's arm and whispered to her.

'What's Phuong saying?' asked Anna.

'In a word: typhoon. They're common around the Danang coast during the monsoon.'

'You're joking! So what do we do? I don't want to sit in this car and be speared by a tree, thanks.'

'I'll back up, find a place to turn around,' said Sandy.

'Not towards the beach – that's where the wind is coming from. What about tsunamis? We could get caught in a tidal wave,' said Anna, remembering horror stories she'd seen on TV of events similar to this.

'That's earthquakes, not typhoons.'

'Is there a village close by where we could shelter?'

'Not that I know of.' Sandy started reversing, and the girls cried out as the wheels bumped over a ditch. 'Can't see a damn thing. You'll have to guide me, Anna.'

'How? If I get out you won't be able to see me and I'll be blown away in this.'

'Take the cords off the kites, quickly. Tie one end around your waist and see if you can lash one end to the bumper bar. They're very strong bamboo straps.'

Anna didn't argue: Sandy seemed to know what she was doing and had taken control. Anna stepped out of the car, losing her balance as the wind whipped at her. Grabbing the door, she righted herself and groped her way to the back of the car and was instantly soaked to her skin. Wiping the running water from her face and eyes she fumbled to tie the end around the bumper bar so she was tethered to the car. She banged on the rear end and began walking beside the car as Sandy inched backwards, guided by Anna's blows.

After a short while she gave three sharp bangs, worked her way to Sandy's window and shouted above the wind. 'There's a clearing. You can do a tight turn.' Anna waved her hand, indicating the direction.

After they turned Sandy hauled Anna back into the car and inched forward, the headlights probing the solid curtain of rain. It was a long slow journey to travel a relatively short distance. Anna had never seen weather like it. The water was starting to gush across the road and the wind was wild. They passed an upturned cart, but seeing no one they continued on as Sandy retraced their way though the countryside till they came to a packed earthen mound running along a paddy field.

'That's it, I remember now.' Sandy stopped the car and got out and peered over the top of the mound.

'Be careful!'

Sandy beckoned. 'Come on. Anna, bring the girls one at a time.'

'Where're we going, for God's sake?' Anna grabbed Phuong's arm and helped her from the car.

'Look, there's a big mausoleum on a rise in the middle of the field. We can shelter in there.'

'What!'

'Just go. I'll bring the other girls.' She spoke quickly to Phuong, who nodded. 'Phuong understands. There should be a sort of crypt thing you can get inside.'

As Anna, still clutching Phuong, headed across the marshy rice paddy, Sandy returned to the car and quickly explained to the three other girls what was happening. In a flash they were out of the car, holding hands tightly, with the smallest holding on to Sandy.

In the driving rain Anna felt her way around the stone mausoleum, which had a small carved obelisk on top. A tiny passage on one side had a narrow flight of steps leading below. Gripping the wall, Anna started down the steps, ducking to avoid banging her head.

'Oh no! It's pitch dark. How are we going to see in here?'

They inched forward, feeling for the steps with their feet, reluctant to move into the musty dankness. As Anna tried to let her eyes adjust to the darkness, she saw an alcove in the stone wall. In it were sticks of incense and a box of matches. The flare from the light flickered around the urns and small statues dedicated to family ancestors. Anna shuddered but Phuong moved forward, curious and not afraid.

'Are you okay?'

Anna jumped as Sandy and the three girls clattered and slipped down the dark stairs. 'Just a minute, I have matches.' She lit another. 'These aren't going to last long.'

Sandy saw Anna's hand instinctively go to her throat and touch the little gold crucifix she'd always worn. Sandy knew it comforted her.

'Is there an altar in there?' Sandy groped her way forward.

Anna held the match aloft. 'There. What's that? A shrine?'

'Quick, let's see.' Sandy moved forward, waiting for the next match.

In the short burst of light they saw some candles on the small altar and quickly lit them and gazed around.

'Ooh, this is spooky,' said Anna.

Two of the girls were looking at the final resting places of half a dozen people. Sandy picked up a candle and explored the small crypt.

'Well, it's damp but no rain. Nothing can fall on us in here.'

Anna didn't answer, hoping that floodwaters wouldn't rush in, praying that something wouldn't fall and block the stairs and their only exit.

'Make yourselves comfortable.' Sandy sat down and leaned against the cool stone wall.

They huddled together as the wind howled and screamed, whipping the rain into spinning spirals of water that lashed the outside of the ornate stone edifice.

'Not like the rain in Sydney, is it?' said Sandy. 'I hope this passes quickly. Sometimes typhoons race across the coast rather than hang about.'

'This rain doesn't sound like it's going anywhere,' said Anna. 'How long is this likely to go on for?'

'Not sure. At least it's not cold, and we had lunch,' said Sandy, trying to be cheerful. She spoke to the girls and two of them raised wan smiles. The other two continued to look terrified. Sandy's worry was that they could get cut off and might not be reached for days. That's if anyone knew where they were. She had a sudden thought. 'I'm going to see if I can get some mobile reception.' She quickly tapped out a text message and hurried up the steps. Turning her back to the rain she pushed the Send button and was relieved to see it had worked.

She couldn't see much and realised that the wind had increased dramatically. She hoped the children and staff at the orphanage were safe and that the buildings weren't damaged. While the mausoleum was strong and offered shelter, it was uncomfortable and they had no food and water, though it struck her there could be some food offerings left on the altar shrine. The thought of staying the night was not appealing, but she knew that driving would be impossible until the wind and rain abated. She just hoped the car was not wrecked.

All they could do was wait and keep the girls' spirits up. At least growing up in central Vietnam the children were accustomed to the vagaries of the monsoon seasons.

Sandy peered through the rain at the waterlogged landscape: the trees bent double; an earthen dyke built to protect the rice paddies now breached so water flowed across fields and tracks and swirled around trees, wiping away the flimsy structures of roadside stalls.

Now soaked, she made her way slowly back down to where the four girls and Anna were huddled on the hard floor beneath the carved walls where Buddha's attendants danced in a centuries-old circle, their movements frozen in the mottled stone.

7

EVEN FROM THE PLANE Tom could tell the city was a vastly different place from that which he remembered from the war years. It didn't matter whether it was called Ho Chi Minh City, its official name, or Saigon, the name everyone used: the place had certainly changed. High-rise hotels, neon signs, roads twinkling with lights and cars: it looked like most international tourist cities. The swift taxi ride from the airport to the city confirmed this: the shops and restaurants, the people and the cars meant he could have been in Hong Kong, Bangkok or Shanghai.

For old times' sake he checked into the Caravelle Hotel, now modernised, but the first place he wanted to go for a drink before dinner was at the refurbished Continental Hotel.

He hadn't walked more than a few metres when he felt the need to stop and reflect. He looked around. Yes, it all came back. This was about the spot where he had so often paused to give a few coins to a girl, probably no more than five years old, who was there nearly every day selling little cardboard baskets of flowers. Like most of her foreign customers, he never took the flowers. Back then there were so many children on the streets, boys selling cigarettes or touting an introduction to their sister in sing-song English. 'You like my sister, sir. Very nice Chinese. Very cheap, sir.'

To his delight, the ground floor of the hotel was still pretty much as he knew it. No major structural changes had been made, although it now had modern interior décor and the outside had been given a facelift. But the mood of the hotel brought a fresh surge of memories. He had a sudden flashback to 1965 when he and some other correspondents had had dinner in a private room at the hotel with Air Vice Marshal Nguyen Cao Ky, who became vice-president after yet another coup d'etat.

He remembered the handsome mustachioed man in the black flying suit and purple scarf. He had been a friendly, shrewd and gregarious man who nonetheless set up public execution stakes in the Central Market as the first step in a campaign to stop racketeers profiteering from the war, and had spent the entire meal justifying his actions. Yes, it had been quite a dinner that evening. One of many extraordinary experiences he'd had in this city.

Over the next few days Tom wallowed in the past as he strolled the streets, all the time conscious of being in a modern tourist city bursting with energy and commerce. Half the time he wondered if he was on Boulevard St Germain in Paris, Rodeo Drive in LA or Fifth Avenue,

New York. He soon wanted to get out of the city and go back to the very different places that had made a really big impact on his life and career . . . Vung Tau and Nui Dat.

He walked to Saigon harbour, glancing up at the old Majestic Hotel where he had spent many a happy hour on the rooftop terrace with other correspondents, and bought a ticket on the hydrofoil leaving for Vung Tau in Phuoc Tuy province. Tom hadn't felt so rejuvenated in years.

While not all the memories of his time in Vietnam were happy ones, it was a time that had shaped him as a journalist and as a man. War changed people. But there had been some great times. Good friends, heroic efforts, stories that touched the hearts and minds of Australians back home as well as fuelling the anti-war protestors. War brought out the best and worst in men. Men who'd never challenged authority, or accepted a dare from a mate, or who'd never shown courage in sport or at work suddenly dug deep and found themselves capable of great acts of bravery. There were insanely mad and funny times and inspirational people who would never be forgotten. How different from the control, the technology, the spin doctors and the organisation behind the media at war these days.

In Tom's day it had fallen to the honest men and women of the fourth estate to tell it as it was. There were those who got close to the action and saw it for them-selves and there were those who reported stories from the safety of their favourite bar. But there was a hint of pride in his reflections. He had not been influenced by editors or the military. He'd tried to find out the truth himself and send back balanced and insightful reports.

It occurred to him that his kids had no idea what he'd done, or been through, from the battlefields to the free-wheeling letting down of hair in bars, hotels and barracks. He grinned. His kids would be quite shocked if they knew some of the stories.

When it had become clear to Tom, after talking with other correspondents, that the Australian effort at Bien Hoa was a sideshow to the deteriorating scene further up the country, he had moved north and saw for himself the massive build-up of American forces taking place through the port of Danang. He flew on helicopters and bombers spraying jungle battlefields in the highlands with chemicals and went on raids aboard Puff the Magic Dragon planes, old C-47 transports fitted out with banks of machine guns, which poured millions of bullets into dense jungle suspected of sheltering the enemy. Then came Agent Orange which denuded the landscape like an atomic bomb had gone off. He recalled the blackened earth, no foliage, the bare countryside a scene of utter devastation.

He had even been in Pleiku when a battalion of the American First Air Cavalry choppered into a valley near the Cambodian border and landed right on top of a North Vietnamese jungle base. The three-day battle that followed was the bloodiest of the Vietnam War to that time. It changed the course of the entire war for both sides. Almost three hundred American soldiers were killed and hundreds wounded. The Americans claimed to have killed and wounded about two thousand enemy soldiers.

Tom had managed to get onto the battlefield briefly. He had talked his way onto a helicopter evacuating American wounded. He flew in through a hail of bullets and clouds of smoke, took in the terrifying scene on the cluttered landing zone, helped load some wounded and came out a shaking wreck, so different from the gung-ho reporter who went in so boldly looking for a headline story.

Later, when opposition to the war began to increase,

176

positive stories got buried. Trying to filter the truth from the official reports was frustrating and it sometimes meant good journalists got moved away from the action or found their avenues to get a story suddenly not available. In contrast there were always the bar Johnnies who rarely left their hotels and certainly took no risks in order to file stories that suited the political climate back at home.

As Tom strolled around Saigon he wondered what some of his old mates would think of the modern, glitzy city and the capitalistic and commercial enterprise happening in Vietnam now. It was a country united culturally, economically and politically and in its own way, it was moving forward.

Now he was freewheeling around the country again. He'd befriended two gorgeous young women and he was getting the old adrenalin buzz. He was back in harness, smelling a story. It felt good. He knew that Sandy and Anna, visiting Danang and Hue, would have very different impressions of those cities and he wondered what they were doing. There'd been a typhoon report in the area so he hoped they were safe. He'd be sure to contact their families as he'd promised the minute he got back to Australia.

There was little hint of the busy wartime harbour as the hydrofoil rose on its floats and churned out into the South China Sea for the hour and forty minute trip along the coast to the beach resort of Vung Tau. During the war it had been the port of entry to Phuoc Tuy Province where the First Australian Logistical Support Group was stationed. Tom recalled visits to the rest in country base at Back Beach. The rest centre, known as the Badcoe Club, had excellent facilities including a swimming pool and volleyball and badminton courts where Tom had enjoyed a game or two. The beach had no surf to compare with home, but for a hundred or so twenty-year-olds on R in C (Rest in Country), Vung Tau's numerous bars and bar girls were a big temptation. The soldiers had been given advice, warnings, condoms and pills to combat venereal disease, but some of the servicemen found that it was their wallets that suffered most.

The hydrofoil was cramped and stuffy as the air conditioning wasn't working, but Tom preferred the peace of the waterway to a crowded noisy drive down from Saigon.

As the hydrofoil slowed Tom was amazed at the hotels, houses and apartment blocks ringing the horseshoe bay beneath the headland where a large statue of Jesus stood, arms outstretched. On the hillside Tom recognised the elegant French colonial white house that had been a holiday home of a one-time French governor and later a local army general. Probably now owned by some wealthy local businessman, he supposed.

Ashore, the first place that caught Tom's eye was an Australian-themed restaurant festooned with coloured signs decorated with kangaroos, koalas and a picture of a bush hat strung with hanging corks to keep the flies at bay. It was called the Swagman Cafe. There were outdoor tables and a blackboard menu advertising burgers, chips and Aussie steaks. He wandered over to investigate and the smell of frying bacon made him realise he was hungry. He dropped his bag and sat at a table.

A pretty young Vietnamese waitress who spoke good English came to take his order.

'What's with the décor?' he asked.

'My father is an Aussie . . . mate,' she answered with a smile and a pretty good imitation of an Australian accent.

'Is that right? Is he around?' asked Tom.

A large man came through the doorway. 'That'd be me. How're ya going?'

'Good. The smell of bacon and fried onions dragged me in,' said Tom, holding out his hand. 'Tom Ahearn.'

'Pat Lang.' He shook Tom's hand. 'You a vet?'

Tom was slightly taken aback at such a direct inquiry. 'Er, no. War correspondent though.'

Pat nodded. 'Figured something like that. More and more people are making the pilgrimage. Beer? Coffee?'

'Cold beer wouldn't go astray,' said Tom. Pat waved to the waitress who hurried to the bar.

'What about you, Dad?' she called.

'I'll have a coffee, love.' He smiled at the girl.

'How long have you been here?' asked Tom.

'Came back to Vietnam fifteen years ago. I was divorced, at a loose end and pretty screwed up. Figured I'd come back to try and find the happy-go-lucky young bloke who first landed in Vietnam.' He paused. 'I wasn't the first to do so, of course.'

'You were based at Nui Dat?'

'Yeah, it was the Australian HQ base. Lot of men saw a lot of action down there. Vung Tau was for R in C.'

'I only had a brief visit there, just as the fireworks started that became Long Tan. I was covering the Col Joye concert and then all hell broke loose,' said Tom.

'Yeah. It certainly did. Too bad the full story never got told. It's taken forty years to get a decent acknowledgment of what we did,' Pat said with some bitterness.

Tom smiled his thanks to the waitress as she put his drink on the table. 'What's your name?'

'I'm called Patsy. After Dad.' She grinned at the red-faced burly man sitting opposite Tom.

Pat's face softened. 'Light of my life, she is. Next to her mother. Her mum was single and struggling to manage with a two-year-old son when I first came to Vung Tau. I kinda hung around and ended up taking 'em all on and started this place.'

179

Tom thought of Barney in Hanoi. 'It's not an unfamiliar story.'

'Back then there were many blokes who wanted to take their girls home. The brass made it as hard as hell, of course. Most liaisons were casual . . . but meant something at the time.' Pat took the tiny cup of short espresso from Patsy. 'As in every war, eh?'

Tom nodded. 'It's the children without fathers one feels for.'

'I might be guilty there. Who knows? A night screwing and boozing with a bar girl and you move on. Must've been hard for them left behind. I s'pose that's another reason I feel an obligation to help.'

'You have a family back in Australia?'

'Yeah. All grown, doing their own thing. The ex-missus has finally given up trying to get any more money from me and is living with some bloke she met at the bowling club.'

'Your children . . . have they visited?' asked Tom.

'Struth, no. They think I'm nuts. And frankly, I'd rather they didn't know that I'm doing quite nicely, thank you,' grinned Pat. 'I go back twice a year and check in; that's enough. This business has been a sweet little earner, passes the time.' He drained his coffee.

Tom glanced around. 'Who does the cooking?'

'I have two young blokes and another girl who do the cooking and wait on tables. My lady runs a travel agency. This was always a holiday spot for the Vietnamese and the French before the war. But once I encouraged a few blokes from my old platoon to come over here for a visit it started a trickle. So we arranged places for them to stay, then they'd come back next year with their wives and families and so we started organising itineraries and so on. Now the trickle is becoming a full flow so we have a growing business. Mostly all vets,' he added.

'Have any come back to stay, like you?' asked Tom.

He nodded. 'There's a group of us. It's a loose kinda organisation where we look after Vietnam vets who do come back and who encourage others to come back because, well, without putting too fine a point on it, it can help straighten 'em out a bit. Settle the ghosts.'

'How many are here? Do they have families?'

'About a dozen of them. They mostly have local women as partners, some like me have started second families. They go back home once or twice a year but most of us think of this as home now.'

'Sounds like you have quite a good life here,' said Tom.

'The pension goes a heck of a lot further. Cost of living is cheaper. And the country might have self-determination and be unified but a white face and a pocket full of dollars buys you a lot of clout and attention.' Pat took out a packet of cigarettes and lit one. 'So, why're you here? You going to write about the anniversary?'

Tom took a swallow of beer to collect his thoughts. 'I've been retired for a while. But when my old editor raised the notion, I thought I'd come back. Vietnam was my first war assignment and in retrospect I realise I got off lightly compared to the servicemen. A few months here and there, saw some action, got a sense of the place and moved on.' Tom paused, deciding against going any deeper into the memories. 'Knowing what we know now . . . how badly the Vietnamese servicemen were treated, the political change, and the long-term effects it's had . . . Hell, they're still paying.' He tried to find the words as he organised his thoughts. 'Fact is, I was here. Maybe I'm thinking the full story hasn't been really told, to the general public anyway. And maybe I owe the men of Long Tan that.'

'Ain't that the truth,' said Pat. 'Some blokes who were here have written stuff, trying to put the record straight, I s'pose. And there are a lot of versions of what really happened at Long Tan. Everyone has a need to deal with their time here in one way or another. Those who weren't here – friends, families, work mates – they can't understand what we went through.'

'I guess some coped with the war better than others,' said Tom.

'You talk to the mob at The Strangled Cow. They've got a story to tell. And they're also involved in planning the fortieth anniversary ceremony.'

'Strangled Cow? Where do I find these fellas?' asked Tom, keen to make contact.

'It's a bar at the St Jacques Resort. Two-star joint where the locals hang out. Lot of the oil-rig workers from Australia and the UK live there on their week off. It's an expat kinda place.'

'So oil drilling is still big business?'

'Bigger. The Russians are the biggest. But they all live in their compound in lockdown. Never socialise and they have a curfew, though occasionally some of the young lads break out and go a bit wild.'

'Is there still a lot of oil out there?' Tom inclined his head towards the South China Sea.

'I reckon. Though Vietnam's been in debt to Russia for its aid so they exported all their crude oil there as debt repayment and got nothing for it.'

'But foreign investment seems to be pouring into this country,' commented Tom.

'Of course. It might still be officially communist, and corruption is still tolerated, but there's cheap labour here and when the economies of Asia crashed, this place became very viable,' said Pat. 'Vietnam is going ahead more than people realise.'

Tom finished his beer and gave Patsy his order for the Outback Burger, chips, salad and another beer.

Pat rose and held out his hand. 'Gotta go. I'll give you Baz's and Cranky's phone numbers. They're the ones organising the whole shebang. Say, you got a place to stay?'

Tom shook his hand. 'Thanks, Pat. I booked in at The Grand. Want to experience where the generals stayed! I'll be back here for a feed though.'

'Good one. But remember: this is a small pond and there are a few people who see things differently from the rest of the mob. But overall we rub along okay.'

Tom nodded. 'I appreciate your advice.'

The Grand was as Tom remembered except for a circular garden in the driveway and smart tables and chairs on the terrace of the elegant white building built by the French. Across the road, beside a landscaped park, holidaymakers strolled. Tourist boats bobbed in the bay protected by the peninsula that stretched into the South China Sea. Oil rigs were silhouetted on the horizon but Tom noticed there were still some traditional fishermen mending their nets on the beach.

The lobby was bedecked with orchids and leather chairs, but after checking in Tom was amused to find the rooms were still quaintly old fashioned. The dining room had been updated and the bar was a far cry from the dim, red-lit room with girls pushing their 'You buy me Saigon tea', the overpriced drink of tea or lolly water that earned them money. And all had a practised sob story to soften a soldier's heart. The more tea they ordered, the more drinks they persuaded the servicemen to buy, the more money they made for the bar, but their own cut being small, most of the girls sold their favours as well.

Tom had spent only a short time in Vung Tau during the war, doing a heartwarming story on the recreation centre where the fighting men relaxed by swimming and playing volleyball on the beach or else were able to sit under a palm tree with a cold beer. The seedier side of Vung Tau's bars and clubs was not mentioned.

During the war he'd driven down Route Two from Nui Dat, past the villages smelling of fish drying in the sun. It was a bit over half an hour as he recalled, but the Australian base and the resort town had been planets apart.

After a walk around the promenade along the water-front, Tom pulled out the phone numbers Pat had given him and rang the two key men – Baz and Cranky – and made an arrangement to meet them at five at their local bar, The Strangled Cow.

He had a feeling that these men would open a wider window onto the story of the men who'd fought in that rubber plantation at Long Tan a short distance away.

The rain had finally eased. Anna appeared to be asleep, propped against the wall with a girl on either side, their heads in her lap. Sandy had an arm around Phuong who was curled beside her; Hong was asleep with her head in Sandy's lap. After the soughing wind, the quiet-ness was oppressive. The candle had burned low, almost spent.

Sandy shifted slightly to ease her aching back and suddenly caught her breath. There was a sound outside.

It came again – a soft thump. Then a metallic sound, a wheeze.

Someone was at the entrance. Sandy eased Hong's head off her lap and quietly edged up the stone steps of the crypt. At the top she saw the silhouette of a figure against the grey dawn. It was shapeless, with no form but the head of a man.

'Who's there?' she called.

The figure jerked and stumbled backwards in shock. 'Eee oww.'

Sandy stepped into the rain outside to see the cowering figure of an old man wrapped in a long plastic cape.

In Vietnamese she said quickly, 'Have no fear, old man. We are sheltering from the storm.'

The man stopped and peered at her and took a step forward. 'Who are you?'

'I am a visitor to the orphanage. We got caught at the beach. My friend and I have spent the night with several of the young girls. Where have you come from?'

The man nodded and came closer. He was drenched despite the shroud of plastic. Mud clung to his legs. 'I am looking for my water buffalo. The rain has been very strong. My home is full of water.'

'Where do you live? Is the road passable?'

He shook his head. 'Is that your motor car over there?' He inclined his head towards the road, which was indistinguishable from the waterlogged landscape. The defining parameters of paddies, road and pathways were all just part of the muddy sea.

'So we can't drive.'

'Not for a day at least,' he answered.

Anna called from the steps below them. 'Sandy, who's there?'

'It's okay. A farmer.'

'Were you coming in here to rest?' Sandy asked the man.

He nodded. 'I have spent the night rescuing my pig and chickens. My family are in the top floor. They are safe.'

Sandy had seen houses that had a small hatch and a loft area where bags of rice and supplies were stored. She could imagine the farmer's wife and children sheltering up

185

there as the waters ran through the ground floor of their house. 'It's dry in here. Are you going to stop till daylight?' she asked. The old man looked exhausted.

He nodded. 'This is a good place.' He followed Sandy downstairs.

'How do you know it?'

The girls were awake and stared as the old man shook off his wet cape. He gave a smile and greeted them. The girls giggled and returned his greeting.

'What did he say?' asked Anna.

'They have chosen a hard bed for the night.'

The old man went to the shrine, reached for the matches, lit several sticks of incense and prayed quietly. Then he sat down.

'I asked my ancestors to look after us.'

'Your family are in here?' asked Sandy.

The old man spoke in English for the first time. 'Yes. Long time. We very old family here.'

The group settled down again, making themselves as comfortable as they could.

'When it's daylight, can we walk home?' asked Phuong.

'It's a long way. We'll have to wait till the water has run off the road and we can drive the car. It won't be long,' Sandy comforted her.

'I'm hungry,' said Hong.

'Your car has been washed off the road,' said the old man in Vietnamese to Sandy. 'It will be hard to get going.'

'What did he say?' asked Anna.

'The car is stuffed. Something will get sorted,' said Sandy more cheerfully than she felt.

Anna closed her eyes. What a nightmare. Nevertheless, a calmness, a feeling of resignation, came over her. There was nothing she could do. She glanced at Sandy, who was smoothing Phuong's hair as she chatted to the old farmer. She was seeing her friend in a new light. Sandy had always been the capable and adventuresome one but their escapades had never been, well, life threatening. While she had no idea how they were going to get out of this creepy place, she had every confidence Sandy would find a way.

Sandy had been listening as the old man quietly told her the history of his family. As he paused, Sandy asked him to tell it in English so Anna could understand.

'My English not so good,' he said. 'American English.'

'You fought in the American war?' asked Sandy.

He nodded but did not elaborate, except to say, 'Big fighting south from here. Where you from?' He studied Anna.

'We come from Australia.'

He sucked his teeth and nodded his head. 'Good people. Australian soldiers good men. Not like Americans.'

'Why do you say that?' asked Anna.

'Australian soldier bury our dead. They stop and do this. Many Australian soldiers in Phuoc Tuy.'

'Is that where you were?' asked Sandy, trying to figure out if he fought for the South Vietnamese or if he was a VC supporting the North in their liberation campaign.

'I fight for my country. Vietnam now free. Good place. Why you come here?' He motioned to the dozing girls. 'You help these children?'

'Yes. I worked for an Australian organisation – HOPE – helping Vietnamese people. We raised some money to start the orphanage as many children are left alone and are very sick,' she said.

He looked at Anna. 'You Viet Kieu. Where your family, your ancestors?'

Anna shook her head. 'I don't know.' She didn't elaborate.

'Very bad. Not good you don't pay respects to ancestors. That one, there. He my ancestor.' He pointed to the carving of a dragon with the head of a phoenix.

'So tell me more about your family. You were saying they came from Hue? And had some connection with the emperor?' Sandy picked up the threads of his story.

'Which emperor?' asked Anna.

'Emperor Tu Duc. Very famous.'

'Yes. We went to his tomb. Really beautiful,' said Anna.

'So who was your ancestor?' asked Sandy.

'He was servant at the palace. He one of many, many. They buried the emperor and so must die.'

'The story goes they were all beheaded so as not to reveal where he is really buried,' said Sandy.

Anna beat her to the next question. 'So how do you know what happened to your ancestor if he was killed?'

'He had a wife and she must be worried when he go away to bury emperor. So she cut his hair and kept it.' He pointed to one of the markers in the wall. 'She got no bones to bury but his hair in special box there. Hair come back to his village so his family honour him.'

'Very sad story,' said Anna.

'No. Big honour for our family.'

'So possibly the emperor is buried somewhere between Hue and this province?' asked Sandy.

The farmer shrugged. 'Probably go to mountains. Many hiding places.'

'Too bad your ancestor can't tell you the location,' grinned Anna. 'You'd be a very rich man.'

The farmer smiled. 'Maybe. Is better the emperor have all his possessions for the next world.'

'Seems to me he had quite an excess in this life. Might do him good to go without so much in the next,' Anna said to Sandy.

'I think the karma of one's deeds counts for more,' said Sandy, then turned to the proud farmer. 'And your family? They are farmers too?'

'My son works on rice paddy. I have not enough land to give to number two son. He a fisherman. My girl is married; I have two grandson.' He smiled. 'When water go down, you come to my house. We can eat something.'

'That would be good,' said Anna.

The girls were trying not to complain at feeling stiff and hungry.

'Is it morning yet?'

'Maybe. I'll go and look and see if we have any phone messages,' said Sandy.

The landscape was still watery in the pale morning light. But as she gazed around she could see where the water had receded. The mound of mud that had been the barrier between the rice paddies and the road was discernible. If the old farmer had managed to wade across it, they could too. But where to? The car sounded a write-off as far as transport. She hoped the hire company was understanding and that her insurance would cover any damage.

Sandy turned on her mobile phone. The battery was nearly flat but there were two messages. One from Kim saying he'd received her message. The other was an SMS from Jean-Claude asking if they were enjoying themselves. She texted back. 'Not really. We've spent the night in a crypt in middle of a rice paddy. Waiting for flood-waters to recede. All OK tho' we can't drive. Will walk out soon I hope.'

She waited a moment in case Jean-Claude replied, and he did almost at once: 'Send directions to your location. I will try to help.'

She didn't know what he could do from Danang as the roads were impassable, but she tried to describe

189

where they were as best she could. She also sent Kim a message asking him to contact the orphanage and tell them they were all safe. She tapped out the message quickly as to talk at any length would have used the last of her mobile battery. At least the word was out there.

'We've made contact. Kim is on the case,' said Sandy cheerfully as she went back into the gloom of the crypt. Light was beginning to filter down the stairs.

'But he's in Hanoi,' said Anna.

'Jean-Claude also knows. I think he's in Danang. I don't know what he can do but it's a start. Anyway, at least people know we're safe.'

'I go look for my buffalo.' The farmer got up and rolled his rain cape. 'You come to my house.'

Sandy's inclination was not to impose but the girls got to their feet. 'We would be grateful if your house is not too damaged.'

'It will be mud. But my wife can cook something.'

'Anything hot would be wonderful,' said Anna.

They got up and filed out after the farmer who pointed across the soggy paddy. 'We go that way, near dyke. In middle is all water.'

'Lead on. At least it's stopped raining.' Sandy suddenly stopped and made the introductions and shook hands with the farmer, who introduced himself as Mr Nguyen.

'Would you be related to Madame Nguyen who owns a silk shop in Hoi An?' asked Anna.

'No. Nguyen very common name in my country. Name from emperor dynasty,' he added with some pride.

Holding hands with the girls who tucked their skirts and long pants up as high as they could, Sandy and Anna sloshed behind Farmer Nguyen as he set out across his land. There was a lot of damage but he assured them everything would recover quickly. The land was used to being flooded and water drained away quickly. They reached the road which was knee-deep in water, and the farmer in the lead stopped and pointed.

There was their car, washed off the road into a stand of bamboo but upright and undamaged. Standing next to it was the farmer's water buffalo.

'Want anything from the car?' asked Sandy. 'A swim-suit perhaps?'

'I'm not going near that beast,' said Anna firmly.

The farmer hurried to his animal and, talking calmly to it, nudged its head and the old buffalo trudged behind him, its weighty feet sinking into the soft ground as it waded through the water urged on by Farmer Nguyen. Once the buffalo felt the firmer surface of the road beneath its feet, it stepped along more quickly.

It was still early but other people began to appear on the road, wading through the water to see what damage had been done as well as seeking fresh supplies.

Farmer Nguyen turned off and pointed to where terraced fields had been neatly laid out. His house stood on the high side of the slope. It was a solid structure with a thatched roof but the yards around it were in a sea of water which had obviously flowed through the ground floor. As they got closer they could see his wife and daughter-in-law pushing large brooms to clear the mud from inside.

The family welcomed the girls warmly and after hearing how they'd spent the night, offered them hot tea and a bowl of noodle soup that was warming in a large pot on the stove.

Sandy thanked them profusely as they stood around tucking into the very welcome food. When they'd finished, the girls asked for brooms and rags and offered to help with the clean-up.

The chickens were handed down from the coop in the

roof and the pig was released. By mid morning the sun had come out and the countryside looked a lot more welcoming.

'It's still going to be days before we can use the road though,' said Anna. 'Where do we go from here? Ask if we can sleep in the vacated chicken coop?'

'I'm going to walk back down the road. I know there is a small town further inland and I should be able to get some help to pull out the car,' said Sandy.

'Do you want me to come with you? It's a bit of a hike.'

'No, you stay here with the girls and the Nguyens. It'll probably take me a couple of hours. I just wish I could buy some food for them from somewhere,' said Sandy.

'There might be hawkers on foot. People are very enterprising,' said Anna. 'Anyway, there's plenty of rice here.'

Sandy went back the way they'd come, noticing the water had gone down in the few hours they'd been at the Nguyen's farm. She reached the car and carefully unlocked the driver's door. She was worried about the angle of the car but it was firmly wedged against a wall of muddy soil. She looked at the swimsuits, kites and remnants of their day at the beach and wondered how hard it was going to be to get back to the orphanage, let alone get their flight back to Hanoi.

She trudged along the road feeling hot and uncomfortable in the steamy humidity as the temperature rose when there was a noise behind her. She turned, wondering what kind of vehicle or motor was running. A boat?

A motorbike was pushing through the water over the road, sending out a yellow bow wave. It was a big old bike with wide handle bars and fat heavy tyres and it rode high and easy, making steady progress. Sandy waved madly to attract the rider's attention. It was a hundred metres away when the driver saw her and sped towards her.

For safety she stepped off the road, sinking into the mud, which threw her off balance. As she staggered to her feet, gluey red dirt smeared up to her armpits, the motorbike slowed and stopped. The rider, a man in equally muddied jacket and goggles, stopped, propped the bike, and pulled off his helmet.

Jean-Claude beamed down at her. 'You're looking particularly elegant this morning.'

Sandy simply stared at him, the realisation taking a moment or two to sink in. 'How did you get here?'

'On my bike. Your directions were very good.' He held out his hand. 'May I help you out of there?'

Sandy suddenly realised how she must look. 'Yes, please. I must look a mess. I didn't know if you were going to stop and I didn't want to get hit by that wave of water.'

He reached over, grasped her hand and helped her back onto the road. They stood grinning at each other.

'If I wasn't so filthy I'd hug you,' Sandy said. 'How did you get here so quickly?'

'I was only a little way up the coast at a fisheries conference. Lucky, eh? How was your night in the mausoleum?'

'Actually, not that bad.' She took the towel he pulled from under his seat and tried as best she could to wipe off the mud. 'A farmer took us to his house this morning. I was walking back to see if I could find someone to pull our car out.'

'Hop on and I'll take you back to the farmer's place. How far from here is the orphanage?'

'Inland about an hour's drive. I hope they didn't get hit as badly as we did.'

He kicked over the motor, which had a strong, throaty roar. 'The typhoon skimmed the coast and headed back out to sea. It was a pretty narrow corridor of damage. You were lucky to find shelter.'

Sandy swung onto the broad seat behind him and grasped his jacket as the bike slewed slightly and took off. It was too noisy to speak, so she nudged him and pointed as the Nguyen's farm came into view. There were more people moving about, on oxen, by horses, pushing bicycles and trying to start a few stalled motor scooters. Life was getting back to normal, but there had been a lot of wind damage.

Anna was stunned to see Sandy walk in with Jean-Claude. 'If it wasn't for the mud on that black jacket I'd say you were our white knight coming to the rescue,' she joked.

It was decided that Jean-Claude would make two runs with three at a time on the bike back to the orphanage. The orphanage's phone line was out, but Kim had sent word via HOPE to the villagers nearby, who had passed on the news that the girls were all safe. The hire car company was contacted and arrangements made for the car to be retrieved and taken back to Danang for repairs. Jean-Claude had collected their possessions from the car and they gave the kites to the Nguyens for their grandchildren.

The smallest of the girls sat in front of Jean-Claude, another behind him, with Anna at the rear holding onto his jacket. They waved as the bike took off, ploughing along the waterlogged road.

Jean-Claude returned after lunch to collect Sandy, Phuong and Hong.

'How're things at the orphanage?' asked Sandy.

'Bit of the main roof is gone, windows broken, the classroom flooded. Nothing money and manpower can't fix.'

'Oh dear. Money is a problem.'

'I'm sure there'll be a way.' He smiled. 'Ready to hit the road?'

Sandy turned to the simple farm couple who'd been so generous and welcoming. She thanked them, but when she proffered money they shook their heads. Sandy knew the money would be welcome and useful. She turned to Jean-Claude. 'What good people they are.'

He shook Farmer Nguyen's hand and in fluent Vietnamese thanked him profusely.

'Farmer Nguyen's ancestors are very important. One worked for Emperor Tu Doc,' said Sandy, knowing how highly the old farmer regarded his ancestor's claim to fame.

Jean-Claude gave a slight bow towards the old man. 'Thank you for being so kind to my friends and the young girls. You have made your ancestors proud.'

As Jean-Claude negotiated the road back to the orphanage with Phuong balanced in front of him and Hon behind, Sandy held tightly to his leather jacket. She wished she could find a way to raise funds to help the orphanage as she knew how stretched HOPE's budget was. Once they headed inland, apart from a few broken trees, scattered palm fronds, rubbish, discarded plastic sheets and damage to flimsy stalls and shops, the impact of the typhoon was less obvious. People were busy repairing and cleaning up and picking up the threads of their lives.

In the village near the orphanage there wasn't the same water build-up so there was little flooding, but the wind had taken its toll. Nevertheless Sandy was still upset to see the damage.

As Jean-Claude pulled up everyone came running and the two girls were welcomed back as heroines returning from a big adventure.

'I'm sorry we didn't get back for the celebrations,' said Sandy to the staff.

The woman in charge smiled. 'The girls have coped very well with a difficult situation. I think they have showed great maturity, don't you?'

'I'll say. They weren't as scared as I was,' said Anna.

'That's because they understand respect for ancestors.'

'I know HOPE will try to get some help with repairs as soon as possible,' said Sandy.

'We will manage. The children have lived in far worse conditions.'

'I've got a working bee going,' said Anna. 'What are the plans – once you clean up?' she said, looking at Sandy's mud-caked clothes.

'Stay and help, I guess. What about you, Jean-Claude? How can we thank you?' began Sandy.

'It was lucky I was close by. I'm heading off to see some farms and investors before going back to Danang.'

'Investors?' Sandy's interest was aroused. 'Do you think they might be willing to make a donation to the orphanage? For repairs?'

Jean-Claude smiled. 'Come with me and ask them. I'll bring you back this afternoon.'

'I'll wash and change clothes. Is that all right with you, Anna?'

'I've plenty to do here. I can't get as excited about shrimp farms as you. Thanks again, Jean-Claude. By the way, whose bike is it?' asked Anna. She knew it was the sort of bike Carlo would adore.

Jean-Claude looked at Sandy. 'It's mine. A slight indulgence but it has proved useful in getting around in a country where the majority are on two wheels.'

Sandy laughed. She wouldn't have picked the suave Frenchman as a bike fan. 'Well, we're glad you have it. Can I buy you lunch as a thank you?'

'Au contraire. I will take you for being so brave. I'll wait for your transformation.'

'I hope it's not upmarket – best I can do will be a clean dress.' She was suddenly glad she'd thrown a sundress in her backpack.

Jean-Claude was familiar with the district, taking detours, weaving through villages until they came to an area outside Danang which was being developed with several multi-storeyed apartments, a huge shoe factory and a shopping complex. He parked outside a building with yet to be occupied shops on the ground floor and offices above. Sandy glanced around at the glass, chrome and mirror fittings trying to imagine the clutter of merchandise typical of Vietnamese shops in these cold and modern surroundings.

'I'll wait outside while you conduct your business,' said Sandy. But Jean-Claude propelled her forward.

'No, please, I'd like you to observe and give me feedback on these characters,' he said. 'They want me to encourage overseas companies to invest with them in a deal for a large shrimp farm and processing plant here. The shrimp will be frozen and exported.'

'That sounds an expensive investment.'

'It's been the product of choice for a high return. While small operators have gone bust, these guys see farming on a bigger scale will overcome the problems that family farms run into.'

'You mean they'll be able to pour expensive chemicals and antibiotics in to treat any disease?' said Sandy.

'Their plan is to make money,' said Jean-Claude. 'And they think I can help them make this project happen so they're being very nice to me. This is why I thought they might be inclined to make a donation to your orphanage.'

Sandy nodded. 'Let me be the judge.'

Jean-Claude gave her a quick nudge as they went into the reception area, which smelled of fresh paint. 'Money for a worthy cause does good, no matter where it comes from.'

By the time the meeting was over, Sandy was not inclined to want to be in debt to the men Jean-Claude had introduced her to. He had spoken of her work with HOPE and, while they had nodded their heads politely, Sandy could tell philanthropy was not on their agenda. They were among the new breed of Vietnamese businessmen out to make a killing no matter what they left in their wake.

As they walked outside, Jean-Claude said calmly, 'You're not impressed.'

'I don't know enough about their plans, but it was obvious to me that on several key points – environmental issues, displacement of family rice farms, the deal they're offering workers – they're inevitably slanted in the factory's favour. What's in it for you?' she asked.

'Personally? Nothing. It's just part of my job to be supportive of these enterprises and try to guide them towards doing things more equitably and sustainably. My family's business is seafood, but times have changed and some new businesses want quick money with no responsibility. My job is to try to strike a balance.'

'And if they don't, then no funds from your people?'

'Like I said, we try to find a balance between getting new industries started and making a profit, as well as being accountable.'

'Capitalism rules, okay?'

'We might have to think of somewhere else for your donation to the orphanage.' He changed the subject. 'Are you hungry?'

They rode along a quiet path between some trees and jungle that threatened to choke several small huts and a narrow strip of waterway that looked too boggy and wet to get close to. A simple wooden canoe skimmed past poled by a bare-chested man in shorts and conical hat. Soon they came to the river, where a dozen small colourful boats were moored at a landing bedecked with flags. Jean-Claude was immediately accosted by boat owners but he silenced them when he said in Vietnamese that he was looking for a friend.

A man standing on the narrow stern of a boat tied in close to the bank waved and called to Jean-Claude. Taking Sandy by the hand, he helped her into the boat where she sat on a small wooden seat in the bow.

'You can sit in the little cabin out of the sun,' said Jean-Claude.

'I can see more from here,' said Sandy.

As they pushed off from the bank Jean-Claude pulled out two conical hats, handed one to Sandy and put the other on his head. 'Let's be tourists. This is a pretty river.'

'You know this area well?'

'I've been here for holidays a few times. My grandfather owned a house downriver. It's now a restaurant.'

'A bit out of the way, isn't it? Or just a local place?'

He grinned. 'The people who come like it to be out of the way. Gentlemen with lady friends.'

'Oh, so am I one of your lady friends you bring here?' asked Sandy lightly.

He looked serious. 'I've never brought anyone special here before. Because it's so tucked away, the restaurant escaped the notice of the tourist industry for a long time. My mother used to live here as a very little girl and I like to think of her life here, carefree and privileged. But of course many Vietnamese were exploited so that the French could live in such comfort.'

They sat watching the river narrow and then they turned off the main channel into a quieter stretch of water. There were a few huts on stilts at the water's edge, a fish trap set between poles, some boats pulled into the bank and a fairly substantial wooden jetty. As they got closer Jean-Claude pointed to a beautiful old house. Tall French doors opened onto a stone terrace and Sandy could make out tables under shady umbrellas.

'It's gorgeous,' exclaimed Sandy. 'How did your family feel about leaving such a lovely place?'

He shook his head. 'I don't believe my family left under the best of circumstances. They walked out and the house was sold for a song and sat empty for a long time. A clever entrepreneur lives in it and runs the restaurant. Ironically, it's now known for its excellent French cuisine.'

Sandy was intrigued and rather touched by Jean-Claude's bringing her here. He made no reference to his connection with the house and listened politely as the elderly waiter gave a potted history of the place, which had once belonged to a former French colonial bureaucrat.

Jean-Claude ordered in French and passed Sandy a glass of fine French wine. 'The wines are still good here. Not all French wines in the country are the best. They might be old but haven't been stored properly. On the whole you're better off ordering Australian wines.'

'I've discovered that. But they're pricey compared to home. And on HOPE's salary I didn't often bother.'

They touched glasses and Jean-Claude talked more about his family and his connection with Vietnam. He refilled them as the appetiser was served and asked Sandy, 'What about you? Tell me about your childhood.'

Sandy waved his question aside. 'Nothing much to tell. Not very interesting, I'm afraid.'

'Your friend Anna, you seem close. You're old friends, yes?'

'Our fathers are good mates. Anna was born in Australia, but our dads are very different.'

'I am very close to my papa. My mother is . . . difficult,' said Jean-Claude. 'Are you close to your father?'

Sandy hesitated. Jean-Claude's green eyes were soft and he seemed so interested, so . . . caring. Or was she reading more in his expression than he intended? Perhaps it was the second glass of wine combined with Jean-Claude's gentle probing that caused her to talk quite openly and honestly about her feelings.

'It hasn't been easy, ever since I was little. From as early as I can remember, Mum has been saying to my brother and me, "Don't upset your father. He's in one of his moods."'

'How bad were they?'

'He was always short tempered. And you never knew what would set him off. I can remember being at the beach or at family picnics and all of a sudden he'd just get up, stomp off, leaving me crying, wondering what I'd done wrong.'

Jean-Claude reached over and covered her hand with his. 'It had nothing to do with you.'

'I know that now.'

'Have you ever talked to him about this?'

Sandy shook her head. 'I think my mother tried and warned us off trying. Of course there were good times too,' she added hastily. 'Once I teamed up with a gang of girls from school and was invited to a party. Dad drove me and stayed there to have a chat and a beer with some of the other dads and he seemed just like them. It was such a happy day – I've never forgotten it.'

'How does your brother get on with him?'

'He's younger than me and finally immersed himself

in sports Dad had no interest in.' She sighed, and sipped her wine. 'I think our relationship became one of caution, a civil veneer. I was made very aware of "appropriate behaviour" and spent all my time avoiding upsetting him.'

'And so you chose a job that would take you far away from your home,' said Jean-Claude.

'I didn't plan it that way; it just seemed to be how things worked out,' said Sandy.

'Sometimes we do things without knowing why but in retrospect they seem planned. Because it is the right thing to do.' He leaned back as their main course was put before them. 'Have you ever spent time alone with your father? A holiday? A trip?'

Sandy shook her head. 'Family holidays were hard enough.' She suddenly felt close to tears. The conversation had brought back old hurts.

Jean-Claude sensed her struggling to regain her composure. 'Try your duck; it's highly recommended.' He began talking about other places he'd been to in South-East Asia, places she hoped to see one day. He was interesting and amusing company and the time passed quickly.

At the end of the meal Sandy smiled at Jean-Claude. 'Thank you.' But she was thanking him for letting her unburden herself as much as for lunch.

When they arrived back at the orphanage the sun was setting. Anna welcomed them with the news that the hire car company was sending another car the following morning so they could drive to Danang to catch their flight to Hanoi.

Jean-Claude kissed Sandy on the cheek. 'Drive with care. I will send you a message. Perhaps we can meet again soon.' He mounted the muddy bike and, blowing kisses to the little girls giggling by the doorway, drove out of sight.

8

As Kim whipped through the early evening traffic on the highway from Noi Bai Airport and through Hanoi's outer suburbs Sandy sighed. 'Thanks for meeting us, Kim. It's great to be back in the arms of the grand old dame again. I do love Hanoi.'

'Looks good to me, too. I'm a bit over rice paddies,' agreed Anna.

'So when do you start running Barney's?' asked Kim.

'After we get the crash course. How about we go there tonight to eat? Then we'll be behind the counter.'

'And in the kitchen. I hope the chef who works with Lai won't mind my trying my hand at a few dishes,' said Anna.

'I'd say the skill is going to be in the way we'll have to serve up a lot of different dishes with limited space. I'm always amazed at how those women whip up meals out of a basket and a brazier on the street,' said Sandy. 'I'll be dealing with front of house. I hope the staff and regular customers will be understanding while Lai and Barney are away.'

Kim glanced at Sandy. 'You've done a lot of things since you've been here. Did you ever imagine you'd be managing a cafe?'

Sandy laughed. 'Well, after HOPE I've learned to be flexible, roll with the punches. Anyway, this is not a career move. Just helping out a friend.'

'We'll all drop over for a meal,' answered Kim. 'Even wash up if you're stuck.'

'Thanks. No freebies – even for friends. Well, coffee maybe,' answered Sandy. 'Spread the word.'

'Will do. I'll catch you guys later for dinner.'

He dropped them in front of the laneway leading to the courtyard of Sandy's apartment, and as they came to their building Sandy glanced up at the front window.

'Did you leave a light on, Anna? I thought we checked everything was off. The electricity is so ropey I don't like leaving anything on.'

'No. I'm sure everything was off.'

Across the courtyard Mrs Minh, who was the unofficial caretaker of their small building, was emptying a bucket of soapy water onto her precious potted plant and she gave them a big smile and funny little wave.

'What's that mean, do you suppose?' said Anna.

'She's pleased to see us back. They're always so interested in our comings and goings she was probably bored without us around.'

They lugged their bags up the twisting steps, past the floor where the Tran family's altar was set up in an alcove by the front doorway of their apartment. Rows of shoes and many sticks of burning incense and candles were a sign that all the family was visiting. But as they got to the door, Sandy stopped, the key poised as she was about to put it in the lock.

'The TV is on. And the lights. Do you think Mrs Minh came in and made it look like someone is at home?'

'Bit of cheek without asking us. And running up the power bill,' answered Anna. 'Do you think we should knock?'

'Why? It's my place. If it was a thief they wouldn't have the lights and TV on.'

'It is the right flat, isn't it?' Anna suddenly asked, looking around the darkened hallway illuminated by a hanging light bulb. The building was such a higgledy-piggledy jigsaw of little apartments, stairs, landings and levels it was easy to get confused.

Sandy turned the key as softly as she could and flung open the door. Anna peered over her shoulder. It was Anna who reacted first.

'Whaat! What're you doing here?' she shrieked.

'How did you get in?' demanded Sandy, striding into the main room.

Carlo took his feet off the coffee table in front of the TV and gave a broad grin. 'Ah, the ol' Italian charm works just as well in the exotic east, it seems. Hiya, sweetheart. Aren't you pleased to see me?' He stood up, holding out his arms.

Anna ran to him as Sandy brought in their luggage and closed the door. 'This is a surprise, Carlo.'

He squeezed Anna's buttocks. 'A good one, I hope.'

Anna had felt rattled with the unexpected shock of seeing Carlo, then pleasure, then a faint annoyance at his not telling her. 'So who let you in?'

'I got here yesterday. Your description of this place and the address made it easy to find and I talked the old duck downstairs into letting me in. I showed her photos of us and got the taxi driver to translate.' He released her and spread his arms, 'Hey, give me some credit, babe. So, Sandy, pleasant little hole in the wall you have here.'

'Thanks, Carlo. It might have been nice if you'd told me, asked me, if you could stay here. As you see, there's not much space.'

'Don't get shirty, Sandy. If it's a pain for you then Anna and I will find a hotel.'

'How long are you staying, Carlo?' broke in Anna, 'Maybe we could have a few days in a hotel . . .'

'Honey, if you can take leave for a couple of weeks, or however long you plan on hanging around here, so can I,' he said with a smile. 'You girls'll thank me.'

'What about your work?' asked Anna.

'Carlo, what will you do with yourself? I think you'll be bored: this place isn't your scene,' said Sandy evenly, trying not to show the displeasure and annoyance she felt. 'Anna and I do actually have to work quite long hours at the cafe. We promised Barney to look after his place for him.'

'That's why I'm here. What do you two girls know about running a bar?'

'What do you?' countered Sandy.

'More than you think, I reckon. C'mon, it's a guy thing. I bet I've spent a lot more time in bars and bistros than you have,' he said, pleased with himself.

'I won't argue with that,' said Sandy, putting the kettle on to boil for coffee. Strong coffee.

'Carlo, there's a big difference between Barney's and the Italian espresso bars you hang out in,' said Anna. She sat beside him. 'Sandy and I'll be working long hours; we won't have much time together. You should've asked me, waited till I was free.'

'I'll hang out. You were raving about the sights. So I'll be a tourist. Might even do a bit of business.'

Sandy took her bag into her bedroom. 'It's not that

easy, Carlo. This is a communist country and they are very big on red tape.' She started pulling her dirty clothes out of her bag, wondering whether Carlo had really missed Anna, or had simply come to check up on her. She glanced at the dried mud on her clothes from her tumble in the rice paddy to avoid Jean-Claude's motorbike and found herself smiling.

Anna came to the doorway. 'Sands, I'm sorry if he's going to be a problem,' she said softly. 'We can share my bed in the alcove.' She gestured towards the tiny space that served as the guest 'bedroom'.

'Well, if you're sure.' Sandy was not going to offer her bigger bed and be pushed out of her space by Carlo. His presence dominating the little flat was bad enough. 'It's a pity he didn't let you know. I'm sure you'll both want to sightsee a bit, but we did promise Barney . . . '

'Oh, I'm not trying to get out of it. I'm looking forward to it. Carlo will just have to do his own thing for a bit. We'll work something out,' said Anna unconvincingly.

'There's no way I want Carlo trying to move in on Barney's. He has no idea about this country,' said Sandy firmly.

'Well, let's take him with us to dinner tonight so he understands what we're committed to doing,' said Anna.

The cafe was buzzing. A lot of the local clientele were there to see Barney and Lai off, and tourists, seeing the crowd and laughter, chose to wander in rather than patronise other places they'd passed.

Anna introduced Carlo to Barney, who threw Sandy a questioning look.

'Carlo just dropped in to Vietnam unexpectedly. It won't interrupt our plans,' she said quickly.

Barney raised an eyebrow. 'Well, Anna, he is your

boyfriend, and he's come a long way. Are you sure about this? Won't you want to spend some time with him? Maybe I could find someone else to help Sandy. A bit late notice, though,' he began.

'Absolutely not. We promised to run this place for you and we will. I'm looking forward to it,' said Anna, steering Carlo to a table.

'Then have a bite to eat and come and get the run of the kitchen and meet Ho,' said Barney.

'Ho is the chef? No relation to Uncle Ho?' joked Anna. She'd been fascinated at the almost beatification of communist leader Ho Chi Minh who was regarded as a benign, wise old leader, the father of the nation.

'No. He's a bit dour: he got nicknamed Ho, Ho, Ho one Christmas as a joke. We don't think anyone has seen him smile.'

Sandy and Anna ordered spicy noodles and introduced Carlo to Kim and several of the expat regulars. After the hurried meal they were just about to go to the kitchen when Sandy was tapped on the shoulder by the American gallery dealer Charlie Ralston.

'Charlie! How good to see you. You're back from the hills. What've you been up to?' said Sandy, giving him a quick hug.

'The usual. Actually it was quite an interesting trip. Miss Huong knows every artisan in every village, it seems. We found some wonderful pieces. Including a few treasures.'

'I'll have to come and have a look. Always dangerous going into your place,' she said. 'Anna, you remember my friend Charles?'

'Please, it's Charlie.'

'Charlie, this is my partner, Carlo Franchetti.'

Carlo shook hands as two other friends joined them and they squashed around the table.

'We'll have to excuse ourselves, we're getting a crash course in keeping Barney's afloat,' said Sandy. 'Just while he and Lai are away.'

'Great. I heard there was a bit of a problem in Canada, great of you guys to step in,' said Charlie.

The girls went to the kitchen and Anna glanced back to see Carlo looking a bit glum as the conversation at the table hummed along about people and places he didn't know.

Sandy noticed it too and wondered how long it would take before Carlo managed to make himself the centre of attention.

Ho, the chef, was a wizened little man who looked, to Anna, as if he'd been smoked. His skin was tough, brown and stretched tightly over his body. She imagined sticking a fork him and hearing him pop and juices run out like an overcooked sausage. Barney introduced them and Ho nodded and mumbled a greeting, his mouth showing gaps between yellow teeth.

'He understands some English. More than he lets on, I think,' said Barney. 'These are the kind ladies who are going to help out while we go away to Canada,' he said to Ho.

Ho nodded again to Sandy and Anna. 'Me cook. You work.'

'There's the menu. No new dishes,' said Barney. 'Ho, no make trouble. Miss Sandy, Miss Anna be Mr Barney and Mrs Lai. Ho boss of the kitchen, okay?'

Ho nodded yet again but his miserable demeanour didn't change. Barney ran through the basics of the kitchen system, the food ordering, how the roster for the two waiters and waitress worked.

Lai appeared and thanked the girls. She led them out to the rear courtyard, which was her domain. 'I have one girl run this business here. Travel and tourist information,' she explained. 'You don't need to know about that. I show you how to look after money, and here are keys.'

'Front door ones?' asked Sandy.

'No, this one for grog cupboard; this one for trouble men,' said Lai.

Sandy and Anna exchanged a glance as she opened a cupboard that held the liquor supply and a locked black tin box.

'What's in there?'

Lai put a finger to her lips. 'I explain later. We keep separate some cash from the restaurant. If we need to pay trouble men, we use this.'

'Trouble men?' asked Anna, giving Sandy a look.

Barney appeared behind them. 'She means standover men. Occasionally we get an eager-beaver new copper or other local trying to stake his bit of territory. It's cheaper to pay 'em off with little regular bribes. When they get too greedy and try to up the ante, I call in a few favours from people up the line. Don't worry about it. While we're away we've organised protection.'

'What kind of protection?' asked Sandy, feeling uncomfortable about this, though she knew well enough that some local officials were neither too proud nor too rich to organise 'business security protection' scams.

Lai interrupted. 'We are very grateful to you. Do not give any credit. Do not buy food from anyone other than our regular suppliers. And do not let Ho be boss. Here is menu list.'

Sandy glanced at Anna. 'No new dishes? Ho cooks all these things?'

'Don't let him try anything new. Lai always super-vises the menu,' said Barney.

'Right,' said Anna. 'I was hoping to try my hand at cooking a couple of dishes. Will Ho teach me some of these?'

Lai waved a hand, fanning herself in an agitated manner. 'Ah, no. Ho doesn't let anyone else to cook.'

'He's seeing this as an opportunity to prove he's capable of being number-one chef. Ho wants to run his own restaurant and has grand ideas, so keep an eye on him,' said Barney.

Sandy was seeing the chef as a bit of a liability. 'Well, at least he's used to preparing meals for any number of people. What about my end of the business?'

'Come with me.' Barney led them to the little office under the stairs where he kept the books and ran the financial side of the business. By the time they had listened to Barney's instructions, made notes on book-keeping, wages, ordering and a few tips on special customers, an hour had passed.

Sandy and Anna returned to the main cafe to find, as Sandy had expected, Carlo holding forth, telling a story about some exploit where he'd made a killing on a deal, hinting at putting one over on an Italian 'mob'. Sandy knew he was using the Australian vernacular but she realised those listening assumed he meant some mafioso group in Italy. Carlo was prone to exaggeration.

'I have a few schemes I might float while I'm here,' he said airily, and turned to Charlie. 'Say, what're the treasures you've found out in the sticks? I buy and sell stuff; maybe I could unload something in Australia for you.'

'It's not quite as simple as that,' said Charlie politely. 'My clientele ask me to find special objects for them. We prepare pieces as a museum would. Or people come in looking for something that has a particular provenance. Rare pieces.' He paused and added, 'There's a lot of paperwork involved in exporting artworks. But we consider that we are promoting the cultures of all the peoples of Vietnam.'

'Paperwork, that's a pain, isn't it?' said Carlo. 'In my

import–export business I tend to look for ways to cut some corners.'

'If you're considering doing business here, you might want to visit your trade commissioner to acquaint yourself with the way business is done in Vietnam,' said Charlie.

'Good advice, buddy,' said one of the expats. 'Find out the guidelines and then do research into how and when they can be bent.'

'Know who you're dealing with, that's the trick,' added another. 'Who can be trusted and how far they can be trusted. Takes a while.'

'Carlo is only here on a short visit to see Anna. I doubt he'll be doing any business. Right, Carlo?' Sandy gave a tight smile.

Then Anna spoke up, recognising the annoyance behind her friend's smile. 'Please excuse us. We had a busy evening and we start work tomorrow. I hope you'll all keep dropping by to give us moral support,' she said to the group.

There was a chorus of agreement, and a round of goodbyes. Sandy and Anna farewelled Barney and his wife, wishing them a safe trip and hoping that all would turn out well with their daughter in Canada.

'Don't you worry about a thing, Barney,' Sandy assured him. 'We'll be here from opening to shutting up shop and will keep a close eye on everything.'

'It'll be fun and a great experience,' added Anna.

Barney and Lai exchanged a look. 'It's hard work. And you have the number of Lai's uncle if there are any problems.'

'There won't be. Go, and don't worry,' said Sandy firmly. 'I'm sure you'll get everything sorted out.'

Sandy, Anna and Carlo walked home talking about the cafe and how they'd juggle their time.

Carlo was quiet and Anna asked, 'Are you tired from the flight? You don't have to hang around the cafe from morning till midnight.'

'You girls have no idea what you've let yourselves in for. It's a good thing I'm here.'

'We'll manage, thanks, Carlo,' said Sandy quickly.

He gave a short laugh. 'Listen, as soon as Anna told me what you were doing I hopped on a plane. What makes you think you can run a bar? It's a crazy idea. It's not just dishing up noodles. Have you been there when that joint closes down? I bet it's a different scene from your little social supper of this evening.'

'I haven't stayed past eleven,' admitted Anna. 'Have you, Sandy?'

Sandy stepped off the footpath into the whirl of after-dinner traffic and Anna confidently followed. 'Yes, I have. It's not the sort of place you seem to think it is, Carlo.' She turned to admonish him but Carlo was still standing on the footpath behind them, a sea of bikes, scooters and cyclos between them.

'Shit! Don't these bastards ever stop?'

Anna laughed. 'Just walk slowly, don't hesitate. They'll go round you.'

Muttering under his breath, Carlo weaved his way across the road to join them. 'Idiots. How many people are killed on these roads every day?'

'Actually quite a lot,' said Sandy matter-of-factly. 'About a 747's worth each week across the country.' She strode ahead.

Anna took his hand. 'Don't mind Sandy. Sweetie, I know you're trying to help us, but just go slowly, okay?'

'You'll be glad I'm around, mark my words,' said Carlo. 'You two are babes in the wood.' He squeezed her hand. 'Speaking of babes, you're looking hot. And I'm feeling horny. You've been away too long.'

'We should go somewhere romantic before you leave. Halong Bay maybe,' said Anna. 'I just hope you can entertain yourself while we're running Barney's.'

'Don't you worry about me. I have a few plans,' said Carlo.

They shut the laneway gate and walked through the dark courtyard.

'I bet that nosy old bag is watching – what's her name? Mrs Minh? How can you stand this communal living?' asked Carlo.

'They're our friends. We look out for each other and they've been very helpful. It's how it is here,' said Sandy shortly.

Carlo leaned over and whispered in Anna's ear. 'She must have PMT. Miserable bitch.'

'Shut up, Carlo,' whispered Anna as Sandy went up the stairs ahead of them. 'Don't try to run everything. You've just arrived.'

'You haven't seen anything yet, caro. This country is ripe. Just opening up. I can smell opportunities.'

Anna didn't answer. Carlo wouldn't be in Vietnam long enough to embark on a business project. But she was worried what he'd do with himself while she and Sandy were at Barney's. Why couldn't he have contacted her before impulsively jumping on a plane, she thought. But, as she knew, no one could tell Carlo what to do.

As arranged, Tom turned up at The Strangled Cow bar a few kilometres out of Vung Tau. The sun was setting, turning the clipped wet lawns a shining emerald. He followed the noise and laughter to the poolside bar, where there were strings of coloured lights around a thatched roof supported by wooden poles over a long bar.

Most people were clustered around the bar, but some

couples stood apart on the lawns in intense conversation. It was a scene he recalled from years ago – large western men, beers in hands, leaning close to dainty, pretty Vietnamese girls. But instead of the ao-dai or, in his day, the daring mini skirt, these girls were wearing cut-off jeans and skimpy tops. A couple of kids raced past and he saw they were an attractive mix of Caucasian and Vietnamese. The girls behind the bar had the same bright lipstick and sharp look he remembered well. Behind their fast smiles and repartee was a machine calculating every cent a customer was worth and what they might extract from them in the course of the evening. He heard the click of billiard balls and glanced at the pool table where some kids were playing. In the old days he'd been one of many to lose heavily in games with the bar girls.

A man stepped forward as Tom approached. Stocky, tanned, silver-haired, but trim and fit in shorts and a T-shirt. He was in his fifties, Tom guessed.

'Tom Ahearn? I'm Barry Malden. Baz. We spoke on the phone. You're the journo?'

'Right. Good to meet you. Thanks for taking time to fill me in on the Long Tan ceremony and the background.' They shook hands and Tom looked around. 'This must be the local hang-out. Nice that it's away from town. I thought the cab was headed up country.'

'Yeah, we all live around this area. This bar is the base for a lot of the oil workers, local blokes who come in and out on a regular basis. It's safe for the kids. Friday night is barbecue night – hope you'll stay on. Now, who'd you like to meet? I asked a few of the regulars to come and yarn to you.'

'That's good of you. No rush – can I talk to you for a bit?'

'Sure. What'll you have to drink?' Baz signalled to one of the girls behind the bar.

Tom sensed that the easy-going Australian wielded some influence. A beer and a refill for Baz were swiftly handed over, the crush at the bar parting for him to reach over for the drinks. Baz had an air of authority; he was a man used to getting his way. Tom wondered what rank he'd held and assumed he'd been an officer.

Suddenly a little boy, about nine, nudged Baz, holding up a coloured picture. 'Dad, lookit, my picture.'

Baz ruffled the boy's hair. 'That's terrific. Todd, this is Mr Ahearn, visiting from Australia.'

The boy shook hands and Tom smiled. 'Pleased to meet you, Todd. Are you a budding artist?'

'Project for school.'

'Where's Ky? She looking after you, mate?' Baz glanced around and then smiled at someone across the room. 'Off you go, finish your work and we'll have some tucker. I'm talking to Mr Ahearn.' Baz added a phrase in Vietnamese and the boy nodded.

'Good looking boy,' said Tom.

'Yeah, he's a great kid. I'm enjoying being a dad this time around,' said Baz.

'How long you been here?'

'Came back ten years ago. My first marriage busted up when the kids were in high school. I wasn't much of a father, or a husband. Coming over here turned my life around. At first not for the best. I met a local Viet girl and she wanted to get married and go to Australia. So we did. She had relatives there so I thought she'd adjust. Boy, did she ever – she had everything sorted out quick smart. Todd arrived and she moved in with her family and before I knew it, I was out on my ear. She'd fleeced me for the lot. I stuck around because of him, but two years later she had a boyfriend, handed Todd over to me and took off. So I brought him back to Vietnam and stayed here.'

'Does he see his mother?'

'Yeah, she's re-married so he goes back to Perth to visit a couple of times a year. But this is home now.' He nodded at a pretty young Vietnamese girl sitting with his son. 'That's Ky; I teamed up with her two years ago. Very sweet girl.' He watched Tom glance at Ky who looked barely twenty-one, and he gave a wry smile. 'Don't know how long she'll stick with me. As long as I keep doling out money . . . ' He gave a small grin. 'There simply aren't available mature women around here. All married and settled.'

'So what's the story with the Aussie veterans here?' asked Tom, steering away from Baz's personal life.

'There're half a dozen of us who live here permanently. We have a nice lifestyle. Most of us have second families, informally or legally. My mate Cranky married a Viet girl and he's been embraced by her whole family – even old Uncle who was a VC.'

'Do they talk about being on opposite sides in the war?' asked Tom.

'Hell, yes. They've gone over every inch of where they were when, and what they did. They've concluded they must have taken a shot at each other somewhere along the line.' Baz chuckled, then added, 'The Vietnamese are amazing people. The war was never going to be won by the US, no matter what the Americans poured in. The Vietnamese were fighting for their country, their families, their future. Yet they're very forgiving. They've had enough – seven hundred years of wars. They've moved on, not like some of us poor bastards.'

'Do you mind if I make notes?' Tom pulled his notepad and pencil from his pocket. 'So, have you blokes here moved on, as you put it?'

'A lot of us have. Most Vietnam vets have come to terms with their experiences. They were young and resilient. But some of them haven't.'

'Even after all this time?'

217

'Pain's pain. Fresh as yesterday. I've met some blokes who haven't had a decent night's sleep since the war. They live in waking nightmares. Trouble is, they don't, can't, share it with their families.'

Tom nodded. 'I was a correspondent and the war was a pretty scary place. At one point, in ninety days I made sixty-two 'hazardous' flights. Insane flights if you ask me. In twenty different types of aircraft. I was shot at, forced to land with engine trouble, helped to load wounded and dead, and, once, was three feet off touching down in a minefield.'

Baz nodded. 'Yeah, we admired you blokes who didn't have to be there, who tried to tell it like it was, when you could. For us the experience was compounded by the way we were treated by the Australian government.'

'As we now know,' said Tom.

'It soon enough became an unpopular war, especially when they brought in conscription. It was a bloody lottery – literally. Your birthday coming out of a barrel, for chrissake. Some go, some stay. Crazy. We flew out of Amberley at midnight and were made to wear civvies and the next day we're in a war zone. Then, one day, our time is up but even the government didn't want to know us when we came home. I was shoved on a Qantas plane to Sydney and asked where I lived. I said my mum was in Melbourne. And they told me I'd be on a train the next day so they'd put me up in some motel for the night. Bugger that, I said, I'd hitch if I had to. I was going home. One minute I'm knee deep in mud on a battlefield; twenty-four hours later I'm sitting at home having a baked dinner. My head was scrambled.'

'I s'pose the blokes sent home by sea had a bit more time to adjust,' said Tom quietly.

'Not everyone adjusted, mate. Not after what we saw. In a way it was worse coming back here, even after decades, and seeing what we did to these people, to the country.' He drained his glass. 'I was pretty shocked. What the hell was it all for? And yet we were made welcome. That's when I decided to try to do something. At least in our neck of the woods. The rural areas were badly affected by the war, as well as by the years of isolation from the west. So I approached the People's Committee to see what kind of help could be given and how to go about it.'

'Must have been a slow process. Was it welcomed?'

Baz grinned. 'Yeah, it took a while, but once I decided to base myself here and they realised I was genuine and I was getting help from Aussie vets and organisations, then our group was made official, in 1994.'

'So what are you doing?'

'Fundraising, first up. Now we get government help from Australia as well. Essentially we try to provide practical aid and assistance. We built a school, put toilets in houses, set up agricultural projects, medical facilities and a kindergarten. Where we see a need we try to help. Our objective is to improve relations between the peoples of Vietnam and Australia.'

And you're back in command, running things, and doing a good job too, thought Tom. 'And on a personal level?'

'I think all the blokes who come here agree – we want to make some restitution for what we did to this country. Payback time. It helps us too.'

'And Long Tan?'

'That's been another battle. A cross was raised at the site on the third anniversary of the battle and stayed there while Aussies were stationed in the province. Then it was moved to the local museum. For twenty years servicemen have been coming back and the Long Tan cross was the focal point. So in 2002 we got the cross renovated, raised funds and, with the co-operation of the Vietnamese, we unveiled the memorial. We also raised funds to improve the local roads and make it easier to visit.'

'I assume there are certain protocols to be observed by visitors?' said Tom.

'Yeah. You've got to have a permit, medals are not to be worn, and they like to keep groups small. The plaque is kept in the local police station and brought out by the guides for visitors with the permit to pay respects and then it's put back. To keep it safe. Anyway, we're knee deep in negotiations for this fortieth anniversary.' He sighed. 'Everyone from the pollies, bureaucrats, business people, locals, veterans' organisations – everyone wants to have a say in the ceremony. Naturally the vets feel they should have the main say. We want to start the service at three-forty when the battle started. So we'll see.'

'Long Tan is finally getting recognition back home,' said Tom.

They were joined by two other veterans, Cranky and Ed, who sat down with their beers and talked of their own experiences of fighting in Vietnam and how it had affected their lives.

'Bloody dreadful when I look back on how miserable I was and how it affected my family,' said Cranky. 'That's how I got my nickname. By the time I'd lost my wife, my house and quit my job I had nothing to lose so I agreed to come over here.' He shook his head. 'It was cathartic. So I stayed.'

'We see blokes who come over here release a lot of bottled-up agony and go back new men. Many don't want to ever come back again; others get a different perspective and want to encourage other mates, bring their families over,' added Ed. 'I'm a widower; my kids are all happy and settled back home; they don't need me. So I retired over here and I have a little boat. I live on my own – it's a good life. I see enough of these blokes each week to appreciate my peaceful life.'

'So do you see your role as encouraging veterans to come back? To make this pilgrimage?' asked Tom.

'It's a good way to honour your mates and if some vets are having problems they can talk to us,' said Cranky.

'There is a mob back home who've been helping blokes deal with the trauma. Not the professional service people, but a group of fellow vets,' said Baz. 'They go bush and talk. It's run by blokes who know what they're doing. Seems to help.'

'Some blokes I know just couldn't cope with city life after the war so they got jobs up north in isolated areas where they didn't have to see people very often,' said Ed. 'Being with nature and animals rather than crowds of people made it easier.'

They all fell silent for a moment, each reflecting on their own experiences till Baz spoke up.

'Hey, barbie's going. Grab a plate and some food, Tom.'

They settled at a table, Baz's young son, Todd, squeezing in beside his father, who handed him a sausage wrapped in bread.

With another round of drinks, the men began exchanging stories with Tom, asking where he'd been during the war. They all talked about the girls they'd met, the escapades, the characters, the narrow escapes. The bleak and fearful times were not mentioned.

For Tom it was a memorable evening. He was a good raconteur with a fund of stories that went down well with an appreciative audience. In the taxi going back to The Grand he knew he'd have a headache the next morning, but it had been a long time since he'd been able to share an evening with men who'd been in the same place at this particular time in their lives. The memories had come pouring back.

He debated about going to the Long Tan memorial on his own, but decided to wait until he came back and went to the anniversary commemoration, and write about the impact of the event by sharing it with the men who'd fought there on 18th August 1966. He wondered if entertainer Col Joye would be there and then he remembered the soldier he'd interviewed in the hospital the day after the battle. Phil Donaldson. Could that be Sandy's father? Tom began to see another angle to his unfolding story on the return to Long Tan.

Settled on the back verandah with a pot of tea after touring his garden, Tom took a biscuit and munched it thoughtfully. His wife, pleased to have him home, watched him chew slowly.

'C'mon, Tom, out with it all. Your trip to Vietnam: what was your biggest impression?' asked Meryl eagerly.

Tom finished his biscuit and downed a mouthful of tea. He'd already told Meryl about Hanoi and Saigon, of his adventures with Sandy and Anna in Halong Bay and of the veterans in Vung Tau. Now, sitting in the sunshine of his quiet suburban backyard, Vietnam seemed far away. And yet, he didn't feel he had totally left it behind; nor did he feel completely back at home since arriving in Australia the day before.

'It seems as if I could just step outside and order a bowl of noodles in the street. I keep listening for the jangle of bicycle bells. Everything here smells strangely clean. I think I'm still in transit.' He smiled. 'Lots of impressions. Biggest I s'pose are the changes. I kept flashing back to how it used to look. Lots of memories of people and places I knew then.'

'And how is it today?'

'Terrific. You'd love it. For a tourist, for anyone, it's great.'

'So you're definitely going back? There's a good story there?' asked Meryl. While it had taken Tom hours to get back into the rhythm of their lives and onto Sydney time, he seemed to have more get up and go than she'd seen in a long time.

'Yeah. Several stories, though I guess they're all entwined. Met some beaut people. In fact, I had an idea.' He grinned at her. 'I thought you might like to go back with me – as a birthday present.'

'To Vietnam! For my sixtieth! Gosh, yes. How wonderful. It's quite safe, isn't it?' she added. 'I mean from a health point of view?'

'Look at me. Didn't get a tummy bug or feel crook the entire time. The food is even better than I remembered. Seriously good tucker – and some very upmarket places to eat. Not to mention the shopping. I can guarantee that you won't be bored while I'm trailing around doing my thing.'

Meryl leaned over and gave him a kiss. 'How exciting! Thank you, Tommy. It will be the best birthday present ever! It means a heap to me. I know Vietnam is a special place to you and I'm thrilled I can share it with you. Where are we going? Just Long Tan? Or other places too?'

'We'll move around. I have to check in with some veterans. First I'm going to see Anna's and Sandy's fathers, the girls I met over there. Great kids. I went through my old stories, and I think I interviewed Sandy's father after the battle.'

'Are you sure? What a coincidence.' Meryl had been bemused to find Tom had befriended two young women on his travels.

Tom went inside to his desk, brought back a red folder and pulled out a pile of yellowing carbon copies of stories he'd punched out on an old typewriter before sending them off with cans of film and sound tapes. 'Here's my Long Tan stuff. At the hospital I came out on a chopper with Col Joye and we went to visit the boys who'd been wounded and airlifted from Nui Dat to Vung Tau. Listen to this.'

Slowly, in his broadcaster's voice, he read from his old script.

20 August 1966
This is Tom Ahearn reporting from South Vietnam.

It is believed eighteen Australians were killed in a surprise attack on a platoon in the Long Tan rubber plantation near the Task Force Base at Nui Dat. The wounded have been evacuated to the field hospital at Vung Tau in Phuoc Tuy province. Entertainer Col Joye, who had been performing in the area, was among the first to visit the wounded in hospital. He spent time with Sergeant Phillip Donaldson of Sydney, who had been one of the first to encounter the North Vietnamese Regular Army.

[Tape insert Donaldson] 'We thought there'd been a small unit of VC in the area . . . but the enemy were wearing khaki uniforms. The penny didn't drop till afterwards that they were regular army. It was bad . . . some reckoned we were outnumbered twenty to one. Bloody dreadful. There's not much cover behind a rubber tree, mate! When we first walked in on patrol, we could hear the music. We were pretty upset at missing the concert, so it's been a big thrill to meet Col Joye. I'm hoping I can get back into the action with my platoon as soon as possible.' [End tape insert]

The full extent of the numbers involved on both sides in the battle fought in the Long Tan rubber plantation is yet to be confirmed. But it's been a defining conflict for the

men of the Sixth Royal Australian Regiment. Sergeant
Donaldson's spirit is typical among the wounded men I
met today. But they carry the knowledge that many of
their close mates died at Long Tan.

This is Tom Ahearn reporting.

'And that Phil is your friend Sandy's dad?'

'Yeah, I think so. Anyway, I'd like to meet him and
find out for sure. Seems like he had a bad time of it. Like
a lot of the vets who came back from Long Tan.'

'So how are those who went to live in Vung Tau cop-
ing?' asked Meryl.

'I'm really impressed with what they're doing.
They've all started over – new families, a new life. But for
most of them who go back, it's a matter of coming to
terms, settling ghosts, finding some peace.'

Meryl was thoughtful. She'd married Tom several years
after he'd returned from working overseas in other Asian
posts after Vietnam. But she'd never really asked what effect
being there during the war had had on him. 'What about
you? You saw some awful things, I suppose. Were you close
to the fighting? Did you have problems then?'

Tom put the script back in his old red folder, filing
away the memories. 'Yeah. Before I met you.' He got up
and left the verandah, leaving his tea, and she knew the
subject was closed. Going to Vietnam with him for her
birthday while he covered the story of the anniversary
might be good for both of them. After years of marriage
it was ridiculous that there were things they'd never
talked about, never shared.

She wondered what Tom had been like as a young man
in his twenties, before she'd met him. At least Tom had got
over whatever troubles he'd suffered during the war, even
if the memories had been rekindled.

9

SANDY LEFT THE FLAT early, deciding to go for a run around the lake. It had been a while since she'd been to Hoan Kiem with the early risers but she needed a break as it had been a restless night. She imagined Anna was feeling tired, too. Carlo's love-making sounded very demanding. And in the proximity of the tiny flat, there was little privacy. Sandy didn't blame Anna: she'd heard her trying to shush Carlo, but he had taken no notice. It was clear that Carlo's staying in her flat wasn't going to work. Perhaps he and Anna could move into a hotel or a small furnished apartment.

Then she found the solution. She knew that Barney and Lai wouldn't mind if Anna and Carlo stayed in the apartment above the cafe. It was a cute funky place. Barney had kept many of the famous old paintings as well as acquiring new ones. Barney would probably be pleased someone was staying at the premises full time from a security point of view. Cheered by this simple solution, she broke into a fast jog, turning her mind to their first day as cafe managers.

At the flat Anna was remonstrating with Carlo as he rummaged in Sandy's kitchen cupboards.

'Doesn't she have any decent coffee? I'm not drinking the mud they call coffee here.'

'Carlo, you're not listening. We have to find a place of our own.'

'What for? From what you say, we'll hardly be here. You'll be at the cafe during the day; I'll be there in the evening.'

'You don't have to do that . . . ' began Anna. But Carlo leaned over and kissed her as he held up a can of coffee. 'Good old Starbucks. Who brought this?'

'An American friend of Sandy's, I suppose. When people come to visit they always bring something. I brought Vegemite and honey,' she added pointedly. So far Carlo hadn't produced any gift from home. He ignored the comment and began making the coffee. 'What do you want to do today?' she asked.

'I'll cruise, get the layout of the city, bit of a feel for the place. Where's Charlie's gallery?'

'Why do you want to go there? You've never been interested in art.'

'I smell a deal. Y'know, these eastern artifacts, quality stuff, can fetch good money. He's only dealing with the US, but there're a lot of rich Asians at home who must want to collect these sorts of things.'

Anna didn't argue. Carlo had a nose for a business deal. He was always full of stories, schemes, ideas. She just wished one of them would make the financial killing he was always promising. 'There's a map and brochures on the coffee table,' she said. 'You have to look around as there are so many different types of things to buy. You see one thing and think it's great then you find another that's better and so on. I always get confused and can't remember where I've seen what. Write it down. You should check out the good-quality lacquerware: it's gorgeous.'

'Sweetheart, I'm not buying souvenirs. You need to go to the source for merchandise.'

'At least see what's available. What people make here. You really need to travel round the countryside. Every place has its own specialty, from marble and ceramics to fish or soy sauce.'

'Forget food. I've got that covered. And I'm sticking with Italiano, thanks very much.'

'You wait till you taste pho and some of the traditional dishes. Yummy.' Anna put on a piece of toast to cook.

'Why don't we check out the breakfast joints?' Carlo put his arms around her. 'Or go back to bed?' He nuzzled her neck.

'Carlo, cool it. Anyway I hear Sandy downstairs talking to Mrs Minh.'

'Doesn't that old bag ever sleep? Doesn't she have a family to look after?'

'Of course she does. There're three generations in that flat of hers. This is a crowded city; have a look at the buildings, the way people are crammed in. But it's more their way of life, the extended family, everybody living and working together. They don't like being alone,' explained Anna.

Carlo gave her a quizzical look. 'You suddenly know a lot about this place.'

'Yeah, well, you can't help it, living with Sandy. She's been here so long and working with HOPE she knows stuff. And I'm observing things myself,' she added.

Carlo poured his coffee. 'Yeah, well, don't get too attached. This is a one-off visit.'

'Why do you say that?' asked Anna, surprised and a little defensive. 'It's a fascinating place; there's no way I'm going to see all of it in one trip. Sandy might stay on here longer, so I could come back.'

Carlo gave her a look. 'You haven't seen Italy yet. Now that's a really great scene. Don't get too many ideas about this place.'

'What do you mean, "ideas"?'

'Look in the mirror, Anna. You're a great-looking bird. Bella, bella. But even if you're half one of them, you weren't born here. Just don't feel you have any links here in Vietnam, that's all.'

'But I do!' exclaimed Anna. Then, shocked, she stopped to consider her spontaneous reaction but decided not to pursue it with Carlo. 'Like you have links to Italy. Your family came from there. You like going back there. You know your heritage.'

'That's different.'

'How?'

'I have family there; we do business there. I live with my heritage every day,' he said patronisingly.

Anna heard Sandy's footsteps in the hallway. 'I probably have family here, and I'm starting to learn about my heritage too,' said Anna quietly.

'Fine. Just don't bring it home. Our kids are being raised on pasta not rice.'

Before Anna could answer, Sandy came through the door. *Our kids* rang in Anna's head. Carlo had never formally proposed to her; there was an understanding that they were a couple but Carlo had always hedged about any commitment until he'd made a motza and could afford to live the way he dreamed.

'Hi, guys. You got breakfast under control, Anna?'

'Yep. Want a coffee?'

'No, thanks. I had one down at the lake.'

'Carlo wanted to go out for breakfast. Maybe I'll take him there.'

'Fine. I'll go over to the cafe and get the keys from Barney. He's opening up and then they're heading out to the airport. I want to make sure the early staff are there. I'll just have a quick shower and change.'

'I'll see you there after breakfast,' said Anna.

When Anna arrived, the cafe was already half filled with regulars as well as several tourists.

Sandy handed her a set of keys. 'Barney and Lai are worried about security here at night. They wondered if one of us would consider staying in their flat upstairs. I was thinking, maybe you and Carlo . . . wouldn't mind . . . ?'

'Of course not.' Anna was relieved that the problem of accommodation was solved so easily. 'That'll mean that Carlo will be able to hang around and close the bar.'

'Anna, it's great Carlo has offered to help . . . but, you know, we're in charge,' began Sandy diplomatically, but Anna held up her hand.

'I know. Don't worry, he won't be a hassle. He's got ideas for his import–export business. He'll keep himself busy.'

Sandy didn't want to know what ideas Carlo was exploring, but she was glad he didn't plan on being around the cafe all day.

The hours sped by with a steady stream of customers and a long discussion with Ho over the menus.

Later in the day Anna moved her and Carlo's belongings into Barney's flat. She was amazed at the murals, the collection of paintings, the different coloured walls and a few pieces of handmade and decorated furniture that filled the small rooms. She studied the framed photographs that lined one wall of the staircase showing the original owner posing with some of the now-famous artists he'd befriended. There was a picture of a younger Barney wearing snowshoes in wintery Canada. There were pictures of Barney in the cafe with groups of men – obviously Vietnam veterans. This made Anna think about Sandy's dad. She wondered if Tom had made contact with her father and Phil.

Carlo returned in the late afternoon and went upstairs for a nap, saying all the walking had wearied him and he was still jetlagged.

In the early evening, Kim dropped by and filled Sandy in on news of everyone at HOPE. 'Cherie has gone to Cambodia for an NGO's meeting. Tuk's baby is due any minute so there's a little tea party for her tomorrow if you can make it.'

'Of course. I'm sure Anna can manage for an hour or so without me.'

'How's it going? Everything seems pretty normal.'

'So far, so good. I'm staying on top of everything, just so the staff know they can't sit out the back with a cigarette too often. You have to keep reminding the girl about taking away dirty coffee cups, wiping down tables. People don't want to sit down at a table covered in dirty dishes,' said Sandy.

Kim nodded. It seemed strange to see Sandy, whom he'd seen directing groups of people digging ditches and wells, getting babies vaccinated, arranging food supplies, helping fishermen launch their new boats, giving speeches, writing reports and briefing committees suddenly fussing about dirty coffee cups. 'You're enjoying it, then?'

'Actually, I am, especially the contact with people.

No wonder Barney always parks himself out the front and socialises.'

'That's because Lai is out back running things,' said Kim. 'How's Anna doing?'

'She's watching Ho like a hawk. I don't think he's very happy about it.'

Kim laughed. 'I hated being the underling when I worked in a food joint in Honolulu when I was at college. Say, there's Rick Dale. I haven't seen him for weeks. I might go and join him.'

Refreshed and smiling after his nap Carlo wandered into the bar. Rubbing his hands together he set up some glasses and a bucket of ice, which Barney always insisted was made from filtered or boiled water – 'To keep the tourists happy. Clean water and no MSG. House rules.' Carlo then helped himself to a bottle of American lager, without bothering to pay, pushed a slice of lime into the top and joined Rick and Kim.

'Anyone care for a drink? Name your poison. I'm tending bar.'

'I'll have a beer, thanks,' said Rick.

Kim nodded. 'A light one for me, thanks. I don't think you've met Rick, have you? He's been living here buying Vietnamese art for a gallery in New York.'

'Enjoying Hanoi?' Rick asked Carlo.

'Crowded. Crazy traffic. Colourful. Could be that this place has real potential for an experienced importer,' he added.

'So what are you after? I heard you were looking for merchandise to export to Australia,' said Rick.

'I could be. Who told you that?'

'Charlie. I do some work with him and Miss Huong.'

Carlo leaned forward. 'So what sorts of things sell well, fetch high prices?'

Rick smiled. 'Depends on the collector. One man's

treasure . . . might not be of any interest to someone else. Some people buy as an investment, others because it's rare or unusual, something no one else has. Others buy because they're passionately interested in certain things.'

'And they'll pay top dollar?'

'Sometimes. Some collectors can be eccentric. I heard of a fellow in Tokyo who collects Buddhist sculptures, really old Tibetan paintings and porcelain from a particular period. Stashes it all away in a basement where no one else can see it except him.' Rick lifted his beer. 'If a collector is missing one piece from a set of something, they might pay handsomely to get the missing item.'

'How do you find these people?'

'Ah, that's where the expertise comes in, eh, Rick?' interrupted Kim.

'But what if someone has something to sell – how do they find a buyer?' persisted Carlo.

'I guess they take it to a reputable dealer, like Charlie. He'll check if it's authentic, that it's not stolen, looted, whatever. Some pieces have turned up that are seriously valuable. He has quite often donated pieces to museums because they're culturally significant to Vietnam,' added Rick.

'You on the lookout for antiques, then, Carlo?' asked Kim.

Carlo got up to get some nuts and snacks. 'I'm in the market for anything that sells, mate.'

Anna stopped by the table and greeted Kim. As he was about to introduce Anna to Rick she smiled and said, 'Hi, nice to see you. We met at the art show. I've now met your friend Charlie. I still haven't had a chance to visit his gallery. Have you met Carlo?'

Rick nodded. 'You both must go to Charlie's gallery. It's a great insight into Vietnamese culture. Are you planning to go to see the hill tribes?'

'She's a bit busy right here,' said Carlo, setting more bottles of beer on the table.

'Maybe when Barney gets back,' said Anna. 'Sandy said it's well worth a visit.'

'I hear you went to Hue and Hoi An,' said Rick.

'We did. Got caught in a typhoon.'

Rick grinned. 'Monsoon season. You're getting the full experience, eh?'

'And now this. I've had more adventures here in a couple of weeks than I've had in a year at home,' laughed Anna.

'Lucky I'm here to keep an eye on her now,' said Carlo.

'Ah, you're in safe hands with Sandy,' said Kim smoothly. 'Besides, it's good to go home with a few different experiences under your belt. Running this place might be an adventure too, eh?'

'Could be,' agreed Anna. 'Ho the chef is a bit of a challenge. See you later.'

The cafe was filling with the pre-dinner crowd. Sandy was seating people, suggesting what food to order and chatting in Vietnamese or English to locals and visitors. In the kitchen Anna was dishing food onto plates under Ho's close instructions. Carlo circulated, taking drink orders, making suggestions, spruiking the wine list.

Sandy passed him and whispered, 'Be sure to write down what drinks are going to what tables. And that includes what you're drinking too, Carlo.'

It was past midnight. A few people lingered on, sipping coffee and drinks. Carlo had joined one table where an American couple and two German girls had teamed up to compare places to sightsee and shop. Anna brought Sandy a plate of food as she sat in the rear writing up the receipts.

234

'Here, you've hardly eaten. Try this.'

'Thanks. Yum, smells good. What is it?'

'Ho's favourite noodle dish . . . I added a couple of things myself. Behind his back – he's a tyrant over letting me help.'

'Don't upset him, Anna. I heard him shout at Carlo at one stage. What was that about?'

'Carlo helped himself to some food. Don't worry, Sands. I'm keeping track of what we're eating and drinking. There's not much left over. Ho is very frugal. And he cooks everything from scratch, which is good: there are no pots of food being wasted.'

'See if you can get Carlo to bring me the bar bills. I'd like to wrap this up. I'm exhausted. I feel like I need six pairs of eyes and hands.' Sandy yawned. 'Tell Ho to clean up; we'll close the place soon. It's mid week; I doubt there'll be any new customers.'

Sandy ate her meal and took the plate into the little kitchen and thanked Ho. The chef wiped his hands on the long white apron he'd wrapped over his black trousers and began to complain about Anna. She was watching too closely, 'stealing' his recipes.

'Nonsense, Ho. She's helping – she admires your skill. She is not a chef; she's not opening a restaurant.' She let him complain as he cleaned and put away his knives, threw his apron into the cleaning pile and pulled on his black mandarin-style cotton jacket. He picked up a box filled with fresh vegetables, bottles of sauce and plastic containers of cooked noodles and rice.

'Where is that going, Ho?' Sandy pointed at the box.

'I take. Mr Barney say yes, I take food from kitchen. No good for tomorrow.'

'The vegetables will still be okay. Is it for your family?' asked Sandy, not wanting to upset him but equally not wanting to be taken advantage of by the cranky little chef.

Ho glared at her and broke into a torrent of rapid-fire Vietnamese that left Sandy struggling to make sense of his outrage.

Anna appeared in the kitchen. 'Is everything all right?'

'I merely asked what he was going to do with that box of food he's taking. He's accusing me of attacking him, not trusting him. He's threatening to walk out. Mr Barney always gave him permission and so on. I still don't know what it's all about.'

'Just calm him down, Sands. Who cares about a few leftovers?' sighed Anna.

Sandy pacified the chef as best she could and went and washed her plate. Without saying goodbye, Ho left the kitchen with his box of food. It would probably make meals the next day for his family, Sandy surmised. Ho was paid a decent wage and the tips and surcharges were shared by all the staff. But Sandy was too tired to argue.

When she went back into the cafe, her heart sank. A new group of people had just arrived and Carlo was busy opening a bottle of wine for them. They looked to be Vietnamese businessmen, dressed in suits, but now with ties loosened and all very upbeat. Sandy went over and welcomed them in English but politely informed them that the chef had left and the kitchen was closed except for snacks.

The men shrugged. They'd been out to a dinner, celebrating a new business deal and so were only interested in drinks.

'They're in transport,' Carlo told her. 'Trucking. Very good business apparently.'

Sandy studied the men, trying to get their measure. There was something about them she couldn't put her finger on. Especially one of them. He smiled too much. His English was sprinkled with American colloquialisms.

He boasted about the new Vietnam and how those who knew the 'right' people were making their fortunes. He talked of plans for new highways, mountain tunnels and the movement of freight across borders.

When Sandy asked what kind of freight they moved around the country, he shrugged and answered, 'Supply and demand. We not only move goods: in many cases we supply what is in demand. Which is why we got into transport.' He continued to be vague about what sorts of goods they trucked, adding, 'We move crops, food, merchandise across our borders. The roads are poor, not so safe. We also use rail and are looking at moving in bulk in our own ships and, soon, planes.'

In Vietnamese one of them said to him, 'Ask her if she wishes to import or export from America.'

'She is not important,' he answered quickly. 'Our friend here is more interested.' He inclined his head towards Carlo.

Sandy pretended not to have understood the brief exchange in Vietnamese. But she had met these sorts of businessmen before and quickly realised they probably had dubious business integrity and were ready to exploit regulations and opportunities in the rapidly expanding Vietnamese economy by whatever means they could.

'So you work for the government?' she asked.

The leader of the group nodded. 'We have government contracts. But there are now individuals in Vietnam who prefer to capitalise on their hard work and sell directly. Like in the west.' He smiled, giving Sandy the impression that they were not above side-stepping government laws.

She asked, 'Would you like anything? Coffee?'

To her annoyance, they ordered tea and coffee, and asked for 'light food'.

'What's light food?' asked Anna, who had just tidied up the kitchen and let the waiter go home.

'Sweets, snacks, what've you got?' said Sandy. 'Peanuts, anything. I'm telling Carlo when they've finished the wine, that's it. We're closing.'

Anna quickly produced fruit with cold sticky rice topped with a sweet liqueur; peanuts, crackers and a spicy dip; and pickles sprinkled with chillies. She grilled chicken satay sticks that had been left in a coconut marinade in the fridge.

Carlo and the men were in deep conversation and the food quickly disappeared. Sandy knew Carlo was about to open more wine, but she turned off the lights outside the cafe, locked the bar area and she and Anna moved the tables and chairs inside. The men took the hint and put money on the table and shook Carlo's hand. He escorted them outside as they got into cars, handing their business cards to Carlo.

'Why'd you shove them out?' grumbled Carlo. 'They would've spent money on booze. Influential people like that can bring in business. The night is young. What we need is music in here. Bring in the late crowd.'

'This is a cafe, not a nightclub, Carlo,' said Sandy. 'We're closing up. Besides, we don't want to encourage that kind of clientele. Next thing they'll be asking for bar girls.'

Carlo went to say something, but changed his mind. 'Want a nightcap, eh, baby?'

Anna shook her head. 'I'm going to bed. Do you want Carlo to take you home, Sandy?'

'No, thanks. I'll grab one of the cyclos out the front. Perhaps you can open up in the morning?'

'Sure thing. You go for your run. See you when you get here,' said Anna.

'Thanks for today. And for whipping up the late-night supper for the suits,' said Sandy.

Anna grinned. 'They fancied themselves, didn't they?'

'They're serious business people. Could be useful,' said Carlo, as he headed upstairs. 'See ya, Sandy.'

Sandy picked up her handbag. 'I wouldn't trust that mob as far as I could throw them, Anna. From the bits of conversation I heard I'd say they're moving illegal freight or exploiting government contracts to skim the cream for themselves.'

'Ah, they didn't know you spoke Vietnamese?'

'No. Tell Carlo not to have anything to do with them. Not that he'd have any reason to talk business with them,' said Sandy.

'Of course not. He was just being sociable,' said Anna. 'Night, Sands. We got through the first day okay, huh?'

'Yeah. See you tomorrow.' Sandy headed outside and hailed a cyclo. She was tired and anxious to get back into her own space. Much as she enjoyed Anna's company it had been a while since she'd had the flat to herself. They'd got through their first day at the cafe, but Sandy hoped Carlo would find his own interests and not consider himself a third partner in running Barney's.

When Tom phoned Anna's dad, Kevin, he found him chatty and friendly.

'Well, it's good to hear that the girls are having fun and doing such interesting things. I really appreciate your phoning me,' said Kevin.

'No trouble. I promised Anna I'd let you know that I met them both. She's a lovely girl.' He went on to describe the trip to Halong Bay and the fun the three had had there. Then he paused. 'If you don't mind my asking, does she know much about her mother's side of the family? The subject came up and I didn't know if it was a sensitive area or if she really doesn't have the whole story.

I thought her being over there, you know, might have sparked some curiosity.'

Kevin sighed. 'It crossed my mind too. What she knows about her mum is from Thu's time here, after we got married. I always assumed Thu would fill in the gaps and talk to Anna about her family in Vietnam. But Anna was so young when Thu died, it never happened.'

'It must have been hard on you,' said Tom quietly.

'Yeah. Thu's aunt and uncle were great in the early years. After they died Anna never seemed to have any curiosity about her mum's family.'

'Have you never wanted to go to Vietnam yourself?' asked Tom.

'Not really. Didn't serve there, like Phil, so I thought I'd go if Anna wanted, but it never came up. I was surprised about this trip, but I think she went because Sandy asked her. She would have gone had it been Timbuktu. And I'm glad she's having a break . . . from her job, from Carlo. Mind you, he's gone over there now.'

Tom was very surprised to hear this news and he could tell from Kevin's tone that he didn't really approve of Carlo's rash trip either.

'The girls are running a cafe for a friend of Sandy's,' said Kevin. 'That's going to keep them pretty busy.'

'Of course. It's a pity now that Anna's in the country she doesn't try to get in contact with her mother's family. Do you know where the family comes from or whether she has any relatives there now?' asked Tom.

'Don't know about the family currently. But I got the story from Thu. There's even a photo of her grandmother's family. Don't know who's alive. I know Thu escaped Vietnam from some island.'

'And Anna didn't take that information with her?' Tom, the ever-curious journalist, was amazed at Anna's lack of curiosity.

Kevin had wondered too, but hadn't pushed the subject. 'I figured she'd come to it when she was ready.'

'Maybe Anna will change her mind before she leaves Vietnam,' said Tom.

'Maybe. I'll find that envelope with all Thu's papers in it. You never know. Thanks again for calling.'

Tom hung up realising that Kevin was right. Anna had to decide in her own time. Tom was thoughtful. Too often when we did want to know answers to questions about our past, those who held the answers were no longer around. Anna had a great opportunity right now, to search for her family, especially with Sandy's help.

Sandy's father, Phil, wasn't home when Tom rang the Donaldsons but Tom explained to Sandy's mum, Patricia, why he was ringing and she was eager for news.

'I'm so glad Sandy is having a good time with Anna. They're very close and it's been a while since they've had time together. Did Sandy say when she might be coming home? She's a bit vague in her emails.'

'I don't think she's made any definite plans,' said Tom. 'She and Anna are running a friend's cafe and have plans to travel around the country a bit more.'

'How is Anna finding Vietnam?' asked Patricia. 'I mean, she has a family history there.'

'I spoke to her father and I think he was disappointed that Anna doesn't show much interest in her mother's family. Some of them could still be around,' said Tom.

'What a shame. Her aunt and uncle were lovely people. Suffered terribly; and of course Thu had an awful time when they escaped. But they're all dead now. Who knows if anyone is left.'

'Kevin said he had papers, even a picture. That's a start. I'd be wanting to go back to the village they came from and

241

see what anyone knows,' said Tom. 'But then, I'm a nosy journalist. As a matter of fact, I am going back. I'm writing a story about Long Tan. It's the fortieth anniversary.'

'I know. Phil was invited, but of course he won't go,' said Patricia.

'That's a pity. I met some terrific fellows over there who are living there and say more and more veterans are going back. Making the pilgrimage to settle the ghosts, they call it.'

Patricia Donaldson was quiet for a moment, then said, 'I really wish he would. Some of his mates are right as rain, got on with things, seem content, happy. Phil, well, he still suffers nightmares, you know.'

'Going back could help him. I'd like to talk to him. Do you think he'd be willing to see me?'

'Oh. My goodness, I don't think so. Please don't mention I said anything. He's a very proud man. Did Sandy speak about him?' she asked cautiously.

'It was my mentioning that I'm doing a story on the Long Tan anniversary which brought it up. In fact, I have a feeling I might have even interviewed Phil in the field hospital at the time. I was thinking it would be a good angle for my story to meet him again. If he was up for that, of course,' said Tom.

'Dear me, no. I can't see him ever going back there. And please don't mention we discussed it, if you do speak to him,' said Patricia.

'Well, I would like to see him. Could I come over? We don't have to mention this phone call,' added Tom.

Patricia hesitated. 'I shouldn't agree, I mean it's not my place. But if you were just to turn up. Knock on the door, out of the blue. Early one evening, then . . . I mean . . .'

'Sounds like a good strategy. Sandy was very keen I meet you both. And hopefully I will be seeing her when I go back, so . . .'

'Perhaps it'd be best not to mention you're writing anything,' said Patricia.

'I'll come by on Wednesday,' said Tom.

'Goodbye, Mr Ahearn.'

Tom hung up, struck by the timidity of Patricia Donaldson compared with the strong, outgoing personality of her daughter.

Tom thought carefully about how to approach Phil Donaldson and finally decided to just play it by ear. He took his tape recorder, just in case, photographs from his recent trip and a brochure put together by Baz and Cranky about the vets' group in Vung Tau. He arrived with a bunch of flowers for Patricia.

Phil answered the door and listened as Tom introduced himself, explaining the reason for his visit. Phil reached for the flowers and thanked him, but Patricia was quickly behind him.

'How very nice of you! Do come in and have a cup of tea, won't you? We'd love to hear about Sandy and Anna first hand.' She had Tom through the door before Phil could react.

Seated on the back patio, the tea things ready on a tray, Phil and Tom sat silently as Patricia bustled in the kitchen.

'So, she's all right over there, then? I don't understand why she's hanging around if her job has finished,' started Phil.

'She and Anna are having a ball. Sandy has a lot of friends; she knows the country well, speaking the language and all. I think it's opened Anna's eyes.' Tom paused. 'It seems strange to me that Anna isn't taking the opportunity to find out about her mother's family.'

'Why should she? They chose to come here and be Australians. She's not one of them. She has nothing in common with their lifestyle, culture, mentality,' said Phil. 'All they want is money if they know where you're from.'

'That's a rather jaundiced view, Phil. But then, I guess your opinion is coloured by your time in Vietnam.' Tom saw Phil's mouth tighten, but plunged on. 'I think we've met before. I was at Long Tan covering the Col Joye concert. I was at the field hospital with Col and I seem to recall chatting to you.'

Phil's face registered fleeting emotions but he swiftly regained his composure and in a non-committal voice said, 'Yeah. I was there. I talked to a journo. Was that you? It's a small world,' he said, adding, 'I was still in shock. Didn't hit me for some time, what happened . . .' his voice trailed off.

'Yeah. It affected a lot of men. Still does,' said Tom softly. 'But a lot of them have finally come to terms with it, with themselves.'

'I wouldn't know about that.'

'You might like to look at some material a few of the Australian vets in Vung Tau have put together. I met blokes who went back. Made a big difference in their lives,' said Tom.

'I wouldn't go back there.'

'What's helping, too, is that finally Long Tan is being recognised as a pretty important battle.'

'Bit bloody late.'

'Is it? There's an opportunity to help a lot of veterans, their families and the people of Phuoc Tuy.'

'That's not my concern.'

Tom wondered if there was any point in persisting with the taciturn man. He tried to smile. 'You're a bit of a challenge, Phil. I'd love to make a small wager on how you'd react to going back to Long Tan.'

'You can forget that. All I wanted was to get out of that lousy place. Why would I want to go back?'

'Do you ever consider why, what it was all for, the consequences?'

'Bloody oath, I do. What a waste of men and money. Stupid political ambitions that conned us all. None of us had any real idea what we were really fighting for . . . Stopping the spread of communism? All the way with LBJ? Saving the South Vietnamese . . . Who were they? What's it done for them? The country is all commo now. I lost good mates, for what?'

'Then you need to go back, see what it was for, where the country is going. How the people feel. Move with the times, Phil. You're stuck in 1966. Come back with me and give me your opinion. Good, bad, indifferent,' urged Tom. 'There are probably a lot of men who feel as you do. Check it out. It might show you that actually the whole stinking mess did serve a purpose, that it wasn't a lost cause.'

Phil didn't respond for a moment but stared into the distance. Then he said, 'Tell that to the blokes who died. Not going to bring back my mates, make me feel any better,' he said.

Before Tom could answer, Patricia bustled out with the teapot and warm scones.

'Here we go. Tea. Tom, milk? Sugar?' She looked from Tom to her husband. 'Is something the matter?'

'Tom here is trying to persuade me to go and visit that shit-hole of a country where I lost my best mates and lost myself, as well,' Phil said bitterly.

Patricia poured milk into her husband's cup and glanced at Tom, who nodded, before she added milk to his tea. 'It's a different place now, love. If so many men are going back there and tourists, it must be . . . a special place.'

'Your daughter is very attached to the country,' added Tom, stirring sugar into his tea.

Phil's eyes blazed. 'Attached! She's got no reason, no right, to feel anything about the place. If anything she

245

should hate the place.' He clamped his mouth shut, holding back the words.

'Like you do?' asked Patricia. 'That's not fair. Maybe we hate what it did to you.' She took the cloth off the warm scones. 'There's jam and cream. I'll top the pot up.' She walked away.

'Sandy understands, she really does. I think she'd give her right arm to travel round the country with you. Seeing it now might ease some of the memories you have.' Tom picked up his tea. 'I was there too, mate. I went all over the south. I saw what happened to them, and to us. Believe me, this trip has been an eye-opener. I'm glad I went back. And I'm keen to go again. To Long Tan. Many of them are going to be there. And, like you, it won't be easy for some of them. But they've got the guts to go.' Tom drained his teacup. It had been a difficult little speech.

'It's not going to change anything.'

'If you go back there? Yes, it will. And then again, if you don't go, you'll never know, will you? Seems to me you haven't got anything to lose by going. You can't feel any worse than you do now, right?'

'I don't see that it's any of your business,' said Phil, looking into his cup.

'That's true. I promised your daughter I'd pop in and see you both. I guess I got a bit carried away.' The implication that Sandy knew her dad wouldn't take any notice of the invitation hung between them, unstated.

Tom rose and held out his hand. 'I'll be there at that reunion. I'll tell your platoon mates you couldn't make it.'

Phil stood up and briefly shook Tom's hand, saying gruffly, 'Don't worry about it.'

Tom wanted to say something else, some last remark that might change Phil's mind, something profound, something that would crack open the bottled-up hurt and anger in the man standing opposite him. He searched for the words, but none came.

'I'll tell Sandy I met you. Thanks for your time. I'll just say goodbye to your wife.'

Patricia had been watching from the kitchen and walked with Tom to the front door. 'Thank you for coming.'

'I couldn't seem to find the right words.' He almost smiled. 'Bit of a let down for a writer.'

'Tell Sandy her dad will be okay. He hangs in there. And I'm here,' said Patricia.

Tom looked at the pale quiet woman who had lived for years with a man in a lot of pain, yet had never complained. 'It can't have been easy for you.' For a moment he was tempted to suggest she go to Vietnam and visit Sandy but he figured she was not a woman to do anything without her husband's acquiescence. She might be the quiet strength of the family, but she'd never step outside the boundaries laid down by Phil's difficult moods and behaviour. 'You should talk to some of the other wives sometime. They've got stories to share.'

'Oh, I don't know about that.' She gave a small smile. 'We manage. Give Sandy a hug for me. And I hope she'll be home very soon.'

'I'll do that. Thanks for the tea.' Tom pulled the Vung Tau information kit from the folder under his arm. 'I'll leave this with you anyway. Good day.'

Patricia watched Tom drive away. Phil had disappeared into his garden shed. She washed up and put away the tea things, wiped the kitchen bench, then, drying her hands, she pulled open a drawer. Beneath receipts and papers she pulled out an envelope and re-read the letter inside. On the bottom of her shopping list she wrote down the phone number from the top of the letter and returned it to the drawer.

A little later, she appeared with her shopping bag. 'I'm going down to the shops. Do you need anything, Phil?'

He stuck his head outside the shed. 'No, thanks. You walking or driving?'

'Thought I'd walk. For the exercise. It's just a few things. I'll go to the centre later in the week.'

'Righto.' He disappeared back inside the shed.

Patricia bought a few groceries, then went into the phone booth next to the bus stop and took out a handful of coins. She spoke for ten minutes and emerged looking rather pleased with herself. She crumpled her shopping list, dropped it in the rubbish bin and walked briskly home.

Days and nights became blurred for Sandy and Anna as running the cafe swallowed their time and attention. Ho was becoming increasingly difficult and screamed at Carlo if he spent any time talking to Anna or watching him cook. Carlo maintained the chef was stealing food; Ho objected to being 'spied on'. So Sandy and Anna were relieved when Carlo started disappearing for meetings and making connections with an eye to business opportunities.

'Who's Carlo meeting with?' Sandy asked Anna as they carried out the tables and chairs one sunny morning.

'No idea. People he met through those businessmen that came the first night. I think he's been over to Charlie's gallery. And he said he was taking Rick to lunch to pick his brains.'

Sandy didn't say anything but she couldn't see Rick having much in common with Carlo. He was the high-art end of the market whereas Carlo, with limited knowledge, was after flashy, fast-turnover merchandise.

*

248

Carlo returned after lunch and announced he was onto something.

'And what might that be?' asked Sandy.

'Ceramics!' He swept his arms apart with a flourish.

'You mean bowls, pots, urns, garden tubs?' asked Sandy. 'Or art pieces?'

'You got it. Garden stuff. Costs peanuts here; sells for heaps back home.'

'Is that going to be a big outlay?' asked Anna. 'And who's going to buy it?'

'C'mon, Anna, just about every landscaping place you can think of. Water features, statuary, marble stuff. I'm doing a deal. A couple of containers and I'll make a killing.'

'Where are you sourcing all this stuff? Have you seen it?' asked Sandy.

'It's around. I've seen samples. I'll be going to the factories though.'

'Like the ones we saw on the way to Halong Bay . . . Bat Trung, Mr Thinh's place?' asked Anna.

'Be prepared for the factories, Carlo. They're small backyard operations. Not big, slick, mass-production factories like at home,' said Sandy. 'So you have to be sure what they produce meets the standard every time. Proper glazes and so on.'

'Who put you onto this?' asked Anna. 'It might be good. Don't you think, Sandy?' she asked.

Carlo butted in. 'Listen, I know a good deal when I see it. I have big plans. There's furniture, you name it. These people make stuff quick and cheap. I should get some Italian designs for them to reproduce. Cheap but classy.' He headed for the kitchen. 'I'll just grab a snack. I'm off to meet the woman who owns the two trucks I'll be using. She knows all about this stuff.'

'Carlo, get something to eat from the kitchen

upstairs,' called out Anna. 'Ho is really touchy about you helping yourself in his kitchen.'

'It is Ho's domain,' agreed Sandy, as there came a crashing and banging of metal pans and Ho's shouting above it.

Before they reached the kitchen to find out what was going on, Ho bolted out waving a large knife. He ripped off his apron, flung it on the floor and stabbed the knife into the top of the bamboo bar, all the while shouting in Vietnamese. He yelled at Sandy and ran from the cafe.

'What's going on? Carlo, are you all right?' Anna raced into the kitchen.

Carlo was sitting at the small table used for food preparation, calmly slicing a cucumber over a salad. 'The man's a nutter,' he said.

'What happened?' asked Anna. 'Why did he get so upset?'

'I said I wanted something to eat. He said I wasn't to eat *his* food, so I told him I'd take something out of the box he was *stealing* from here.' He pointed at the plastic box Ho took home each night with leftovers and spare food.

'God, like a pair of kids,' muttered Sandy behind Anna.

'What did Ho say?' Anna asked Sandy.

'He said he quit. Finished. No more. Mr Barney always let him take the box.'

'It's no big deal, is it? Taking home food for his family. You shouldn't bait him, Carlo,' said Anna. 'So what do we do now?'

'That food isn't for his family. I reckon he sells it,' said Carlo.

'Why do you say that?' asked Sandy, trying not to lose her temper and thump Carlo as he sat there unconcernedly munching through his salad.

250

'Well, I know something you don't. He gives it to a young kid who has a mini van filled with food stuffs. It's some sort of scam. I've seen Ho handing it over.'

'You mustn't accuse Ho in front of the staff: he loses face,' said Sandy. 'Anna, you'd better start planning the dinner menu.'

'So you don't think Ho will come back when he calms down?' she asked.

'Not today. I'll find out where he lives and go and make the peace. And you'll have to apologise, Carlo,' said Sandy.

'Bullshit.'

Sandy walked out of the kitchen as Anna tried to calm Carlo and get him to admit he'd done the wrong thing, but Carlo shrugged his shoulders. It was no big deal.

The two waiters crept around the kitchen as Anna started the meal preparation.

'The special tonight is Aussie bubble and squeak and a Thai-fry,' she told Sandy.

'Sounds hideous. What's in it?'

'Bubble and squeak is bits of vegetables dipped in a tangy batter and fried and the Thai-fry is like stir fry but with lemongrass, coconut and peanuts. Chicken or beef.'

'Whatever you say, chef.' Sandy smiled.

Halfway through the evening Ho walked in the front door of the cafe, eschewing the back door he normally used, sat at a table and picked up a menu. He was dressed in casual pants and a long-sleeved white shirt.

Sandy played along, greeting him and putting a tumbler of water on the table, asking him what he'd like.

Ho ordered three dishes including the special Thai-fry. Sandy went into the kitchen. 'Anna, drop everything and get these out there as fast as you can. A fussy customer.' She didn't say who it was.

Anna had a cotton scarf knotted over her hair, her face was shining with perspiration, but she seemed to be enjoying herself. 'Hey, right. I'm onto it,' she said, and chopped the carrots even faster.

Ho watched the meals and snacks come out of the kitchen noting the waiters were moving more quickly than they ever had before, as if they were competing with each other. Sandy watched him as the waiter put his food in front of him. Ho poked through the Thai-fry with a chopstick, breaking open a fritter and sniffing it. He tasted each of the dishes, chewing slowly, but left most on his plate. He asked to pay and for a bag to take the food away with him.

Sandy handed him the doggy bag and waved aside his money. 'It has been an honour to serve you, Ho. I hope the food was acceptable. Anna is trying hard, but your presence in the kitchen is missed greatly.' She spoke in Vietnamese, trying to strike a balance between politeness, but not kowtowing to him either. 'I have asked Mr Carlo not to offend you, or to upset you in the kitchen in the future should you agree to return to your chef duties.'

Ho looked mollified and announced he would think about it.

She smiled and said, 'I will see you tomorrow, Ho. Good night.'

Outside on the street Sandy saw a young man standing by the mini van just as Carlo had described. Ho handed him the food bag. The boy gave a slight bow and drove away.

When the main rush was over and Anna came and joined Sandy for a coffee, Sandy told her about Ho.

'Really! The cheeky old thing, sitting there and ordering my special. God, I hope he liked it.'

At that moment Carlo sauntered back into the restaurant. Anna told him what had happened with Ho.

Carlo shrugged. 'Who cares.'

'Well, what have you been doing with yourself?' asked Anna.

'Babe, this country is ripe for the plucking and with the contacts I've made, I reckon I can do it.'

Sandy looked askance. 'I don't think that's quite the right attitude to take, Carlo.' She thought how little Carlo knew about Vietnam and suspected that he was way out of his depth and she wondered if Anna thought the same.

10

CARLO WAS SPENDING LESS time at the cafe, but when he was around he preferred to hold forth at the bar as mine host. Sandy asked Anna where Carlo was going and what he was doing but she knew little.

'He says he is meeting people and being introduced to the way things are done, that's all I know,' said Anna. 'Though he has said he wants to go to Hoi An. I hope he doesn't do too much without me.'

'I can't see why he wants to go to Hoi An. Sure it's a big tourist town, but I can't see that it would send Carlo into raptures,' said Sandy. 'Nothing in it for him.'

'I'd love to show him some of the places we know about. Maybe go up to the hill country,' said Anna. 'There's still so much to see here.'

Sandy heard the wistful note in her voice. 'Listen, if

you want to take off for a bit with Carlo, we'll manage. Ho is back and we can get one of the waiters to do a double shift,' said Sandy.

'No, no. I like working in the cafe. Ho is letting me watch now and I'm learning heaps. I'm going to the market with him tomorrow morning at some ungodly hour. It's just that, well, a short romantic break with Carlo would be nice,' sighed Anna.

'Listen, why not take a couple of days and whizz down to Halong Bay? He wanted to see the factories in Bat Trung. Take him to see Mr Thinh; he will know who are the more reliable pot people,' suggested Sandy.

Anna laughed. 'Pot people. I never thought Carlo would be into making his fortune out of garden pots.'

'Maybe not a fortune, but it's a start. Anyway, I never thought he'd make a fortune out of importing pasta and olives,' said Sandy.

'It's not just the food side of the business. The wine side of it is lucrative,' said Anna a little defensively.

Sandy knew Carlo's father really ran the business and so far none of Carlo's big schemes had ever come off. But if he was smart, maybe he would do well exporting from Vietnam provided he found the right merchandise at the right price. 'Okay, whatever. But go down to Halong. Kim has some good contacts down there too. He's coming in at lunchtime – we'll pick his brains.'

Kim bowled in with a flourish of roses and gave both the girls a quick hug. 'Put them by the cash register so you see them a lot,' said Kim, then scanned the room and smiled. 'Say, business is booming: not a spare table. Barney will be pleased.'

'Yeah, we hope so. We've saved a spot for you in the back courtyard if you don't mind sitting in the B section,' said Sandy.

'Hey, I'm not going to quibble. Can you sit and chat a minute, Sands? Haven't seen you since you took over. How're you enjoying being in hospitality?'

'The flow of good coffee is nice,' said Sandy and led Kim to the rear of the cafe. 'To be honest, Kim, this experience has cured me of wanting to run a food place, if ever I did. But Anna seems to be loving it.'

'How's the Italian lover-boy doing? He's noticeable by his absence.'

Sandy looked at Kim's sympathetic face and thought what a good pal he had become. Then it occurred to her that Kim hadn't talked much about his personal life since she'd left HOPE and she wondered if he'd found a new girlfriend after his last ill-fated love affair with a Brazilian volunteer. He was such a nice person, attractive in his mix of Korean and Hawaiian blood. Stocky, olive skinned, a great smile and dark warm eyes. 'I have to confess, life is smoother when Carlo is busy. He's hooked up with some business people.'

'Didn't take him long to make contacts.'

'He says they do business here and in Saigon too, I believe. Tentacles everywhere.'

'What sort of business?'

'You name it,' said Sandy. 'Construction, transport, import, export and they seem to have lots of fingers in lots of pies.'

'Sounds like people Carlo would find useful. Sorry, I don't mean to be rude about Anna's boyfriend. But he just has a manner . . . well, you know what I mean.'

'I do. Don't worry about it, Kim. Actually it's nice to share thoughts with you. I don't like to upset Anna, as she thinks the sun shines out of him. I've always thought she could do so much better, but there you go. We all know couples and wonder what one sees in the other.'

'That's for sure.' Kim gave her a quizzical look. 'And what about you, Sandy? No one on the horizon?'

'Not even looking, Kim. I don't want to get into a relationship when I'm about to leave the country.'

'Are you?' He wondered about Sandy's hanging around in Vietnam after her contract with HOPE had finished. Most staff took off home or went for a holiday. She didn't seem in any rush to leave, and the visit from Anna gave her a reason to stay on longer. Sandy was so capable, efficient and compassionate, and he suspected she didn't appreciate how beautiful she was in her casual blonde Australian way. If Sandy tried she could have any man she wanted, he thought. Even me. He knew Sandy liked him as a friend and colleague. She would probably be quite shocked if she knew how easily he could fall in love with her. But rather than lose her he stayed in the role of close confidant. 'What about the Frenchman? Heard from him?'

'Jean-Claude? Yeah, sort of. He's gone to Cambodia and Laos. He's busy with his life and business.'

He smiled at her and changed the subject. 'Do you want me to sound Carlo out? About contacts, what he's doing? If I can help, let me know.'

'Thanks, Kim. I don't want Carlo to rush into some mad business scheme. Though it's hard to tell Carlo anything. He's been in the country ten minutes and thinks he's got a handle on everything. Not that I want to stifle his entrepreneurial dreams. In fact, he could be onto the good idea of importing garden pots and ornaments into Australia. But he needs to cover all the fine details.'

'Sandy, worrying about Carlo and his business prospects shouldn't be high on your agenda. You have enough on your plate,' said Kim gently.

'I'm thinking more of Anna. She's my friend.'

'She chose Carlo,' he reminded her.

'I think he chose her and he's bulldozed right over her. Anna's too nice for her own good. Always making excuses for him.'

'Well, that's something you can't control either. The scales will fall from her eyes eventually,' advised Kim.

'I just don't want her to get hurt. But you're right: I do have enough to get on with. Especially if Anna is taking a couple of days off.'

'I'll help in the evenings if you want.'

'Thanks, Kim. You're such a good mate. I'll yell if we need help.'

'Any time.'

Anna found going to the markets with Ho a more stimulating experience than wandering around the Hoi An markets with Sandy snapping photos of the colourful scenes. Ho was well known to the Hang Da market stall-holders who shouted out to him, asking questions about the attractive Viet Kieu with him. He called back that she was his assistant who had come from Australia to learn how to cook real Vietnamese food. Anna knew she was being discussed and was quite surprised to see Ho almost grinning, enjoying the attention.

He drove a hard bargain and showed Anna how to test which vegetables were fresh. He taught her how to tell the difference between seafood caught the night before and that which had been there several days. Fruit was chosen carefully. Ho turned and inspected each piece as much for its aesthetic qualities – shape, colour, appearance – as for the ripeness and taste. He kept aside five mixed pieces to put on his personal altar, then he moved on to the spice section. Food needed the right spices, the right 'music' to go with dishes, he told her. Depending on the lunar month, food required certain spices. Anna had never seen such an array. Ho rattled off several combinations: ground beetle essence and shrimp paste for rice noodle soup, mandarin peel and fennel with clamworms, oysters and clams from the river with sweet knotweed. His favourite combination was cinnamon, chilli, basil, lemon juice and shrimp paste.

But, he told her, it was wrong to put incorrect herbs with certain foods. Dog meat must have galangal, sweet rice paste, basil, coriander and shrimp paste. Anna still couldn't cope with the idea of eating dog and Ho quickly assured her they never served dog at Barney's. He was bemused by the small things that caught Anna's eye, like cooked food being sold in 'take-away' containers of folded or woven banana leaf.

On the way back to Barney's, Ho stopped at a com binh dan – a streetside eatery – for a bowl of savoury rice gruel. Between mouthfuls Ho commented on the growing trend of families, workers, students, people from all levels of society, to eat at these 'fast food' places.

'When I grow up everyone eat at home. It tradition. People no have money eat like this,' he said. 'Now people got money. This new way to eat.'

'But isn't all the family eating at home important?' asked Anna.

Ho shrugged. 'For festival and special time. Me chef, I want people eat outside places.'

Anna laughed but didn't ask Ho about his dream of owning his own restaurant, especially as things had just settled down after the blow-up with Carlo. She didn't want to raise another touchy subject.

After the markets Ho returned to Barney's and Anna decided to spend an hour or two exploring before getting ready for her next shift. She wished that Carlo was with her, but he had dashed off early that morning to visit the ceramic makers in Bat Trung.

'Back this evening, kid. We'll catch a bit of moonlight then, right?' he'd declared brightly on seeing her disappointment at the sudden trip. Anna had wanted him to visit Mr Thinh's pottery factory but he had dismissed the suggestion, saying that his contacts knew best. Nevertheless, he had agreed with her suggestion that the two of them get away for a couple of days to Halong Bay – as long as she organised it. So Anna had contacted Captain Chinh, and booked the *Harvest Moon* for the middle of the week, when it would be quieter and the trip would be more romantic.

She wandered into a district she didn't know well – leafy trees, French colonial architecture, a few offices housing overseas companies and expensive expat homes behind wrought-iron fences. There was an elegant French bistro, a few local food stalls and a motorcycle repair shop spilling across the sidewalk. Then she spotted a discreet sign above red-framed wooden doors – La Porte Rouge. In the window there was a display of carved wooden posts with abstract symbolic faces and she realised she had stumbled across Charlie's gallery. However, the door was locked and a handwritten sign announced it would open at two.

Nice hours for some, she thought. Oh well, she'd come back another day.

She hailed a cyclo that had been following her down the street and asked the driver to take her to West Lake. Once through the Old Quarter, Anna pointed to the causeway between two lakes which was lined with trees, pagodas and small parks. A myriad of open-air restaurants were serving the local delicacy – West Lake shrimp cake – so Anna settled at a table and placed an order. She was sipping her favourite jasmine tea and had closed her eyes in blissful appreciation when someone stopped beside her. Turning, she recognised Rick Dale.

'Sampling the opposition?' he asked.

'I suppose I could say it's research,' she laughed. 'I was just exploring. Near Charlie's gallery, in fact, but it's closed.'

'Charlie and his wife have gone to Sapa for a few days and Miss Huong is on a field trip. I'm due to open up at two. Another staff member is coming by to continue some work for them.'

'So you're minding the shop? Would you like to join me? I've ordered a shrimp cake. Probably far too much for one person.'

Rick pulled out a chair. 'Lovely. I'm helping to authenticate some old writing on several artifacts. I'm not much of a salesman, but I'm happy to be there for them. Where've you been?'

'The markets with Ho, our chef. That was quite an experience. I can't believe how different food, cooking and eating are here compared to home.'

'Yeah, fast food takes on a whole other meaning. The food is so healthy here. Toss in some fresh greens, home-made noodles, peanuts or tofu, a few bits of meat, chicken or shrimp and you have a fantastic meal in a minute.'

'Don't forget the spices for flavour. I had a lecture about what goes with what from Ho this morning.'

'So you don't mind chilli, nuoc mam, ginger?'

'And the rest. No. I've developed a real taste for this food. Must be in my blood, I guess.' She gave a small smile and Rick studied her and seemed about to say something, but changed his mind. 'Where were you going?' she asked.

'Oh, a few errands. And I was planning on a bite to eat, so this is opportune.' He ordered a coffee and asked, 'How's it going at the cafe? Has your friend Carlo found enough to keep him busy?'

'We had a bit of a hiccup with the chef, but things are running smoothly for the moment. Carlo has gone down

261

to Bat Trung: he's interested in exporting ceramics to Australia.'

'Yeah, he mentioned that. Said he had contacts. He seems quite enterprising,' said Rick casually. 'You said at that art show where we met that you weren't so interested in art.'

'Not knowledgeable. That's Sandy's field.'

'You can get sucked in. Especially in a place surrounded by art. Everywhere you look you see art here. From the colours of buildings, to the food displays, to the decorations on pagodas, and the clutter in the streets. Then in the hill country Miss Huong finds carved burial markers. Even wooden steps up to a house on stilts have a story carved in every step. It's a land of stories. There's a story behind the shape of mountains, lakes, how a piece got its colour.' He stopped, slightly embarrassed. 'I suppose it's like your Aboriginal legends where everything in the landscape has a story about how it got there from the creation time.'

Anna looked at the shrimp cake which was put on the table. 'I have to confess I don't know much about Australian Aboriginal history and stuff. I'm a city girl. Where in the States are you from?'

'California. And if you're going to ask if I know much about Native American history, I don't. I know more about Buddhist art and history.' He took a bite of the fried shrimp cake. 'I bet it's fun for you to be finding out about your Vietnamese heritage. Is that one of the reasons you came over here?'

'What makes you think I need to know my Vietnamese heritage?'

Rick was surprised at her defensive tone. 'Oops, sorry. I just assumed. I know one shouldn't, but as you're part-Vietnamese I thought you were exploring the country's culture.'

'I'm learning to cook traditional Vietnamese food. That's enough.' She sipped her tea. 'I know very little about my mother's family here. I suppose my father has some details.'

'I have a friend who was adopted and can't trace his biological parents. He got married and adopted a little Chinese girl, and there are no records about her either. She was abandoned in a gutter. It rips him up. He's always saying if there was any way he could find anything at all about his family or hers, he'd do anything to know.' He paused and added gently, 'One day your children might want to know about their grandmother. Don't you think you owe them that?' When Anna didn't answer he said, 'I'm sorry. I'm being presumptuous. Is it a painful story?'

'I'm not sure,' said Anna quietly. 'My dad said my mother, who was a boat refugee, had a terrible time but once she settled in Australia and married Dad, she never wanted to look back. She had an aunt and uncle in Australia too, who escaped with her. But they're both dead now.'

'Well, your dad would know her story! He must be waiting for you to ask, Anna. Sandy would help you.'

'I know, I know. It's never seemed important. Well, not part of my life. I know it sounds silly, but I came here on the spur of the moment for a holiday with Sandy. I missed her and I could take time off work. I didn't feel any real connection with this place until I got off the plane.'

Anna stopped. She had surprised herself, not only at telling Rick this, but at how easy it was to talk to him. Carlo didn't want to hear about her feelings very often, and he certainly did not want to hear about her Vietnamese heritage.

'Talk it over with Sandy,' Rick suggested and changed the subject as he could see Anna looked a little confused and he didn't want to upset her. 'By the way, I was going to ask if you and Sandy want to come to a function on Friday evening. Another exhibition, at the Fine Arts Museum, quite a big do. It's a gorgeous building if you haven't been in there. It's not a high-art place, but fine art for all people. It will be sort of formal, lots of dignitaries and so forth. But it could be quite interesting once the speeches are over. There's a cultural dance troupe, great food and a rather interesting show of the art of the Dong Son civilisation.'

'It sounds terrific, but I'm not sure both of us can leave the cafe,' said Anna, genuinely disappointed. 'Sandy would love it, I'm sure.'

'She knows the museum pretty well; I was thinking it might be of interest to a new visitor, like yourself. It's early, six till nine, and you don't have to stay the whole time. You could be back at Barney's by eight. Anyway, see what you can work out. I'll drop by with an invitation. Carlo is included too, of course.'

'Thank you,' said Anna, knowing Carlo wouldn't be at all interested. 'I am trying to learn a bit more about art, which is why it would have been interesting to go to Charlie's.'

'I could take you through if you like. Or there's a really interesting small museum close to the Old Quarter. It's mostly ceramics – the good old ones.'

'That'd be good. Maybe I could get some information for Carlo!' She laughed. 'By the way, aren't all old ceramics valuable? Just because of their age? I mean, how old are we talking?'

'Most of the ones worth big money are fifteenth century or earlier. But they go up to the nineteenth century, which are more common and not so valuable, of course.'

'That's still pretty old,' said Anna. 'I'll settle the bill, unless you'd like more coffee?'

'No, let me. I helped myself to your shrimp cake,' said Rick.

'Just as well, it was huge. No, I insist on getting lunch. In exchange for the ceramics tour.'

'Okay, you've got a deal. Now, I have something to show you near here.'

It was a small building, one of the old narrow tube houses, stretching back from the street. Two floors were devoted to glass display cabinets, but it was an informal kind of museum. Rick showed a pass in his wallet to the guard at a small desk inside the doorway.

'What is this place?' asked Anna, as there was no sign on the door and it didn't appear to be open to the public.

'It's a ceramic history of Vietnam held by the state archives. Vietnam was not recognised for a long time as having its own unique ceramic traditions. It was assumed it was derivative because of Chinese influence for so long. Some old stone pieces were found at Bac Son dating to the middle of the Stone Age, ten thousand years ago. On Friday you'll see some lovely Dong Son pieces from between the seventh and ninth centuries.'

'These look so lonely sitting in a glass case, yet once they were probably used every day in a family,' Anna said, looking at the unglazed pots and jugs.

'A lot of Vietnamese ceramics were traded to Thailand, Burma, the Philippines and Indonesia as burial pots,' said Rick.

Anna laughed. 'I know all about re-burying the bones of ancestors after staying in a mausoleum one night!' She studied some of the pieces, then turned to Rick. 'How do you suppose they invented pottery?'

'I suppose primitive people noticed when fire went through it left the ground baked hard,' said Rick. 'Then they started digging holes, making simple shapes. See these old bowls for holding rice are shaped like cupped hands.'

'I like the blue-and-white pieces. I love this dragon: it's a standing jug.'

'It's a fifteenth-century ewer, a pouring vessel, from Hanoi. The dragon is a common theme in Vietnamese mythology,' said Rick. And, reading from the label on the glass case, he continued, 'This was from a shipwreck found about fifteen years ago off Hoi An.'

'Wow, would there still be treasures under the sea waiting to be found?' asked Anna.

'I guess. They call that coast the Dragon Sea because of all the typhoons. So there're probably old junks sitting around the bottom of the South China Sea filled with ceramics from Vietnam's golden age between the twelfth and sixteenth centuries. The blue-and-white ones you like so much, they're worth a mint. Before this scholars hadn't realised the skill, scale and quality of early Vietnamese ceramics. Despite ten thousand years of Chinese domination, the Vietnamese still made ceramics in their traditional way, and just adapted some Chinese styles and motifs.'

'I saw an old one like that at Mr Thinh's,' said Anna. 'And in a shop in The Royal Hotel in Hoi An. Well, I think they were old.'

'These are the rare ones collectors and museums are after. The nineteenth-century blue-and-white ceramics are more common and not worth as much.'

'A hundred years seems pretty old to me for a dish.'

'Nice, but not nearly as valuable as some of the older pieces. My discerning customers in New York really only want these pieces. Compare the glazes and the work done on them and you'll see there is a difference.'

'It's an amazing blue,' agreed Anna. 'And these yellow-and-green ones?'

'Various areas specialised in different pottery styles and glaze colours. Though the terracotta red is probably the earliest. And some of those ancient ceramic centres are still going, like Bat Trung. But now it's become an industrialised business using imported techniques. The sorts of places Carlo would be dealing with,' said Rick.

'After seeing this, those modern urns and pots seem rather clumsy,' said Anna.

'Functional. And cheap. Anyway, if you come on Friday night, you'll see some truly beautiful stuff.'

'I must get Carlo to come, so he can appreciate the history and background to ceramics here. Rick, thanks so much. This has been great.'

They walked outside into the heat and humidity. 'Hope I didn't bore you. I'll drop the invitation off at Barney's. See you Friday.'

Anna watched him walk off, head and shoulders above the bustling locals, thinking what a nice American he was. She hoped Carlo would come to the show. Carlo always jumped first, thought later. It would be good if he could do a bit of research, acquire some knowledge, not only about the ceramics industry, but about how to deal with people and do business in such a traditionally polite society.

When Anna arrived in the kitchen, Ho greeted her and said, 'You cook; me teach.' Anna grinned and put on an apron.

Under Ho's watchful eye Anna learned to fold sweet sticky rice cakes in dried banana leaves ready for steaming.

Carlo stuck his head around the kitchen door. 'Ciao, bella, I'm hooome. What's for dinner?'

'Nothing – you've missed lunch. How was it? You're back early.'

As if to reinforce the point the cafe was empty and most people were at work or taking a siesta, Ho took off his apron. 'I go home. Come back five o'clock.'

'Bye, Ho. These steam for two hours, yes?'

As the chef nodded and hurried away, Carlo came behind Anna and gave her a squeeze. 'So, baby, miss me?'

'You've only been gone five hours. What did you think of Bat Trung?'

'What a dump. Hideous pollution. But there's a new industrial area nearby and that's where they're making all the garden stuff. Statuary, pots, fountains. Have to say it puts Rome to shame.'

'Is it heavy? Expensive? What about shipping it to Australia?'

'Nah. It's mock stone and marble. Some real marble stuff but you can't tell the imitations from the real thing. Got to give it to these people, they can copy anything.'

'They do have their own history of ceramics going way back; they didn't just copy Chinese or Thai stuff, you know,' said Anna.

'Yeah, well, who cares? Getting your hands on that old stuff, that's not easy. Unless you know a source,' said Carlo, rubbing the side of his nose and giving her a conspiratorial wink. 'I'm not an antiques dealer. I'm an ornamental garden supplier. I think I'll get a beer. Yeah, today was pretty productive. Mr Anh and Mr Mai know their stuff. They're going to be silent partners.'

'Carlo, what does that mean? You don't have to put up the money, do you? Buy all the stock, the shipping of it? And where're you going to store it? Sell it?' Anna sounded worried.

'Chill, babe. These guys know what's what: they have a business base in Sydney – a warehouse, the works.'

'So what's in it for you? Why do they need you?'

'Hey, c'mon,' he called from the bar as he opened a

beer. 'I'm the Aussie man. I run the operation. I just need to find a location big enough and in the right area where people are into landscaping. Not those Macmansion people with no yards. I'll hit all those fancy designer people who do flash homes.'

'Carlo, are you sure you know what you're doing? This is a bit different from what you've been importing,' said Anna as she put rice cakes into the bamboo steamers over simmering water. She wiped her hands.

'This will be my business, not my father's. I'm starting with this kind of stuff but I can see myself getting into all kinds of products – furniture, textiles, maybe even art. You wait.'

'What about the legal side? You have to form a company with these men. How does all that work?'

'Don't you worry about that side of things. Mai and Anh, we need each other and we got both ends covered.'

'Talk it over with Sandy, maybe Charlie, people who know how things work over here.' Anna knew that Carlo tended to rush into things. Over the past couple of years there had been several enthusiastic ideas that hadn't eventuated or had fallen through because he had failed to think deeply enough and hadn't conducted feasibility studies.

'Listen, my darling, trust me. I have the best advisor on my side. I feel really lucky. Coming here is going to set me up back home.'

'So you should thank me. Or Sandy.'

'I came because I missed you.' He gave her a hug and nuzzled her ear. 'If Sandy wants to hang around here I could possibly find her a position. She could be useful. Speaking the lingo. Hmm.' He considered the idea. 'Yeah. Could work. Say, what're you doing? How about going upstairs?' He gave her a playful pat on her backside.

'I can't leave till Sandy gets back. Oh, by the way, we're invited to a smart party on Friday night. At the Fine Arts Museum, very upmarket.'

'I dunno. Find out who's going to be there. Doesn't sound like my sort of thing – or yours. Fine arts, that's more Sandy's scene.'

'I think it'll be interesting. I'd like to go. Rick and Charlie will be there. Sandy and I can't both go and she's been to these things. I mightn't get another opportunity.'

'Whatever. I'll decide later. I've got to go and send some emails.' Carlo headed for Barney's small office leaving Anna pondering his latest idea. She wondered just what he knew about Mr Anh and Mr Mai, two of the obnoxious businessmen who'd been in the cafe the other evening.

Tom was watering his roses when Meryl brought the portable phone out to him.

'A man about Vietnam. The story you're doing. A Mr Tassie Watts.'

Tom took the phone. 'Hello, Tom Ahearn here.'

'Mr Ahearn, Clarence Watts here, from Hobart. Just call me Tassie. I'm ringing about the Long Tan bash. I hear you're doing another story about it.'

'Another one?' said Tom.

There was a hint of a chuckle down the phone line. 'Yeah, you did one of the first news stories about the battle, I believe. In fact, I think we met back then. You remember that Col Joye show?'

'I certainly do.' Tom sat down on a garden chair.

'Do you remember being kidnapped? You and Col?'

Tom burst out laughing. 'I certainly do, Tassie. You were the bloke who jumped us in the rain. Had Col singing for you and all your mates before we got out of Nui Dat.'

'The very one. I've seen you on TV, heard you on the radio over the years. My wife never believed I nabbed you and Col.'

'So what've you been doing with yourself? Did you stay in the army?' asked Tom.

'Strike me, no. I was glad to get home. Ran the family farm outside Launceston then bought a small pub. Retired now, grow a few apples. Got grandkids. The usual domestic disaster.' He laughed.

'You sound a happy man,' said Tom.

'Yeah, we did all right, my wife and me. Can't say the same for all the blokes who were there. Like Phil Donaldson.'

'Ah,' said Tom. So this was how Tassie had got in touch with him. 'Did Phil call you? That's excellent.'

'No. Patricia Donaldson rang me when the old fella wasn't around. Told me about your visit. She really wants him to go to the anniversary. He's been depressed for years and she thought a trip back would either fix him or stuff him completely. She sounded pretty keen.'

Well, good on you, Patricia, thought Tom. 'Yes, I thought so too. Don't think she has much sway in that partnership though.'

'She had the guts to ring me, hoping I could talk him round. I'm going to be at Long Tan of course.'

'So, have you spoken to Phil? He was pretty dead set against the whole idea.'

'No. I thought I'd pay him a visit as I'm coming to Sydney anyway. If that doesn't work I'll bring out the heavy artillery.'

'What? Threaten him or kidnap him?' asked Tom.

'No, I'll turn up on the doorstep with Maxie, the old chaplain. Don't know if you met him.'

'I remember him. He must be in his seventies at least.

271

Astonishing how it all seems like yesterday. I was just in Vung Tau. Bloody marvellous what some of those fellows are doing. Getting the vets to go back there, pay their respects, come to terms with things after all this time.'

'Yeah, I know Baz and Cranky. Their group has done some good work for the local folk in Phuoc Tuy too.'

'They told me after what had happened to the people, their villages, the countryside, they wanted to make some sort of restitution,' said Tom.

'Reckon it helps the blokes almost as much as the local people, that's for sure,' said Tassie. 'It's good to see something positive come out of all that mess. Yeah, most blokes I knew did their service and went on with their lives. But some old mates are still hiding nightmares.'

'I couldn't agree more. I reckon a human-interest piece on the big event would make a good read. Do you think you can convince Phil to go back?' said Tom. 'He's a very private man. Not very communicative.'

'Let's hope Maxie can sort him out,' said Tassie cheerfully.

'Phil's daughter is in Vietnam. Very bright, sensitive girl. Was working for an NGO. Maybe she has an idea,' said Tom.

'Yeah. I'll bet her old man can't have been too easy to get on with. Patricia's had to deal with it all her married life. You know they were just engaged when he was conscripted for national service?'

'So you'll let me know how the meeting with Maxie goes then? How are you going to handle that? Won't Phil baulk if Maxie turns up on the doorstep? And if you ring in advance he'll probably just go out.'

'Ah, we can probably hijack him, get him to some do. Leave that to us. We're pretty resourceful,' said Tassie.

'Yeah, I remember,' laughed Tom. 'Give me your number and we'll keep in touch.'

The invitation to *A Celebration of Early Vietnamese Ceramic History* arrived at Barney's addressed to Sandy, Anna and Carlo. It was on thick expensive paper, trimmed in red and gold, and listed a string of dignitaries who would be the honoured guests as well as an outline of the evening's proceedings. The dress was *Cocktail*.

'Sounds wanky,' said Carlo. 'You girls go.'

'One of us needs to be here,' said Sandy. 'Anna, you'll enjoy it: the museum is stunning. The building was a French boarding school for the daughters of the wealthy. Now it is used to display the contemporary and emerging arts as well as paying homage to the ancient and folk pieces. It'll be a lovely evening.'

'Right. Then I'll go. What will I wear?'

'We'll find something. Carlo, you should go – it'll be a great experience.'

'I have paperwork, meetings, a dinner with one of the partners in our new business venture,' he said importantly, making the invitation seem a frivolous non-event.

'Ask Rick to escort you. Or Charlie,' said Sandy, a little annoyed that Carlo was opting out of the event.

'No: I'll dress to kill and use a proper taxi,' said Anna, suddenly determined to make the most of the invitation. 'I'll make it short and sweet and be back by eight or so.'

'We'll have everything under control,' said Sandy, pleased Anna was going despite Carlo's indifference.

'I'll be like Cinderella and race home from the ball and do the dishes, I promise,' laughed Anna.

*

273

By late on Friday Anna still hadn't decided what to wear even though Sandy had offered to loan her a couple of dressy outfits.

Carlo was entertaining Mr Mai and another man at his favourite corner table at Barney's and the early evening rush had yet to start.

Sandy called from the bottom of the stairs to Anna. 'Come on, Anna. Aren't you ready yet? I've got the taxi organised.'

'All right. I'm coming down.'

Sandy paused. There was something about Anna's voice. She sounded nervous, which Sandy put down to going to a formal function on her own. She wished she'd asked Charlie or Rick to swing past and take Anna with them.

Carlo went to the bar to get drinks as the waiter on duty idly wiped a table. The waiter's hand stopped its circular motion as he looked towards the staircase.

Anna descended from Barney's flat, taking the narrow steps slowly. She was looking down so she didn't see the smile spreading across the waiter's face, Sandy's hands fly to her mouth or Carlo looking shocked.

Anna seemed to float. Gracefully she arrived at the bottom of the stairs and dropped her hands to her sides.

She was wearing the classical ao-dai she'd had made in Hoi An. The chocolate wide-legged silk pants were topped with the long cream silk tunic split above the waist revealing a glimpse of midriff skin. Her slender neck looked even more swan-like as she'd twisted her hair into a smooth chignon and secured it with an ornate lacquered chopstick pin. She held a small silk bag and her feet, in dark embroidered silk shoes, glittered at the hem of her pants. When she lifted her eyes, a slight smile hovering, Sandy noticed that Anna had accentuated her eye make-up, highlighting the slight slant of her big dark eyes.

274

'Anna! You look gorgeous,' breathed Sandy.

The waiter dropped his cloth and broke into applause.

Anna's eyes flicked to Carlo, whose face had darkened. He was clearly stunned.

'What the hell . . . Is it fancy dress?'

'No, it's dressy. This is a formal ao-dai.' But her bravado wavered slightly as she sought Sandy's eyes. 'Does it look okay?'

'Fabulous. You're dressed exactly right. Very appropriate. Come on – jump in the taxi; you don't want to miss a thing.' She bundled Anna past Carlo, noticing the approving glances from Carlo's two companions at the table.

'You mean that, don't you, Sandy? I still feel a little uncomfortable about it all.'

'Anna. I love you! Go and have fun. Say hi to Rick and Charlie. Tell them to keep the predators away from you. They'll be over you like flies. Fantastic!' She slammed the car door shut, elated with Anna's dramatic and gutsy effort. As the taxi pulled away Sandy grinned. Damn, I'd love to see how she goes, she thought. She turned and marched back into the restaurant, smiling broadly. 'What a star, eh, Carlo?' she said.

'Anna's not going to pass as one of them. What does she think she's doing?'

'Maybe she's taking a big step forward,' said Sandy. 'That was more than just a change of clothes. She's finding herself.'

'Crap,' said Carlo and carried the drinks to his table.

The elegant colonial mansion was floodlit and soft lights shone through the tall shuttered windows on three floors. It was set back from the road with a lush tropical garden in front. The driver told Anna the Asian-style

275

eaves on the roof and portico had been added after the French left.

She was greeted by a bowing attendant who took her invitation and ushered her inside where she was introduced and taken along the reception line of dignitaries. Waiters with trays of drinks hovered and guests were drifting around the gracious rooms and up the delicate spiral staircase. Discreet signs pointed guests to the various collections on the three floors.

Anna stood to one side, sipping her drink and admiring the setting and ambience while she decided where to start viewing the exhibits.

A voice at her side and a gentle touch on her elbow surprised her. 'Anna, I'm so glad you came. Wow! You look stunning.' Rick was smiling admiringly.

'Thank you,' said Anna shyly. 'I didn't expect to be coming to a function like this when I packed my bag,' she said. 'Sandy talked me into having this made in Hoi An; I'll probably never wear it at home.'

'You should,' Rick said. 'It not only looks fantastic on you; you have a right to wear the ao-dai. It's part of your heritage. Now, where would you like to start?' Still holding her elbow he led her across the beautiful old tiled foyer. 'Shall we work through the exhibits in chronological order? Starting with the kingdom of Champa, the Dong Son civilisation, the early Ly dynasty – that's eleventh and twelfth centuries – then the Mac, Tran, later Le and Tay Son dynasties – which brings us up to the eighteenth century.'

Anna laughed. 'Sounds like we'll be here for days.'

'It does take time to really see everything on every floor. But there's a special section on the second floor, which is what tonight is all about. Come on, let's get started.'

They made slow progress, stopping in front of displays for Rick to give a brief description, pausing to greet people, while Rick introduced Anna and she explained what she was doing in Hanoi. Anna spotted Charlie and Miss Huong and they melded into an appreciative group.

'It is a wonderful setting,' said Miss Huong. 'I love coming here, especially in the daytime. So airy and light.'

'Food's good too,' said Charlie, taking an hors d'oeuvre from a passing waiter's tray. 'How's that friend of yours with the interest in ceramics doing? Making any progress?'

'Yes, I think so. He's visited some area not far from Bat Trung, where there're new factories making the sorts of things he's after,' said Anna.

'Ah, yes. Well, no one makes anything like this anymore, do they?' commented Charlie with a sweeping gesture. 'No wonder there's a hungry market for collectors.'

'Perhaps it's better that old things be in a place like this, rather than in private collections,' suggested Anna delicately, knowing Charlie had been an avid collector.

'Most of the time, yes. This is the culture, heritage, history of the country. It should be on display for the people to learn about and admire. But in some cases the role of collectors has been to rescue and save artifacts that otherwise might have been destroyed.'

'Trouble is, they don't always want to give them back,' said Rick.

'Human nature. There will always be wealthy individuals, even corporations or museums and galleries, who wish to own something rare and old,' said Charlie. 'But private collectors are also patrons. They assemble collections initially out of passion, but which might end up being endowed to a university, gallery or museum. Even displayed in a hotel or corporation's offices. The collection often says a lot about the collector.'

'Which is why the eccentric collector intrigues me,' said Rick.

'Indeed. There are strange ones out there who do not wish to share their passion. The black hole into which missing artifacts can disappear. Shall we?' He took Miss Huong's arm. 'We shall continue our meander. See you for the speeches, no doubt.'

'Missing? Or stolen?' asked Anna as Charlie strolled away.

'Plundering temples, robbing graves, stealing from museums: it's always gone on. And still does,' said Rick. 'One of my fields is forgery, recognising the fakes. It's getting harder as technology helps the forgers. There are a lot of museums around the world that've paid for very expensive fakes.'

'So what do they do about it?'

Rick steered Anna onto the terrace above the portico overlooking the gardens and sat on a bench. 'It's not simple. You can't return an object to the forger who has sold it through reputable dealers or established a provenance for the piece. Sometimes a serious professional might authenticate something truly believing it to be genuine. Other times, well, money changes hands.'

A waiter refilled their glasses.

'What a strange world,' said Anna, 'but I must confess I find it rather intriguing.'

'It can sometimes sound like a movie – tomb raiders, hidden treasures in shipwrecks and digs, smugglers, a rich collector sending thieves on a mission to steal something they covet. And it can be as simple as a farmer turning up a sod and unearthing a huge treasure. And then it's a race between the archaeologists, the finders, the collectors, the dealers, the state . . . a free-for-all, whether there are rules or not.' Rick got up. 'Let's go downstairs, I'd like to hear what the heavies here have to say.'

Following the speeches, the announcement of a large donation from a museum benefactor and what Rick called the usual art-fart chat, people began to disperse, finishing the food and wine, or taking a more leisurely tour of inspection.

Charlie caught up with them. 'Miss Huong is gathering a group together for supper. Would you like to join us? Some interesting people for you to meet, Rick.'

'Sounds great. Anna?'

'Thanks, but no. I'd better get back to Barney's and help Sandy. It's been a really interesting evening. Thanks for the invitation, Rick. And thank you for your company, Miss Huong and Charlie.'

'My pleasure,' said Charlie. 'And by the way, you look transcendent. Just lovely. Wear that more often. Goodbye. See you about no doubt.'

'I'll see you to a taxi.' Rick walked with Anna to the portico. 'Anna, what Charlie said just now. You do look beautiful. You always do, but it's nice seeing you in traditional dress. Now you've taken this step, why not go further? Think about your family, eh?' He kissed her lightly on the cheek.

On the way back to Barney's Anna thought about what Rick had said. The idea of trying to find some family, some remote relatives, began to impose itself more forcefully than previously. But would she be opening a can of worms? Perhaps she could just find out exactly where her mother came from and quietly visit the area.

The taxi driver spoke to her in Vietnamese. She glanced at the meter and handed him money, understanding what he was saying and realising how her Vietnamese vocabulary was improving.

Carlo was hovering by the bar pouring drinks for a customer, his companions having left. 'So how was it? Did anyone ask you for a drink? Did they mistake you for staff,' he joked.

'It was very interesting. You should have been there: you might have learned something,' Anna retorted.

'Get that gear off and give Sandy a hand; she's going nuts out in the kitchen. Been a busy night. Thought you'd be back earlier,' he grumbled.

'I was busy time-travelling between the tenth and eighteenth centuries. Oh, never mind.' She hurried upstairs to change.

Much later, as she lay curled in bed, in a state of half sleep and half wakefulness, Anna dreamed of statues of serene Buddhas, many-armed bodhisattva gods, dragons and tigers, and heard the throb of massive Dong Son drums that shivered through her body. But she was shaken awake by the insistent nudging and nuzzling of Carlo.

'I was asleep.'

'I'm not. C'mon, cuddle me.'

'Carlo, I'm tired. I don't feel like it.'

'You're tired because you went to a party and now you don't have time for me.'

'I worked till after midnight, you may recall.'

'So who'd you see there?' Carlo rolled onto his back.

'At the party? A lot of people you don't know.' She yawned.

Carlo grunted. 'What'd they say about your getup?'

'Everybody thought I looked very nice. That I should wear it more often.'

'Not with me. Don't go getting any ideas about this Vietnamese stuff.'

'But I'm half Vietnamese! Maybe I can wear it in your shop to sell your frigging Vietnamese pots and water features,' she answered, and rolled on her side.

Carlo didn't answer, but he was thinking, finally muttering, 'That's not such a silly idea. Get some Vietnamese birds from Cabramatta, put them in slinky pyjamas, yeah, could be a bit of an attraction.'

'I was joking.'

'Yeah, me too,' said Carlo. But Anna knew he wasn't.

'Enjoy your break, Anna.' Sandy hugged her as Carlo fussed with the luggage for their trip away together.

'I feel bad, leaving you to manage without me. Are you sure?' Anna asked again.

'Bit late to change your mind: the bags are in the car; the driver is waiting. C'mon, Anna. Let's go. See ya, Sandy.' Carlo got in the car.

'Are you positive you'll be fine?' repeated Anna.

'I'm sure. Kim has offered to help in a pinch. All the staff are on standby in case we get busy. Ho has his sleeves rolled up. Listen, we'll miss you, but we'll cope. Enjoy Halong Bay. You and Carlo need time together.'

As they left the city behind, Anna relaxed and held Carlo's hand.

When they passed a wicker shop with furniture stacked outside, Carlo pointed. 'See, that stuff'd sell well at home.'

'You want furniture? Very good wood furniture here. Very cheap,' said the driver.

Carlo nudged Anna and said in a low voice, 'I tell you, there's so much stuff here. A couple of container loads and we'll make a killing. Easy.'

'Listen to what your partners say,' she advised.

'Hah. I know what I'm doing; I'm the businessman.'

The driver suggested they stop in Bat Trung for a coffee break. But Carlo refused to go to the popular handicrafts workshop where all the tour buses stopped for coffee. The government-run shop had good prices for all types of handicrafts from jewellery to linen, clothes, paintings and pottery, and visitors could see girls and women embroidering clothes and gifts.

'Tourist stuff,' said Carlo, to Anna's disappointment.

'Well, as we're in Bat Trung, come and visit Mr Thinh's pottery, as you didn't when you came here before. His place produces beautiful ceramics, both modern and traditional.'

Reluctantly Carlo followed Anna, who remembered the way to the little studio and factory.

Mr Thinh was delighted to see Anna again and with his limited grasp of English welcomed her and Carlo. He was clearly impressed with the interest both his visitors showed in his work and displayed with pride examples of the classic platters, bowls and dishes for which the area was famous.

'It's nice enough,' said Carlo. 'But it's niche market stuff. I'm after high-turnover goods.'

'You want niche, look at that beautiful platter. That's a rare one. Sixteenth century. There are a few around. I've seen two others like that,' said Anna.

'Since when have you been into stuff like that? How much is it worth?'

'What a collector wants to pay, I guess.' She pantomimed money and asked Mr Thinh how much.

He indicated it was not for sale, but then wrote a figure on a piece of paper and showed them.

'You're joking,' said Carlo.

'If someone wanted it, like a museum, I suppose that's what they'd have to pay.'

'So where did you and Sandy see the others like this?' demanded Carlo.

'In a ritzy antique shop in a hotel owned by a rich woman called Madame Nguyen. And . . . on an altar in a little pagoda where we met a nearly blind nun. We might go there.'

282

He grinned. 'Would she notice if it went missing?'

'Carlo!' exclaimed Anna.

It wasn't until Captain Chinh and his nephew Hung had them settled on the *Harvest Moon* that Carlo finally looked impressed. It was a sunny day, a cool breeze pushed the junk across the bay and as they came close to the limestone karsts jutting from the seabed, Carlo admitted, 'Bloody amazing. How'd you be, abseiling down one of those monsters?'

There was one other couple on the junk, from Sweden, on their honeymoon, who smiled and made it clear they too wished they were alone on this trip. They sat on the other side of the deck where Hung served them drinks and snacks. Anna remembered how she and Sandy had shared such a good time with Tom. Was it because they were all Australian? She half wished the old journo was with them now. He was good company and they'd had some great discussions. Carlo was happy just to drink, take in the scenery and try to send text messages on his mobile.

'There's no reception out here. Try when we stop for the night,' said Anna. 'Who are you trying to reach, anyway?'

'Business, baby.'

After Captain Chinh and Hung had anchored the junk close to some of the stark peaks punctuating the sea, they all ate dinner together on the deck under the stars, and the Swedish couple retired early. Anna, too, was tired and after telling Hung about the joys and challenges of running Barney's she decided to go to bed and read. She said good evening to Captain Chinh and Hung, and kissed Carlo.

'I won't mind if you wake me up when you come to bed,' she whispered.

'I might stay and drink up here for a bit. Very pleasant.' He raised his glass and Hung sprang forward.

'Don't drink too much: you might get seasick down below,' advised Anna.

As Carlo fell into bed she knew it was late and he'd had too much to drink.

'What kept you?' she asked.

'You were right – there was good mobile reception. But here I am, babe.'

He made eager love to her. Afterwards Anna turned on her side and slept soundly, lulled by the motion of the wooden boat and the gentle creaking of the hull.

Anna was up early and left Carlo snoring lightly. Only Hung was about. She greeted him warmly.

'So, how has business been for you and your uncle?'

'The tourist season here has been good. We lost some days with a typhoon,' answered Hung.

Anna sipped her coffee and, as no one else had appeared on deck, asked Hung, 'Do you go to Hoi An?'

'It's a pretty place. Untouched from war. Very lovely. You went there?'

'It was the first place my friend Sandy took me, after here.' Anna hesitated. 'I asked because I thought I saw you there. On a boat coming up the river.'

'I have been there for business. So, how are you enjoying Vietnam? You have been many places?'

Anna sensed he had shifted the conversation and seemed less friendly than when they'd been on the *Harvest Moon* before. 'A few. There's a lot still to see. I might have to come back next holidays. I want to show my friend Carlo where we went before. Can we do that? To the grotto and up to the pagoda, to see the blind nun?'

Hung shrugged. 'Last time, there were no other

284

tourists . . . now the Swedish pair, I don't think they will want to climb up.'

'So we'll let them stay on board. Be alone,' Anna said. 'They're on their honeymoon.'

They exchanged smiles. 'Of course. Going into the grotto, that is not something we do every time,' said Hung uneasily. 'But if your friend wishes to climb, the nun will be pleased to receive visitors.'

Now that she was so close, in this mystical bay with its strange formations, Anna felt an overwhelming desire to meet again the serene and wise old nun on the peak.

II

SANDY SAT AT BARNEY'S small desk and logged on to his computer to check her emails. She was pleased to see there was one from her mother. It had been a week or more since she'd heard from home. She skimmed through details of the weather, health and family until she reached the gist of it.

> *It was a lovely surprise to have a visit from your acquaintance Tom Ahearn and hear news of you first hand. He had a good chat with your dad and I was surprised – and a little nervous – at him talking about the war and this reunion, anniversary or whatever it is at Long Tan. You know how sensitive he is about the war. Tom is writing a story; in fact, did you know when Tom was a correspondent over there he thinks he actually interviewed Dad*

when he was in the hospital! Anyway, Dad listened but I don't think he's keen on the idea of having anything to do with it. I confess though, later I called one of the organisers – Tassie Watts – he was in Dad's unit. Your father got a letter from him about the reunion. I know he'd do nothing, so I did. Hope it's not interfering but from what I've heard it seems it would be good for him to get back in touch with his old mates. Share things, you know?

Wow, Mum, way to go, thought Sandy. Patricia was not usually the type to 'interfere'.

Then a few days later a lovely fellow called Father Max turns up. And would you believe it, Dad was thrilled to see him! Turns out he was the chaplain over there and helpful to Dad when he was in the hospital. So they talked and then Fr Maxie – as they call him – took him off to lunch at the pub. Apparently Maxie had planned it and there was Tassie and two other chaps from Vietnam, not sure if they were in Dad's group too, but anyway when Fr Maxie brought him home, they'd obviously had a good time! Dad hasn't talked about it to me much, of course, but said it was 'all right'. I went down to the shops and called Tassie the next day on his mobile and he said it had gone well and they were working on him. I hope that means getting Dad to go over there. I really think it would be so wonderful for him to go with his mates. So what do you make of all this, then?

What indeed, thought Sandy as she skimmed through the last bit of the email dealing with domestic trivia. What a train of events Tom had started. She didn't believe her father would make a trip to Vietnam, but at least it seemed he was talking about the war. She'd never known him to go out for a beer with his mates from those days.

Anzac Day was just a public holiday, a day to stay at home or work in the car yard. Sandy sent a quick email to her mother saying she thought it all sounded great and to keep her in the loop.

It was a torpid, still mid morning. The street was quiet. Ho had gone to the markets for some last-minute fresh items for the lunch menu. There was only an elderly man with coffee and cake reading his newspaper in the cafe.

Sandy took a coffee outside to sit in the sun and think about all this news. The idea of her father coming to Vietnam, with his hatred of the war, was hard to adjust to. And the thought that she might have to accompany him to the reunion made her uncomfortable. And she thought he'd feel the same.

But then she started thinking about her dad visiting Saigon. She began to think of nice places in the city to take him. She didn't know if he'd ever been there. If he was at Long Tan he must have known Vung Tau. Did he have any pleasant memories of Vietnam at all? She suspected he wouldn't want to come to Hanoi, which was a shame as she loved this city. But the north had been identified as enemy territory so it might be hard for him to cope with that. God, the idea of taking her father around today's sophisticated Saigon would be an eye-opener for him.

She felt a stir of pleasure – this could be a chance for her to get close to him, share things, talk about, well, whatever. She had no illusions of him talking about his war experiences or the two of them madly bonding like they'd been to some therapy group. But it would certainly be a change. And this Tassie Watts sounded like he knew what he was doing. Sending the chaplain to see Dad. Good one.

A car pulled up outside and the occupants emerged, walking purposefully into the cafe. The two men wore outfits of deep olive green and dark glasses. Sandy assumed their outfits were uniforms, but none that she recognised. They had sophisticated communication gear hanging off leather belts and wore solid boots. There was some sort of logo on their shirt pockets. The cloth badge had a rearing tiger and some initials around it that meant nothing to her, and their peaked hats looked a cross between those of the police and the military. They took the table nearest the kitchen door.

Sandy approached them, smiled and asked in English if they wanted to see the menu.

'Coffee.' They sat on the edge of their chairs, not taking off their sunglasses or hats.

Sandy asked if they wanted local or American and then went in the kitchen where the waitress was working. She put the small cups with condensed milk in the bottom ready for the thick local coffee in its small drip percolator and wondered who the two men were.

One of them was now standing at the doorway looking into the street. The other glared at the elderly customer, who got up and left. Sandy asked the man at the table if they wanted something to eat.

He shrugged. 'We no come for food. We come for payment.'

Sandy looked at him blankly. 'Payment? What for?'

'Security. Monthly security. Mr Barney pay every month.'

'Oh. Of course.' The protection pay-off or whatever Barney paid these goons for. 'I thought Barney said he'd paid. He's away, you know.' She continued to speak in English as she tried to remember what Barney had told her. The seated man called to his partner in Vietnamese, 'The owner is away. We can double the price for this girl.'

The other man strolled back and sat at the table,

giving Sandy a demanding look. 'You bring money. Then coffee.'

Sandy went to Barney's small alcove office where he'd put the money for these payments. A pile of dong secured by a rubber band was in a plain envelope. She went back to the table, annoyed that her knees were starting to shake and wishing Ho was back. She put the envelope in the middle of the table.

'I'll get the coffee.' She returned and put the two coffees on the table.

The envelope had gone. The first man spoke with some anger. 'That not correct money.'

'That's what Mr Barney paid,' she said firmly.

He shook his head. 'Price go up. Security more expensive now.'

Sandy heard the scrape of a chair as someone sat at an outside table. 'I'm sorry. I don't have any more money. This is not my business. I have given you everything Mr Barney said to hand over.'

One of the men lifted the coffee drip off his cup and began stirring the thick coffee. 'Some American dollars then.'

'No. I don't have American dollars.' She heard someone come into the cafe behind her. Another customer, thought Sandy with relief.

The top man leaned forward and snarled in a low voice, 'You get American dollars. We come back.'

Sandy knew they were taking advantage of her and if she didn't make a stand they would keep harassing her. Moreover, she didn't want to set a precedent that would mean Barney had to keep paying. More boldly than she felt, she said, 'Can I see your identification? What is your company?'

One of the men rose out of his chair. 'You no ask questions.' He glanced behind Sandy and sat back down.

Sandy turned around to deal with the customer.

Jean-Claude was holding a menu. 'Bonjour, mademoiselle. I would like something to eat.' He raised a questioning eyebrow.

Sandy smiled, guiding him to a table by the entrance. 'Of course, let me tell you what we have on special today.'

'Is everything all right?' whispered Jean-Claude. 'What do those men want?'

'Money. They're standover merchants. Let me deal with it.' She raised her voice and rattled through any dishes she could think of.

He ordered fried spring rolls and lotus tea and pretended to gaze into the street, ignoring the two men.

As Sandy passed their table to go into the kitchen, one of the men grasped her wrist. 'You do as we say or we make trouble for this place.'

Sandy snatched back her arm and spoke loudly in Vietnamese. 'No. There won't be trouble. If you are security, you are supposed to look after Mr Barney. He has been good to you and he has paid you.' She enunciated the last phrase emphatically and strode into the kitchen. Shaking, she grabbed her mobile and rang Jean-Claude. 'What're they doing? Who should I call?'

He chuckled. 'They're leaving. Didn't like the coffee, I guess.'

Sandy joined him as the car with the men sped away.

Jean-Claude kissed her on each cheek. 'I'm impressed. Very bold of you to call their bluff. Did you give them any money?'

'Just the regular payment that Barney told me to. They thought they could double the price and con US dollars out of me.' She sat down. 'That was scary.'

'You didn't look the least bit scared. Their faces were shocked when you rattled off all that Vietnamese. But still, you might want to keep an eye about in case they cause trouble.'

'Oh, great. And just when Anna and Carlo are away too.' Ho poked his head out from the kitchen, letting her know he was back. 'Did you really want spring rolls?'

'No. But I will take the tea.'

'What are you doing in Hanoi?' asked Sandy after she ordered tea and a strong coffee for herself. 'How were Laos and Cambodia?'

'Interesting. I've been investigating the status of the mangrove wetlands. During the 1990s, the investors from Thailand financed a black tiger shrimp aquaculture operation that devastated the mangroves. The giant ibis, among other wildlife, has almost disappeared. It's an example of poor farming practices we don't want to see repeated in Vietnam. So now I am moving to Hanoi for a while. I have a lot to do here in the north and I have to work with government officials – and that, as you know, takes time. But of course I will still have to travel down the coast. What are you up to? Where's Anna?'

'She's gone to Halong Bay with her boyfriend. Of course, you don't know about Carlo! When we got back from Hue he was waiting for us in my flat. They've both been helping in the cafe. Anna loved Halong and thought Carlo might chill out and like it. But I'm doubtful.'

'How could you not like such a magical place?' said Jean-Claude.

'Carlo's more into business than sightseeing,' said Sandy.

They settled themselves at a table and Sandy filled Jean-Claude in on Carlo's surprise visit and his plans to export landscaping items to Sydney. The waitress put the tea and coffee down and gave Sandy a big smile. She had told Ho about Sandy and the standover men.

'Jardinières. That could work, provided he has a good manager this end. What are Anna's plans?'

Sandy looked thoughtful for a moment. 'Go back to her public service job. I don't think marriage is an immediate option. I hope not.' She smiled. 'You should have seen her the other night: she went to a function and wore an ao-dai. She looked stunning. Carlo was furious.'

'That she looked beautiful? A jealous man is an insecure man.'

'No, I think it was her flaunting her Vietnamese heritage. And he is probably insecure here,' said Sandy. 'He just hates to lose control.'

'Anna seems very compliant,' said Jean-Claude. From what Sandy had told him, Anna's boyfriend sounded a bit of an ass, but then, there was no accounting for the men some women chose to love. 'Whereas you!' He grinned. 'Chasing off the standover dogs. They went out of here with tails between their legs.'

'Do you think so? I'm worried they'll be back with reinforcements or something.'

Jean-Claude touched her arm. 'Don't be. They're young and full of bravado. They'll try it on other establishments on their beat. They're probably grateful there weren't other people in here to see them lose face. You aggressive western woman, you.'

They laughed, and Sandy relaxed and told Jean-Claude about the email from her mother.

'It would be good if your father came here,' said Jean-Claude. 'For you and for him.'

'Don't think it's going to happen. Anyway, we'll see.'

'I came over this morning to ask if you would come to dinner with me this evening. Or tomorrow, before I leave for the south.'

'I'd love to,' said Sandy. 'But I'll have to check with Ho. With Anna away I don't want to leave him understaffed.'

'We could make it a late supper, after the kitchen has slowed down. Say around ten?'

'How very European. Where did you have in mind? Not a lot of places stay open so late,' said Sandy.

'I could cook for you. A cassoulet, some good bread, a nice wine.'

Sandy was curious about the place Jean-Claude had just rented. 'Sounds wonderful. Give me the address and I'll come over.'

'I also have tickets to a concert at the Opera House. But perhaps we can leave that for another time.'

'That would be fantastic. You can't spend time in Hanoi and not go into that great building,' said Sandy.

Jean-Claude's apartment was in a complex that had been built in the style of the French-colonial era. A security gate in the wrought-iron fence opened onto a small tiled courtyard with topiary trees in brass pots on either side of the entrance. Sandy pushed the buzzer for apartment five and Jean-Claude's warm friendly voice gave her instructions about how to get into the lobby and then into a quaint iron-cage lift that swayed slowly upwards.

He opened the lift door and welcomed her with a kiss. 'The elevator isn't speedy, but in keeping with the ambiance. This is rather a new building. It's heartening that there weren't too many hard feelings towards French architecture.'

'It's just lovely,' said Sandy, taking in the understated but expensive elegance as she followed him down a carpeted hallway lit by two small, tasteful chandeliers.

As Jean-Claude flung open the door to number five, Sandy couldn't help stifle a gasp. 'This is gorgeous. Are they all like this?' She glanced around at the all-white, airy living room, scattered with antique rugs, dark-blue sofas and a deep armchair covered in a rose chintz pattern. It was an open-plan apartment with the dining area to one side and a long granite bench top dividing off the modern kitchen. A hall led around a corner to the other rooms.

'It's not huge by western standards but you know what apartment buildings are like in Hanoi: long and narrow. Interestingly, the builder–designer is from Hanoi and he lives in number three. Has the best view, of course. But I have a glimpse of the lake out there. Now, how about a glass of wine?'

'The builder is Vietnamese? Who else lives in this building?' Sandy was staring at the walls, which were hung with an eclectic collection of paintings, and she noticed a lot of sculptures standing about on shelves and on the coffee table.

'Mostly Vietnamese, but there is an attaché from the French embassy and an American couple. Some apartments are owned by companies. I assume most of my neighbours work for corporations or high-end companies. There's an intriguing woman downstairs, although she isn't here often. I think you've met her. Madame Nguyen, from Hoi An.'

'She gets around! What do you think of her?'

They settled on the lounge in front of the bay window, which looked over the city.

'She's smart, obviously, because she's rich and successful. She's into construction, got silk shops and dabbles in antiques. I saw a particular piece in a gallery and when I wanted to negotiate, she turned out to be the dealer.'

'Did you get it?' Sandy glanced around at the many pieces of art.

'Mais, non. She was too tough for me. But you, you're interested in ceramics? Why aren't you working in that field?' Jean-Claude asked bluntly.

Sandy settled into the scattered silk cushions, reached for her glass of wine and took a sip before answering.

'I didn't want to be stuck indoors, cataloguing, doing dry stuff. At home the museum and gallery scene can be pretty suffocating. Petty and corrosive. Lots of infighting and having to suck up to potential donors and so on.' She shook her head. 'Not for me. I wanted to travel.' She paused. 'You're a bit of a collector,' she continued, waving an arm around the room.

'Oh, I'm only an amateur. And not all of this is mine. Some of it comes with the apartment. But you can't live here and not be interested. There's so much visual culture in your face all the time.'

'Do you know Rick Dale? He's a nice guy. Works as an art buyer for a New York gallery. He's the one who invited Anna to the Fine Arts Museum,' said Sandy.

'In her ao-dai. I would have appreciated that,' said Jean-Claude. 'I'd better see to the food. I hope you're hungry.'

'I should be, it's late enough,' said Sandy cheerfully.

He laughed. 'You Australians, you're so up front. In French society people play such games. In France you ask someone if they want something to eat or drink and they say no, thank you. So you ask again. No, no, I am fine, thank you. So you persist, please, do try, do have a little something. And they reluctantly say, well, if you insist, when they wanted it all along. Australians, when they ask if you want something and you say, no, thanks, that's it – they don't offer again.'

'We don't play the game,' laughed Sandy.

'At least you know where you stand. Come to the table. If you like, the guest bathroom is down there.'

Sandy washed her hands and peeped into the large bedroom, which looked rather masculine, and a small study that must have been the second bedroom. One wall was lined with crammed bookshelves. For a seafood man, Jean-Claude seemed very cultured.

They sat at the dining table and over dinner talked of

many things. She learned about his family, what a matriarch his mother was and how she had taught Jean-Claude so much about the finer things in life.

'My parents came from well-to-do families. My grandfather did well in Vietnam, although it was difficult for my mother when her parents lost everything and had to start over again back in France. She dislikes my being here trying to help farmers.'

'We have that in common,' said Sandy. 'My father hasn't ever said it directly to me, but he resents my being here too. Sees it as helping his old foe, I s'pose. I hope I don't ever get into such a closed mindset and refuse to be flexible and move on.'

'That's something the Vietnamese have taught me,' said Jean-Claude softly. 'Not to hold grudges. Let's have a nightcap.'

She helped him clear the table and they settled back on the sofa. He put some of his favourite CDs into the machine and they talked quietly, lapsing into companionable silences occasionally. Sandy told him about Carlo and Anna and her disquiet about Carlo being the right man for Anna. As he hadn't met him, Jean-Claude made no comment but listened carefully to all she had to say. Sandy felt at ease and comfortable with him. His arm was along the back of the sofa and she leaned against him. His soft voice with its seductive accent was like honey, soothing and mellow. She finally uncurled her legs.

'I must go: it's late. I have to be at the cafe early in the morning.'

His arm dropped onto her shoulders and hugged her tighter. 'If you must.' He nuzzled her ear. 'It's been a delightful evening.'

'It has been for me too,' said Sandy, turning to him as he lowered his head and kissed her gently. It was a tender kiss, not forceful, not demanding. They drew apart in the soft light from the corner lamp and she saw his slight smile and questioning eyes. She leaned forward and kissed him and this time his mouth was seeking and more urgent. She kissed him again and he wrapped his arms around her, pulling her to him.

It felt natural and exciting. The thrill of passion shivered through her and she did not resist when he led her to the bedroom. She lost track of time as they explored each other, whispered, and surrendered to the sensations of abandonment in their love-making.

Afterwards he held her tightly and stroked her hair. 'Spun gold, it's like sunshine on my pillow.'

Sandy glanced out at the lightening sky. 'Daylight – I'd better leave.' She slipped out of bed.

'Stay. I will take you back early. Sleep a little while; I'll wake you with coffee.'

Sandy pulled on her clothes. 'No, no. Go to sleep. There's bound to be a fellow sleeping in his cyclo outside. I'll be fine.'

She couldn't explain it to him, but she did not want to stay. It felt too much of a commitment. She'd been down that track before. Giving herself over to falling in love. And the problem had always been that it was someone on the move, from another part of the world. A brief crossing of paths, different cultures, backgrounds and heritage. Both finding themselves for the moment in the same place, coming together, and deep down knowing it was just for now and not forever.

She wondered what it would be like to have a love affair based solely on sex, eating and existing from day to day – the basic things, finding food, shelter, warmth – without being able to communicate. That would simplify matters and strip things down to the essentials. And do away with the complications that arose from miscommunication, unfulfilled expectations, or the lack of commonality.

But then she thought back over the evening, how easy it had been talking with Jean-Claude, the comfortable, easy environment, the awareness that here was a man used to the better things in life and yet who was equally at home in the rougher, rural parts of the country.

Somehow she'd associated Jean-Claude's family connection with the seafood industry as being a bit coarse – rough fishermen, smelly boats and tough characters, not above acting dangerously or provocatively to achieve their ends. But he wasn't like that at all. He appreciated culture. He was a citizen of the world.

Now dressed and anxious to leave, she leaned over the bed where Jean-Claude was drifting off to sleep and kissed him lightly. 'It's been lovely. Thank you.'

He jerked to wakefulness and flung back the covers. 'Merde. Sorry. I was falling asleep. Wait, I'll drive you.'

She gently pushed him back down on the bed. 'No, no. If I can't find a cyclo or a taxi, I'll call you to come down and drive me.'

'You're sure? Sandy, I'll telephone you tomorrow.'

'It's all right, Jean-Claude,' said Sandy. She blew him a kiss. 'Go back to sleep.'

She shut the apartment door and pushed the button for the wrought-iron cage. As it rattled to the ground floor for a moment she hoped Jean-Claude might have thrown his pants on, run down the stairwell and be there at the ground floor to fling open the lift door and sweep her into his arms and insist she return to his bed.

Instead she found the foyer empty. Once the lobby doors hummed shut behind her she had no way of re-entering unless she buzzed Jean-Claude's apartment. She went out into the quiet street, the only light a buzzing neon sign on a nearby building. She glanced up at the sky, comforted by the first streaks of pale sunrise.

Along the street there was a cyclo, its driver curled on

the seat under the canopy, a plastic sheet flung over him. Sandy knew that he had a change of clothes and a few simple possessions tucked under the seat that was his home. Gently she shook the handle bars and in Vietnamese asked if he was working and could take her across the city.

Sleepily the driver flung back the cover, rubbed his eyes and began haggling over the fare. Sandy laughed and against her normal practice agreed to his outlandish price. He pedalled slowly through the near-empty streets. Sandy marvelled at the difference riding through the sleeping city was compared to the hustle and bustle of the day. The metal doors of most shops were locked and bolted. People slept in many of the doorways or in their cyclos. An occasional bar sign flashed, and here and there, a pedlar fanned a small brazier getting ready for a new day. The high-rise hotels and bigger shops had lights glowing but little movement. When they reached Sandy's block all was dark save for a single light above the gate across the alley. She asked the cyclo driver to wait until she had unlocked the gate, then thrust the required dong into his hands.

The stairs to her apartment were dark but, after feeling her way up the twists and turns she knew so well, Sandy arrived at her door, key in hand, and was swiftly inside. How small and shabby her apartment seemed compared to Jean-Claude's, but then she was living as most of the locals did and not in some mock-French extravaganza.

As she fell into bed the phone rang.

'I just wanted to make sure you were safely home,' said Jean-Claude.

'Thanks for thinking. And it was a lovely evening.'

'Sweet dreams, chérie.'

'G'night, Jean-Claude.' She hung up, glancing at the clock to make sure the alarm was set to wake her in time for work.

*

Hung paddled Anna and Carlo into the luminous grotto at the base of the karst.

'See, Carlo, isn't it amazing?'

'Yeah. Weird. Is this a kind of smuggler's cave, eh?' he said to Hung.

Hung laughed. 'Maybe. Good hiding place for a boat. There are many such places in Halong. Special places. This one my favourite place. Only show special people.'

'Bet he says that to everyone that comes on their boat,' said Carlo. 'What else is there to see?'

'We can climb to the top of the peak,' said Anna. 'It's beautiful, but best is the little pagoda with the old nun. I so want to see her again. She's nearly blind and lives there alone. I just felt some sort of connection with her.'

'I'm not climbing a mountain to see some blind nun who probably doesn't speak English. Any fish in here?' he asked Hung.

Anna was disappointed. 'You don't have to talk to her; just come up and look at the view.'

'It's only more of the same, just higher up. I'll hang with Hung and the others.' He grinned at the captain's nephew.

'Maybe Carlo would like to see your village while I'm at the pagoda,' suggested Anna.

'Sounds good. Okay, Hung?'

Hung guided Anna onto the path that led to the peak. 'You do not want me to translate for you?'

'I'll practise my French,' answered Anna. 'She speaks a little English. We'll manage.' She just wanted to be in the company of the serene nun again; indeed, she felt a sense of urgency and the need to see her. The image of the little nun and the feelings she'd aroused had popped into Anna's mind several times since they'd first met.

The climb was steeper than Anna had recalled,

maybe because this time she didn't stop to admire the view but pushed continuously upwards. When she reached the path to the pagoda, silhouetted against the bright blue sky, she stopped to catch her breath. There didn't appear to be anyone else up here, so she walked around the pagoda calling out.

The room where the nun lived was empty, though Anna could smell freshly baked bread. The vegetable patch was well tended and watered, and the fruit trees were flourishing. It really is a mini paradise, thought Anna. Far below, the bay glittered and tourist boats were dotted around the mysterious peaks that shot from the sea.

Anna walked around the garden to the edge of the cleared land where a bamboo fence held back the untamed trees and undergrowth that spilled down the hillside. On the other side was sheer, bare rockface. She continued across the clearing to the pagoda and slipped off her shoes and stepped inside. It was cool and tranquil. As she walked to the altar the figure of the tiny nun came to the front.

'Hello. Bonjour encore,' said Anna. 'I'm Anna. I was here a few weeks ago with my friend Sandy and Hung. You gave me a little green Buddha.'

The nun broke into a smile and nodded. 'You come back again. Good, good. Your friend, she speak Vietnamese, she here?'

'No, just me.' Anna reached out and took the nun's hands in hers.

The nun lightly touched her face, reminding herself who Anna was by touch and the sound of her voice. 'You are well? Happy?'

Anna nodded. 'I am happy to see you again. How are you?'

The nun gave a gallic shrug. 'Comme ci, comme ça.

Visitors are coming. It is good for my English, oui?' She smiled. 'Before, not so many. Many days I am here alone.'

'You're becoming famous,' said Anna, thinking the little nun probably preferred her solitude before the tourists started coming.

The nun handed her a bundle of incense sticks. 'You make prayers and then we sit.' She walked slowly away, the swish of her cotton garment like a small sigh.

Anna lit the fragrant sticks and bowed her head. She didn't make specific prayers for herself or anyone else, but merely stood, letting thoughts come and go, allowing the peace and the sensations of this special place to wash over her.

She went outside. The sun was bright, blinding her for a moment.

'Miss Anna. I am here,' called the nun.

Anna went to the seat beneath the tree that over-looked the vista of the bay, its karsts of rocks partially dressed in green shawls of foliage. In the distance she could see the tender from the *Harvest Moon* speeding towards Hung's village. She sat beside the nun.

The nun lifted an arm and pointed across the huge bay that opened into the South China Sea. 'Long way to your home. You go home?'

'Yes. Too soon. I would like to explore a lot more of Vietnam,' said Anna.

'There are many things to find in our country. Some time, you find these things inside.' She tapped her heart. 'No this way.' The nun tapped her eyes and her head. 'Answers are always in here.' She smiled as she leaned over and touched Anna's heart.

'Mmm, I have many questions to think about I sup-pose,' said Anna slowly. Carlo, her work, her future, her family: all jostled for attention in her mind. Anna reached down, picked up the little cloth bag she'd brought with

303

her, pulled out a parcel and handed it to the nun. 'A small gift. I didn't know what to bring you.'

The nun clasped her hands together in a gesture of thanks and delight. She lifted the package to her face and inhaled, her face breaking into a smile. 'Ooh, les fleurs.'

'It's lavender soap,' said Anna shyly. She had also brought some chocolate and fruit with her but thought feminine luxuries would be a rarity for the nun who lived so simply.

The nun opened the package and caressed the cake of soap. 'Merci.'

They continued to sit in the sun in silence for a few more moments. Then the nun took Anna's hand and, looking across the bay, she said, 'We meditate now. You know?'

Anna nodded. She had done some yoga classes and knew a little about relaxing meditation but was unsure what the Buddhist nun expected of her. So she shut her eyes and lifted her face to the sun filtering down through the branches. This time there wasn't the confusion of rushing thoughts and feelings. She felt very calm, detached almost, as if watching a movie.

She saw lush green rice paddies where a water buffalo slowly trudged, she saw a rubber plantation, coconut trees, a strip of empty beach, thatched roofs of a village, neat white buildings lining a dusty road, people eating, an old woman with a bamboo pole and baskets weaving between the bicycles and motor scooters. She saw two little girls dressed for school, one holding the hand of an older brother and the other holding the hand of the little brother. An old lady waved to them, watching them leave the gate of their white house. It was a scene of everyday living in a peaceful rural town.

Why did she feel she had seen this place, knew those children? Anna wanted to follow them. Her conscious mind was telling her it was a scene glimpsed in her travels with Sandy, while her subconscious was telling her it was something more.

She had lost all sense of the time she'd sat there beside the nun, but slowly Anna's eyelids fluttered open and she drew a long breath as she refocused on the scene before her. She turned and the nun took her hand.

'You saw your home?'

Anna shook her head. 'It wasn't Australia, but it seemed familiar. Maybe some place I've seen since I've been here. Why would that come to my mind, I wonder?'

The nun shook her head. 'You have not been to this place. But you must go. You know where is this place?'

Anna shook her head. 'It was very green, pretty houses . . . '

'You know the home of your mother?' asked the nun.

'My mother?' Anna stared at her. 'No, I don't know where she came from. You think . . . you think I imagined her village? But I know nothing about it. She never talked to me about where she grew up. How would I know what her home was like, where it was?' Anna felt her voice rise.

The nun merely nodded and pointed at her heart. 'In there knows the place of your mother. You must find this place. Is it not why you come to this country?'

'No, not at all! I don't even know where she's from.'

The nun folded her hands calmly in her lap and said simply, 'Now it is time. You must go there.' She turned to Anna. 'You have no memento, nothing of your mother?'

Anna's hand went to her throat, to the fine gold chain around her neck. 'I have this,' she whispered, and pulled out the chain with the small gold crucifix hanging from it. She leaned forward and showed it to the nun.

The nun touched the little cross. 'Who did it belong to?'

Anna felt close to tears. She felt ashamed, like a chastised child. 'It belonged to my mother who brought it

305

from Vietnam when she escaped with her younger brother who died on the journey. That's all I know. I'm so sorry. I wish I knew.' A tear fell from her eyes.

The nun patted her hand. 'You will know, soon enough. You must make this journey.'

The nun rose and took Anna's arm as they made their way back to the pagoda and went inside. She nudged Anna forward. 'Buddha is listening. Go, make prayers for your family. The family of your mother. It is what has brought you here.'

When Anna left the pagoda, the nun was waiting. Anna impulsively took her hand and kissed it.

'Thank you. I will somehow let you know what happens. I will come and visit you again.'

The nun smiled. 'I will know. From my seat over there I can see very far.'

Anna nodded and set off down the path, understanding what the nun meant about seeing. Despite her near blindness she had inner sight, a knowingness. And for a moment or two she had shared it with Anna. And now Anna knew there was no turning back. She had a promise to keep, to herself, to the nun – and to her mother.

Captain Chinh spotted her at the small strip of rocky beach at the bottom of the peak and paddled over in his canoe to take her back to the *Harvest Moon*. Carlo and Hung were still at the stilt village. The other couple had not wanted to go and were 'resting', he told her, grinning.

Anna was glad Carlo was away with Hung. She stretched out in a deck chair to think through the emotions churning inside her. Was this the reason she'd felt the pull to come back here? To see the little nun? It hadn't been in her mind to find her mother's family, if any were left, or the place she came from. Or had it been buried so deep in her subconscious that she'd blocked it out? But now it was out in the open, and curiosity began to nibble at her.

There was no reason why she shouldn't try to find out where her family had come from, as Tom, Sandy and Rick had suggested. She wondered at her reluctance. She wasn't ashamed of being half Vietnamese and as far as she knew there wasn't any stigma attached to her mother's story other than that the escape on the boat had been a terrible experience and, of course, little uncle had died.

Anna needed to talk to her father. Had he been waiting for this call ever since she arrived here? She felt a rush of love for her dad, always cheerful, generous and good hearted. How hard it must have been for him, raising her after losing his wife. Her grandmother and dear Uncle Quoc and Aunty had been a tower of strength to them both. But she'd never realised how lonely Kevin must have been and how loyal he'd remained to Thu's memory.

Growing up there'd never been a hint of another woman. It was Anna as a teenager who'd encouraged Kevin to 'date'. He'd had a few lady friends at the club, played golf with another, but that had been it. He'd never pushed her to embrace her mother's heritage, other than when as a little girl it had happened naturally in their blended family.

He talked in general about Thu but he made it clear that when Anna decided, he'd share whatever she wanted to know. Mentally Anna had put her mother in a box marked 'Private' and had tucked it away. Suddenly she felt she owed her dad.

First she'd talk to her father and then to Sandy. This had been a momentous morning, but she knew she wasn't going to tell Carlo. She didn't know how to explain what had happened to bring about this urge to embark on a family quest. But did she want Carlo to ridicule or sabotage the idea. Already she was making plans. Once they'd finished at Barney's she'd enlist Sandy's help to travel to wherever it was in Vietnam that her mother had left when she'd fled all those years ago.

Anna was sleeping in a deck chair when Carlo and Hung returned to the junk.

'How about a beer, Hung?' said Carlo. 'Celebrate a good morning.'

Anna opened her eyes. 'You're back. How was it?'

'Terrific. Interesting,' said Carlo.

'Really?' Anna sat up, surprised at his enthusiasm, as Hung handed Carlo a beer and gestured to Anna. She shook her head. 'No, thanks.' She lay back and closed her eyes. After a moment she said, 'My morning was good too. Really special.'

'Great,' said Carlo with little interest. He reached for his small backpack. 'Brought you a present.'

'Oh, how sweet of you, Carlo.'

'Well, it's only something of interest, not a proper gift,' he added, handing Anna a chipped blue-and-white plate.

Anna looked at the pattern and turned it over, trying to make out the markings on the back. 'Is it real? I mean this looks like one of those that were at the potter's. And in the antique shop at The Royal. Where did it come from?'

'That's what I'd like to know. I just bought it from a little girl in the village selling shells.'

Hung joined them. 'You are interested in such things?'

'Not really. Anna and Sandy are into antiques. It looks kinda old. I'm a businessman,' said Carlo.

'The plate is no good: it is broken,' said Hung.

'Yeah. Though it's amazing that these so-called hard-to-find old dishes are floating around. Anna says people pay big bucks for this kind of stuff.'

308

'Only in mint condition,' said Hung. 'This one no good. Throw it away.'

'I can't throw it away; it's a gift,' said Anna.

Carlo glanced at Hung. 'You know about antiques?'

'What sort of business do you do?' Hung asked Carlo.

'Import–export. I'm looking to export ceramics, those big garden pots and anything else of interest that will turn over some dollars.'

'The ones made in Bat Trung and at the factories further out?'

'Yeah. You know about them?'

Hung nodded. 'Yes, but antique porcelain get more money than garden pots.'

'For sure. But finding rare plates isn't so easy. Unless you know a source?'

Anna stared at Hung. 'Do you think there are more of these plates somewhere?'

Hung shrugged. 'There are fakes around, but they are easy to pick. I hear people talk. There are stories.' He waited as Carlo sat listening, giving the young Vietnamese man a steady look.

'How would you sell them, if you came across a cache of old blue-and-white plates? Like this, but in mint condition?' Carlo held up the broken plate. 'I mean, really old, not made twenty years ago.'

'Carlo, you don't know anything about antiques,' interrupted Anna.

'Listen, I'm in sales. There's a market for everything.'

'Of course there's a market for antiques. But you have to know people. The right people, surely,' said Anna. 'What do you think, Hung?'

Hung lifted his shoulders. 'I'm just a boat boy. I would find a dealer. Someone who makes a business of selling things. Not in a shop. But to special people,' he said casually.

'You mean private collectors?' said Anna.

'That's right,' Carlo jumped in. 'You'd have to find someone who's not going to rip you off. As the supplier you end up being the bottom of the food chain. Maybe I should look into this, eh? What do you think, Hung? Could you help me find a source of these old things?'

'Ah, then I would be the bottom of the food chain,' smiled Hung.

'It's gotta start somewhere,' said Carlo smugly. 'If you had a stack of these things, you could walk into a gallery or an antiques shop and sell them for a tenth of what they're worth. Or, you can set yourself up in business, but you have to be an expert to know what's what, plus you have to have credibility, prove where you got them – expensive. Better to move merchandise quickly, take the money and run. Move on to something else.'

'Carlo, you're not selling cars or biscuits,' said Anna.

'Baby, don't tell me how to do business,' said Carlo.

'You could give them away to a museum,' said Hung innocently.

'Would you?' asked Carlo.

Hung laughed. 'No.'

'Rick told me this country was trading ceramics way, way back. I told you that you should have come to the show at the Fine Arts Museum,' said Anna to Carlo. 'So it's natural there'd be plates like this still around.'

'They do not make them like this anymore. They are rare and worth a lot of money,' said Hung. 'If you could buy a small shipment and send them to Australia, you would do very well, eh?'

Carlo eyed him. 'Like what? How many?'

Anna looked from one to the other. There was a match between them, unspoken information being batted back and forth. 'What are you saying, Hung? Do you know where there are more of these? In good condition?' asked Anna bluntly.

'There could be pieces available. But it is business between us. Not to be spoken about with others,' said Hung.

'Carlo . . .' began Anna.

Carlo hadn't broken the look he held with Hung. 'Hey, business between men. How many pieces?'

'Maybe two dozen. Plates, bowls and a few dragon jugs. All good quality. Very old. Worth many, many thousands of US dollars.'

Anna gasped. 'So much money! Where are they from? Are they stolen? Carlo, you don't want to get mixed up in anything . . . illegal,' said Anna.

Hung shook his head. 'Not stolen. Been in the sea. Shipwreck. A big old junk off here.' He pointed out to sea. 'Maybe five, six hundred years ago.'

Carlo took a sharp breath. 'Shit. Really? Who knows about it? Where is it? I'd have to raise a lot of money. What's the wholesale price? And who's involved?' he asked quickly.

Hung shrugged. 'The fisherman who found it has disappeared and the cargo gone. Maybe hidden somewhere.' To quickly re-establish his position he added, 'The government takes anything dug up or found like this. These pieces are in, er, storage. I can deliver to you.'

'What about paperwork? Guarantees that they're the real thing? Got to have all that in order to export them,' said Carlo. 'And I'd have to see the merchandise first. Arrange its shipment and disposal. That is, provided it's genuine and my, ah, investors agree. It will take a little time.'

'Carlo! Where are you going to get that kind of money?' exploded Anna. 'You're mad.'

Carlo spun and said to her, 'Anna, baby, this is

311

business. And you don't know anything about it, so just butt out. Okay?' He turned his attention to Hung. 'Where is the transaction to take place? There must be out of the way places here? Your village?'

'The cargo is not here,' said Hung.

'Where is it?'

'It is safe.'

'Safe! Where?' demanded Carlo. 'Why doesn't anyone give you a straight answer in this country?'

'I need to talk to others,' answered Hung.

'And the price?' persisted Carlo.

'Maybe I show you. Very nice antiques,' smiled Hung.

'Carlo, I want to see them too!' said Anna. 'Imagine, they've been in the sea, all these years . . . '

Carlo was after money thought Anna. That's all. Wherever they came from didn't matter. Anyone really interested in buying the pieces would have been begging to see the beautiful old objects rescued from their sleeping place in the sea for so many years. Carlo wanted the deal and wanted to make money. He'd have to talk to his father as soon as possible and convince him he'd really found a goldmine that needed capital.

'Bloody hell,' said Carlo. 'Who'd have thought this would turn up? God knows what else is lying around this backward country waiting to be picked up. I'll go and ask Captain Chinh what's for lunch.' Whistling, he swung below to the compact galley.

Anna fingered the old plate, wondering who had used it, what meals it had been present at. She recalled the similar plate on the altar in the pagoda that looked down on them from the top of the peak. Had someone given it to the little nun for her offerings to Buddha? Did they know its value and had it too come from some shipwreck off Halong Bay?

Anna was uneasy about Hung selling the plates to

312

Carlo. She wondered how trustworthy he was. But then, clever as Carlo kept telling her he was about business, she doubted he'd be able to raise the money to buy them. And what on earth did he know about antique porcelain anyway? He'd talked so often of hitting the jackpot so they could marry, buy a nice house, settle down that Anna decided to let Carlo go with this deal and see what happened. She had more important things to think about. As soon as she could, she'd phone her father and tell him the time had come. She wanted to find her mother's family.

12

BARNEY'S WAS JAMMED, THE outside tables full. In the middle of the room a group had gathered around a large circular table to welcome back Barney and Lai. Anna and Sandy insisted they wait on them and Ho and Anna had prepared all their favourite dishes.

'Man, it's good to be back,' declared Barney. 'You can keep the weather in Canada.'

'Rained all the time,' said Lai. 'But not proper rain like monsoon rain. Misty rain.'

At the large table sat Charlie, Miss Huong, Rick, Jean-Claude, Kim and Cherie – back on duty at HOPE. Sandy, Anna and the two waiters raced between tables and the kitchen. Carlo acted as bartender and was kept busy serving the range of Australian beers that were always in demand from tourists.

Two new arrivals were chatting to Barney. They were middle-aged American Vietnam vets who were members of a bike club. They were riding around Vietnam on old army bikes seeing the places 'we didn't get to see on our first visit'. Jerry had a grey pony tail, Brad a full grey bushy beard. Both wore lightweight black jackets with the elaborate insignia of their American bikers' club called The Retrievers.

In the kitchen Anna commented to Sandy, 'Funny that Barney is friends with two vets when you told me he was a draft dodger.'

'Water under the bridge now, according to Barney,' said Sandy. 'It's forty years ago. They're all trying to help Vietnam, as well as helping each other through what was a bad time.'

Anna knew what Sandy's next unspoken thought was. 'Yeah,' she said, 'be good for your father to come here. Share the pain, as they say.'

When Sandy went back to the table she paused by the two Americans. 'What does The Retrievers stand for?' She thought that maybe they were a group looking for bodies of men missing in action.

'Back at home we pick up strays,' explained Brad. 'People down and out, the homeless, street kids. Take 'em to a shelter we pay for. They get a bed, hot meal, bit of a helping hand – but mostly it's the companionship they come for. One of our buddies has started a similar thing in Saigon.'

'We thought we'd check it out, see if we can help,' added Jerry.

'Why there?' asked Rick. 'Must be plenty of people to look after in the US.'

'Most of The Retrievers served in 'Nam,' said Brad. 'We did a lot of damage. Barney told us about what the Aussies were doing in Phuoc Tuy – helping kids and the local villagers, so we thought we could help out where a lot of us served.'

Sandy put a platter of fish cakes and spring rolls on the table. 'If you're looking for an orphanage to support, you could help us with one near Danang that got hit by a typhoon recently.'

'You don't say? Sure, we'll take a look at that. Whaddya reckon, Jerry?' said Brad.

'You betcha. We're heading that way. A few of our guys were round Danang. Give us the details. We might get a few more guys to come over. Sounds just the kinda thing we were looking to do.'

'I'll put you in touch with the head of the village and the woman running the orphanage. The villagers will help too. It's paying for the materials that's the problem. There's manpower and enthusiasm galore,' said Sandy.

'You got a deal,' declared Jerry.

When Sandy told Anna, she clapped her hands in delight. 'Fantastic.'

But when Anna stopped by the bar to tell Carlo about the plan, he was sceptical. 'How can you be sure they're going to do it? They're a couple of old bikies passing through,' he said.

'Do you want to ask them if they meant it?' said Sandy, overhearing his comment.

Carlo ignored her barb and changed the subject. 'So when do you guys finish up here now that the bosses are back?'

Anna and Sandy exchanged a quick glance. 'We'll talk about it later, Carlo,' said Anna.

'Well, I'm outta here next week. Business meeting.' Carlo gave Anna a hard look. He'd made her promise not to mention anything to Sandy about his possible deal with Hung involving the old ceramics.

'That could work out then,' said Sandy. 'Anna, better get back in there and help Ho: we don't want him losing the plot the first night Barney is back.'

'He's okay. We get on like a house on fire now,' said Anna as she headed for the kitchen.

'What are you two planning then?' asked Carlo.

'We'll talk later. Those people are waiting for their drinks, Carlo.'

Sandy hurried back to take orders. Anna had made her promise not to say anything to Carlo just yet about her plans to find her mother's family. And Sandy wasn't going to drop any hints.

When Anna returned from Halong Bay, she and Sandy had caught up over a coffee. Anna told Sandy that she wanted to share something special and personal with her. Sandy took one look at the light in Anna's eyes and the glow about her and thought that Carlo had proposed. But when Anna explained she'd had a kind of epiphany at the pagoda when she'd gone back to see the old nun, Sandy was surprised.

'What sort of "awakening"? What happened?'

'It's hard to explain. But I've decided I want to find my mother's family. I've rung Dad, he's sending me copies of any relevant papers.'

'Wow! That's great! What did Kevin say?' asked Sandy, thinking this must mean a lot to him.

'He was so pleased. Got a bit choked up. Said he'd hoped I'd want to do this. That being here would kind of provoke my curiosity,' smiled Anna.

'Tom, Jean-Claude, Rick . . . we've all felt that you should dig into your family's past here. It had to be your decision though. That Temple of Nowhere is kind of special. Or was it triggered by something the nun said?'

Anna shook her head. 'Maybe. Anyway, I haven't said anything to Carlo – yet. I'm not sure he'll be too interested. But I wanted to ask you first. If you'd help me.'

'Hey, as if you have to ask! What's your plan? Where was she born? Do you think there are any family still there?' asked Sandy, thrilled for her friend.

'It'll be in the email Dad sends. He said he doesn't know if there's anyone left from the immediate family.'

'Will your dad come over here?' asked Sandy.

Anna shook her head. 'No, he's never wanted to do that. My mother didn't want him to. She was determined to make a new life in Australia – and she did. Dad said this journey of discovery is my thing.'

'What are you hoping to find, Anna?' asked Sandy quietly.

'Look, I know I'm not going to fall in the arms of some lost rellies, or anything like that,' said Anna pragmatically. 'I just want to see where Mum was born and grew up. It's probably changed, but I want to get a sense of the surroundings. Feel I'm walking in her shoes a little bit, that's all. And although she never wanted to have anything to do with her country after she left, I like to think she might be a little bit pleased I'm doing this.'

Sandy reached across the table and squeezed her hand. 'I'm sure she is. Y'know, I remember her quite well. I remember your sixth birthday party – she made all that food – and the games we played.'

Anna looked over Sandy's shoulder into the distant past, seeing again her pale-faced mother with her dark eyes and long straight hair and how happy she'd been watching all the little girls playing in the backyard, under the gleeful guidance of Kevin. 'She was sick then. It must have taken a lot out of her.'

'What do you think Carlo will say?'

Anna dropped her eyes. 'I'm not sure. I'll wait till I know where we're headed before I tell him. You know how Carlo is. He thinks I should ignore anything to do with my Vietnamese background. It makes him uncomfortable. But you're not like that because you knew her. Anyway, I'll need you to translate and for a bit of moral support.'

'Yes, I know. Strange how Carlo expects you to totally accept his Italian family,' countered Sandy, but quickly dropped the subject when she saw the wounded look in Anna's eyes. 'Listen, as soon as we're finished at Barney's, I'm free to do anything, go anywhere you want. Will Carlo mind?'

Anna shook her head. 'Not really. He's got some business things happening.' She wished she could tell Sandy about the old plate and the subsequent discussions with Hung.

They'd left it at that. Now here it was, their final night in charge of Barney's.

Brad and Jerry carefully wrote down details of the orphanage, promising to see what needed to be done and to make it a priority.

As the evening quietened down, Sandy took a break and sat down next to Jean-Claude, who held her hand and gave it a small squeeze.

'It's good to see you,' he said. 'I'm heading to Hue tomorrow. What are your plans? I hope it's not too long before I get back and we can see each other again.'

'We plan to go south too. Anna and I are taking a little trip . . . not sure where to at this point.'

'And Carlo?'

'He has business things to do.'

Jean-Claude glanced over at Carlo. 'He's very confident, isn't he?'

Sandy smiled at the polite description. 'Oh yes, Carlo is very sure of himself. I just hope he doesn't get burned.

319

Doing business in a strange country when you don't know the customs can be difficult.'

'I am happy to offer any advice,' said Jean-Claude, 'but I don't believe he thinks I have anything to offer. We move in very different worlds. I think he's written me off as a fish farmer, so of little value to him. I feel that Carlo is making all the obvious mistakes – he's ill informed about the culture and feels superior. The Vietnamese are very proud and nationalistic. But they have a great sense of humour, are casual, friendly and generous. Well, you know all that, Sandy. The investment climate in Vietnam is very good now and developing long-term relationships with business partners here could benefit him – if he makes friends and earns their trust.'

'You're right, Jean-Claude, but I'm afraid he thinks his time here is for making a quick buck on some deal. Frankly, I think he's got more than the landscaping ceramics in mind. He's socialising with some unsavoury characters.'

'Like anywhere, especially an emerging business world, there are those who try to cheat the system, profit them-selves. And corruption still happens. Certain kinds of people seem to sniff out those who'll work with them in not quite legitimate deals,' said Jean-Claude.

'Those who are basically greedy,' said Sandy. 'Anna thinks Carlo is shrewd and smart. And he can be, but in this country I worry that's he's out of his depth. He'll never admit it though. As soon as Anna has decided where we're going I'll let you know. But I must take Anna to Saigon – it's so different from Hanoi.'

He leaned over and kissed her cheek. 'Take care, sun-shine. I will stay in touch. If that's all right?'

'Of course.' She kissed him, aware of the tingle that coursed through her. But she was determined not to get involved too quickly, as she had in previous relationships that had fizzled out. Jean-Claude was charming and sweet, but she would be going back to Australia soon enough and that could mean the end of it. She didn't want to get hurt again.

'Sandy, this is your last night running Barney's. Now Barney and Lai are back, will Anna and Carlo return to your apartment?'

'Yes,' sighed Sandy. 'Only for a while, we'll be taking off in a few days.'

'Please, stay in my apartment, be my guest. I'll be gone for a week or so. I'd be very happy for you to stay there.'

'Jean-Claude, are you sure? That'd be wonderful.' The relief in Sandy's voice made him smile.

'I can understand how, um, claustrophobic it could be having Carlo and Anna in your little flat, as you describe it.'

She gave him a quick hug. 'I'll be very responsible. Wow, it'll be like a holiday for me.'

'Enjoy. There's a woman who comes to clean. I'll drop off the key in the morning. Take care.' He waved to the others and said his farewells.

'That was a touching little scene,' said Carlo as Sandy passed him. 'Those Frenchmen are smooth.'

'Yes, they have lovely manners. You Italians could learn a thing or two!' she teased.

Barney and Lai were jetlagged and tired, and excused themselves, taking Anna and Sandy aside.

'We've booked into a hotel as we arrived without much notice and it will be late by the time this wraps up,' said Barney.

'We can't thank you both enough. Everything looks wonderful,' said Lai.

'I must say peace seems to reign in the kitchen. Ho is in great spirits. Can't say I've ever seen him so affable,' said Barney. 'What's the secret?'

'He adores Anna,' said Sandy.

'Once we found our feet he's been great. He's taught me heaps,' said Anna.

Lai and Barney exchanged a look. 'Never would have believed it. Hope it lasts – you'd better keep popping back in to see him, Anna. See you tomorrow.'

After Barney and Lai left, Sandy and Anna sat down at the table as the restaurant crowd had begun to thin out. Ho stuck his head out of the kitchen and waved to Anna.

'Better see what he wants.'

In the kitchen Ho was standing with his arms folded, looking serious.

'What's up, Ho? A problem?'

'You finish in Ho kitchen?'

'Yes, is something wrong?'

Ho picked a small package wrapped in a banana leaf and handed it to Anna. 'You good cook. You learn Ho dish, very good.' He gave a little bow.

Anna unwrapped the parcel. Inside were Ho's three favourite cooking implements – a small chopping knife, a large carved wooden spoon and a set of long painted chopsticks. 'Ho, thank you. These belong to you . . .' Anna hesitated, not wanting to offend him by refusing but knowing how carefully he looked after these utensils. She was moved. 'I will use them every day and think of my friend Ho,' she said, giving a small bow in return.

Ho turned and went outside to his bicycle and pedalled away into the night.

'Oh, he's forgotten the food parcel,' exclaimed Anna, seeing the package by the door.

The girl who'd been cleaning up the kitchen picked it up. 'I will take tomorrow morning.'

'Tell me where. I'd like to take the food,' said Anna.

The late stayers had settled in around the bar and one

long table. Carlo had turned off the pirated CDs and had his favourite music playing loudly.

'I'll finish the paperwork in the morning. Carlo, keep note of the bar tab, won't you?' said Sandy.

'I'll clean up Barney and Lai's flat first thing in the morning and then move our stuff back to your place,' said Anna. 'I'm exhausted.' She picked up her gift from Ho. 'I was so touched by this gesture.'

Carlo shrugged. 'A few used kitchen tools. Big deal.'

Sandy and Anna exchanged looks.

'Night, Anna. Don't stay open late, Carlo,' said Sandy.

Anna hugged Sandy. 'Thanks. For everything.'

Sandy fell into bed, listening to the familiar noises outside her flat. How grateful she was that Jean-Claude had offered her his place to stay in until she and Anna set out on their trip to find Anna's family. She must tell Jean-Claude about it tomorrow when he gave her his key.

Anna was sound asleep when she heard noises. Raised voices, then the shattering of glass brought her wide awake. She sat up in bed. Carlo was not there. She pulled on a cotton robe and hurried downstairs to the cafe. There was a light above the bar and two low lights on inside. She could see figures outside standing near the stacked tables and chairs. She saw Carlo talking with two men – no, not talking, arguing. She went through the cafe, hesitating before calling out. She wanted to shout out to Carlo, to ask if everything was all right, but some instinct made her stop. Then she saw Carlo pull something from his shirt pocket and one of the men stepped forward and grabbed his hand.

Anna flung on the lights that lit the front of the cafe, calling, 'Carlo, what's going on?'

'Go back to bed, Anna. It's okay.' He flung an arm at her, gesticulating at her to back away.

Terrified, Anna dashed upstairs, grabbed her mobile and rang Sandy.

Sleepily Sandy tried to understand Anna's breathless garble. 'Anna, calm down, take a deep breath. Tell me again. Is Carlo all right? Where is he? And what's happening? Who's with him?'

'Two men. They look like police or something. What should I do?' she asked worriedly.

'Keep inside. Unless he's being bashed up, let him handle it. Go down again and tell me what's happening. I'll hang on.'

Anna hurried downstairs and peered through the cafe. Carlo had stepped back towards the door to the cafe.

Anna called loudly, 'Carlo!'

He spun around and stuck his head in the door. 'Go to bed. It's okay.'

'Who are those men? What's happening? What was that breaking glass?'

'Just a dropped bottle. Go upstairs, Anna.'

She went upstairs, speaking to Sandy. 'Well, he doesn't seem to be in trouble. They just appear to be arguing.'

'Well he doesn't appear to need your help. I'm sure Carlo can take care of himself. But ring me if you're still worried.'

'Thanks, Sands.' Anna got back into bed and waited. It was another half an hour before she heard car doors slam, cars drive away and the front doors clang shut. Carlo fussed around in the cafe before coming upstairs.

In the dark he slid into bed beside her.

'What was all that about then?' asked Anna.

'You're awake? Good.' He leaned over to caress her.

'Carlo! For God's sake. I nearly called the cops. I thought you were in trouble. Who were those men?'

'Cops! Well, some sort of security heavies. Said they'd been patrolling and checking on Barney's, saw I was outside talking with a couple of fellows and they thought I needed protection. Assistance.'

'What was the argument about?' asked Anna.

'Money. Barney pays them protection money. They were doing their job. They wanted payment. Fair enough, I thought.'

'I hope you didn't pay them.'

'Of course I did. If Barney's been paying, I'm not going to rock the boat.'

'Sandy just paid them! They tried to get a lot more out of her and she told them off. Now you've paid them again!'

'Yeah, well, Sandy doesn't know how to handle people like that. I gave them US dollars and that got rid of them.'

'Now poor Barney is out of pocket and they're going to expect that all the time,' exploded Anna.

'Anna, keep out of business dealings. You don't understand how things work,' said Carlo crossly. 'Go to sleep.'

'Gladly. I'm tired. But you put that money back in Barney's till out of your own pocket.' She rolled on her side with her back to Carlo, who sighed.

'I'll wake you early, eh?'

Anna didn't answer.

However, Anna was up early, dressed and downstairs before Carlo woke and long before the cafe was due to open. She checked everything was clean and tidy, then headed outside and hailed a cyclo. She had an errand to do before cleaning Barney's flat and opening up for the breakfast trade.

She showed the driver the address the waitress had written on a scrap of paper and they set off through the early morning streets. They stopped outside a narrow house on a corner. A small tree struggled at the edge of the road and above it a looping spaghetti tangle of electrical wires hung from a pole with several thick tendrils disappearing into the roof. An elderly woman in dark pyjamas had thrown a bucket of water across the footpath and was busy sweeping it clean. A sign in Vietnamese was painted on the door. It was the correct number so Anna knocked. It was immediately opened by an old man who smiled at her. She held up the plastic bag of food and the basket she was carrying. Nodding and murmuring he led her inside.

There was the smell of cooking, the sound of a baby crying and women's voices in a room down a hallway. Anna passed several rooms with cushions and mats on the floor. In one a woman sat breastfeeding a baby while a toddler played at her feet. The hallway led to an open courtyard where several women were chatting and children were playing. A small fountain splashed against one wall and an altar was set up under the eaves. Off the courtyard there was a bath house and a big kitchen where women were cooking. Dishes of food were spread along a table where older children were helping themselves to bowls of noodles and rice.

'Good morning,' said Anna. 'Does anyone speak English?'

A young woman came to her. 'I do: can I help you?'

'I've brought you food. From Ho, the cook at Barney's cafe.'

'Oh, thank you!' said the girl, taking the bag with the plastic tubs of food. 'He is so good to us. We thank Mr Ho very much.'

Anna followed the young woman into the kitchen and

326

looked around. It seemed very sparse and basic. One dish for each person and few utensils and pots. The meal looked very frugal. 'What is this place, exactly?' Anna asked.

'It is a home for mothers and children who have nowhere to go or who are in trouble. We care for them for a few nights and then they must move on. They come back again, but we try to have space for those who need help, who are hungry,' explained the girl.

'Who owns this place? Do you get money from the government?' asked Anna.

'The old couple over there have lived in this building for many years. All of the family had moved out so they started taking in neighbours in need and the word spread and others came. It's called The Family House.' She pointed to the old man who'd opened the door and the woman who'd been sweeping out the front. 'They are grandparents to anyone who wishes to come here.' She smiled. 'They have many, many children. Everyone here is their family.'

'How nice. So no money is given by the government?' asked Anna.

The girl shook her head. 'No. If they ask for official help, they must get papers. Too many regulations. They are good people who do this from their home, but any donations are welcome.'

'And is it just for mothers and children?'

'That's right. Many are alone because of problems with their husbands. Some of the children live on the street, even from very young. They beg, work, get money. We look after them and then help them go to school.'

'They are very good people,' said Anna, nodding at the old couple. 'But they don't own this house? What will happen in the future?'

The girl shrugged. 'It is hard to say. We pray each day. We manage.'

'Could I light some incense?' Anna indicated the altar. 'I will say a prayer for them too.'

'Thank you.' She called to a little boy, who ran forward with some incense sticks and shyly handed them to Anna.

Anna lit the sticks and placed them on the altar beside the small brass dishes holding pieces of fruit and some rice. She clasped her hands and said a small prayer. Warm feelings washed over her at the recognition of the great goodness people can do if they try.

The young woman escorted Anna to other rooms that contained sleeping mats and rolled bedding. 'Upstairs are some beds and more spaces for mothers and their children.'

'Is there anything the house really needs?' asked Anna. 'Maybe my friends and I could help.'

'You are kind. We can always do with sleeping things. Dishes and some toys, perhaps. My name is Loc.'

'I'm Anna. I'm here from Australia with my friend Sandy. We have been working with Ho.'

'Please, thank Ho for me. He comes once a week to cook a special dinner for us. He is a good man. He has no family anymore, so he cares for us here,' said Loc.

'Really? I didn't know that.' Anna realised she knew nothing about Ho's personal life.

'Yes, very sad. His wife left him and took away his children. He was not a good husband. He drank too much and was harsh to them.'

'Ah, I see.' That explains a lot, thought Anna. 'And you, Loc? You help here also?'

She smiled shyly. 'These are my grandparents. I teach English and help them when I can. But I do not live here.'

Anna glanced at the old couple. 'I hope things work out for you. And The Family House. I'll make sure Barney continues to support you, thanks to Ho.' She wondered if Barney knew what Ho was doing with the leftover food from the cafe. She felt sure Barney would be willing to help even further if he knew the full story. She'd talk to Sandy. 'I have to go back and open the cafe. You should stop by and introduce yourself to Barney. I'll tell him about this.'

'Please, do not get Ho into any trouble.'

'Not at all. It's a shame to see food wasted. I think Barney and Lai will be very happy to know about you. Goodbye.'

The following evening, Anna joined Sandy at Jean-Claude's apartment for dinner. She told Sandy that Carlo was at a business meeting.

'Isn't this a gorgeous place?' said Anna. She gave Sandy a sly smile. 'So, you like Jean-Claude? Could it get serious?'

'He's charming. He's French. But where's it going to go, Anna? He's locked into Vietnam and France. I'm due to go back to Australia to look for another job.' She shifted uncomfortably under Anna's scrutiny. 'Now, show me what your dad sent.'

Anna spread out the scanned emails Kevin had sent her. 'There's some letters and a photo.' Anna peered at the image of a family group. 'That's my mother; she was about fourteen then. Next to her are my grandparents, Mum's brothers and sisters, and other people I don't know.'

'That must be the brother who drowned,' said Sandy, pointing to the little boy holding Thu's hand.

'Van,' said Anna softly. She pulled the chain from around her neck and touched the little gold crucifix. Her face crumpled. 'Read the letter about what happened on the boat. And Van. It must have been so hard for my mother to tell that story to Dad. He's written it all down.' Anna shuffled some of the papers, picking up a printed email. 'Dad also sent me this.' She handed it to Sandy.

> *My dearest Anna,*
> *Here are the relevant documents and personal papers you asked for the other day. Your mother packaged them up with a note for you many years ago. She told me that one day you'd want to look at your family's Vietnamese background. In the meantime I was to look after the few bits and pieces she treasured.*
> *Well, I wasn't surprised to get your email asking for info. I'd been expecting it, hoping for it, for some time and had everything ready to send – hence the prompt response.*
> *It may well be a very emotional trip back to that distant past, so chin up.*
> *I'm very proud of you, my dear girl.*
> *Good luck, love Dad*

'Oh, Anna, how lovely,' said Sandy, looking at the tears welling in Anna's eyes.

Anna nodded. 'I love my dad,' she said simply.

Sandy swallowed and didn't speak for a minute, then, more briskly, said, 'Right. Now the big question is where was she from?'

'Dad says Mum left Vietnam from a village on an island just off the very bottom of the country. Phu Quoc.'

Sandy answered, 'Yes, I've heard of it. We've been planning to go south to Saigon so we can jump off from there. Now, what are Carlo's plans? Have you told him yet?'

Anna looked uncomfortable. 'Not yet. I thought I'd wait till we had worked out where to go, what to do. It's not like we have an address or anything. He'll tell me it's a wild goose chase. He's going to Hoi An. On business.'

Sandy felt she should have probed a bit more about Carlo's activities. She didn't like the sound of the businessmen he'd been mixing with, but she'd been so busy with the cafe. Now Anna's quest was more important. 'Okay then, let's start making plans. We'll go down to Saigon, maybe get a local flight from there.'

'What about your dad, is he coming over for that reunion thing?' asked Anna.

'I don't know. Tom sent me an email to say they'd done all they could, and now Dad'll have to make his mind up. But he'd better do it soon. Anyway, I really don't think he'll come.'

'But Tom is coming? Is he bringing his wife?'

'Yep, they're leaving soon. Maybe we can hook up with them in Saigon. You might have a story for him,' said Sandy with a grin.

Anna rubbed her eyes. 'I don't know. It seems a long shot, but if I could at least see the place my mother lived, maybe even find their house . . . '

'One step at a time, Anna,' cautioned Sandy. Surely an island village was a small place. She hoped there'd be someone alive who knew the family and could give Anna some information. The photo would help.

That evening Jean-Claude rang Sandy to see if she was settled in and she told him about their plans to visit the village where Anna's mother had lived.

'After all this time, do you suppose she will find any answers? A pity she waited so long. Her family here probably don't know what happened to her mother and the little brother,' said Jean-Claude.

'Sure, it's a long shot and Anna isn't expecting to find anyone living, but she's quite excited. She just wants to see where her mother lived. That's important.'

'It is. It's how I feel when I go down to the river house where my grandparents lived,' said Jean-Claude.

Sandy recalled the beautiful old terrace restaurant as well as the lovely house in Hue. 'Do you miss your family? You seem so settled here.'

'Ah, but I go to France very often. For business and to see my family. The world is a small place now, eh?'

'If you have money. The global village doesn't always extend to the poor,' said Sandy.

'The internet has shrunk our world though. When are you coming to Ho Chi Minh City?'

'Fairly soon. Carlo says he is going to Hoi An. Anna doesn't think he'll be interested in coming along to trace her family.'

'Call on me if you need me,' said Jean-Claude. 'I like Anna and she's your friend. So I want to help you.'

'Thanks, Jean-Claude.'

'Let me know your plans so I can adjust mine. I hope you're comfortable?'

'Of course I am. You must let me buy you dinner as a thank you.'

'I'm happy to help you but I won't say no to the dinner offer.'

'Terrific, Jean-Claude,' said Sandy, and felt a surge of affection for him. 'I'll let you know our plans.'

Sandy called in to the HOPE office and told Kim about their plans to try and find Anna's family.

'I've never been to that part of the coast down south, but it sounds like a fishing village. Is that where the refugee boat left from?' he asked.

'Most probably. That's the sort of thing we hope to find out. I just had an email from Tom and he's very keen for us to follow it up. He's very fond of Anna, I think.'

'Didn't Anna's mother have any documents, like a birth certificate and such? Surely they'd have a few more details,' said Kim.

'No, they probably went without papers or they were taken off them. They were robbed by pirates. And worse,' said Sandy.

Kim was thoughtful. 'I've started to wonder about my family history. I'm a mixed-up Hawaiian. I suppose some of my family were sent there to work in canefields and pineapple plantations. It's never bothered me: everyone I knew was the same. Well, I hope Anna finds what she's looking for.'

'We'll let you know. Don't know how long we'll be down south.'

'And your father, is he coming to Vietnam?'

'It seemed so for a minute. But he's procrastinated and may have left it too late. Can't get all the paperwork done, visas and so on.' Sandy had mixed emotions about the news from her mother and Tom about her father. She wanted what was best for her dad, but deep down the thought of being responsible for him during what would be an emotional time disturbed her. For the moment, she'd concentrate on Anna's family.

They tried to do as much homework as possible, using the internet with Sandy calling her contacts to discuss the best way to go about this search.

'I wish there was a telephone directory system,' sighed Anna. 'So many don't have a phone.'

Sandy made contact with the provincial governor, but his district covered many villages and towns, and he was of little help. The surname Thanh was not uncommon. He suggested they contact the nearest police station and 'knock on doors'.

'There doesn't seem much we can do until we get there,' said Sandy.

They booked a flight to Ho Chi Minh City leaving at the end of the week. The night before they left they joined Carlo at Barney's for dinner. Carlo was driving down to Bat Trung to meet a representative of the Vietnamese company which would make all the arrangements to ship his merchandise to Australia. He'd then go to Hoi An as, he said, he had a lead on some other products. He didn't elaborate and Sandy didn't ask. Anna had kept quiet, unhappy that Carlo still insisted she say nothing to Sandy about the antique plates.

'But Sandy could be helpful. She's my friend; we can trust her,' Anna had pointed out to him.

Carlo had been adamant. 'It's not just me involved. There's Hung and his associate – whoever that is. I reckon they've got more than they're telling me. Hung swore me to secrecy. So long as I get my merchandise out of the country, that's all I care about.'

'So will this company who are shipping the garden pots also send the antique ceramics?' asked Anna.

'Are you crazy? No, that requires special paperwork. Hung will let me know. But that's a thought. I could combine them in the same shipment and save money.'

Barney took Anna to one side. 'Good luck with your search. I hope things work out for you.'

'Thanks, Barney. I'm not sure if we'll find anyone, but I feel I have to try,' said Anna.

'Listen, thanks too for telling me what Ho does with the food from the kitchen. I never worried about the stuff going out. I figured he needed it, and, hey, anything to keep him happy. He was a handful. But you've brought about a big change in him. We didn't know about his family troubles. He's a real loner.'

'He has no family anymore so I think he's trying to make it up to The Family House.'

'Yeah, the nice girl from the house came by. Lai and

334

I will go over and see what else they need. We might be able to help them.'

'That would be great, Barney.'

Sandy also had a quiet talk with Barney as she went through the paperwork with him and told him about the visit from the protection men and the incident with Carlo.

'He's replaced the money, that seems in order. But they'd better not try to get extra money or American dollars out of me,' said Barney.

'I worry about what exactly Carlo's doing. But you can't tell him anything,' said Sandy.

Barney patted her shoulder. 'He'll learn. They're good people here, but there are many levels of power and corruption. Not that all western companies are squeaky clean either,' said Barney cheerfully. 'The bottom line rules. I'm only in business for the hell of it! Lai is the business head. Tell Anna and Carlo to pick her brains, any time. Good luck in the south. Check in when you get back.'

Saigon was an eye-opener for Anna and Sandy enjoyed showing her around. They stayed in a modest hotel and spent a full day cruising the elegant high-end shops – silks, French accessories, exquisite embroidered linens, lacquerware. They stopped for lunch at The Lemongrass bistro and arrived back in their hotel room to find messages from Jean-Claude and Tom.

'Tom and Meryl arrive in a few days. Great. We should be back from the south by then,' said Sandy.

'What's the note from Jean-Claude?' asked Anna, flopping on the bed among her shopping bags.

Sandy tore open the envelope he'd sent to the hotel. 'Oh my gosh, how sweet!' she exclaimed.

'What?'

'He's treating us both to a session at some fabulous spa here. L'Apothiquaire. He says it's in a cute hundred-year-old building and they use their own handmade products from Bordeaux. We are to relax before setting out on our big adventure.' Sandy shook her head and grinned at Anna. 'Nice of him, huh? Let's book for tomorrow.'

'That's really nice. We'll have to get him something as a thank you,' said Anna, wishing Carlo was as thoughtful. He was good with splashy gifts on public occasions like birthdays and Christmas, always making a big show to family and friends. But he rarely bothered with sweet surprise gestures, which was why the gift of the broken porcelain plate had so surprised her.

They splurged on a superb dinner, managing to get into the Temple Club, which rarely had empty seats. Anna was entranced with the little alley lined with lanterns that led to the entrance of the former Chinese temple where they were ushered upstairs to a cluster of dark-timbered rooms with antique fixtures lit by red-and-gold lanterns. Reproductions of 1920s advertisements featuring doe-eyed Chinese girls were framed in vermilion.

'All very Indochine, isn't it?' whispered Anna.

'The food here is heavenly,' said Sandy. 'Different from the food Ho does: more Vietnamese high cuisine.'

The following day, after visiting L'Apothiquaire, they flew directly to the island of Phu Quoc, landing at a small airstrip in the township of Duong Dong, boldly designated as the capital. The island was barely fifty kilometres long.

As they flew over it Anna and Sandy exchanged a surprised look. Palm-fringed white sand beaches stretched below them, one seeming to go forever, lapped by an azure sea. A township was dotted with red roofs and past a rubber plantation could be seen a luxury resort. At the far end of the island a pristine beach was deserted save for fishing boats hauled onto the sand where fishermen were repairing their nets.

'It's a big island: look at the ridges in the centre. Must be as big as Singapore,' marvelled Sandy. 'What a find.'

They settled into their budget accommodation which was close to the beach, fronting a narrow sandy road that wound through the sleepy town. There were some noodle shops and a few simple cafes.

'No bars, no discos, no cinema, power boats, casino, or commercialisation – how brilliant,' said Anna.

'We can hire a motorbike or there's a local bus that mooches round the island, though its timetable is a bit erratic,' said Sandy. 'Where do we go first?'

Anna was tempted to opt for a swim but thought they'd better start their search somewhere.

'Let's get a moto and scoot around the island, get a feel for the place,' suggested Sandy.

With Anna perched behind her, Sandy headed the motor scooter out of town, following the coastal road. They were both stunned by the magnificent unspoilt scenery.

They stopped for lunch at a powdery white beach where a few stalls sold cold drinks and snacks. There was an open-air, thatched-roof shack on the beach with tables under the palm leaves. They ordered the local speciality of small chilli crabs, fish cooked over an open flame, boiled rice served in a woven leaf bowl and a tall glass of green coconut milk.

'What a stunning place,' sighed Anna. 'So idyllic.'

As the owner cooked their meal and served them Sandy chatted to him about the history of the island. It had been colonised by the French in the nineteenth century until the Japanese invaded during World War Two.

'The French tried to keep us and Cambodia wishes to

own us as we are located close to it,' he told them. 'In the American war thousands of VC prisoners were put in a war camp here. Now many Vietnamese come back here to make holidays.'

'It's what I imagine the South Pacific and Asia must have been like thirty years ago,' said Sandy. 'Are there any people who were here in 1978?'

The owner, a man in his fifties, looked thoughtful and rubbed his chin. 'Maybe some people in a village or in the hills in the north. But many people from here escaped. Many boats took people away.'

Sandy and Anna exchanged a quick look. 'Do you know anyone who was organising these escapes?' asked Anna.

He picked up their empty dishes. 'I might. Why do you want to know this?'

Anna quickly explained and he nodded sympathetically. 'Ah, this might be difficult. Or it might not. I shall ask.'

Sandy quickly wrote the name of their hotel and their mobile phone numbers on a corner of the food-splattered paper table cloth, tore it off and handed it to him.

They continued their tour, returning over the northern hills and stopped briefly at a temple dedicated to a local resistance leader who helped sink a French battleship in 1861.

Back in town they wandered along the simple main street leading to the beach.

Locals were sitting outside their shops and houses, chatting at the ease of the end of the day before darkness demanded meals and preparations for the next day. Sandy overheard a conversation as they walked past two women. One told the other, 'The Viet Kieu is looking for the family of her mother.'

Sandy paused and greeted them politely in Vietnamese and asked how long they had lived there. When they replied all their lives, she asked if they could speak to them. The women smiled and shrugged. One asked Anna a question and she looked to Sandy.

'She wants to know the name of your family,' said Sandy.

'Thanh. Grandfather Van Thi and Uncle Quoc. My mother was Thu. She was nineteen when they escaped from here on a boat.'

'Where they go?'

'To Australia,' said Sandy.

'Ah. Australia.' They sucked their teeth and nodded. One woman pulled out a rolled cigarette from a pocket in the flowered pyjama top that matched her pants. They looked at each other and spoke for a few minutes.

'What are they saying?' asked Anna tensely.

'The names are not known here. But Mr Hang might know. He helped people escape by boats. Where can we find him?' Sandy asked the women.

They conferred and seemed to agree and pointed up the hill. Sandy thanked them and she and Anna turned and began walking in the direction the women had shown them.

'A lot of people left from this island to escape,' said Sandy. 'It cost a lot. Money or jewellery were the exit visas. It's unlikely that any records were kept, but perhaps he knew the family.'

Mr Hang lived in a modest house on top of a small rise overlooking the sea. A bird cheeped in a bamboo cage outside the green-painted door to the small ochre-coloured house. A teenage girl opened the door and stared shyly at the two foreigners.

Sandy asked if they could speak to Mr Hang. The girl said her grandfather was busy but she'd ask. She hurried away and shortly after a wiry, bandy-legged older man wearing glasses and a battered khaki pith helmet came to the door.

Sandy greeted him and told him what they wanted and briefly outlined Thu's story.

'It was a very long time ago. Many people left from here. We tried to help as many as we could. Then other people came to make money. Their boats were no good.'

'Could we speak with you, please?' asked Sandy. 'It means very much to my friend.' She indicated Anna, who smiled hopefully.

He nodded agreement and led them through the small house to a back area where he'd been tinkering with a very old bicycle. He drew up three low plastic stools and they all sat down, their knees higher than their bottoms.

He began as if delivering a lecture, detailing the background to independence in 1975 after North Vietnamese troops marched unopposed into Saigon and by 1976 reuniting the country as the Socialist Republic of Vietnam. Later, tens of thousands of South Vietnamese were put in re-education camps; the private property of Chinese and Vietnamese merchants and upper class people was confiscated and the land was controlled by collectives to create a socialist economy in the south. 'This was when so many fled from the oppression. Your family too.'

'Is there any chance you knew her family? Thanh,' said Sandy.

'I do not recall such a family living here. So many came here from other places. Some had to live here until they could leave. By then unscrupulous people smugglers were taking people's money, all their savings, and sending them away in leaking boats. I wonder how many survived and started new lives,' he sighed.

'Anna's mother survived but her little brother did not. They were attacked by pirates.'

Mr Hang nodded. 'It became a bad problem. Does your friend know the name of the boat or who was in charge? Any dates when they arrived in Australia?'

Sandy asked Anna, who pulled the papers from her bag and quickly skimmed the story of the nightmare boat trip Thu had told Kevin.

'She says here the boat captain, Tan, tried to turn the boat away and argued with the men.' Anna looked at Mr Hang. 'Ask him if the name Tan means anything.'

Mr Hang was already nodding. 'Yes, yes. I know him. He was a good man. Did not take too much money or steal from people. I used him several trips.'

Anna handed him the photo of her family, pointing out Thu and Van.

Mr Hang nodded. 'I believe I remember them.'

'Where did they live?' asked Sandy eagerly.

He shook his head. 'They are not from this island. They came from some other place.'

Anna's face fell when Sandy translated. 'How would we find where they came from?' she asked, close to tears after thinking they'd almost found Thu's home.

Mr Hang stood up. 'I am a teacher. I wished to help people. I pretended to be a poor fisherman, but because I am educated I felt that one day these people and their families would want to know the fate of their relatives as family is so important to us. The country was in such turmoil. No one knew who to trust. So I kept records of those who left in my boats.'

'You kept records? Where? Can you look for us, to see if the Thanh family is listed?' asked Sandy excitedly.

Mr Hang called to his granddaughter. 'We shall take tea while I look.'

Sandy and Anna sipped their tea, which the young girl had put on a tray on a stool in front of them, as Mr Hang had disappeared indoors.

'You'd think he'd be far richer if he was charging people to get away,' said Anna.

'This is quite a substantial house and it all happened

341

thirty years ago. He's probably lived off what he made then,' said Sandy. 'I doubt he would have gone back to teaching under the new regime.'

After they'd finished their tea and a long half-hour had passed, Mr Hang returned with a ledger book. There were columns of names, dates and details written in Vietnamese.

'It was in 1978 – just before the monsoon rains. One of the last to leave that season.'

Sandy caught her breath and managed to ask, 'Are they listed?'

Mr Hang read out the names of Thu, Van, Quoc and Aunty as one family group.

'What else can you tell us?' asked Sandy quietly.

He squinted through his glasses. 'They lived here for some months waiting their turn for a boat. They travelled a long way to get here. As many did. No one took much notice of this island then. Other places where boats left from were not so lucky.'

Sandy and Anna were holding their breath.

Mr Hang looked at Anna. 'Your family came from a village outside Dalat, in the Central Highlands.'

Sandy let out her breath. 'The name of the village?'

'Bao Loc. It might not be there anymore. But then again, it may be.' He smiled and closed the ledger. 'I wish you good fortune in finding your family.'

They stood and Sandy and Anna gently shook the old man's hand, giving a small bow of respect.

'Tell him I am very grateful for what he has done for my family – and many other people,' said Anna formally.

'You must pay your respects to your mother and your ancestors,' he told Anna.

'I will,' said Anna. 'I promise.'

Deep gold and red-ringed clouds hung over the sea in

the last of the sunset as they walked slowly back to their little hotel.

'I guess we book tickets to Dalat,' said Sandy.

Anna's hand went to the chain around her throat that held the gold cross. 'I know we're going to find her home. I just know it. I promised the nun at Halong I would do this. Find her.'

'We'll do our best, Anna,' said Sandy. 'We're close now.' She just prayed the village was still there. And that someone remembered Thu and her family.

Anna stood at the far end of the beach by herself where a few fishing boats were hauled up on the sand in the shelter of a small cove. She stared across the blue waters of the Gulf of Thailand. So this was where her mother had helped her little brother into an old boat that was to take them to a new life.

13

SANDY AND ANNA FLEW back to Saigon, leaving the magical island behind but wishing they could have stayed longer. As they checked into their hotel Sandy received a text message from Tom.

Meryl and I have arrived in Saigon. Where R U?

'Hey, Tom and Meryl are here,' exclaimed Sandy. 'Shall we meet them for lunch?'

'I guess so,' said Anna. 'But can we make the booking to Dalat first?'

Sandy knew Anna was anxious to press on with the search for her family. 'We'll see if we can get a flight tomorrow. I'll book us a hotel room in the centre of Dalat. You'll have to fill Tom in on your news.'

'I don't feel I have a whole lot to tell him . . . yet,'

said Anna. 'But it will be good to catch up on news from home.'

The four met at a pretty little garden restaurant specialising in French food and chose a table on the vine-covered patio at the back of the quaint old building. The floor was made of cool ochre-and-blue tiles; ferns draped out of blue-and-white porcelain pots; the table cloths were starched embroidered white cotton; and there were small fresh orchids on each table.

'How elegant,' said Meryl. 'What an amazing city. Did you see all the flower shops? Masses of fresh flowers banked all along the footpath!'

Tom smiled at Meryl, who was trying to take in all the sights and sounds of the exotic, sophisticated city. 'Thought we'd hit the better end of town first,' he said. 'Now fill me in on your news, then I'll cover the scene at home.'

Sandy and Anna took turns telling him about running Barney's, and how Carlo was moving ahead with a business deal, and Anna finished off with her latest news about looking for her family.

Tom clapped his hands in approval. 'Excellent. Good one. So when are you off to Dalat?'

'As soon as we can,' said Sandy. 'Now what about my dad? Thanks for going to see him.'

'Ah, that's been quite successful. Prised open a long-closed can of worms there, I'd say. That Tassie Watts and Father Maxie have been working on him.'

'So Mum said. But what about the anniversary? Is he coming over? He's not saying much to Mum,' said Sandy.

'Hard to say. I think there was a bit of a break-through with him getting together with his old mates. I did have a bit of a private yarn with your mother,' said Tom. 'His case is not uncommon.'

'Must have been difficult for your mother,' said

Meryl gently. 'Hard when you see someone you love suffering and you can't help them.'

'He didn't want help. Or didn't think he needed it, I guess,' said Sandy slowly. 'It was just the way he was. Moody, quick tempered. Very private.'

'I think his mates explained to him there were other vets just like him. But he didn't seem convinced anything could change,' said Tom. 'He was in two minds about coming over here when we left. We were a bit busy the last week before leaving and then Patricia rang us to say he was thinking he might go, but had left it too late. Hard to get a visa quickly.'

Sandy didn't answer, feeling guilty at the rush of relief that her father wasn't coming after all.

'Oh, that's a shame,' said Anna. 'But you'll both be there?'

'I'm not going to the actual ceremony at Long Tan,' said Meryl. 'I'm staying in Vung Tau at a very nice new resort. I felt it was more the men's thing. Those who were there.' She glanced at Tom.

'It'll be quite emotional, I think. I'll be hiding my face behind a camera,' he said with an attempt at joviality.

Meryl patted his hand. 'I'm still a bit tired from the flight. But can you give me a few tips on where to go when I've caught up? I thought I'd brave getting out and about, though the traffic looks frightening.'

'Shopping? Sightseeing? Eating?' asked Sandy. 'It's much easier getting around Saigon than Hanoi.' She liked Meryl but could see she was a bit nervous about her new surroundings. But she did enjoy her lunch and told Sandy at least Tom's cooking had familiarised her with Asian food.

'Maybe just sightseeing,' said Meryl. 'Until I get a feel for what's available. And Tom has promised to take me round some of his old haunts.'

'Well, those that are still here.' He grinned at Sandy and Anna, who knew that Meryl would get just the sanitised shiny version of his wild days in old Saigon.

Sandy and Anna hugged them both goodbye, as they were heading to the travel agent and Sandy wanted to drop into the HOPE office to say hello to the small group who staffed the southern branch of the organisation.

'We'll keep in touch. I have my laptop with me if you want to email,' said Tom. 'I'm in work mode now. Maybe you'll have a story for me, Anna.'

'I hope so, Tom. But I reckon your trip to Long Tan will be more than enough,' said Anna, a little uncertain about the feelings her family search were arousing in her.

'We're going to take our time getting down there and spend a few days in Vung Tau, go along the coast. I'll leave Meryl with some of the other wives in Vung Tau for the actual day of the event. Good luck to you both.'

'You too, Tom. See ya.'

'They're terrific girls, just lovely,' said Meryl as Sandy and Anna left. 'I can see why you enjoyed their company. You've been a great help to them, Tommy. Lunch was lovely, but I wouldn't mind a little kip before hitting the streets again.'

'It's the local custom and a very sensible one. C'mon, we'll stroll back to the hotel.'

After booking their flight to Dalat, Anna phoned Carlo to tell him of their latest plan and Sandy did a search for any families named Thanh.

'Doesn't sound too hopeful,' reported Sandy after making a few phone calls. 'The best thing is to just go out to the village – which might be way out. Dalat is in the hills – where it's always spring, they say. The French

347

found it a great retreat from the heat and built exquisite chalets. It's quite a gem of a place.'

'Sounds like the hill stations in India that the British developed,' said Anna.

'I imagine it is a bit. A mountain resort on a plateau that has gorgeous scenery around it – gardens, lakes, waterfalls. Popular place for local honeymooners. Dalat used to have some of the ethnic minorities living there. But not so much now. They're mainly just in the far north of the country.'

'Rick and Charlie told me about them. Miss Huong goes out into the hills collecting old tribal artifacts,' said Anna. 'Old pieces – art, carvings, weavings, old porcelain and such . . . Do they really get high prices in galleries and from collectors?'

'You bet,' said Sandy. 'Le Cong Kieu Street here in Saigon is full of antique shops where all the rich tourists and VIPs go. But every second one sells replicas, I'm told. You have to know what you're buying to pick the genuine antiques.'

'How do they get them out? Isn't there some rule about nothing over a hundred years old allowed to leave the country?'

Sandy stared at Anna in surprise. 'My, you have been talking to Rick and Charlie. The shop arranges the paperwork. I've no idea but money smooths the way, I guess.'

Anna dropped the subject. But she wished she could discuss Carlo's antique ceramics deal with Sandy.

Tom and Meryl arrived in Vung Tau and drove into the Best Beach Resort set on a hillside that ran down to the sea. It was lushly landscaped, the gardens dotted with guest cottages and pavilions.

'I've booked the Cottage Villa,' said Tom. 'View of the ocean, a private terrace with our own jacuzzi.'

When Meryl saw the pretty little villa with its thatched roof and high beams, cool terracotta floors and bamboo furniture with brightly coloured furnishings scattered around the three rooms, she gasped. 'Tom! Can we afford this?'

'Why not? It's your birthday! And this is Vietnam. Still affordable. Though if things like the Cua Lac complex go through that might change. Come and see our private terrace.'

They wandered through the gardens, had a swim in the huge pool, discovered all the other amenities and then headed down to the beach.

Later, ensconced on their terrace with cold drinks, Meryl sighed, 'This is magic. Did you ever imagine when you were here in the sixties that places like this would exist now? That you'd be sitting here, like this?'

'Good lord, no! It's lovely to be here with you enjoying all this. I've been doing some research for my article and it's most interesting. Do you want to hear about it?'

Meryl settled back with her feet up on the chaise longue. 'Give me a brief rundown.'

'The west bailed out of Vietnam in 1975, leaving it a kind of client state of the Soviet Union. Vietnam seemed to prosper but it was all shadows and masks,' explained Tom. 'Many people starved due to the need to support a million-strong army in Cambodia and then with the collapse of the Soviet Union Vietnam lost its foreign support and money. But the Vietnamese are very pragmatic, which brought about a re-think, and the renovation, or doi moi, policy began in 1986. Since then it's gone ahead with huge annual growth.'

'How does this compare with development in China?' asked Meryl.

'It's smaller, but Vietnam has an efficient population and high literacy rate. So the country is concentrating on manufacturing high-tech and specialty export products. And just offshore near here there's a huge new gas-supply industry. I met some of the workers when I was here earlier. A lot of Russians are involved in oil and gas here too.'

'What about the young people?' mused Meryl.

'There's a heap of money floating around and you see kids with mobiles, ipods, expensive clothes. While I suspect a bit of hand greasing goes on at the top with all these multimillion-dollar foreign projects, the core values, family and such, are still very strong. And that's good.' Tom stood up to get them a refill for their drinks.

'So Vietnam is becoming a more affluent country, even though it's still a communist one,' said Meryl.

'Ah, now there's the rub,' said Tom. 'Becoming so prosperous might bring its own troubles again in the future. We shall watch this space with interest.'

'I'm looking at the space over there where the restaurant is,' said Meryl. 'What are we doing for dinner?'

'I'm taking you out to a swish restaurant in town. Get your glad rags on,' said Tom. 'Two more days and I have to head to Long Tan.'

Tom made contact with Cranky and Baz from the Aussie vets group and they arranged for him to meet some of the early arrivals for the commemoration. Cranky picked Tom up at the Best Beach Resort and drove him the forty minutes down to Nui Dat.

'So, is it all coming together?' asked Tom.

'Ah, the usual bun fight. We hate it when the pollies and bureaucrats get involved. And once you've got media and bigwigs coming over who all want their share of the

limelight to justify their trip to the folks back home . . . '
He made a throat-slitting gesture. 'They want to start the
ceremony at a time to suit them; the vets all want it to
start at the time the battle started – three-forty pm. We'll
just do our own thing, I reckon. Do you want to go and
have a look at the memorial before the shindig and
hoopla on the day?'

'Yeah, I would,' said Tom suddenly. He hadn't planned
this but it now appealed to him, to pay his respects quietly
and privately. 'How do we do that?'

'I'll call ahead and set it up. In the meantime, how
about we run around the area, go over to meet some of
the blokes who've already arrived at The Strangled Cow
for lunch?'

'Excellent idea. Sure you can spare the time?'

'Yep. I'm one of the designated media-minders.' He
grinned.

They drove in Cranky's old four-wheel drive along
the rutted red dirt road past fields and plantations,
pulling over to let a farmer with a herd of goats pass. Tom
was quiet, recalling the very different landscape this now
peaceful terrain presented when he'd flown in forty years
before. The outline of the hill caused him to catch his
breath as they drove up to where the helicopter pad had
been. They got out and walked over to the patchy square
of bitumen that remained.

'Luscombe Field airstrip has gone, all fields now,'
said Cranky, pointing. 'Some of the vegetation has come
back. Not like the areas that were hit with Agent Orange:
they still look like a bleeding moonscape. Natural forests
never came back.'

'Hard to believe it all happened,' said Tom softly,
slowly turning a full circle to take in the view. He sensed
that the land was still feeling the agony of the past, those
years when a new style of warfare had inflicted such

lasting scars on the land and its people. To mask his sadness he drew a deep breath. 'Right, let's push on.'

They drove to the site of the base where two lonely gateposts stood as a remnant of what had been a centre of intense activity.

'You know we built the camp hospital over a Viet Cong tunnel complex,' said Cranky. 'Tunnels went for bloody miles. One of the old VC fellas told me they felt safe here as there wasn't artillery fire.' Cranky smiled. 'I had a bit of a quiet get together with some of the VC who were operating round here. My mate Stretch came along, six foot four he is and none of the VC blokes were over five foot. They laughed and asked Stretch, "How'd we miss hitting you?"'

'How'd you hook up with the VC vets?' asked Tom curiously. 'I thought that was going to be part of the big day, the re-meeting of the Vietnamese commanders and our Long Tan officers.'

'Oh yeah, that's all happening,' said Cranky. 'Some of our blokes want them to admit we won and that we didn't just walk into an ambush. Twelve Platoon D Company was sent out after there had been a mortar attack on the base camp compound the night before. We knew there were still VC in the area and wanted to stop any more attacks on the base.'

'And so D Company put an end to any further attacks on the Australian base,' said Tom.

There was no stopping Cranky. 'Yeah, but it turned out to be a bit of a mix-up, to say the least. Eleven Platoon were separated from the other two platoons and then it came under heavy attack from the VC. Many blokes in the platoon were either killed or wounded. Then the monsoon rains came. This was good because it meant that the VC couldn't see the Aussies but bad because it also meant that the USAF, who had been sent

352

in to give them cover, couldn't see them either. They were pinned down and taking casualties.'

'I was at the hospital when they were coming in,' said Tom, remembering his interview with Phil.

Cranky continued to re-tell the familiar tale, looking into the distance. 'The RAAF boys from 9 Squadron did a bloody great job to supply us with ammo and even though the platoon had only six uninjured men they continued to inflict damage on the VC. Then the New Zealanders started throwing artillery on the VC, who were almost on top of 11 Platoon. Must've lobbed more than three thousand rounds right on the bullseye. What was left of 11 Platoon managed to link up with 12 Platoon and their machine gunners were able to deal with the VC. Mind you, it wasn't till after seven o'clock, hours after the battle had started, that reinforcements in the form of A Company finally arrived, because the base commander was too worried about possible attacks on the base to send them earlier. So the tide turned then but . . . '

'By then we'd lost eighteen men – although there were two hundred and forty dead VC,' finished Tom.

'Well, that was all we counted on the battlefield after they'd taken away many of their dead and dying. It's been estimated that the three platoons of D Company had fought off ten times their number.'

'So, Cranky, what do you know about the other side of the story?' asked Tom.

Cranky shrugged. 'My wife's family. Her uncle was one of them. We've re-hashed the battle many times. He's a decent bloke. Lot of the local VC were just protecting their homes and families as he saw it.'

'Is that so? Interesting,' said Tom. 'Could I meet him?'

'Yeah. We have regular family get togethers. I'll ask the missus to set it up. C'mon, few more places to see.'

*

The village near Long Tan rubber plantation was a scattering of simple houses, two small shops, a school and a little hospital next to the most imposing building – the police station. They pulled up outside a smaller building of government offices and Cranky went inside and came out with a young Vietnamese girl in dark pants and a white shirt with a badge on her pocket.

'This is Miss Cong, our guide for the memorial,' said Cranky, adding, 'it's the rule. The Vietnamese are very strict about who wanders into the rubber plantation. They like to have everything well looked after. Now we have to go to the police station.'

Miss Cong smiled and greeted them in good, if heavily accented, English. At the police station she went inside and returned a few minutes later with a metal plaque on a chain and handed it to Tom who was surprised to see it was the replacement plaque from the memorial.

'It's safer kept in the police station. We didn't want it stolen or defaced,' said Cranky. 'The original dedication plaque got lost. This is a pretty good system.'

As they drove to the plantation, Miss Cong gave Tom a potted, accurate history of the battle and handed him a printed leaflet that listed the names of the eighteen Australians who lost their lives and where they were from.

Tom scanned the list of names he'd seen many times before. 'Not one of them over twenty. Seems so young to me now.'

The car bumped along the muddy dirt road. Fields stretched into the distance on one side and on the other, lines of rubber trees stood in precise rows.

Then Cranky pulled over. 'This is it, mate.'

Tom got out and followed Miss Cong who walked briskly ahead describing where tents had once been pitched and where soldiers of D Company had dug in. Two old moss-covered stones still showed the traces of coloured paint where men had written their names and regiments.

Tom trailed behind. It was late morning and the sunlight was filtered through the screen of the tall trees. Tom stopped to look at a metal cup hanging at the end of a spiral cut in one of the trees, catching the bleeding white sap. It was so quiet. He trod carefully, not wanting to break the spell. No breeze penetrated the thick canopy overhead. He broke into a sweat in the oppressive heat and atmosphere of eerie quiet where ghosts still hovered.

Then suddenly through the trees he saw the large white cross with a small fence around it – the Long Tan memorial. Miss Cong hung the plaque in its centre. She brushed the stones in front of it with her hand, picking up a few scraps of paper, a cigarette butt, some leaves, then stood to one side and watched Tom and Cranky approach.

Tom felt his throat tighten. The simplicity of the memorial in this strange green grove was startling and moving. Miss Cong waited as the two men circled the memorial, then she gently ushered them to the front and, to Tom's amazement, asked them to stand to attention. Both men bowed their heads and she stood beside them and then, to Tom's shock, in her sing-song accent, she respectfully recited:

They shall grow not old, as we that are left grow old:
Age shall not weary them, nor the years condemn.
At the going down of the sun and in the morning
We will remember them.

'Lest we forget,' echoed Cranky and Tom.

They all stood for a minute in silence, Tom still trying to accept the fact that this young Vietnamese woman had spoken the hallowed words that every Australian claimed as his own mark of respect to the fallen.

355

'You want a photo?' asked Miss Cong as they stepped away.

Tom shook his head. The scene was etched in his memory for life.

'It is good to remember your people. We do same. Vietnamese cemetery and memorial over that way.'

Cranky briefly outlined the ceremony planned for the 18th August. 'There'll be a few speeches, wreath laying and so on. When the men come here, it can be hard for them. They walk around looking for the spot where they were, where the first shots were fired. Vets who weren't at Long Tan come because they feel the need to honour their mates no matter where they served.'

'It's certainly a special place,' Tom managed to say. The mood and emotion of it had almost overwhelmed him.

He took Cranky's hand and gave it a firm shake. 'Thanks. Thanks for bringing me here.'

'No worries, mate. I know how you feel.'

'You finish your time here now?' asked Miss Cong.

They nodded and she carefully lifted the plaque, wrapped it in a cloth and put it in a plastic bag. 'We look after here very good. Very special place.'

Back at The Strangled Cow on the outskirts of Vung Tau, Tom downed a cold beer.

'Phew, I needed that. I was quite choked up back there.'

'Yeah, gets to me every time, too. You can imagine how it affects the blokes who fought there when they go back in there now.'

Tom took another drink and thought of Phil and his nightmare memories of Vietnam. 'Yes, it would be a hard one to face up to. Very hard.' He thought for a moment. 'I'm still amazed by Miss Cong. To have a young

Vietnamese woman explain the valour of the fighting Australians and be so sensitive in honouring our dead.' He shook his head. 'Vietnam has come a long way in open mind, open heart stakes,' said Tom.

'They respect us Aussies,' said Cranky. 'They respect us for adopting guerrilla tactics. We respect them as good fighters too.'

At lunchtime several of the visiting Vietnam veterans arrived and were introduced. One had come from Perth, another from Melbourne and two from Sydney. Soon they were regaling Tom with stories of escapades and colourful mates during their Vietnam tour of duty. There was a lot of laughter and jokes and it struck Tom again how there was instant rapport between these men who were all so different, yet shared one thing in common that bound them for life.

Over dinner with Meryl, Tom related the day in great detail.

'What an incredible experience,' said Meryl. 'But I can't believe a Vietnamese woman recited "For the Fallen". That's terrible! The men must be turning in their graves.'

'Well, I admit I was shocked at first. But the more I think about it, it's a good thing. She was very sincere and she understood what Long Tan means to Australians. The Vietnamese aren't bitter, they don't hold grudges, they move forward, but they do respect the past. Now, what are your plans?'

'A couple of the wives are going to the ceremony, but I know you'll be working so I think I'll stay here. I might go down there later just with you, when it's quieter.' She hadn't expected Tom to be so emotional about the visit to the memorial. 'I had a nice relaxing day. Baz's partner organised an outing for the wives to some of the sights. You should have seen inside what they call the White

357

House, the elegant house on the hill that was a residence for some wealthy Frenchman in the colonial days. Utterly gorgeous. They certainly knew how to live back then.'

'And did the visiting wives get on with the Vietnamese wives?' asked Tom. Most of the Vietnamese women were second or third wives and all were quite beautiful and generally much younger.

'They were a bit shy at first, but once they took us shopping, everyone warmed up,' laughed Meryl. 'It was a total girls' day out.'

Tom sat with a mug of tea waiting for the sunrise over the ocean below. It was an unsatisfactory brew made from a stale teabag. He should have travelled with his favourite loose tea. But English teapots seemed to be few and far between in Vietnam, although a little Chinese teapot would suffice. He'd ask Meryl to find one. She was still sleeping. He wanted these few moments of contemplation before leaving for the ceremony at Long Tan. A bus had been organised to take a small group of them down before the afternoon event.

He was pleased he was doing an in-depth article for Alistair because it was the stories within the framework of the big story that interested him. He was hoping Cranky's wife would set up a meeting with her VC uncle and he wished people like Phil Donaldson were here as well. He'd spoken to many men and found it intriguing that each of those who'd been involved in the battle had a slightly different interpretation of the events. There had been many versions – from those of the senior officers at base camp, down to the stories from the men in the field. Loyalty to mates and field leaders was of greatest importance in all versions.

But there was resentment over the lack of recognition

for bravery and deeds during the battle. Tom heard how recommendations for a Military Cross had been down-graded to a mention in dispatches. 'Like we were bloody postal clerks doing an okay job,' sniffed one of the men.

Moreover, the fact the men weren't allowed to receive bravery citations from the South Vietnamese government still rankled. 'We got bloody dolls, mate,' said one of the men. 'Even the damn Yanks gave us a Presidential Unit Citation.'

So much pain. So many scars and wounds; physical, mental and emotional.

Tom had thought about this commemoration day and had brought with him a surviving safari suit, the cor-respondents' dress uniform he'd had made by Mr Minh in Saigon in 1966. He had kept this one, a fawn lightweight suit with its double set of pockets, shoulder tabs, neat short sleeves and firmly creased trousers, for sentimental reasons. His pen and notebook fitted in a breast pocket, his new digital camera and tape recorder in side pockets. He thought that he looked pretty smart in the suit and was pleased that it still fitted him, even if it was a little snug. He was still in front of the mirror when Meryl emerged from the shower.

'Tom! You're not wearing that! Where on earth did it come from? Not from home surely?'

'Yep. This is an original. Figured I'd give it one last run and put it back in mothballs.'

'Please don't tell me you want to be buried in that,' chided Meryl.

Tom grinned. 'I figured the blokes would know exactly what I was – a correspondent.'

Meryl shook her head, but she was touched at his sentimental gesture and she realised that she knew very little about that period of Tom's life which had meant so much to him. 'The bus will be here soon. I won't plan on dinner with you. I imagine you'll be kept busy down there.'

'Yeah. There's a chance I could get up to Cranky's wife's home village and meet some of her relatives. They were VC in this area.'

'Really! How ironic.' She gave him a kiss. 'I hope today goes well.' She watched Tom leave, chatting to the others getting on the little bus, always interested, always curious about other people and everything going on around him. 'Taking it all in', as Tom was fond of saying.

There was a crowd of about one hundred and fifty people, maybe a few more, who had come for the event. Tom spoke to the Australian Consul-General, other dignitaries, a commander from the former South Vietnamese army, as well as the head of the local Phuoc Tuy Province, and several younger members of the Australian media who were covering the day. There was talk about the meeting lined up between the two Australian platoon leaders and the Viet Cong battalion commanders.

Tom overheard one of the young journalists comment, 'These old soldiers never stop fighting the damn war, do they? There's nothing new to write about.'

A veteran standing nearby, dressed in a casual jacket and jeans, spun around to face the young man. 'Listen, kid, you be damned glad we didn't give up. You should learn when to stop making smartarse comments and listen. You might learn something. I was in that battle and when I got back to camp, leaving my best mate dead on the battlefield, a young reporter started asking stupid questions. You know what I did? I shoved my rifle in his belly and nearly shot him. Instead I picked him up and slung him up in a rubber tree.' The veteran walked away from the stunned journalist.

Tom walked up to the young man. 'They left that journo strung up there till someone took pity on him and cut him down. I was there too. These men here today, every one of them has a story. Tune in, mate.'

Speeches were made; wreaths were laid; tears were shed. Men embraced. Others talked quietly or stood alone, remembering. Some walked every inch of the plantation, recalling in photographic detail what happened on that day forty years before. Occasionally they paused, fighting back tears as they saw, as fresh as then, a mate fall, or recalled how close they'd come to dying, pointing out where they'd lain as bullets whistled past or thudded into the rubber trees that provided such inadequate protection from the onslaught.

Tom watched the ceremony from a sideline, seeing the emotions play across faces as they repeated in unison 'Lest we forget'. Then silence. It was all over. Phil had missed it.

The official party was ushered through the plantation; others began to trickle away in small convoys, heading to gatherings in bars and restaurants.

The sun and light had gone and now the green gloom enveloped the quiet plantation. The few men left walking through it were silent, or spoke in hushed voices. This was hallowed ground; ghosts claimed this country now. Tom was watching a group of tourists walking quietly around the plantation and was about to leave when he saw three men coming along the dirt track towards the large white cross. The one in the centre stopped and turned around. The two other men stopped, leaned close and put their hands on his shoulders in a comforting gesture.

Curious, Tom walked through the trees, wondering who these latecomers were. As he drew closer he stopped in shock. The man being supported by his mates was Phil. He looked distressed. Then Tom recognised one of the

361

two men, despite the years since he'd last seen him. There was no mistaking Maxie, the chaplain. Tom realised the other man was Tassie Watts, his one-time kidnapper. They'd got Phil this far. But the final few steps seemed just too hard.

Tom didn't want to interrupt but moved closer and heard the soothing murmur of Maxie's voice shattered by a cry from Phil.

'I can't do it, mate. No way,' sobbed Phil, holding on to a rubber tree, shaking his head.

'You've come this far, Phil. You owe it to yourself, to your mates. A few more yards,' urged Tassie.

Phil's face was anguished. Frantically he looked around him, fearful the enemy was still out there. He seemed to be back there, in the battle, seeing his mate take a bullet in the temple and fall beside him, blood spurting onto the red mud.

'Bastards!' he screamed, rubbing his face against the trunk of the tree, eyes closed, trying to erase the sights, the sounds, the confusion and that incessant monsoon rain streaming over all of D Company.

'There's no one there, mate,' said Maxie, shaking him gently. 'Just us, your friends. We're with you. It's over. Gone, mate.'

Phil opened his eyes and stared around the deserted plantation.

'C'mon, let's do this together.' Tassie unhooked Phil's arms from the tree. Firmly he and Maxie put their arms around his shoulders and waist, and walked forward.

Tassie quietly counted, 'Left, right, left,' and their steps fell into unison.

They walked past Tom, not seeing him, but Tom saw the tears streaming down Phil's face, his eyes riveted on the big white cross, drawing him closer. The three men reached the open ground and stood at the base of the cross, their arms still around each other. Phil's shoulders were heaving and Tom could hear the deep sobs racking his body.

The wreaths and the plaque were still in place. It was dim and still; shadows from the trees recalled the shapes of men who'd sheltered there long ago. Tom lifted his camera as a beam of blood-red sunset light penetrated the canopy, a glowing shaft that, for a moment, backlit the cross, its shadow falling at the feet of the men who stood there.

Slowly Phil calmed and he straightened his shoulders and the men on either side of him dropped their arms to their sides. Smoothly Phil lifted his arm, his chin went up and he snapped a firm salute. Tassie and Maxie saluted also. Following Phil's lead they bowed their heads, each making a silent prayer.

Tom found he'd been holding his breath and as he let out a long sigh he realised he hadn't taken a photo. He slipped the camera back in his pocket. The three men began to walk around the memorial, pointing in the direction from where the first shots of the battle had rung out. Phil was looking around, talking and remembering. Tom heard him chuckle and slowly walked from the trees to join them.

'G'day, Phil. Glad you decided to come,' said Tom, reaching out to shake Phil's hand and give his shoulder a warm squeeze.

'Yeah. Reckon you had a lot to do with this,' said Phil. 'Didn't think I'd make it. But Maxie pulled a lot of strings to get the paperwork through.'

'Phil was on the plane before he knew it,' grinned Tassie. 'I'm Tassie Watts, old mate of Phil's. We spoke.'

'I recognised you.'

Tassie laughed, knowing that Tom was alluding to his kidnapping of Col Joye. 'Bet you're getting a story or two today.'

'Yes, indeed. But I'd say the best story is seeing you here, Phil. Does Sandy know you're here?'

'Nah, unless she's got an email from Pat. We'll catch up.' Phil appeared more interested in walking around the plantation, looking for familiar landmarks, than he was in the whereabouts of his daughter.

Maxie drew out an envelope filled with photos and the men pored over them. There were men posing outside their tents, a haul of enemy weapons, enjoying a beer at the R and C base in Vung Tau. Phil began recalling stories of Shorty and Sting and the 'Boot Camp'. Tassie hummed the Nancy Sinatra hit 'These Boots Were Made for Walking'.

Tom took out his notebook and began to write.

By the time they left the plantation it was nearly dark. Tom joined them in Tassie's four-wheel drive and they headed to The Strangled Cow to join Cranky and the rest of the men. Phil continued to talk and reminisce, pent-up memories and stories pouring from him.

The stopper was out of the bottle, thought Tom. While he was here and with those who'd been there too, Phil felt safe. They shared a common language of experiences and camaraderie. How would Phil cope and adjust back on his own at home, wondered Tom.

Later, as the level of noise rose with the consumption of alcohol, Tom took Maxie aside and asked the chaplain for his impressions of Phil and what lay ahead.

'I've seen this before, that's for sure,' said Maxie. 'He'll hit a low not long after he gets back. He'll need the support of mates back at home for a bit. Help him readjust and accept. That should have happened when the men first got home years ago,' he added. 'Most coped with picking up their lives. Many, like Phil, didn't. There's a tribe of them at home, living on pills, dealing with nightmares, sleepless nights, broken marriages. But there's more help now.'

'Counselling, support groups?' said Tom.

'Yes. But nothing beats the help the men give each other. Phil should go to one of the vets' bush camps.'

'Where are they?'

'Scattered round the country now. In more remote and unspoiled areas. It's a network of places that have sprung up led by Vietnam veterans but they welcome veterans from all wars. Places to chill out, take time out, share stuff. It'd be good for Phil. There's one called Cockscomb in the hinterland of the Queensland Capricorn coast. It would help Phil settle in at home, knowing there's a place he can go when he needs to.'

'Sounds bloody terrific. You could chat to him about it. When the time's right,' said Tom, glancing over to where Phil was getting happily drunk.

The following morning Phil, Maxie and Tom were having a quiet talk over very strong coffees when Tom asked Maxie how he had been able to persuade Phil to come to the ceremony.

Maxie glanced at Phil. 'Why don't you tell him, Phil?'

Phil was quiet for a moment, then said, 'It was you and Tassie showing up. We went to the pub and started talking. Figured I needed a bit of support, I guess. For the first time I could tell someone how I felt. The guilt.'

'Guilt?' prompted Tom.

'Yeah, that I didn't die.' His face crumpled slightly with the painful memory. 'My best mate was blown up in front of me; he was the forward scout. Bits of Gordon just suddenly flew through the air. He was right in front of me when it happened. Next thing all hell broke loose when we were hit by the VC. I couldn't go back for him because the VC were everywhere but I've always felt I should have done something. Why him? Should've been me.'

Maxie touched Phil's arm. 'Nothing you could do,

mate. But pray. Gordon wouldn't blame you. Guilt: get rid of it.'

'Plenty of men feel just as you do, Phil,' said Tom.

Phil drew a deep breath. 'Well, I'm glad I came. Felt I owed it to them all. But I'm ready to go home.'

Cranky drove Tom and Meryl up the hill above Vung Tau to a simple residential suburb of modest homes that had great views over the bay. His wife greeted them at the door and they shook hands.

'We're having a barbecue out the back. Too many of us to fit around the table.' She smiled.

A handsome boy of about ten raced out to greet them.

'This is my son, Dzung,' said Cranky proudly. 'Keeps me young and fit.'

Tom shook hands with the boy, who led him outside. 'You like football?' Dzung asked.

'I follow a team in Sydney. What game do you play?'

'Soccer,' came the prompt reply. 'Dad's one of the coaches.' Then in Vietnamese he introduced Tom and Meryl to his family. Turning to Tom, he said, 'This is Aunty Bao; my cousins, Dinh and Hanh; and this is my great-uncle, Trong.'

Tom shook hands with the Vietnamese man with white hair and smiling eyes. 'Pleased to meet you.'

Trong didn't speak English, so his young great-nephew translated for him. 'I am glad to know you. Are you a veteran of the American war?'

'No. I was in Nui Dat in the war writing for the newspapers and radio.'

When he heard this the old man nodded. 'I too was in Nui Dat.' He straightened. 'D445 Regional Force Battalion.'

Cranky came and joined them. 'Is Dzung doing the honours? He's a good lad.' He ruffled the boy's hair and sent him to fetch fresh drinks. 'Trong was out there. At Long Tan. Part of a small group of local VC. He's told me how they were joined by a big mob from the north – regular army along with other VC units. We were bloody outnumbered ten to one.'

The old VC fighter understood the gist of what Cranky was saying to Tom. Dutifully, Dzung, who'd returned with a tray of drinks, translated again. 'Australians fought very hard even though outnumbered. They are good fighting men. Hard fighting men. After Long Tan, our commanders did not go near Phuoc Tuy.'

Trong went on to explain how they lived in the tunnels and the forest, climbing trees, tapping out messages on tree trunks to alert their scouts to the movements of the Australian patrols. 'Australian men good fighters, clever fighters. Like Vietnamese, fight jungle warfare.'

'That's a compliment, Tom,' said Cranky.

'How do you feel? Knowing your wife's uncle was probably trying to shoot you back then?'

Cranky shrugged. 'We all do what we have to do. He and I are the old boys now. Everyone in the family looks up to us. They respect age and elders here,' he smiled. 'It's nice. To Dzung, his great-uncle and his father might have fought on opposite sides but we are both men to respect.'

Later, as they were getting ready for bed, Meryl commented, 'What a nice family. That Dzung is a sweet boy. Though Cranky is old enough to be his grandfather, rather than his dad.'

'Dzung has his old uncle. And he has Cranky. He loves them both. That's where the hope for the future of this country is. Be nice if we oldies got that sort respect in Australia.'

The next day Tom and Meryl took a trip down the

Mekong. Tom considered flying to Dalat to see if he could track down Sandy and Anna but there was no answer to his mobile phone messages so he concluded they were out of range.

He and Meryl had a farewell drink with Father Maxie in Saigon.

'I hope you're planning to come back, Meryl,' said Maxie.

'There's certainly a lot to see. Tom really wants to take me to Hanoi.'

'Next trip. I've got to turn this story in and I want to touch base with Phil after he's been home a couple of days,' said Tom.

'Be good if he'd get up and see Cockscomb. Kind of debrief. He's been through a lot here,' said Maxie.

'Cleansing though, don't you think?' said Tom.

'Hopefully so. But it can also bring a lot of repressed fears and anger to the surface – they should be dealt with in the appropriate way. The boys at the vets' camps understand all this. I'll make contact with them and have a yarn to Phil,' said Maxie.

In the plantation that had seen so much activity, all was quiet. A rubber tapper moved down the rows of trees, emptying the cups of the sticky white sap. A farmer shepherded a small herd of goats along the muddy roadside.

At the memorial the stark white cross was without its plaque; wilted flowers and rain-soaked ribbons and cards – their sentiments now blurred – lay scattered. Long Tan plantation was empty.

14

ANNA DECIDED THE ROLLING lush hills of Dalat, with its old stone churches, colonial villas, misty lakes, flower-filled gardens and parks, was like walking into a picture book.

'You can see why it was so popular as a summer retreat. A French physician started the move up here round 1920. I think the setting and some of the villas look Swiss,' said Sandy, gazing over the lake from their hotel window. 'It's honeymoon heaven for someone from a crowded city like Saigon. And there are lots of tourist attractions.'

'It's lovely, but we didn't come to sightsee,' said Anna a little anxiously.

'Let's take a stroll anyway, get lunch and work out a plan,' suggested Sandy reassuringly.

They walked around the town admiring the buildings

and the pretty parks, including an orchid garden famed for its blue orchids, and settled in a small but smart restaurant for lunch.

'How are we going to get to my mother's village?' asked Anna as soon as they'd ordered.

'We've a couple of options. Let me make some inquiries,' answered Sandy, pointing to coloured flyers, a brochure and some business cards she had put on the table. 'I'm onto it.'

After flicking through the brochure highlighting the lakes, treks and unusual attractions of Dalat, Anna wished she was just a tourist. Now she was worried that they wouldn't find anyone connected with her family, or anyone who had known them. And nervous that they might. Would they remember the teenage girl Thu and her brother Van after all this time?

Walking back to their hotel, Anna stopped. 'Hey, smell that.'

'Gum trees!' exclaimed Sandy. She pointed to a valley. 'Yes, they planted eucalyptus trees after all the deforestation during the war. They grow quickly. The Australian government has given heaps of them to Vietnam.'

'Reminds me of home,' said Anna.

They passed a cafe and Anna was amused to see some local boys dressed as American cowboys hanging around. They waved and called out, offering to pose with the two women for a photo. Several other young men lounged at outdoor tables in the shade sipping the local coffee. Parked beside them was a variety of polished motorbikes. They all wore red-and-blue windcheater jackets with a small insignia on them.

One got to his feet, and beckoned them with a big smile. 'You want a tour of Dalat and all around?' he offered. 'Good price, good time. We're Easy Riders, the real thing.' He held out a photo album.

Sandy stopped. 'That's it! Of course.'

'What! Are you nuts? I'm not going anywhere with a bunch of bikies,' protested Anna.

'Not just bikies – Easy Riders. They're famous,' said Sandy. 'A group of English-speaking, charming, fun tour guides who take you off the beaten track . . . well, kind of.' She strode up to the young man while his partner, an older man, stayed seated, his legs up on a plastic chair, smoking a cigarette and reading a newspaper. 'Hi, yes, we might be interested.'

The young man held out his hand. 'I'm Chip. You want to see sights of Dalat or go down to Hoi An? Saigon? To see the Montegnard tribe people?'

'I'm Sandy. And this is Anna. We're not tourists really. We're looking for a village.' Sandy showed him a small map with the village circled.

Chip studied it, looking puzzled. 'Nothing much down there. Getting close to the jungle. Wild country. Why you want to go there?'

'We're looking for Anna's family. Her mother was born there.'

'Ah!' Chip was immediately interested. 'Where you from?' he asked Anna.

'We're from Australia.'

'First time in Vietnam?' he asked Anna.

She nodded.

'You like our country?'

'Yes. Dalat is very beautiful.'

'City of eternal spring. Always cool, always pretty,' said Chip. 'Except when it rains. Come and have coffee, very good coffee from a plantation down there.' He waved towards the sloping green hills. 'You meet my partner, Dun.' He led them across the street. 'Not his real name. Dunhill is his favourite cigarette.'

Dun, the older man who'd been reading, dropped his

feet from the chair, folded his newspaper, stood up and, taking off his granny glasses, gave them a big smile. Chip made the introductions, filling him in on where the girls wanted to go.

'I've never been there. Not on tourist itinerary,' he grinned.

'That's good. We like to find new places. No tourists: that's Easy Rider way,' said Chip.

'So who are you?' asked Anna, still not convinced that teaming up with two strangers on bikes was a sensible option.

'Please, sit.' Dun ordered coffees all round as Chip opened the album and began showing them photos and testimonials including letters and emails from previous customers. 'We just started to do this with friends who had bikes and now we have over seventy Easy Riders. We make sure our guys are high-quality people. Our bikes are excellent condition. Other people try to be like Easy Riders, but not so good,' explained Chip.

'Can you ride a bike? Or go pillion passenger?' asked Dun. 'It will be a difficult road to get to where you want to go. Take long time.'

'Really! Well, I can't ride a bike on my own,' exclaimed Anna.

'Where will we stop? It sounds a bit remote,' said Sandy.

'We bring everything. Very simple. You have backpacks?'

'No. And what are you going to charge for this?'

Chip deferred to Dun, who thought for a moment. 'This different, not usual way. Fifty dollars a day. US dollars. Each.'

'Including food and accommodation?' asked Sandy.

Chip nodded. 'I'm a good cook. I do Aussie barbecue.'

'It's a deal,' said Sandy.

Over coffee each man gave his potted life story. Dun's was the more interesting. Now in his fifties, though he looked younger and very fit, he had once studied architecture but the communist government saw no call for his talent and he was forced to join the Vietnamese army in the invasion of Cambodia. After several years of fighting he was sent to East Berlin to become an industrial chemist.

Dun shrugged. 'What use to me is that? But I study hard and when the Berlin Wall go down I came back here and I work selling things, do some digging jobs. Then I meet the Easy Riders.' He spread his arms as if to indicate that he'd found his life's work.

The four conferred a little more as Chip and Dun studied the map and suggestions were made as to what to take.

'Would you like a quick tour around Dalat now? Free. No charge,' said Dun. 'Get used to the bike riding.'

'Why not?' said Anna. If this was the way they were going into the wilds of Vietnam, with two strangers on the back of motorbikes, then the sooner she got used to it, the better.

Sandy travelled with Dun. Anna cautiously got on the back of Chip's Russian Minsk motorcycle, which he kept polished and talked to like a favourite pet. They were whisked around the city and the popular tourist spots of Hang Nga guesthouse, with its eccentric rooms, the Valley of Love, the Lake of Sorrows and Xuan Huong Lake, the modest summer palace of the last emperor, Bao Dai, with its décor frozen in the 1950s, as he had left it. They were also taken to the Lam Ty Ni pagoda but declined to buy a painting from its solitary monk, who had, Dun said, painted over a hundred thousand pictures. They loved the flowers, bonsai and parks scattered throughout Dalat.

Anna began to relax and stopped clutching Chip in a death grip. They ended up at the central markets.

'We buy food; you look around: nice walkway around the markets,' said Dun. He grinned at Anna. 'You okay on the bike now?'

'Yes. But I'm wondering about all the things we have to take with us.'

'We borrow backpacks for you, okay?'

'Sure, that'll be fine,' said Sandy. 'I suppose we'll be riding most of the day?'

'Yes, we stop when you need to and when we find good places. You will see beautiful waterfalls, if you want to take a picture, you tell me,' Chip said to Anna. 'Though we cannot take you tomorrow morning because we are already committed to some French tourists'.

Anna clearly looked disappointed.

'But, hey, we could go as soon as we have finished with them. Not too long to wait.'

So Sandy handed over money for supplies and they all agreed to meet at Sandy and Anna's hotel after lunch the next day.

The girls strolled around the markets commenting on the wonderful local fresh fruit and vegetables and the difference between these and other city markets.

'This was probably the main city where your family used to come,' said Sandy. 'Might have been an annual trip or something. Selling things, stocking up. No supermarkets near their village!'

The thought hadn't occurred to Anna and she looked about with new eyes. But it was hard to equate some of the kitschy tourist attractions with the way it must have been for her grandparents.

'I'd like to have been here in the 1930s at the Hotel Du Lac, swanning around in a silk tea gown and floppy hat smothered in roses, sitting on the terrace while my lover rowed to me across the lake in a striped blazer and white flannels,' declared Sandy.

'Maybe Jean-Claude's grandparents came here,' said Anna.

'They probably did,' said Sandy. 'I'll ask him next time we talk.'

'Speaking of men, I wonder how Carlo is doing? I'll check in with him tonight. Tell him we'll probably be out of contact for a few days,' said Anna.

It was bright and sunny when they set off wearing the jackets they'd bought in the market. Sandy and Anna were amazed at how much fitted onto the bikes and they shouldered their backpacks and settled themselves for the ride. Dun led and they zoomed out of town and were swiftly among the rolling hills that looked over the patchwork of pretty valleys with neat vegetable gardens, racing past pine forests, and coffee and rubber plantations. They stopped at a pretty waterfall where a sheet of glittering silver splashed in a clear deep pool. They sat on flat rocks to enjoy afternoon tea while Chip pointed out a rickety bamboo bridge that crossed the falls behind the curtain of water, daring them to try it. Anna preferred to take photos of the spectacular setting.

Dun pointed towards a pass through the higher ground. 'Over that side we go down, very steep. Then we turn off from the tourist way and go into different country.'

It was a tiring afternoon. The girls clung on as the bikes slewed down a rutted steep track, crossing streams and slippery rocks before climbing into thick jungle where the sun didn't penetrate. Dun pointed to tracks in the mud, which he guessed were made by wild boar.

'Did you say boar or bear?' shouted Sandy in his ear.

Dun lifted a hand and swivelled a wrist. 'Maybe boar, maybe bear.'

Birds were raucous but unseen as the bikes passed. They were in their territory now. Anna cowered as a group of gibbons shrieked from a treetop and was glad when they came out onto a small plateau into late afternoon sunlight and stopped for a break.

Anna and Sandy got off the bikes and stretched. 'Wow, look at that view,' said Anna. 'Have to take a picture. We're on top of the world.'

Dun pointed to where the edge of the plateau dipped. 'Over there, we go down a little way to a valley and a small river. The village is in there somewhere.'

They put on their backpacks but as Chip tried the starter his motorbike spluttered and refused to start. And refused to start several more times.

'Oh great,' groaned Anna.

'No worries, mate,' he mimicked and, talking soothingly to his bike, as if to a dear friend, he took out his tool box and tinkered.

Dun didn't offer to help, but lit a cigarette and sat on the side of the track. 'Chip not let anyone touch his bike,' he explained.

It took over an hour before Chip's bike was coaxed back to life and they roared away along an unsealed track winding through lightly forested hills.

Anna realised that this was virgin territory. In her travels in Vietnam she'd come up against signs of war everywhere – scrap metal merchants waving metal detectors over old battlefields; village memorials and city edifices to war heroes or museums that told of a long history of wars. She had seen amputees: women and children still bearing the signs of the effects of Agent Orange – as did the landscape. Much of it was either still naked and burned or reforested with unnatural woodland or plantations and still hiding untold hundreds of unexploded landmines. Yet this was a place that was serene and seemed untouched by the sorrows of war.

The small road came to a fork and they stopped.

'Do we toss a coin?' asked Sandy.

'What's the map say?' asked Anna.

'This isn't on the map,' answered Dun.

'Anna, you decide,' said Sandy.

Anna closed her eyes, swung her arm and pointed.

'To the left. Let's go.' Dun revved his bike and set off in the lead.

But it quickly became obvious that this was not a path used by many vehicles. They were now following another stream and, rounding a bend, they came to a small bridge. A waterfall trickled into a broad pool, which looked to be a place regularly used as the grass and bank were flattened as if animals drank there and there were remains of a fire pit.

'What a great place to stop,' exclaimed Sandy. 'Can you drink the water?'

They went to the pool and Dun knelt down and cupped his hand, tasting the water. 'Very good. From a spring in the hills. Local people use this. Can't be too far from a village.'

'Let's fill our water bottles,' suggested Sandy. 'I'd rather take my chances drinking this than well or village water.'

It was getting late and after crossing the bridge they were riding through a wooded area when Chip suddenly pointed. A dog raced towards them, barking as it ran alongside. Up ahead a figure was trudging beside the road, a man bent under the weight of a huge bundle of twigs and brush wood balanced on his head. Chip stopped and spoke to him and the man, who barely glanced at them, pointed ahead and resumed walking.

The two bikes whizzed past him and through the trees in the last light of day they could see dwellings and lights and smell smoke. Dogs came running and barking; foraging chickens flew out of their path.

The first thing they saw was a tiny stall, a kind of bush kiosk, selling drinks and cigarettes. An old woman in dark blue pyjamas with a quilted jacket over them sat beside the stall, smoking. Then they heard the deep resonance of a gong.

'There's a temple here,' said Dun. 'Do you want to take a look?'

They parked the bikes and walked past the kiosk where several children stopped playing and stared at them. There was the smell of cooking and through the trees they could see palm-leaf shacks and a few small houses. In the centre of a clearing there was a large rough-wood pavilion-style temple, where half a dozen monks were standing around outside, smoking. The elder monk was lighting incense sticks before a large statue of Buddha. When he struck a large brass gong the younger monks stubbed out their cigarettes, folded their robes across their arms and stepped into the pavilion. They sat in the lotus position on mats and with eyes closed, began chanting prayers in deep throaty tones.

Anna and Sandy stood watching, fascinated. Anna discreetly took a photograph.

The old woman from the cigarette stall came over and nudged Sandy and Anna, encouraging them to go and sit with the monks. To Sandy's surprise, Anna kicked off her shoes, stepped into the rear of the open-sided temple, sat down behind the monks, folded her hands, lowered her head and seemed to become lost in meditation.

Dun came back from talking to some locals and said quietly to Sandy, 'We've made a wrong turn. The place your friend is looking for is along the other road. We must go back. But it's too late today so we can stay the night here. It is a rural monastery. Is this okay?'

'I don't think we have much choice as it's nearly dark. Who do we speak to?'

'There are two Buddhist nuns who run this place and look after the monks. The young monks stay here for several months and then move on. Come, this way.'

The nuns were preparing the monks' evening meal in a simple two-room house with a loft above, and they greeted Sandy warmly. A long table lined with plastic chairs was set outside under a shelter. To one side there were several tiny huts, each just a room big enough for two with a sleeping mat and a small window. At the rear there was a bathing and toilet block. Through the trees they could see other houses linked by a dirt path. The lives of families, school children and animals all swirled around this small hamlet dominated by the rustic temple.

A nun showed Sandy where they could sleep and wash and invited the visitors to share their simple meal.

'We have food,' said Sandy. 'May we use the kitchen when the monks have eaten?'

The nun nodded and returned to her duties.

When the last sounds of the monks' prayers had rumbled and droned away, Anna joined Sandy.

'That was special,' said Anna. 'That chanting vibrated right into me; it calms the mind. I feel really focused.'

'Ready for whatever tomorrow brings, eh?' said Sandy.

'I am.' Anna pulled the gold chain from around her neck with the little cross on it. 'I could feel this against my skin. Like it was alive. Weird. So what are we doing tonight?'

Sandy looked at Anna's glowing face. She seemed different somehow. At peace in her heart perhaps, thought

Sandy. She realised she'd been worrying about how Anna would react to whatever they might find tomorrow. Now she could tell that Anna would take whatever happened in her stride. 'We're staying here; it's pretty basic. Dun and Chip are getting cleaned up. There's a bath house. And we can cook in the nuns' quarters after the monks have eaten.'

'Great. I might just walk around a little bit. Maybe buy some cigarettes for the monks.'

Sandy watched Anna stroll away, thinking how different she was from the woman who'd first arrived in Hanoi just a few weeks ago.

The monks ate and then retired early to their sleeping quarters. They would be up at three to meditate and pray till sunrise. The village head man joined the two women as they ate their dinner and nodded enthusiastically as Sandy and Anna asked about the village where Anna's family came from.

'It is where the school is. Much bigger than here,' he said. 'There is a small market, more people. A big bus stops there; it doesn't come through here. We must ride or walk to the village to catch it.' He pointed to a converted army truck. 'The children go to school in that.'

'Sounds quite a fairly big place. Have the same families lived there for many generations?' asked Sandy.

He shrugged. 'Some. But after the war the government moved many people or sent them to re-education camps. Farmers were probably better off than anyone with an education. Your family might not be there anymore. Life was hard.'

Sandy translated this to Anna, who said, 'Not all my family left Vietnam. I suppose they couldn't afford it. As far as I know some of them travelled from here to the coast, to the southern tip, where they left on a boat.'

Dun spoke up. 'Vietnam is changing. Not so many changes in the countryside, but even here it is different.'

'Mum was very happy in Australia. But I hope she would be pleased that I am finding out about her home in Vietnam,' said Anna.

Afterwards in a hut, Anna and Sandy spread out the groundsheet and rubber mat Dun had provided and covered themselves with a thin blanket.

'My yoga mat is more comfortable than this,' muttered Sandy. 'Will you sleep okay, Anna?'

'Yes, I will. It's been a long day. I'm exhausted.' Anna reached across and found Sandy's hand. 'Thanks, Sands, for bringing me here.'

'Whatever you find, I hope it's what you want,' replied Sandy.

'I realised when I sat with the monks this evening that it doesn't matter. I've somehow made a connection with my mother just by making this trip. It's the journey, not the destination. Whatever I find will be okay.'

'I'm glad, Anna. Good night.'

The next morning the four ate a simple breakfast, thanked the nuns, waved goodbye to the monks and retraced the path to the fork in the road.

Now they passed through open countryside and the road became wider. They saw people on bicycles, carts drawn by oxen and, at the edge of a field, two young children sitting astride a plodding water buffalo waved to them as the bikes roared past. Eventually they saw in the distance a group of buildings and a busier flow of traffic.

It was a sizeable village of possibly two thousand people or more. Built around a main market square, it seemed a pretty place. Some houses had a business at the front – motor repairs, food stalls, fruit and vegetable vendors, as well as general merchandise – and there appeared to be several eating houses as well as a cafe with plastic tables and chairs outside. In side streets, trees had been planted and children and dogs played in front of solidly made homes. A police station, a school and a neat pagoda all faced a small park where several men had set up a badminton net and were engaged in an energetic game.

The two bikes cruised up and down the main street, around the square and down several laneways, then turned back into the centre of town.

'The police station,' said Sandy. 'Let's start there.'

The officer on duty was a bit taken aback and somewhat surprised at the sight of the two girls. Sandy explained quietly in Vietnamese and in some detail who Anna was trying to find.

'But why? After so long?' he wanted to know. 'What documents do you have?'

'Ah, nothing very official,' said Sandy, knowing the bureaucrats' love of paperwork. 'A letter from her mother before she died and a photograph.'

The officer held out his hand. 'Show me the letter.'

Anna shook her head. 'It's personal.'

The policeman, unable to understand her, glared and shrugged his shoulders. This was outside his normal duties.

But Sandy stepped in, saying smoothly, 'It's from her mother who was very sick and knew she wouldn't see her daughter grow up, get married and have children so she wanted to say many things in this letter.'

The police officer nodded, his expression not softening, but he didn't press further. 'And what is the name?'

'Thanh,' said Anna, and waited.

Was it a flicker of recognition on his face, or curiosity? 'The photograph?'

Anna took the picture from the folder she'd pulled from her backpack and passed it across the counter.

He stared at the picture, lifting it closer to study it, then put it back down. 'I do not know any of these people.'

'It was a long time ago,' said Sandy. 'Is there anyone by the name of Thanh living here?'

He nodded. 'Yes. It is not so unusual a name in Vietnam.'

'What's he saying?' interjected Anna, seeing his slight nod. 'Is there a local phone book?'

Sandy was as impatient as Anna but she resisted the impulse to push him along. 'How or where could we find any Thanh family here?'

He sucked his teeth and looked thoughtful. 'The square. There are old men who sit outside Son's cafe. Thanh Vu Tan goes there. Ask for him.'

Sandy retrieved the photograph. 'Thank you. Thank you very much.'

In the sunshine, she pointed back towards the town square. 'Son's Cafe next stop.'

At the cafe two old men were sipping coffee, engrossed in a deep discussion. Newspapers were spread on a table. At another several men were playing cards. Two young women gossiped nearby. Dun and Chip discreetly settled themselves at a table and ordered food and coffee, watched their bikes and waited for further developments.

Sandy approached the two men with the newspapers and asked if they knew Mr Thanh and they pointed to the card game. Respectfully she asked if she might interrupt the game and inquired if the players knew a Mr Thanh. Immediately three of them pointed to a fourth man sitting beside them. He had white hair, a nut-brown face and sharp black eyes. He frowned and looked uncomfortable at being singled out.

'Good morning, Mr Thanh. We have come from Australia, seeking my friend's family.' She gestured towards Anna, who gave a hopeful smile. 'Do you recognise anyone in this picture? It was taken in Vietnam in the early seventies.' She passed him the photograph and all the men leaned over to try to get a look at it.

Anna watched him, holding her breath. He didn't react at all. But as she felt her shoulders slump in disappointment, he asked through Sandy, 'Who are you related to in this picture?'

'Pull up a chair and sit with him; point out who they are,' whispered Sandy.

The men made room for Anna to sit next to Mr Thanh. Slowly Anna pointed. 'Thu, my mother.'

'*Me*,' translated Sandy in Vietnamese.

'My grandmother.'

'*Ba ngoai*.'

'My grandfather.'

'*Cong noi*,' said Sandy.

'My mother's brothers and sisters. This is my mother's little brother, Van. He died on the boat on the way to Australia.'

'Her mother is still in Australia?' he asked Sandy.

'Her mother died when she was seven years old. She married an Australian,' answered Sandy.

As Sandy continued to translate, he looked grave, but said nothing.

Anna continued, 'This is my great-aunty and this is my great-uncle. My grandfather's brother.'

The old man studied the picture in silence for almost a minute then put it on the table and took a long look at Anna before putting a finger on one of the men in the photograph. 'This is me. These are my two brothers.'

Sandy touched Anna's hand. 'Anna, this is your great-uncle. Your grandfather and Uncle Quoc's brother.'

Anna blinked and they gazed at each other, the old man rather surprised, slightly bemused. Anna bowed her head in a gesture of respect. 'How do you do, Great-uncle.'

The man pushed back his chair and rose; Anna did the same. Awkwardly, formally, they embraced. Sandy quickly translated to the others this news and there was an immediate outburst of chatter. The other men stood and shook Anna's hand and then moved to another table, leaving them alone.

And so they settled to the details of the story. Great-uncle was polite but not effusive as Sandy translated.

'My brothers and I were born here. Your grandmother came from the north. When she married your grandfather she lived with my parents.'

'Here? In this town?' asked Anna. 'Is the house still here?'

He nodded and went on. 'I married and moved away.' He looked over Anna's shoulder. 'I was very different from your grandfather. We had different ideas. He was a teacher, a man of words. I was a worker, and a fighter.'

'Where did you fight?' asked Sandy, sensing what was coming.

'I did not like what the French had done. Our family and Anna's mother's family were Catholic. Because of the French I renounced that religion. I went to fight with the communists to get rid of the colonists,' he said to Sandy with a clear sense of pride.

'And the American war?' asked Sandy quietly. 'Did you fight against them as well?'

He nodded. 'I went south to fight. I was Viet Cong,' he said proudly. 'My family did not agree. When the communist government took over, I came back here to reclaim my home. But the family had all gone. I did not know where, except they were escaping. They did not want the new Vietnam.'

'So you stayed. Are you married?'

'I have a wife. My children have gone away to the city for good jobs.'

There was silence as Anna digested all this.

'It must have been quite a big split in the family, but where are the rest of Anna's relatives?' Sandy asked.

He shrugged. 'I don't know what happened to them all after the war.' He studied Anna. 'So your mother, she married an Australian man? You are Viet Kieu.'

On hearing this Anna's shoulders slumped. So there was no one left but this old man.

Great-uncle continued, 'Good fighting men. I fought against Australian men.'

'My father fought in Vietnam. He was at Long Tan,' said Sandy.

'I was D445 Regional Force battalion.' He smiled for the first time. 'Also in Phuoc Tuy. Maybe we fought your father?'

'I wouldn't know. My father never talks about the war.' She glanced at Anna. 'My friend has come a long way to find her family. Could you show us the family home?'

Great-uncle studied the young women as he came to understand more fully the extraordinary background of the relative who had suddenly come into his life. 'It is my home. When I returned everyone had left. I reclaimed the house. I worked for the government resettlement program.'

'It would mean a lot to Anna if she could see where her grandmother lived as a bride and where her mother was born and grew up.'

'It is a simple house,' he said, then stood, spoke to his friends and walked from the cafe. 'Please, come.'

Anna grabbed her bag and they told Chip and Dun to wait for them.

386

'Find somewhere for us to stay tonight. We won't want to leave straightaway,' added Sandy.

'We'll have to leave early in the morning to get back to Dalat,' said Dun. 'Or there might be a bus that suits you better. We'll check it out.'

They walked slowly: Great-uncle had a limp, a souvenir of the war, he explained briefly.

Sandy continued probing as they walked. 'Tell us about Anna's grandfather.'

'He was educated better than me as he was the older son. He did not like the Communists. And his Catholic wife.'

'Has the town changed much since those days?' asked Anna.

'A little. Modern things. There are some buildings from the French days; more people came here after *doi moi*, to start businesses. Many who went away did not come back. There are new people. Some from the city, but there are many poor people who farm. We are an independent nation now. Our own masters,' he added with pride.

They turned down a side street and Anna stopped. 'It's here, isn't it? The house?'

'What makes you say that?' asked Sandy.

'I just know it.' Anna took the camera from her bag as her great-uncle confirmed the house was indeed a little further down the street.

The house had two storeys. The doors and shuttered windows were framed in wooden fretwork painted mustard yellow. There was a gnarled cumquat tree in a glazed pot by the front door – a gift for Tet, from New Year celebrations so long ago it had become a bonsai. A patch of garden to one side was dominated by a large tree.

Anna began taking photographs and Great-uncle softened slightly. 'I remember your mother, Thu. She was a pretty little girl. She climbed that tree. Your grandmother did not approve of that.'

Anna clung to this bit of information as if it were gold. She photographed the tree, then went to it, rubbing her fingers along its trunk before resting her cheek against it. A tear trailed down her cheek.

An elderly woman opened the front door looking quite startled at the unexpected visitors and demanded to know who the foreigners were. Her husband explained and she looked at Anna curiously. 'Tell her it is our house now. She has no business here.'

Sandy stepped forward and politely introduced herself in Vietnamese and apologised for the intrusion. The woman was taken aback at the blonde stranger speaking her language.

'It would mean a lot if my friend could see inside the house. Her great-uncle says it has not changed very much. She is a visitor to Vietnam; she came just for this purpose. She can go back to Australia and be happy in her heart to know where her family came from,' said Sandy gently.

'They won't make trouble,' Great-uncle Thanh assured his wife and strode indoors. Reluctantly the woman invited Sandy and Anna to follow her inside, leaving their shoes at the door.

'Give me the camera,' said Sandy. 'I'll take pictures for you.' She could see Anna was in a bit of a daze at the speed of events and the rising emotions at every turn.

It was a fairly large house compared with houses they'd seen in other small towns and villages. And while the kitchen and bathroom facilities were antiquated, the rooms were big and somewhat formal. But what fascinated Anna was the old furniture made from intricately carved wood which she assumed had been there since her grandmother's day. She ran her hand over the chairs and table where her mother had sat as a little girl, trod gently on the narrow stairs and was shown the small bedroom that her mother had shared. She bent to peer out the window at the view over the village to fields and hills and wondered what her mother had dreamed when she'd looked out from there as a child.

Sandy took photos of the kitchen and lounge room and asked if the dishes and the large blue pots had belonged to Great-uncle's parents. His wife didn't know and didn't appear keen to elaborate.

'Are there any photographs or personal belongings Anna could see?' she asked Great-uncle.

He thought for a moment then went to a bedroom and came back with a small box. In it were two framed photographs, one of his parents on their wedding day and one of a family gathering at a Tet celebration dinner. They all studied the picture carefully, finally identifying most of the family, including Thu aged about three.

Sandy asked if they could photograph the pictures and they carefully took them from the frames and wrote down all the names.

After an hour there Anna could barely speak. She was glad Sandy was doing most of the talking. She felt so overwhelmed by being this close to her mother's family and the house where she was born. It had made the trip utterly worthwhile.

Impulsively as they made their farewells, Anna gave Great-uncle a quick hug and walked to the roadside.

Sandy was writing down Anna's address to give to the elderly couple when Great-uncle's wife came from the kitchen and thrust a small plastic bag into Sandy's hand. 'For the girl.' She turned and went back into the kitchen.

Anna and Sandy walked slowly along the little street. Anna glanced back only once towards the house as they turned the corner onto the main thoroughfare.

'Was it worth it? Even though he didn't tell us exactly where your grandmother's family came from?' asked Sandy.

Anna nodded, still very moved. 'It's enough. I want to talk to my dad.'

'Will you contact Great-uncle again? I can write a letter for you,' offered Sandy.

Anna shook her head. 'Probably not.'

Sandy handed her the plastic shopping bag. 'His wife gave me this when we were leaving.'

They stopped and opened the bag. Inside was a small porcelain cup with a flower pattern around the edge and a book.

'What's the book?' asked Anna.

Sandy leafed through it. 'Vietnamese poetry.' Then she looked at the flyleaf. Written inside was *Thanh Ho Truong*. 'It belonged to your grandfather. They seem to be romantic poems. Maybe he read them to your grandmother and your mother.'

'Do you think this cup belonged to my mother?'

'I think Great-uncle's wife felt sorry for you and grabbed the first thing she could find that had some significance for you,' said Sandy.

Dun had booked them into a small guesthouse and he suggested they look at more of the town. So they hopped on the bikes and circled the town and its outskirts, all the while Anna calling for photo stops and thinking, Did my mother come here? Where were her friends? Where did she play?

They were told the original schoolhouse had burned down and the new government school was built only ten years ago. Then, at the very edge of the northern end of the town on a slight rise, they came to a pretty white church with a small spire.

'Chip, stop please. I want to go in there,' said Anna.

They parked the bikes and Dun and Chip lit up cigarettes and waited.

'I bet that was built by the French,' said Sandy.

'Looks pretty old. I'm surprised it's so well kept. The communists cracked down on religious freedom and even after reunification the Vietnamese government still insists on control over religious institutions. Amnesty International got involved with a case of persecution of a priest here who's still under house arrest.'

'The controls are still pretty tight then,' said Anna. 'Not what the tourists see.'

Sandy went up the steps to the entrance of the Catholic church. 'Well, shall we go in?'

The double wooden doors were partially open and they went into the vestibule. Sandy was surprised to see that not only had the church been preserved but it was obviously being used. There were candles on the altar and flowers in vases at the side. However, it was empty now and she let Anna go ahead to genuflect before the altar and sit in the front pew. Sandy tip-toed out, leaving Anna alone with her thoughts and prayers.

'Do you guys want to do your own thing? Anna and I will walk back to the guesthouse,' Sandy said to Dun and Chip.

'If you are sure; it will take about forty minutes,' said Dun. 'We'll talk later about leaving in the morning.'

'We'll check out best places for you to eat dinner,' added Chip.

Sandy turned to take a photo of the little church and found a Vietnamese priest standing at the side door smiling at her. He greeted her in French.

Sandy spoke to him in Vietnamese. 'Hello, Father, is this your church?'

'I like to think so,' he said. 'I was away from Vietnam for many years and I am happy to come back. You have come to worship?'

'My friend is inside. Do you know the history of this church?'

'Ah, yes. It was started by a French missionary in the 1890s. It was closed by the communist regime. A priest stayed in the district so he could be near his faithful and watch over the safety of his church, but he had to obey the new laws. He died two years ago. I have come to replace him. In the last few years there is more tolerance and religious freedom, but restrictions remain.' He smiled. 'Your friend, she is a tourist, like you?'

'Her mother came from here but fled to Australia because they were afraid of the communists. She came here in the hope of finding traces of her family. And she has just found a great-uncle.'

The old priest turned to go into the church. 'Ah, then I will give her a blessing. Please, come in.' At the entrance Sandy stood aside for the priest to enter, but he stopped and took her hand. 'The old priest who used to live here kept a register of births, deaths and marriages. There may be some information in it. Tell your friend she might want to study these records.'

Sandy stared at him. 'I will tell her, Father. We're leaving tomorrow.'

He patted her hand. 'When she is ready and has the time. The register has been kept in a safe place. It will always be available at this church.'

Sandy sat in a back pew as Anna knelt again and crossed herself, murmuring responses to the priest. When she walked from the church, her face was tear stained but she was smiling.

'What a sweet man. I should have taken Vietnamese lessons before I came. Perhaps I might when I get home.'

'Oh, so that's on the agenda?' said Sandy.

Anna looked at her. 'I think so, Sands. There's still a lot I want to know about this country.'

'There's a lot more to learn, for sure.'

'And what about you?' asked Anna, nudging her.

'I bet there's a lot more to learn about Jean-Claude too. It's hard to leave Vietnam with him still here, isn't it?'

'It's going to be hard to leave for many reasons,' said Sandy lightly. 'C'mon, we have to walk back: I sent the boys off.'

Over dinner in a small local restaurant specialising in cuisine similar to that of Dalat they invited Dun and Chip to share their meal. The two men were curious about what had transpired through the day and asked Anna, who gave them a brief outline of what she'd found out.

'So you will come back here again?' asked Dun. 'Or is this the end of the story?'

'There's a lot to absorb,' said Anna truthfully. 'I hadn't planned on any of this and then it became a bit of an obsession. But now I feel more peaceful. I don't know if I'll come back, but if I do it will be with you guys.'

Chip raised his glass. 'And you come on the Easy Riders!'

'We won't tell tourists about this place. It's your village, Anna,' said Dun.

They laughed and Sandy decided to keep the news about the register in the old church to herself for the time being. It would be a gift to Anna at an appropriate moment sometime in the future.

From Dalat airport, while waiting for their flight back to Saigon, Anna rang Carlo.

'Hi, how's it going?' she asked.

'Where've you been? Good thing you told me you'd be out of contact: I was starting to think you'd been kidnapped. Hey, you're not going to believe the deal I'm putting together here.'

'Where are you?'

'Babe, still in Hanoi. Didn't go to Hoi An. Things are

393

happening here. I've lined up some great antiques which can be shipped out with the garden stuff. And I have a lead on some really hot pieces. Like out of the Egyptian tombs!'

'Carlo, what are you talking about? First of all, before you settle on those antiques, who's checked they're the real thing and not fakes?' asked Anna worriedly, watching Sandy ordering them coffees.

'I'll get them checked. I know what I'm doing. Anyway you'll be able to see the goods.'

'What would I know? Why not get Rick Dale to examine them?'

'Good thinking, babe.'

'And what do you mean about pharaohs and tombs?' asked Anna. 'What about the garden pots and landscaping pieces?'

'That's all under control. Listen, have you heard of the Thang Long archaeological site in Hanoi?'

'Thang Long archaeological site?' She raised her eyebrows and took the paper cup of coffee from Sandy.

'It's one of the most important archaeological finds in Vietnam's history,' said Sandy. 'Right in the middle of the city. Who's that?'

'Carlo,' whispered Anna and Sandy's eyebrows shot up.

'What's he doing there?'

Carlo could hear Anna talking to Sandy. 'Hey, listen, shut up about this, okay? Don't repeat this to Sandy. It's a huge excavation of a whole citadel, thirteen hundred years old. They found it five years ago but kept it quiet for a year. Now it's a major thing. But, babe, get this, in that first year before they let the news out and before they got, er, really organised, I'm told quite a few pieces kind of went walking.'

'Stolen?'

'Be quiet. Who knows? They were taken away for

testing or something. There's a whole damned city in there: who's going to miss a few terracotta dragon heads? I got a lead on them.'

'Carlo! This is way out of your league. You're crazy,' cried Anna, rolling her eyes at Sandy.

'Listen, this country is a goldmine, wide open. We'll talk – and other things – when I see you. Can't get to Saigon though. Too much business up here.'

'But you can't be in Vietnam and not see the south. Just a few days together and then we'll go back to Hanoi.'

'Ah, babe, some other time. What I'm doing is really important for us. Can't you give Saigon a miss and get back here?'

'So aren't you going to ask me how things went, what I found?' asked Anna.

'Oh, yeah, right. Bet you didn't find your mother's family. Needle in a haystack job, right?'

'No. Yes. I didn't exactly find my mother's family . . .'

'See. Wild goose chase. So what'd you do then? You were outta touch long enough.'

'Carlo, I found my great-uncle. My mother's uncle.'

Carlo paused for a few seconds then resumed brightly. 'What do you know. Well, good one, Anna. When you know what time your flight gets in, call me then, huh? I might have more news.'

'All right, sweetie, will do. Bye.'

'So what did he think? About the family search?' asked Sandy.

'Typical Carlo,' said Anna. 'If he's not involved, he's not interested. But at least he asked.'

Sandy nodded and sipped her coffee, thinking if it were her she'd be in tears or shouting at him. Anna was so forgiving, so patient, when it came to Carlo.

'Dad will be interested though,' said Anna. 'I can't

wait to sit down with him and the photos and everything. What messages have you got?'

'God, I haven't even turned my phone back on!' Sandy pulled out her phone and waited for all her messages to run through. After some time she put the phone in her bag.

'Three from Jean-Claude. Kim called and so did Cherie. And . . . there's a message from Tom about my father. Dad went to the commemoration of Long Tan after all but is on his way home now. Tom says that he's sorry he missed me but he wanted to get back to Mum.'

Anna stared at Sandy in shock. 'God! He came. And you weren't here. Oh, Sandy, I'm so sorry. It's my fault . . . '

'No, not at all. I'm just so glad he came. I wonder how it went. I must call Tom and Mum and find out what happened. No, to be really honest, I'm glad I wasn't with him. I don't think I would have been much help. I think we both would have been embarrassed.'

'It must have been a big deal for him,' said Anna softly. 'Well, tonight will be phone home and talk to parents night, eh?'

They finished their coffee in silence as their flight to Ho Chi Minh City was called. Each was thinking of family and of the men closest to them – especially their fathers.

15

Anna now recognised the familiar landmarks on the drive from Hanoi airport and as the taxi turned in to the one-way street that led to Sandy's apartment, she yawned.

'I hope Carlo isn't in yet; I'm so tired, emotionally drained. I don't even want dinner. Just to go to bed. I'll call Dad in the morning. But, Sands, I feel badly about putting you out of your flat.'

'Are you kidding? I'm wallowing in luxury at Jean-Claude's place. So nice of him to let me stay there.'

'When do you see him again?' She gave Sandy a big grin.

'No idea. That man flits about like I can't believe.'

'We haven't done too badly in the flitting department,' said Anna. 'I must send copies of the photos of us all to Dun and Chip.'

'They enjoyed it too, I think. Different from the normal customers' trips,' said Sandy.

The taxi dropped Anna off at Sandy's flat and continued on to Jean-Claude's affluent district. Sandy let herself into the security lobby, glided up in the quaint lift and went into the apartment. And froze.

The lights were dim; soft music was playing; she noticed the fresh roses; and there was the smell of food. Oh lord, she thought, he's entertaining a woman. She turned and, as gently and noiselessly as possible, opened the front door again.

'Where're you going?' Jean-Claude came into the main room.

Sandy put a finger to her lips and whispered, 'Sorry to barge in. I thought you were away and I know you thought I was in Saigon.'

'No, I didn't. Anna phoned me to say that you were coming back here this evening. Thought I'd surprise you with dinner.' He took her bag and kissed her on the cheek. 'I'm anxious to hear your news. Anna sounded elated but she said she'd let you tell me all.' He took her hand and led her to the sofa. 'Sit down; I'll dump this. There's cold champagne waiting. I thought this called for a celebration.'

Sandy sank into the plump cushions and found her heart was still racing. Anna had set this up. She took the flute of champagne and grinned at Jean-Claude. 'I thought I'd walked in on a tete-a-tete.'

He looked quite shocked. 'Sandy! Who would I be entertaining?'

'I don't know, Jean-Claude. You must know lots of attractive women here.' Sandy realised she knew so little of Jean-Claude's life. With all of his travelling around the country, he must know women everywhere. And what was his life like back in France, was there someone patiently waiting? He was too appealing and successful to be unattached.

'Of course I do.' He sat beside her. 'And I have business contacts with successful and interesting women from all over. And I'm always being invited to dinner parties and functions to meet unattached young ladies.' Seeing Sandy take a gulp of her champagne, he took the glass from her hand and put the champagne on the table beside his. He lifted her hand and kissed it. 'But, Sandy, none of them interest me like my adorable Aussie.' He pulled her to him and gave her a long, hard, passionate kiss. 'I've missed you.'

Sandy was flustered and her heart was thumping again.

Jean-Claude topped up her glass. 'Here, sip this. It's too fine a vintage to gulp. And tell me everything. Is Anna happy?'

Sandy drew a deep breath and began to relax. She smiled at Jean-Claude, took a small appreciative sip of the French champagne, curled her legs under her, settled into the cushions and reached for his hand. 'Let me tell you all about it.'

By the time she'd shared Anna's story with Jean-Claude, had dinner, tidied the kitchen together, talking all the while, it just seemed natural that they slip into bed together, wrapped in each other's arms.

'You're tired. What a few days it's been for you,' murmured Jean-Claude.

'Sitting on the back of a motorbike over those rough roads there and back wasn't too comfortable either,' said Sandy sleepily.

He stroked her hair and nuzzled her neck. 'Much as I want to make love to you, sleep tight, my darling.'

Sandy smiled and closed her eyes and was almost instantly asleep, locked in Jean-Claude's gentle embrace.

Jean-Claude watched Sandy drift into a deep sleep, her breathing slow and steady, before smoothing her tumbled hair and settling himself to sleep beside her. He had never felt so protective of a woman before, yet Sandy was one of the most independent and capable women he'd ever met. He hoped that the phone call with her father went well tomorrow. Phil Donaldson's visit had been so brief and Sandy, despite what she said, felt guilty she hadn't been with him to share some of the experience. Jean-Claude thought of his own elegant and particular parents and considered what they would think of Sandy. His father would be enchanted, but Sandy might not be the woman his patrician mother would choose for her son. Tant pis pour toi, Mama, he smiled to himself: this is the one.

When Sandy awakened the next morning, she found that Jean-Claude had left and there was a rose on his pillow beside her. She made coffee and phoned her mother.

Patricia answered the phone and was relieved to hear her daughter's voice. 'Sandy, pet, it's been ages without any contact. You must have been way out in the bush. How are you? How is Anna? What news?'

'It's all good, Mum. First things first: how is Dad? How did it go? I was so upset I missed him. I had no idea.'

'Yes, it was all a bit sudden, thanks to Maxie getting the visa through. He's jetlagged and I think still chewing it over. But he's glad he went. He hasn't gone into a lot of detail but he said he'd caught up with old mates from his unit and I think that meant a lot to him.'

'Has he changed at all? Do you think it did him good?'

'Oh, Sandy, love, it's too soon to tell. But he's proud of himself for going. And so am I.'

'Oh, me too,' said Sandy quickly. 'I hope he comes

back. And brings you, then I can show you some lovely places.'

'But aren't you coming home, dear? What about your work?' asked her mother, sounding worried.

'Of course. I have to come back. And get another assignment or look for another job. I haven't saved very much.'

Patricia knew Sandy wanted to work overseas rather than stay in Australia so she changed the subject. 'Now, tell me all the news about Anna. Did she find any of her family?'

'Yes, she did!' Sandy quickly told her mother and suggested that Patricia give Kevin a call and see how he was feeling about the news.

'Well, well, isn't that marvellous. Hard though, when she couldn't speak her great-uncle's language. What was the place where her mother came from like?'

'Simple, a big village. But quite pretty. The house probably hadn't changed since her mum's day, so that was nice.'

'And what did Carlo think?'

'Ah, he didn't go with us. He's got some business deal going.'

Patricia had only met Carlo a few times and although she thought of Anna almost as a second daughter she wasn't overkeen on Carlo. 'I always find him so boastful. I was sorry he chased her over there when she went. I wanted you girls to have fun together. Just the two of you, like you've done since you were little.'

'We did, Mum. Especially on this trip.'

'And what about you, Sandy? Met any nice Australian boys over there?'

Sandy smiled. Her mother was always worried she'd marry a foreigner and live away from Australia. She wanted grandchildren and all the family over for Sunday lunch each week. 'I know two Americans and a Frenchman.'

'No one special?' probed Patricia.

'I rather like the Frenchman. Jean-Claude. You'd like him too.'

'Is he coming here?' she asked hopefully.

'I doubt it, Mum.' Sandy sighed. 'I'll try to get hold of Dad another time, then.'

'All right, pet. Take care.'

Sandy called Anna. 'I need to pick up a few things: can I stop by the flat?'

'Of course. Have you had breakfast? And we want to get in touch with Rick Dale. What's his number?'

Sandy bought some of her favourite croissants from a nearby bakery and waved to Mrs Minh as she went through the courtyard and up to her flat.

Anna was still in her nightdress in the kitchen as Sandy let herself in. 'Mm, those smell good,' said Anna. 'Tea or coffee?'

'Another coffee would be nice. Here's Rick's number. Is this something to do with the Thang Long site?'

Anna put a finger to her lips and inclined her head towards the bedroom. 'Carlo is getting dressed. He's grabbing breakfast on the run. A meeting.'

Carlo appeared and grunted at Sandy.

'Don't you want some fresh croissants, Carlo?' asked Sandy.

'Nope. Gotta go. You got that number?' Anna gave him the piece of paper with Rick's number on it. 'See you later.' He left, closing the door none too gently.

'He's grouchy; what's up with him?' asked Sandy.

Anna reached for a croissant. 'Oh, he has the shits because I wasn't paying enough attention to him. I was tired. His male ego is dented,' she said cheerfully. 'Hey, I spoke to my dad; he's so happy for me.'

'Let's ring Tom. Tell him your news and get the full story on my father at Long Tan.'

Tom was delighted to hear from Sandy and Anna and wanted every detail about finding Anna's great-uncle. 'That's brilliant news, Anna! I'm looking forward to seeing the photos. Meryl and I are going over to see your father when we get back home. I wonder what he thinks of Phil's trip to Long Tan.'

'Dad and Phil are friends,' said Anna. 'But they only talk cars, we girls, and sport. So I doubt he'd share much.'

'What're your plans?' asked Tom.

'Carlo has to sort out a business deal and I'm just lazing around. I'll let Sandy fill you in on her stuff. Take care, Tom.'

'Hey, Tom. You missed a great trip. On motorbikes, too!' laughed Sandy.

'Maybe next time. Anna sounds so pleased; it's a great outcome. Very clever of you to track down the family,' said Tom. 'What do you know about Carlo's business deal?'

Although Anna had gone to have a shower, Sandy lowered her voice so that her friend would not hear. 'I know he's planning to export garden pots. But I think there's something else going on.'

'Keep me in the loop. I'm intrigued.'

'How long before you leave Saigon to fly home?'

'Only a couple more days. What are your plans?'

'I don't know, Tom. I just hate to leave here, but I don't really want to renew my contract with HOPE. I'd like to try something else. And I don't want to work in Australia.'

'And Jean-Claude, would he be a factor in your reluctance to leave?'

Sandy laughed. 'You're a smartie, Tom. Yes, actually. He's lovely, but I can't see us melding our lives, careers. He might have a lady waiting back in Brittany or Paris.'

'One way to find out, Sandy. Ask,' suggested Tom.

'That's not very subtle. We'll see. I have a little time yet. After Anna leaves I have to run a week-long orientation for all the new HOPE recruits.'

'Good luck with it, Sandy. I'll visit your mum and dad and send you a report.'

'I'd appreciate it, Tom. When I do get back there, I'd love to see you and Meryl.'

'Of course, kiddo. The greatest pleasure I had in Vietnam was meeting you two gals.'

'Thanks, Tom.'

Around mid morning Anna got a call from Carlo. 'Can you come down to the Harp coffee bar at the lake? I'm meeting Rick. I think you should be here.'

'Sure, happy to.' Anna walked the few blocks to the lake, pausing to peer into the window of her favourite shop, which was filled with dainty embroidered linens. She thought of the gifts she'd take home for friends and the things she'd like to have in her own home one day.

Rick and Carlo were seated at an outdoor table, deep in conversation. As she joined them Rick jumped up.

'Hi, Anna. Good to see you. Congratulations on finding some family here. That must be pretty special.'

'Oh, Carlo told you? Yes, it was. Wonderful.'

'I didn't actually get the details but, when you have time, I'd love to hear all about it.'

'Some other time, Rick. Now, listen, Anna, there's an opportunity here,' interrupted Carlo.

'Vietnam seems full of opportunities for you. What do you think, Rick?' Anna smiled at the American.

'Carlo has a lead on some real antiquities from Thang Long that seem to have, er, gone astray. Frankly, I think that it's too risky to be involved with these pieces. They are relics that show that Vietnam was a prosperous, cultured nation with centuries of continuous occupation. The government is planning big celebrations for the one-thousandth anniversary of the founding of Thang Long in 2010.'

'What exactly is Thang Long?' asked Anna.

'It's a legend. King Ly Thai To chose the site for his new capital by the Red River and when he saw in the sky a golden dragon flying into the clouds he named it Thang Long, which means Rising Dragon. Hanoi, today.'

'Very auspicious,' said Anna.

'The thing is, this is such a big deal that any objects associated with it are going to be carefully scrutinised. I wouldn't touch them,' said Rick firmly. 'Now, these old plates that you're interested in are another matter.'

Anna gave Carlo a questioning look. He lifted his hands as if to say, I couldn't help it. 'Babe, Rick is the expert. We need someone we trust to confirm they're the real deal. I can't fork out a pile of my father's money for nothing. Isn't that what you do, Rick? Authenticate antiques?'

'Could you do it? Carlo will pay you, of course,' said Anna.

'I'll deal with this, Anna. So, Rick, what do you think? Your expertise would help a great deal.'

'My fee depends on how many pieces and their value. So you want me to come to Halong Bay with you to see some antique plates that you'd like to buy? What do you know about them?' asked Rick.

Carlo said smugly, 'I'm going to purchase a shipment of fifteenth-century, perfect-condition porcelain that has come from a wrecked ship off Halong Bay. I've finally struck the big time. This will be the deal of my life.'

Rick let out a small whistle. 'Well, there are certainly people who would pay handsomely for Vietnamese porcelain, provided they thought it was pretty rare. And genuine.'

'In other words, as long as it can be properly authenticated,' said Carlo.

'Yes, it's important to be able to give provenance to a piece especially if it was made to honour an occasion, an event or an emperor. Or was a tribute for an emperor,' said Rick.

Anna was thoughtful. 'Actually, when you mentioned an emperor I thought of the story of the emperor who was secretly buried with all his treasure – we joked about finding it. And when Sandy and I sheltered in that mausoleum from the typhoon we met this old farmer who said his distant ancestor was one of the slaves who buried the emperor.'

Carlo jumped in, 'And the secret was passed down in the family!'

'No one would keep that secret for generations,' said Rick. 'Greed rules. That would be too powerful a secret to keep. I doubt that there ever was a treasure and even if there were, it would be long gone by now.'

'Okay, now what if the farmer happened to dig up something in his rice paddy or whatever? That's how stuff is found. That's how they found Thang Long in the middle of the city for chrissake!' exclaimed Carlo.

Rick nodded. 'It's true. That is how finds are made. Either an educated guess or sheer luck.' He grinned. 'I am very particular about accurate documentation – as far as possible – to authenticate a piece. In the case of a shipwreck, if anything is left of the ship, that would help. Sometimes these pieces are easier to identify.'

'What about the pattern?' asked Anna.

'If it's the dragon phoenix,' said Rick, 'that's highly significant and sought after.'

'Do you suppose there are any of those?' asked Anna.

'You'd have to go through every piece in the shipment. When do you get hold of the porcelain?' said Rick.

Carlo chewed his lip.

Anna knew what he was thinking: that Rick might tell him that the pieces weren't genuine after all. 'How are you going to sell them?' she asked. 'Not on eBay, I assume?'

'I've heard of chunks of Angkor Wat in Cambodia up for sale on eBay. Fake or stolen, you wouldn't know. No, I can put Carlo in touch with two dealers. They'll place his goods around the world. Some might find their way into a museum or art gallery's collection,' said Rick. 'There's actually a pretty well-oiled system of . . . distribution.'

'No questions asked?' said Anna.

'Rick provides the bit of paper that guarantees the age and origin,' said Carlo, triumphantly.

Rick smiled at Anna. 'Something like that.'

Carlo leaned back in his chair, his hands behind his head. 'You get paid for saying something is old and it's such and such. You tell 'em what they want to hear. Who's to say you're right or wrong?'

'Another expert.' Rick smiled calmly. 'And experts disagree all the time. I have to be very sure or I lose my reputation.'

'Wouldn't Charlie be able to verify these plates?' asked Anna suddenly and was surprised at Carlo's swift response.

'No way. And he's not to know about this, Anna,' said Carlo sternly. 'You could blow this whole deal and I'd be bust. Broke.'

Rick was unfazed. 'I respect Charlie enormously. He's made his money, and now he's more of a philanthropist and curator. But I'm not sure that he would entirely approve of what we are doing.'

'He'd probably donate the whole lot to a museum,' cut in Carlo. 'We're in business.'

Anna was silent. She supposed it was all legal

enough: the finders-keepers principle. It seemed to be accepted that many people bought old pieces without looking too hard at how they came onto the market. But it seemed a bit, well, sneaky. And while she was surprised Rick was willing to be involved, it was his job to find special pieces for his rich clients. Many people did it in Vietnam and other parts of South-East Asia. It seemed quite common. Finally she asked, 'So how do you send them out of the country?'

'That's all taken care of. The right customs' hands have been greased. Paperwork is in order. We take delivery in a few days, move them to Bat Trung and ship them to Sydney with the garden goods. Piece of cake,' said Carlo.

'Where do we pick them up?' asked Anna. 'Can I be there? I'd like to see them too.'

'Halong Bay. Hung's taking us to meet his boss to complete the deal. And yes, you'll be there. A bunch of foreign tourists seeing the sights.' He laughed. 'And of course you want to make a pilgrimage to see your nun friend, right?'

Rick looked bemused. 'Which nun is that, Anna?'

'She's nearly blind, lives on top of one of those mountains poking out of the sea. Weird,' said Carlo.

'Then that's a very good reason for us to all go down there, isn't it?' Rick stood. 'Let me know when the details are all set. In the meantime, I have to get back to the day job.' He reached over and took Anna's hand, giving it a small squeeze. 'See you in Halong, Anna.'

When Rick had left Anna said firmly, 'Sandy has to come. We have to tell her.'

Carlo scowled, but he knew she was right. 'Tell her we need her along to translate. It's no big deal: Hung has the goods stowed and we're taking delivery. If I don't buy them plenty of others will. Working with Rick means it's all legit.'

The mention of Rick Dale's name gave Anna a sense of confidence.

'By the way, Hung's uncle doesn't know, so say nothing. Just say nothing to nobody. Be a tourist,' warned Carlo.

'If we're supposed to be tourists, then Sandy should bring Jean-Claude. I'd feel more secure,' said Anna.

'What the hell for? The fewer people who know the better. And nothing is going to happen. We just have to be discreet about getting the goods from where they've been stored so no one asks questions.'

'All right then. I'll tell Sandy and ask her to keep it to herself.' Anna was uncomfortable. She knew if it were her she'd confide in Jean-Claude and because she guessed that he was devoted to Sandy he'd want to watch out for her – and her best friend. Anyway, a trip to Halong Bay was something to look forward to. And if things worked out, maybe this time Carlo would strike it rich.

As Anna suspected, Sandy was not enthusiastic about Carlo's haul, as she called it.

'Why all the secrecy? I'm surprised Rick is involved. Bribing customs, government officials . . . I know it goes on.' She wanted to say she wasn't surprised that Carlo was mixed up in all this but kept quiet as Anna was still hoping Carlo was going to pull off a deal to make money rather than fall in a heap – which seemed to have happened so often. 'Tell me what you know,' she said briskly. 'And of course I'll be there. We love Halong Bay, right?' She smiled to herself and thought wild horses wouldn't keep her away.

'Carlo doesn't want you to say anything to Jean-Claude. Is that okay? And how're things with you two?' asked Anna, quickly diverting the topic of conversation.

'He's great. Really great. It's going to be so hard to say goodbye.'

'So it's au revoir for a short time. You'll get back here, I just know it,' said Anna. 'Do you love him?' she asked suddenly.

Sandy thought for a minute. 'Y'know, Anna, I think so, then I think, how do I know? I've had some relationships, quite passionate, but deep down you sort of know it's not going to last – and that makes it all the more intense. With Jean-Claude it's passionate, the sex is wonderful, he's terrific to be with and talk to, he's tender, I care about what he does, I hate the idea of not seeing him again.'

'Jeez, Sandy, stop right there. That's enough! If that isn't love, what is? You'd better hang on to him. That's the bottom line for me, when you can't imagine not being with that person, he's the one.'

Sandy didn't comment about Anna needing to be with Carlo. Instead she said, 'If he is the one, what do I do about it? I can't force myself into his life. He knows I'll be going back to Australia.'

'Propose to him! Ask him whether he wants to be with you,' said Anna.

'I couldn't do that! Anna, what an outrageous idea.' Sandy shook her head, laughing. 'Now, listen, when are we off on this little jaunt to Halong?'

'Soon, I think. Thanks for doing this. Your speaking Vietnamese will be a help and I'll feel better if you're there. Carlo is so counting on this; I'd hate to see anything go wrong now.'

'And when the shipment has left, you'll both go back to Sydney. What about his plans for exporting all the garden pots and things? I think that's a better business than diving into antique objects d'art!'

'That's all happening too. The antiques are apparently

410

being shipped along with the garden ceramics. It's funny he hasn't mentioned bella Italia for ages. Sees himself as quite the Vietnamese specialist,' she said.

'You do know Carlo well,' Sandy said, thinking Anna had also accepted his faults as part of the package. Maybe she was hoping a splash of success would change him and that he wouldn't be so pushy and boastful. Privately Sandy doubted it: Carlo was Carlo. Though she'd never say it to Anna, Sandy just kept hoping the scales would one day fall from her eyes. If only someone else would sweep Anna off her feet.

Sandy sighed. 'Let's hope everything goes the way it's meant to, eh?'

Jean-Claude was still in Hanoi and Sandy continued to stay with him while Anna and Carlo used her flat.

'Tonight, may I take you to dinner at The Metropole, in their wonderful Le Beaulieu restaurant?' Jean-Claude asked.

Sandy loved the gracious elegant hotel that reminded her of the Raffles in Singapore, though on her HOPE salary she'd rarely eaten there, only enjoyed cocktails around the pool and on the terrace. 'What a treat. Is this an occasion? Are you leaving town again?'

'No, I'm trying to delay going south,' he said. 'You're causing me to neglect, well, postpone, my work. And I don't mind a bit.'

'So, if you're going to be around, I was going to suggest coming to Halong Bay with . . . ' she stopped. 'Never mind. Anna and Carlo are going. Forget it.'

But Jean-Claude picked up the concern in her voice. 'What is it, chérie? You look worried.'

'I am. But I'm not supposed to tell you anything,' she said miserably.

'A promise? There's something bothering you. You can trust me; you know that.'

'Yes, I know I can. So just hear me out, okay?' Swiftly she told him all she knew. 'I think Anna is a bit worried. Carlo really doesn't know what he's doing, so he asked Rick to come in and authenticate the goods, which was smart although Carlo's annoyed he has to pay him, I think.'

'Such things are not uncommon. Here and in Cambodia too. I've been offered temple pieces but you never know if they've been hacked out of an old temple or are a fake. Either way I wouldn't want to own one. Other people don't feel the same way.'

'Oh, Rick's sure the plates are probably genuine; otherwise, why would they let him see them? Fifteenth century. Very valuable.'

'How much has Carlo put into this deal? I didn't think he had that kind of money?' asked Jean-Claude.

'Anna wasn't sure but she thinks it could be well over a hundred thousand. He expects to double his money. Well, his father's money.'

'Carlo must have been very persuasive, or his father has more love than sense,' commented Jean-Claude. 'Perhaps it will all be fine, but this transaction at Halong Bay sounds unusual. I would like to be there. Can't I come, make it a romantic interlude for us?' he cajoled, leaning over to kiss her.

'I'd really love you to be there, too. But then Anna would know I've told you. And so would Carlo, and that would get Anna into trouble with him,' said Sandy, returning his kiss.

Jean-Claude kissed her again. 'How about I just turn up, surprise you? All I know is you said you were going to Halong Bay with Anna. I am a possessive, jealous, lonely man who can't bear to be away from the love of his life. Mmm?' he murmured, taking her in his arms.

'Sounds good,' sighed Sandy. 'The plan, not the jealous bit,' she added between kisses.

'But you are the love of my life,' he said. And picked her up and carried her to the bedroom.

She wound her arms around his neck, buried her face against him then blurted, 'So why don't we get married?'

He stopped. 'What did you say?'

Sandy pushed her flaming face hard against his chest. 'Nothing, nothing. Forget it.'

He stood her gently on the floor in front of him and pushed his hand under her chin, forcing her to look up at him. 'Did you just propose to me? Mon dieu.'

'Forget it; it just slipped out. Oh, I feel sick.' Sandy rushed to the bathroom and splashed water on her face. Damn Anna for planting the idea in her mind. Her proposal had just popped out.

She walked back into the bedroom trying to look composed. 'I'm sorry, Jean-Claude, forget what I said.'

'No, I cannot. Nor will I let you forget it. Close your eyes.' He took her hand and pressed something into the palm. 'Okay, look now.'

She uncurled her fingers and gasped at the diamond ring lying there.

'I was going to give it to you tonight, at a romantic candlelit dinner, when I would ask you to marry me.' He pretended to look wounded, but his eyes were laughing.

Sandy was transfixed. 'I don't believe this. Really? You mean it?'

He took the ring and slipped it on her finger. 'I didn't just happen to have this lying around. Of course, if you don't like it, we can choose another. That is, if you'll have me?'

Sandy looked at him, her eyes sparkling. 'It's so beautiful. Of course I'll marry you . . . if you'll have me?'

He burst into laughter and swept her into his arms.

*

Rick drove to Halong Bay with Carlo in the front seat, and Anna and Sandy sat in the back.

Sandy nudged Anna as Carlo asked Rick to brief him about Vietnamese ceramics so he could talk with some authority on the subject. They exchanged an amused glance.

'I think Carlo is expecting to get on TV,' whispered Anna, but she was proud of him. He seemed genuinely interested in Rick's history lesson.

'The Vietnamese developed their own style although some of it was derived from Cambodia, India, and China, of course. But they all had different decorative motifs, glazes and methods. Using clay from the Red River valley, Vietnam produced some of the most sophisticated ceramics in South-East Asia,' said Rick.

Carlo nodded sagely.

Sandy was dying to share her news about Jean-Claude with Anna. But she kept quiet as she did not want to let on that Jean-Claude had decided to join them all at Halong Bay.

The four checked into a high-rise hotel at the edge of the bay near to where the tourist boats berthed and they waited for Hung to meet them in the late afternoon as planned. Rick suggested having coffee while they waited. Sandy was the last to come down from her room and found the others in the hotel coffee shop. She and Anna placed their order and walked around the lobby looking at the souvenirs for sale.

'How is Carlo paying for the antiques? I hope he's not carrying cash on him,' said Sandy.

'No, it's some sort of electronic transfer to a bank account somewhere. Carlo's father will send it through when Carlo tells him,' said Anna.

They bought a miniature Chinese junk and a small booklet of stunning photographs of grottos, beaches and the floating village in Halong Bay.

'Look, there's a shot of the Temple of Nowhere,' said Anna. 'I'm going to go up and see the little nun. I feel I owe her so much.'

'How's that?'

'She gave me something I can't describe. A sense of who I am. A certain sense of direction. I don't think I'd have looked for my family if I hadn't met her.'

'She'll be happy to know you made some contact at least. And you stepped into your mother's shoes for just a little while,' said Sandy. 'I'm sure there will be time for you to see her.'

As they were finishing their coffee, Anna suddenly gave a small gasp, and looked shocked. Then she gave Sandy a furious gaze. 'Look, Jean-Claude is here.'

'What!' Carlo spun around to watch Jean-Claude, looking elegant in a casual silk shirt and smart linen pants, come towards them.

Sandy jumped up. 'Hi! What are you doing here?'

He spread his arms. 'Surprise! I've been looking for you. I've called every hotel and every boat operator in Halong Bay. And here you are.' He leaned over and kissed Sandy.

'How did you know she was here?' demanded Carlo as Jean-Claude shook hands with Rick and kissed Anna on both cheeks.

'When my beautiful companion told me she was slipping down to Halong Bay with her girlfriend, I thought I'd come and surprise her. This is a surprise to find you all here,' he said, feigning an injured look.

'Oh, it's just . . . ' Anna was about to say it was a business trip, but Carlo kicked her under the table.

'Just a sentimental trip before we go. Anna has a thing about the old nun down here. We happened to run into Rick,' said Carlo, unconvincingly.

'That's nice. Well, I hope I'm not intruding. What are

you doing for dinner this evening?' asked Jean-Claude and there was silence round the table.

Rick jumped in. 'I'm sure you want to be with Sandy, Jean-Claude. I was planning on taking them out to meet a friend who has some ceramics I thought Carlo might be interested in – for his garden business,' he added. 'Perhaps we can meet you later.'

'I was hoping to steal you for a while. So a late supper, would that suit?' Jean-Claude asked Sandy.

'Sure. Where are you staying? Where shall I meet you? Are there any good places to eat here, Rick?' Sandy was worried the charade was getting too complicated and she wanted Jean-Claude to be close at hand.

'I'm sure Jean-Claude knows better than I do. What are our plans, Carlo?' asked Rick.

'We'll be back here round sevenish. Why don't you meet Sandy then,' said Carlo. 'Unless you'd rather go with Jean-Claude now,' he said with a hint of a smile.

'I'm keen to go out on the bay again. Can we meet later?' she said sweetly to Jean-Claude.

'Of course. See you anon.' He waved to the group and Sandy jumped up.

'I'll walk you out.' Sandy held his hand and whispered, 'That's put the cat among the pigeons.'

'What are you really doing?'

'Anna tells me that we're meeting Hung who's taking us out to meet the big boss on some boat to look at the plates so Rick can check that they're all okay. When he's done that we come back and Carlo gets his father to send the money electronically and we collect the packed stuff in the morning to take to the factory where Carlo has all his garden pots so it can all be shipped back to Australia.'

'So it's all going in one container. Sounds straightforward,' said Jean-Claude. 'What's your hotel room? I'll move in while you're out with the big boss.'

416

Sandy re-joined the others, who all stared at her. 'That was a surprise.' She looked at the impassive faces around the table. 'Look, I didn't know he was coming down. But I had to tell him I was going somewhere! I had no idea he'd want to surprise me.'

'Better keep him under wraps,' said Carlo. 'Until we've done the deal. If there's more merchandise available, let's keep it quiet.'

To Sandy's relief, Hung came striding across the room and greeted them enthusiastically. To anyone observing they looked like a bunch of tourists and their guide.

'The boat is ready. It's just a small launch to take us across this end of the bay. Follow me.'

They walked to the end of the long jetty, where a launch was tied. Hung helped them into the open boat. In minutes they were bouncing across the deserted bay. Most of the tourist boats had headed out earlier in the day and were preparing to moor for the night and the day trippers had not yet made their way back.

As soon as they were well clear of the mainland shore, Hung cut behind a peak and suddenly they were in an expanse of water unseen by any boat or being.

Rounding one of the smaller forested karsts they came upon a large modern junk. Even from a distance it appeared luxurious and as they drew closer it looked brand new, made from polished teak, with rich red sails and large portholes indicating spacious staterooms below. Once they were beside the junk it loomed as high as a double-storeyed building.

Sandy and Anna clambered aboard, awed by the glowing brass fittings, the smell of polished wood and a sweet drift of incense. They were ushered into the main stateroom which had low lights burning and red velvet drapes pulled across the windows, screening out the end of the day. It was lavishly appointed with plush lounges, a long teak dining table with matching chairs and several deep armchairs. The carpet was thick, there was ornate carving in every detail of the woodwork and several framed silk paintings that looked to be very old Chinese scenes which were hung between the windows. A huge carved and painted silk screen stood in one corner. Dotted around the room and piled on the table were items covered by gold silk sheets.

An elderly waiter dressed in a white jacket and black pants passed around glasses of sweet wine and tiny savoury delicacies, and indicated that they should be seated. They settled themselves around the extraordinary room and Carlo glanced at Anna, slightly raising his glass towards her as if to say, 'See, I've made it this time'.

Hung pointed at the covered items on the table and a large box on the floor. 'There they are.' But he made no move to show them and, like the rest of them, waited, sipping the fine French wine.

There was a slight flurry as a door was opened by the elderly waiter who bowed as a figure emerged. She was dressed in a red silk ao-dai, jewels sparkling. Her hair was swept sleekly up onto her head and her bright red lips stretched in a somewhat smug smile.

'Madame Nguyen!' exclaimed Anna.

Carlo gave his broadest smile. Rick stepped forward, took Madame Nguyen's hand and introduced himself and his companions.

Sandy also rose out of her seat. 'How lovely to see you again.'

Madame Nguyen coolly acknowledged the greetings and took a seat at the table. A glass was set beside her by the obsequious waiter. 'Thank you all for coming. So, we have business to conduct.' She waved towards the table.

'Mr Dale, I believe you are something of the expert. I trust you will appreciate the treasure Hung has assembled for you and Mr Franchetti.' She gave a brief nod in Carlo's direction, then turned her head to a crew member by the door who leapt forward and swept off the light gold covering from the table.

Even Rick had to swallow hard at the display of exquisite ceramics: blue-and-white polychrome, green glazes and a dull grey primitive stoneware. They all got up and circled the table.

'May I?' asked Rick, wanting to lift a piece to study it more closely.

Madame Nguyen waved a hand. 'Certainly. This is a very nice collection, don't you agree?'

First Rick lifted a blue-and-white dragon jug, then a lotus bowl. He turned over several of the dishes with their simple but classic pattern. 'These are not dishes used by farmers. These are made for the tables of nobles. Very high quality. Lovely.'

Carlo was anxious. 'So, what do you think, Rick? Do you think these pieces have a market?'

'I do indeed. Collectors are curious people. They can be quite eccentric in the specifics of what they collect. Some want something from the earliest period; others have no interest in plain peasant objects, no matter how old. But these pieces will be in great demand.'

'What's in the box, Madame Nguyen?' asked Carlo.

'Plates, platters, bowls. Pieces I believe you could turn over for a good price.' She indicated the plates. 'You can quadruple your investment fairly swiftly. A good enough return?' She raised a thin pencilled eyebrow and Carlo was quick to concur.

Sandy and Anna sat on the sidelines, watching and listening. Sandy thought perhaps Carlo had pulled off the big one and thanked the heavens that Rick was present.

Anna was watching Carlo with love and admiration. He'd really hit the jackpot this time.

Several pieces were carefully passed around. Sandy and Anna recognised a plate that was similar to the one they'd seen in Madame Nguyen's shop in The Royal Hotel in Hoi An. There was further discussion. Rick spent time admiring some pieces at great length, fingering the porcelain, turning them over, holding them under a light to see better, wondering who these pieces might have been made for.

Carlo began to get fidgety. 'So, Rick. Everything is okay by you? I think we should be moving on. Hung?' He turned to Hung who had sat quietly in the background letting Madame Nguyen do all the talking.

'When you are ready, Hung will take you back. These items will be carefully packaged and marked in several crates. Naturally, we will not seal the crates, so you can inspect their contents in the morning,' said Madame Nguyen in a business tone. 'If everything is to your satisfaction, Mr Franchetti, you will arrange payment this evening by electronic transfer and tomorrow, when everything is confirmed, you will take the merchandise away with you. Hung will bring you back here and you may make a final inspection and take the crates away with you. Is this satisfactory?'

Carlo stood, anxious to make arrangements for the settlement. 'Sounds cool to me. Rick?'

He nodded. 'Tomorrow you can settle up with me. We'll leave your antiques at the gardenware factory and continue on to Hanoi. You seem to have your shipment under control.'

'Yep. All's in order. Next time I see these dishes it will be back in good old Sydney. Thank you again, Madame Nguyen. Pleasure doing business with you.' Carlo pumped her hand enthusiastically and didn't appear to notice when she withdrew it with a pained expression.

Hung ushered them out. 'It's dark; be careful getting back into the boat.'

'Hey, don't drop any of the dishes back in the briny,' joked Carlo.

'They will be treated like gold and packed very, very carefully. We know how to deliver such items around the world. Don't worry,' declared Madame Nguyen, who then disappeared below.

As they chugged to the mainland Sandy glanced back at the shadowy shape of the big junk, a dark smudge, its oily yellow lamps gleaming over the dark water. She couldn't wait to tell Jean-Claude what had transpired. She wished she could talk about it to Anna, who sat clutching Carlo's hand. Both of them looked somewhat starstruck. As if their wildest dreams were about to come true.

There was a brief meeting in the lobby of the hotel. Each of them was playing it cool and calm.

'So what's the plan for tomorrow?' asked Rick.

Carlo stiffened his shoulders, assuming an air of authority. 'I will contact my father at once to transfer the money. Depends on Hung when we go back.'

'Early. Everything will be very carefully packed, ready to be collected from Madame Nguyen's junk.'

'Is she staying in Halong Bay?' asked Anna.

'No, she will not be staying after she's concluded her business with you. She has many other things to attend to,' said Hung. 'She is returning to Hoi An.'

'Apparently she has a very beautiful home in Hoi An,' said Sandy. 'She was building a lot of places. She has diversified interests.' She gave Hung a questioning look.

'A lot of things are stored in her home at Hoi An, but they are also dispersed throughout the country. And much further,' said Hung. 'Madame Nguyen is a clever lady. Very smart. I am lucky to know her.'

'How do you know her?' asked Sandy.

'Ah, it is a long story. My Uncle Chinh knows her from many years ago. She became very rich after her husband died. Her husband was Uncle Chinh's relative. Madame Nguyen looks after the family. She did not have children.' Hung smiled. 'She is very good to me.'

Anna smiled and nodded. Family was important in Vietnam and who would you trust more?

They agreed they'd all do their own thing for dinner. Rick had a friend to look up, Carlo and Anna would find somewhere to eat and Sandy would wait for Jean-Claude.

'Please, Sands, say nothing to Jean-Claude. Carlo is so pissed off he turned up.'

'Everything is working out just fine. What a trip. That Madame Nguyen is something else,' said Sandy to deflect Anna's comment about Jean-Claude.

Sandy stepped into her hotel room to find Jean-Claude relaxing in front of the cable television. He gave her a hug.

'How was it?'

'Amazing.' She told him every detail.

'So tomorrow morning you go out in the launch, pick up the goods and hit the road. It all sounds too easy.'

'Seems that way. But I still need to smooth things over with Anna. She's a bit hurt and suspicious I broke my promise not to tell you.'

'Why don't you call her after supper and break the news we are engaged,' said Jean-Claude. He took her hand. 'You know, Sandy, this whole scheme seems too good to be true. I know of Madame Nguyen and she is a shrewd and clever operator.'

'Darling, Rick knows what he's doing so I'm sure it

will be fine. For once Carlo might have pulled off a real coup.'

Sandy held the phone receiver away from her ear as Anna's squeals reverberated down the line after dinner.

'No way! That's so fantastic! I told you. He adores you. It's meant to be. Oh, Sands, I'm so happy for you.'

Sandy was elated at Anna's reaction to the news of their engagement. Her friend's annoyance now seemed to be a thing of the past and one day Sandy would confess to her that she had been the one to do the proposing.

16

NIGHT WAS STILL CLINGING to the crevices, caves and craggy karsts, the strange limestone formations that rose from Halong Bay. As grey dawn light crept into their hotel room, Sandy reluctantly wiggled out of Jean-Claude's embrace.

'Ah, Sandy. You are sure you have to be there with them this morning?'

'Anna wants me there. And I admit I'm curious.' She slipped her diamond ring on her finger. 'And besides, now I can show the world we're engaged. The reason you came down here.' Thinking about it, she added, 'Maybe you should come along too.'

He yawned. 'Perhaps that is a good idea. We'll both meet them at the wharf. I don't expect Carlo will be pleased to see me though.'

The sky was compressed with dark rolling clouds as the group assembled at the wharf and settled themselves in Hung's launch. Jean-Claude's arrival had caused some consternation for Carlo, but Anna told him that Jean-Claude had rushed to Halong Bay to propose to Sandy and the two could hardly be expected to be apart now.

'Why couldn't he have waited till they were back in Hanoi?' Carlo muttered.

'Jean-Claude thought this might be a romantic place to pop the question,' said Anna pointedly.

Carlo ignored her remark. 'We're picking up the goods, taking them to the mainland once they're packed. The money has gone through. Rick has rented another car as the crates won't fit in just one.'

In spite of Carlo's pointed change of subject, Anna was thrilled with the way things had worked out and she couldn't see any problem in having Jean-Claude join them. Sandy was hanging on to him like crazy. She'd never seen her so openly besotted with a man. Anna smiled to herself. Sandy certainly had never made a commitment to any man before. Jean-Claude was obviously very special to her.

Boats were still sheltering at their night moorings or remained berthed at the port. Heavy rain looked inevitable as Anna and Sandy sat together in the launch admiring Sandy's ring. Hung handed out the coloured plastic capes that most Vietnamese wore in the rain. They were big circles, wide enough to wear on a bicycle. He was quiet as he headed the boat across the bay. Rick and Carlo exchanged an occasional comment. Jean-Claude studied the scenery.

Once out of sight of the mainland they turned towards the place where Madame Nguyen's junk was moored, in the shelter of two small peaks. By the time they reached the junk it was streaming rain and they were glad to get on board. A crew member took their rain capes and ushered them into a different, smaller stateroom where Madame Nguyen waited, standing beside two crates with a crew member, each one ready to hammer on the wooden tops. The crates looked to be well padded and packed, and on top through the bubble wrap could be seen the blue shadow of a plate.

Madame Nguyen greeted them and thanked them for coming but seemed a little surprised at so many being present. At a nudge from Anna, Carlo introduced Jean-Claude who graciously lowered his head to brush a small kiss on her hand.

'I believe our paths have crossed before,' he said. He had recognised her straightaway as the flamboyant woman who always stood out in a crowd.

She nodded. 'It would appear so. We live in the same building in Hanoi. You have an interest in these particular ceramics?' she asked.

'Not at all. Miss Donaldson is my fiancée.' He flashed a smile at Sandy, who held out her hand to show her ring.

Madame Nguyen barely glanced at her and gave a cold smile. 'Congratulations. Now, excuse me. Mr Franchetti, if you wish to inspect your goods.' She waved a hand towards the crates.

Carlo nodded and stepped forward, giving the impression of being a businessman used to such high-powered deals. He took no more than a cursory glance. 'Yeah, yeah, great. I'm sure everything is in order. My father has confirmed that the money is now in your account.'

'That is so – we too have confirmed it. It has been a pleasure to do business with you.'

Jean-Claude raised his eyebrows. 'Carlo, perhaps, as Madame has left the boxes open, you should just check?'

Carlo frowned. 'Yeah, right. I was just about to do

that.' He lifted a layer of bubble wrap and soft paper and held up a small plate.

Jean-Claude reached for it. 'May I? This is lovely. Fifteenth century you said, Rick?'

Rick took the plate, turned it over and nodded.

Jean-Claude smiled at Anna. 'You will do well with these.'

'It's not her deal. It's mine,' retorted Carlo.

Rick lifted a jug from the top of the second crate, looked at it and felt the layer of plates below it, then carefully re-rolled the jug in the protective wrap and replaced it. 'They're fine. Very well packed.'

At that moment the wind changed and the rain began to lash the junk. Hung glanced outside. 'We should go. Monsoon rain. I am afraid you will get wet even with the capes.'

'This way.' Madame Nguyen led them to the stern of the boat, where a small crane had been readied to move the crates. 'We shall swing them down to the centre of your boat.'

'How rough will it get? This rain is unbelievable,' said Anna, thinking back to the typhoon.

'It's only rain, with occasional wind gusts; the sea is quite calm,' Jean-Claude assured her.

They quickly donned the tent-like rain capes and with Hung in the launch to help them down, they scrambled into it, pulling the hoods of the capes over their heads.

Hung climbed back up onto the deck of the junk and with the help of a solidly-built crew member and the crane dropped the ropes around the first crate and lowered it down to Rick and Carlo. With both wooden crates settled in the centre of the open launch, Hung jumped aboard, started the engine, threw the line back to the crewman on the junk and steered away into the pouring rain.

Sandy glanced back and saw that the big junk was

already hauling up its anchor, but then heavier rain blotted it out altogether.

'Don't run into any of those bloody great peaks in the bay,' said Carlo to Hung, only half joking.

The karsts made dark forbidding shapes through rain that blew around the launch in great wet curtains. Then, as the rain momentarily abated the world briefly appeared.

'There's the roof of the Temple of Nowhere,' exclaimed Anna, pointing to one of the forested limestone peaks.

'There's a boat behind us.' Jean-Claude peered through the rain at a fast-moving white boat churning up a bow wave. 'It's a long way back but going pretty fast for these conditions.'

Hung reached for the binoculars under his seat, took a quick look, then pushed the throttle forward to its maximum, sending the launch powering forward and throwing the passengers off balance.

'What the hell? Hung!' exclaimed Carlo.

Hung took no notice but the boat swerved in a hard curve to starboard, heading away from the mainland and towards the two small karsts in front of the one with the pagoda on top.

'Hung! Where are we going?' cried Anna.

'What're you doing?' said Sandy at the same time.

'Who's in that boat?' asked Rick, but Hung ignored them.

They all sat frozen in shock for a few moments. The white boat changed direction and it was obvious it was following them.

'What do they want? What's happening, Hung?' shouted Carlo.

'Sit down,' snapped Hung, steering towards the small karsts.

Jean-Claude reached for the binoculars and trained them on the pursuing white boat. 'It's probably customs or police. It's impossible to tell in this rain.' He turned to Carlo and shouted, 'Why is Hung running from them?'

'How would I know? We haven't done anything wrong,' said Carlo furiously. 'Hung! What the fuck is going on?'

Another burst of heavy rain swept across the bay, blotting out the peaks and the following boat. They knew that the launch was close to the peaks but in the pouring rain it was difficult to make out where they were headed.

'Slow down, Hung! We're too close to those peaks!' cried Sandy.

'I know this water,' shouted Hung, not taking his eyes from the way ahead. He sped in between the karsts, putting the smaller one between them and the other boat. Then he changed direction again, running straight towards the large peak with the pagoda. The group in the boat now sat gripping their seats, the girls hanging on to Jean-Claude.

'He's trying to lose that boat in this rain,' said Rick.

'But they will find us when we get back to the mainland,' said Sandy. 'What's he thinking?'

Suddenly the white boat loomed through the rain, this time with bright lights flashing. Hung ignored it, swerving the launch around the smaller of the peaks so they were again out of sight of the pursuing boat.

'There's something wrong,' said Jean-Claude. 'Clearly that's a patrol boat. Carlo, what do you know about this?'

'What do you mean?'

Rick spoke up. 'There's got to be a reason Hung is running scared. We've paid for these plates. There's nothing illegal at all in what we've done.'

'You sure there's just old plates in these things?' asked Jean-Claude, touching the crates.

'You saw them. What're you saying?' demanded Carlo angrily.

'One way to find out,' said Jean-Claude, making a move towards the crates.

Carlo slammed his hand down on the boxes. 'Leave it.'

Anna was frightened at the sudden turn of events. 'Carlo, there's something wrong. Make Hung stop.'

Carlo moved forward and tugged at Hung's sleeve. 'Man, what's going on?'

Hung didn't look behind him but swung his free arm, pushing Carlo so that he lost his balance and fell down.

'Carlo! Are you okay?' Anna tried to help him as he struggled to get back on his seat.

'I'll get the bastard for this. Whatever his problem is, it's nothing to do with us,' spluttered Carlo.

Sandy suddenly said, 'I know where he's headed . . . the grotto!'

The view of the peaks was breaking through the slicing rain and they could see the mouth of the grotto at the base of the pagoda peak.

'What's he running from?' exclaimed Rick. 'Let's check these boxes again.'

'What for? You saw what was in them,' said Carlo angrily.

'Only the things at the top,' said Rick. He pulled out a penknife and began levering the plywood top off a crate.

Hung glanced back and made a move as though to stop them, but they were almost at the entrance to the grotto and he needed to pay full attention to getting through the narrow passage. He slowed the launch slightly, judging the level and wash of the water.

Carlo was now helping Rick and Jean-Claude as they

wrenched off the top of the crate and pulled out and unwrapped the top layer, then another and another.

Rick shouted, 'These aren't the ones you paid for! These are cheap copies you can buy in any market.'

'What do you mean?' gasped Carlo. 'What about the rest of them?' He sounded panicky. Elbowing Jean-Claude away he began pulling out blue-and-white plates that now, even to him, looked like cheap imitations of the pieces he'd seen on the junk.

Carlo stumbled to Hung and grabbed him, shaking his shoulder. 'What's going on? What do you know about this? Where're my antiques?' he shouted.

'Look out!' squealed Anna as the launch swung towards the rock face.

'Duck down,' shouted Jean-Claude as the boat flashed through the low arched entrance to the grotto.

It was suddenly quiet as Hung cut the motor and they glided deeper into the eerie green cave.

Jean-Claude and Rick continued delving into the crates when Jean-Claude suddenly gasped. 'What on earth? Oh, mon dieu.'

Rick let out his breath. 'Jesus.'

'Let me see,' screamed Carlo.

Rick and Jean-Claude were holding some packages wrapped in plastic. Rick ripped one open.

Carlo was ashen-faced. 'What the hell is that?' he said in a whisper, looking at the white powder.

'What's it look like?' snapped Rick. 'Dope of some kind for sure. Probably heroin.'

'Throw it overboard,' yelled Jean-Claude. 'Get rid of it, fast.'

Carlo flew into a rage. 'Where's my stuff? It has to be there! I don't know anything about fucking drugs!'

'Drugs! Who put them there? Oh god, this is terrible,' said Anna, starting to cry.

'That's why the police or customs are following us. Carlo, if you're caught with this . . .' Sandy suddenly stopped. 'It's us too. We could be executed!'

'That's right. This stuff is a death sentence.' Jean-Claude spun around to Hung.

'Is this Madame Nguyen's or yours?'

Hung took no notice as the launch slid close to the rock wall at the very back of the grotto.

Rick was ripping through the plastic and tossed several plates over the side along with packets of drugs.

'Just throw the crates over,' said Jean-Claude. 'We don't have time to pick out the drug packets.'

'No way. Stop! My antiques might be in there!' cried Carlo, flinging himself at the crate and pulling out plates in the hope that he'd find what he had paid for.

'Forget it,' shouted Rick. 'It's cheap shit. Worthless. You've been conned.'

'Hung! Look at Hung,' shouted Anna.

Hung had clambered to the bow and had reached for the overhang of a rock ledge and pushed himself out of the boat. The boat dipped and everyone held on fast to keep their balance.

'Let him go. Get rid of the crates,' snapped Jean-Claude and he and Rick elbowed Carlo out of the way and heaved the first crate over the side.

'Oh, Jesus. No!' Carlo struggled with them until Anna grabbed him.

'Stop it! Don't you understand? We can be arrested, jailed for life or worse if we're caught with this!'

Carlo slumped as the second crate went over, his face in his hands.

'Let's get out of here,' said Rick, peering over the side.

'Can you see the crates at all? How deep is it?' asked Sandy.

'Deeper than the karst is high, I'd say,' said Jean-Claude.

'So what do we do?' asked Anna in a frightened voice. 'Where has Hung gone?'

'He can look after himself, stuff him,' said Rick.

'And the patrol boat? They're still out there. Even if they didn't see us come in here they know we have to go back to the mainland sometime,' said Sandy.

They all looked at each other for a moment, the realisation of how close they'd come to being caught with a haul of illicit drugs – and the certain consequences.

'They're going to ask a lot of awkward questions. They must have seen us leave the junk.'

'But did they see the crates loaded on board?' asked Rick.

'Crates? What crates?' said Jean-Claude with an arched eyebrow. 'This is what we do. We're tourists. We were invited to visit Madame Nguyen to see her beautiful junk and now we are going to explore the grotto and climb the peak as Anna wishes to see the nun again.'

'In this weather?' asked Sandy.

'Chérie, you are visitors, you only have so much time to see the sights,' he said with a shrug. 'Rick, start the engine. Carlo? You are au fait with this scenario?'

'I don't give a shit.'

'Well, you'd better,' said Sandy. 'We don't want to be hauled in for questioning. Play along. This government doesn't approve of smuggling. Especially drugs.'

Carlo was shaking his head, still in shock. 'Rick, you checked the plates; didn't you suspect anything?' he demanded.

'Hey, don't start accusing me. The plate and the jug on top were real. It was pretty sharp of them to keep the crates open and appear so upfront. All they had to do was have the good stuff on top and the rubbish underneath,' said Rick as he turned over the motor.

'What if we'd insisted on looking through the entire crate?' asked Sandy.

'Guess they took the risk,' said Rick. 'Jean-Claude who do you think is behind this? Hung?'

'I'd say Madame Nguyen for sure.'

'So do you think the authorities were watching her? Or Hung?' asked Sandy.

'Both of them, most likely,' said Jean-Claude. 'You don't have fingers in as many pies as she does or get so wealthy without a sideline or two.'

'I want to go to the junk and throttle that bitch. Get my antiques back,' said Carlo furiously.

'Forget it. There won't be anything on board. And I wouldn't put it past that crew of Madame Nguyen's to dump you over the side with rocks tied to your feet,' said Rick, steering through the opening of the grotto.

'I saw them pull up the anchor and get underway. They could be anywhere,' said Sandy.

The monsoonal rain had eased once more and as soon as the launch came from behind the peaks they spotted the patrol boat idling in the bay. It revved its engine and raced towards them.

'Here they come. Carlo, sharpen up. Don't look so miserable,' said Jean-Claude.

'Piss off. You haven't just lost a bloody fortune,' snapped Carlo.

'We're tourists, remember. Having a good time,' said Sandy.

'Yeah, right. Say nothing. Let Rick and me do the talking,' said Jean-Claude, very much in control of the situation.

Rick pointed the launch towards the peak with the pagoda, aiming for the strip of beach that they could just make out through the rain.

A horn blared and a voice came through a loud hailer as the patrol boat drew alongside.

Rick idled the engine. 'Something wrong, officer?' he shouted.

'Who are they? Water police?' whispered Sandy.

There were four men on board. They wore khaki and navy uniforms Sandy hadn't seen before. They had holsters with hand guns.

'You, stop your boat. Throw a line, here.' The senior officer reached out for the bow line that Jean-Claude tossed to him. 'Where you go? What you have in boat?'

'Just our gear, sir. We're tourists, looking around.' He shrugged and pointed at the rainy heavens. 'Too bad it's monsoon time.'

'Stand back: we come and look.' The officer clicked his fingers and a younger, agile crew member sprang into the launch.

'What's up? What're you looking for?' asked Jean-Claude.

'You. No speak. Stay there.' The officer pointed at Jean-Claude and spoke in an abrupt tone.

'Ssh,' whispered Sandy. 'He probably hates the French.'

They sat still, Anna and Sandy huddled together as the young officer stepped between them, prodding under seats, lifting floor boards and looking in the engine housing.

'Bag,' he demanded, and the girls gave him their handbags, which he emptied on the floor of the boat.

'Hey, my camera!' exclaimed Anna, but Sandy gripped her hand, telling her to be quiet.

He pointed at the girls' capes. 'Take off.'

Everybody peeled off their rain capes. It was obvious they weren't hiding anything and the young officer gazed at his superior, looking for guidance as to his next move.

The senior officer glared at them. 'Why you visit the big junk?'

'Madame Nguyen invited us to see it. We met her in . . . a shop,' said Rick.

'Silk shop,' added Sandy.

'Where you go just now?' He inclined his head towards the small peaks.

'We were told about the grotto in there. Very interesting,' said Rick.

The senior man spoke in Vietnamese to another crew member, who leapt to lower an outboard-powered inflatable over the side. He climbed in and at barked instructions from the chief, sped in the direction of the grotto. The officer who had searched the launch climbed back onto the patrol boat.

'Can we go now?' said Anna. 'We want to climb up to the pagoda.'

'You stay.' He lit a cigarette. The other two officers didn't take their gaze off the launch and the five foreigners, who sat in the steady rain. No one spoke.

The inflatable returned and the crewman spoke rapidly to the senior officer, who turned and gave them all a hard look. He leaned down and untied their bow rope and tossed it into the launch.

'Be careful who you do business with in my country,' he said sullenly.

'We're tourists. We like Vietnam very much,' said Rick.

For the first time the man gave a cold smile, making it clear he saw through Rick's polite retort. He jerked his head at his man at the helm and the boat roared off.

'What a sinister-looking bastard. What now?' said Rick.

'We go to the pagoda, of course,' said Anna.

'Are you for real?' shouted Carlo. 'Oh, Christ. My father will kill me. This'll bust me.'

'Yes, I think you have certainly been taken for a ride,' said Jean-Claude. 'What interests me is how the goods were going to be collected in Sydney before Carlo took delivery.'

'If they're paying off people this end, they must have someone waiting for it at the other end. The drug haul would have been worth a lot of money,' said Rick. 'I bet Madame Nguyen has done this before.'

'Heavens,' said Sandy. 'What if Australian customs had intercepted it first! We'd be dead meat.'

'There's the little beach, Rick, go in there,' said Anna, still shaken.

'You're not really going to hike up that bloody hill, are you?' grumbled Carlo.

'Listen, do you realise how close we came to getting arrested and probably executed?' snapped Sandy. 'We should all be giving thanks. Especially you, Carlo.'

'Don't blame me; it wasn't my fault,' exploded Carlo. And then his face crumpled. 'You don't know what this means to me. I'm done for. Wiped out. How am I going to pay back my father?' He threw a desperate look to Anna who moved next to him and put an arm around his shoulders.

'Listen, we'll get through this. You've still got the landscaping and garden stuff coming. That'll make good money. And if the worst comes to the worst you can always sell your flat, downsize. Or I can move in and help with the mortgage. We'll manage,' she said soothingly.

Sandy, Rick and Jean-Claude exchanged incredulous glances.

The launch nosed onto the beach and they all jumped out.

'Look, the police guys, they're out there watching us,' said Sandy.

The patrol boat had stopped, and its crew were obviously observing them through the sheets of rain.

'Well, let them,' said Anna. 'I'm going up to see the nun. You coming, Carlo?'

'What for?'

Sandy hesitated, she knew this was Anna's thing, but she didn't want to let her go up there alone. 'I'll come, but wait for you outside the temple, okay?'

'We'll wait here; there's shelter over there near the rocks,' said Jean-Claude.

'They might think we're collecting illicit cargo,' said Rick.

'Let them,' snapped Carlo. He was still angry at Rick and wanted to blame him for this disaster. Anything but admit he'd been conned.

'No, you guys come up to the pagoda. There's some shelter there for you while Anna sees the nun. It's really special. And I do believe we should pay our respects to whichever god looked over us.'

'It was damned close, that's for sure,' said Rick.

'If you want us to come, then we will,' said Jean-Claude.

'I want to get out of this pissing rain,' snarled Carlo.

Anna ignored him and started on the track that wound up the hill. It was familiar now and despite the rain she strode ahead, followed by Sandy, Jean-Claude, Rick and a reluctant Carlo.

Halfway up they paused and from a lookout across the bay saw several tourist boats and the waiting patrol boat. Then the rain swept across the karst wiping out the view. They trudged on in wet and sombre silence.

Anna found her steps quickening as she got closer to the pagoda at the peak. She had so many thoughts swirling through her mind. Her heart ached over the collapse of Carlo's deal. Yet this time it wasn't really Carlo's

438

fault. Everyone had thought he'd do so well with the antiques. In an odd way too, she'd been pleased that he'd taken an interest in a project in Vietnam.

The rain stopped just as they reached the pagoda. Shrugging off their capes they stood quietly in the entrance.

'We'll wait here,' said Sandy softly to Anna. 'You go and find her.'

Anna took off her shoes and walked towards the simple altar. She glanced around, then stood alone, bowed her head and gave a prayer of thanks and lit a stick of incense. As she stood there, deep in meditation, she felt the presence of the little nun beside her. She hadn't heard her softly enter from the side doorway but when she turned she saw the nun smiling at her.

Anna took her hand and lifted it to her face. 'It's me, Anna.'

'I remember. I knew you come back.'

'I wanted to come back and thank you before I leave Vietnam.'

The nun studied her through her watery eyes. 'You find your family?'

'I did. It was not as I expected. But it was good. I saw where my mother grew up. Where she lived and played and went to church.'

The nun nodded. 'So you can tell your children. They will know how it was for you, and for your mother. And what family you find?'

'Only my great-uncle. But he remembered my mother. I'm so pleased I met him.'

She smiled. 'We can believe in many things but we must believe what the heart tell us. You have a true heart, child.' The nun was about to say more but cocked her head to the murmur of voices outside. 'You have friends here?'

'Yes. I will bring them in to give thanks in the temple. And then, can I see you alone for a moment or two?'

The nun took her hand and walked to the entrance where Anna introduced the others. The nun said to Sandy in Vietnamese, 'I am glad your friend followed her heart. She made the right choice.'

'You helped her very much. Thank you. She will go home more at peace,' answered Sandy.

'And your family?' the nun asked Sandy.

'My father came here for the first time since the American war. He came for a special memorial service. I think the visit helped him too.'

In her fractured English the nun addressed the group. 'You all come again to this place. It special place for thinking, deciding on path in life.'

'They come to see you,' said Anna.

'I will always be here. Even after I die. My spirit will return. Now, please, come in.' The nun gestured to them and Sandy took off her shoes and led the way into the pagoda to give thanks.

Carlo was uncomfortable: this felt alien to his Catholic upbringing, but Anna squeezed his hand and so he slipped off his shoes and followed the others.

Anna and the nun left them there and walked to the simple room where the nun lived.

'I wanted to thank you for giving me the courage to make this journey,' said Anna. 'It has become much more than looking for my family. I think I've found myself, as well.'

'You not always find what you expect in life. Accepting what comes – that important.'

'I still treasure the gift you gave me,' said Anna, opening her hand to reveal the tiny green Buddha. 'Thank you for giving it to me.'

The nun closed her eyes, fingering the shape and then

her face broke into a smile. 'It has helped you on your journey.' She rose and Anna thought how much frailer she seemed. Together they walked back to the pagoda, the nun holding Anna's arm. 'And you have decided about your life?'

'Yes. I have.' She lightly touched the nun's hand.

The little nun smiled and seemed content.

Jean-Claude took Sandy's hand as they walked outside where the rain clouds were scudding across the sky, revealing brilliant sunshine. 'What a beautiful place and such an amazing old nun. I sense she has great insight.'

'Anna thinks so. I'm so glad she was able to come back here.'

He smiled. 'So all things happen for a reason. Even for Carlo.'

'You think so? He doesn't see any silver lining in all this,' said Sandy, looking back to where he was pulling on his shoes.

'Maybe he will. Maybe Anna will show him. She's stronger than he realises.'

'I've never felt he was the right man for her,' said Sandy.

'Well, you're the right one for me. I know we will be very happy together,' he said.

'We will be, Jean-Claude.' She reached up and kissed him gently. 'I feel very, very sure.'

Rick joined them. 'Did anyone notice the plate on the altar? It's one of the old ones. Either Hung or someone else has found one of the pieces from the shipwreck and has given it to the nun.'

'It's where it should be,' said Sandy. 'But don't mention it to Carlo.'

Rick led the way back down the track. The patrol boat was no longer in sight.

'They've given up,' said Rick.

But when they got to the strip of shoreline Rick let out a shout and raced to the place where they'd secured the launch. It had gone.

'Hung! It had to be,' cried Jean-Claude.

'The little bastard! He must have escaped from the grotto and now he's taken the boat,' said Carlo. 'I don't believe this. Now what?'

'Good question,' said Rick.

Jean-Claude thought for a moment. 'Tourist boats call here, but who knows when? Mobiles don't work.'

'What about the nun? Maybe she can help us,' said Sandy.

'She just believes in fate and what will be will be,' said Anna.

'No, I think there must be some way of communicating with the mainland. What if a tourist had an accident or something?' said Rick.

'So do we go all the way back up there again?' said Carlo dispiritedly.

'I'll go,' said Sandy and Anna in unison.

The nun was sweeping wet leaves from the pagoda doorway and stopped in surprise as the girls hurried to her.

Sandy explained what had happened and asked, 'If you need help or want to contact someone, how would you do that?'

The nun asked what had happened to their boat.

'The young man, Hung, he brings tourists here? Well, we think he has taken the boat but we don't know why,' said Sandy.

The nun shook her head sadly. 'Perhaps he has been misled by people who promise him money. Money too easy. I hear talk about things,' she sighed. 'His uncle very disappointed.' She lay down her broom and went to her room, returning with a small cardboard box.

'Captain Chinh? You know him?' asked Sandy.

'He comes here many times. Bring me fresh food,' said the nun. 'He good man. He give me this.'

Sandy opened the box.

'What is it?' asked Anna.

'It's a flare. Like ships at sea use. Fantastic. This will work. Who will come if we set this off?' she asked the nun.

'Captain Chinh. Maybe someone from village. They know,' said the nun. 'Someone come.'

On the shore the three men heard the crack and whoosh and saw the plume of orange smoke shoot into the sky across the bay from the peak.

'Hey, well done!' said Rick.

'What do you know,' said Jean-Claude.

'Yeah, but who is going to come? Will they know where we are?' said Carlo.

'Let's wait and see,' said Jean-Claude.

By the time Sandy and Anna had descended, they could see the unmistakable silhouette of a small junk cutting across the bay and recognised the *Harvest Moon*.

'Good old Captain Chinh,' said Sandy.

'We'd better not say anything about Hung's involvement in the plates and drugs,' said Anna.

'Why not? He might know where the little sod has gone,' said Carlo.

Jean-Claude spoke firmly to Carlo. 'That would be foolish. We must not tell anyone about the drugs. Anyway, you can't get back your money or your cargo. Consider it a valuable lesson, Carlo.'

'We could turn in Madame Nguyen. The police will be interested in what we have to say,' insisted Carlo.

'Forget it. Why should we want to incriminate ourselves? Besides, some of them are probably on her payroll. And we have no proof. It was in those crates we threw overboard,' said Rick.

'Move on, Carlo. If you want to do business here it's best not to make waves,' advised Jean-Claude.

'I'm not likely to do business here again,' grumbled Carlo.

Anna put her arm through his. 'Now, c'mon. You say that, but let's see how well you do with the garden pots. And now we have such good contacts and friends here, there could be all sorts of possibilities,' soothed Anna.

Sandy looked at her friend and then at Jean-Claude and shook her head. Anna was always an optimist, always looking on the bright side, always being positive and hoping for the best.

Carlo looked glumly at Anna. 'It's all right for you. You don't have to sell your flat.'

Rick and Jean-Claude couldn't stand it and walked to the water's edge to wave in Captain Chinh as he anchored the *Harvest Moon* and lowered a kayak over the side.

Anna told Carlo to stop worrying until they had spoken to his father. Then she and Sandy left him sitting miserably on a rock as they walked along the little strip of beach.

'How do you put up with him?' said Sandy.

'It's how he is,' said Anna philosophically.

'Anna, you've changed such a lot since coming over here,' said Sandy. 'Don't you feel it?'

'I do. I know it.' She took Sandy's arm. 'I'm so happy you suggested this. I'm going back home with a whole new direction to my life.'

Sandy breathed out a small sigh of relief. Finally Anna had found the strength to separate from Carlo. 'Meaning?'

'I'm going to change my job, strike out with something new.' She beamed at Sandy. 'And I'm just going to insist that Carlo and I get married.'

'What? You're joking!'

Anna didn't notice the shocked expression on Sandy's face. 'Yep. Like I told you, make a stand. He'll never propose. It's silly to wait around for him to have a big nest egg.'

'It might never happen, Anna,' warned Sandy.

'Exactly. So we might as well move in together, economise, rationalise. Two can live as cheaply as one,' she said happily, as if everything were settled.

'But, Anna, this whole fiasco has shown you, yet again, that Carlo is . . .' Sandy tried to find a soft way of telling her he was a loser, '. . . is a risk. This is the perfect time to get out of this relationship and move on.'

Anna frowned. 'No, Sands, I can't do that. I'd never leave him while he's down. I'll stick by him. Look at your mum, how she's stuck by your dad all these years when you know how miserable and difficult he's been.'

'She loves him,' said Sandy.

'And I love Carlo. Listen, I know all his faults. But his heart is good. And he really, really loves me. Remember he came to Vietnam when he thought I needed him. Please try to understand, I want you to be happy for me, as I am for you,' she said.

Sandy bit her tongue. 'I think you're nuts, but there's no accounting for taste,' she said lightly. 'I don't think you should quit your job though, what would you do?'

Anna chuckled. 'Open a cafe. Vietnamese food. Seriously.'

Sandy stopped and stared at her. 'You're mad!' Then she burst out laughing. 'I love it. I don't know how you're going to make that happen. But why the hell not? If you're crazy enough to marry Carlo, then you might as well be crazy enough to run a cafe.'

Anna slid her arm around Sandy's waist. 'And what about you? What are you going to do? What are your and Jean-Claude's plans?'

'To be happy. We haven't talked at great length, but

it's a given we'll both stay here, at least in the short term,' said Sandy. 'I don't know how I'm going to break it to Mum and Dad. Look, Captain Chinh's here.'

Anna and Sandy turned back to where the old boat captain had pulled up his kayak on the beach and was listening to Jean-Claude. It didn't take very long for Jean-Claude and the captain to return to the *Harvest Moon* and bring the rubber ducky to ferry them back to the junk. No mention was made of Hung but Sandy suspected the captain had an inkling of what had happened. Jean-Claude had smoothly explained about a 'misunderstanding' with the launch they'd hired.

When they arrived at the tourist wharf on the mainland Sandy shook the captain's hand. 'We are very grateful. Thank you.'

'And thank you for looking after the nun on the peak. She is very special,' added Anna.

Captain Chinh nodded and smiled. 'You come back to Vietnam?' he asked Anna.

'Oh, yes, it's most likely. I now have family here,' she answered.

Sandy was the last to leave the *Harvest Moon*. As she did she turned back to the old man and said softly in Vietnamese, 'Please give our good wishes to your nephew Hung. And say we hope he will continue with his university studies. It is the passport to a good job.'

The captain lowered his eyes and gave a slight bow. 'I will tell him. Thank you. Safe journey.'

'We'll be back, Captain. Goodbye.'

Back in Hanoi, they met up again at Barney's cafe. Settled at a quiet table for dinner, Barney, Charlie, Miss Huong, Rick, Jean-Claude, Carlo, Kim, Anna and Sandy tossed around the details of what they called the Hung Sting.

'Sounds like Hung's young, greedy and gullible,' said Barney.

'It's not an uncommon story, I have to say,' said Charlie with authority. 'Not that it helps you, Carlo. Madame Nguyen has a reputation – one of stellar proportions. On one hand she's an ultra successful businesswoman, a connoisseur of objects d'art. Socially she's upper echelon, privately an enigma. She is surrounded by dubious large-set "gentlemen" whom one wouldn't want to meet in a dark alley. And the Greek chorus in the background sings of unsavoury dealings.'

'Very poetic, Charlie,' said Barney. 'How unsavoury?'

'Bribes to get approvals for her buildings; people who cross her have been known to disappear or take a long vacation; investors lose, she profits; and the rumour is that drug money is laundered through her more legit dealings. Apart from that, a charming woman.'

'Why hasn't someone knocked her off?' growled Carlo. 'How does she get away with it? At least I'm not the only bunny she's ripped off.'

'That's true enough. It's a highly sophisticated operation on many levels,' said Charlie. 'One suspects she has built this up over a long time and has people planted, working for her or being paid off by her, in lots of official capacities. Her influence probably goes to the very top.'

'She sounds like a Vietnamese godfather,' said Anna. 'But one day she'll come unstuck and her house of cards will collapse.'

'Would be nice,' said Charlie. 'But it's no flimsy house. She has loot stashed around the world, I'd say.'

Miss Huong listened politely before saying quietly, 'Madame Nguyen is a great patron of the arts. She has made several large donations to galleries.'

Barney grinned. 'Well, she sure is one of our more colourful characters.' He raised his glass. 'To more pleasurable company. Congratulations to Sandy and Jean-Claude. Bon voyage to Anna and Carlo. We look forward to your return.'

They all raised their glasses and toasted each other.

Sandy and Kim touched theirs separately, Sandy saying, 'Here's to our work together.'

'No, to you, Sandy. You're amazing. I'm really going to miss you,' said Kim in a rather sad voice. 'By the way, have you heard that those biker friends of Barney's – The Retrievers – have taken on the orphanage as a project? A few more of them arrived a couple of days ago. They'll have that place repaired in no time at all.'

'Oh, Kim, that's great news,' said Sandy.

'See what I mean?' said Anna. 'Give Miss Fix-it here a cause and she's right onto it.'

'So what will you be doing now, Sandy?' asked Charlie.

She smiled at Jean-Claude. 'I have to give a wrap-up, de-brief, pep talk to the new HOPE recruits. Go home and see my folks. Plan a wedding. Maybe start studying a bit more about fish farming. Try to make myself useful.'

Barney raised his glass again. 'To Sandy, who has given so much to this beautiful country.'

'As have you all,' said Sandy, flushing slightly with embarrassment. 'But I've been given far more than I gave.'

'You're a credit to your country, Sandy,' said Charlie. 'NGOs, volunteers, good-hearted people like you are what makes the world a closer and better place.'

Jean-Claude squeezed Sandy's knee under the table, kissed her cheek and whispered, 'I am so proud of you.'

Ho emerged from the kitchen, beaming, holding aloft a platter of chilli soft-shelled crabs. 'Number one course,' he announced, 'for number one friends!'

Anna was the first to taste the dish, and gave it the thumbs up. 'Ten out of ten, Ho. I'll add this to the menu in my cafe . . . one day!'

17

Sydney, two months later

ANNA PUT THE FINISHING touch – a sprinkle of freshly chopped coriander – on top of her crispy vegetable rolls and fried shrimp cakes and carried the platter to the table on Tom Ahearn's back verandah. Meryl, Tom, Phil, Patricia and Kevin all smiled appreciatively. Sandy followed with a jug of fresh lime juice and more icy cold beer.

'What a shame Jean-Claude is in France and can't be here,' said Meryl. 'Anna, this looks and smells fabulous. You're really right to go into business.'

'We're working on it. Carlo's dad has found a take-away corner place that's gone out of business. He's negotiating a lease and I'm sinking my savings into it.' She smiled at Kevin. 'Dad's going to help with the renovations.'

'Count me in, too. I'll help on weekends,' offered Phil.

'And is Carlo going to work there with you?' asked Tom, ignoring Meryl's gentle kick under the table. 'And by the way, where is the lucky man?'

Anna grinned. 'Playing soccer, Tom,' she said. 'He's got big ideas – of course. He wants to recreate Barney's. But we're starting small. Now that we're engaged, his father wants him to be more involved with his business so he can retire.'

'And Carlo is okay with that?' asked Tom.

'Yep. His other business contacts turned out to be really good. The Vietnamese pots did so well, he's going back for another shipment. Actually, the pots have helped Carlo pay some of the money back to his father and he might not have to sell his flat after all.'

'He'll be able to buy more when he comes over for my wedding. You are all coming?' smiled Sandy.

There was a chorus of agreement.

'Wouldn't miss it for quids,' said Kevin.

Sandy looked at her father. 'I have a lot of beautiful places I want to show you this time.'

Phil gave her a fond smile. 'There'll be plenty of time, love.'

'I can't wait to go back,' said Meryl. 'And Anna, where's your wedding to be held?'

'Oh, Carlo had this idea of everyone going back to Italy to a church in a village where his grandparents were married. And then I mentioned the little church in the village outside Dalat. In the end we decided to stay here.' She smiled at Kevin. 'I'm being married in the church where Mum and Dad were married – in Maroubra.'

'How lovely,' said Patricia.

As the platters were passed around again, a brilliant eastern rosella landed on the railing looking for titbits.

Tom leaned back and thought what a typical Australian Saturday it was. But the food and the presence of Sandy and Anna brought back wonderful memories of Vietnam. The women began talking wedding plans and Kevin insisted on clearing the table and stacking the dishwasher.

Tom refilled Phil's glass. 'Let's take a stroll and inspect my roses.'

They admired Tom's garden and stood in silence for a few minutes.

Then Phil shifted his weight and said quietly, 'I s'pose you'd like to know about my trip north?'

'Only if you want to tell me,' answered Tom, who'd been wondering about Phil's trip to the Vietnam vets' retreat in Queensland.

'The best bloody thing is just to know it's there,' said Phil. He shook his head. 'Wish I'd been able to go to such a place when I got back after the war.'

'I imagine a lot of men felt like that, but it's taken decades for people to recognise how many blokes were so badly affected by their Vietnam experiences,' said Tom. 'So how was it? Was it structured in any way?'

'Nah. Blokes just turned up. You can stay a week for a token payment. There are rules about food, cleaning up, that kind of stuff. It's the peace and beauty of the bush and the fact you can just hang out and chill with men who've been through the same thing. You have an instant connection.'

'And that helped you?'

'Being able to talk through things and find out other blokes feel the same. Had the same shit. When I told one chap how I'd tried to join the RSL way back and was told by an old member to "Come back when you've been in a real war, sonny," he said it happened to him too.'

Tom shook his head. 'There's a lot of repairing to do.'

'We're doing it ourselves. Vets helping vets. Some of

them are starting to age, mellowing, I guess. Or years of being on medication for depression and anxiety and stuff has calmed them down. Tell you one thing, though.' Phil glanced back towards the verandah. 'It's made me appreciate Pat a hell of a lot more. So many wives shot through. Couldn't take the moods, the angry outbursts, the drinking, all the rest of it. Several of them said that if they had a woman like Pat they'd be hanging on to her.'

'Have you told her?' said Tom quietly.

'In my own way.' He looked down at a rose bush. 'It's been harder talking to Sandy. She and her brother had a hard time with me. Going to Long Tan was good. Hard, but good for me.'

'You'll go back?'

'Maybe. I've kept in touch with my platoon mates. But Sandy is determined to drag me round the country. Pat's looking forward to it.'

'How do you feel about her getting married to a Frenchman she hasn't known very long and living in Vietnam for a bit?'

Phil lifted his shoulders. 'It's her life. I want her to be happy. He sounds a nice enough bloke. We talk on the phone.'

'A lot's come out of going to Vietnam,' said Tom. 'For all of us. You, me, Anna, Sandy . . . Even Carlo seems to have found his feet after a bit of a fall.'

'What'd you get out of it, Tom?' asked Phil. 'I figured it was a job for you. Once a journo always one.'

Tom thought for a moment. 'I had a few ghosts to lay to rest from the war too. I was sad at what I saw happening to a nation of people with such a wonderful heritage. It's opened my eyes to how a country can survive such devastation. It also makes you realise the bloody futility of all that fighting.'

452

'Yeah. I guess I need to spend a bit of time there,' said Phil and grinned. 'I might have grandkids there one day.'

'Ah, they tend to come home when the babies arrive. But who's to know, eh?'

The two men strolled back to join the group on the verandah.

Sandy watched her father chatting amiably to Tom. She nudged Anna and nodded towards the two men who'd seen so much and were now looking forward to the calmer years to come.

'What a gift Tom's been to us,' she said.

'For sure.' Anna sighed. 'I wish my mother was here to share all this.'

'She might be. Remember what the nun told you . . . that she'll always be around in spirit. I think Aunty Thu is here, too, and that she is very happy you made the journey.'

Anna touched the chain around her neck with the tiny cross. 'You're a good friend, Sands. I'm so glad you dragged me over there. It was a special time.'

Sandy smiled. 'It's not over, Anna. The adventure is just beginning.'

The End